THE HUNCHBACK'S SIGH

CM KERLEY

FIRST EDITION MARCH 2020

THE HUNCHBACK'S SIGH

Cover design by Danielle Nicole

For Steve and the boys

Laurie, 712

THE HUNCHBACK'S SIGH

CM KERLEY

PROLOGUE

The Four Gods of All had watched their beloved creations for aeons, bored. For them, the monotony of the cycles of life were too short to be interesting, too vapid to hold their omniscient attention. After millennia, all but An'dorna turned away. The giantess felt such love for her druids, and such pity for Evram's abandoned mankind, that she embraced them as her own. She watched with sadness when they could no longer stand to live together, too alike and all too different. Curiosity won over despair. She watched as they began creating realms for themselves with arbitrary borders. She quietly cheered as they turned their intellect to understanding the world. They created numbers and used them to make complex machines of wood and metal that were only as limited as the mind of the inventor. Her glee turned to gloom as she watched them repeat the pattern of idea, design and invention. Always the inventions were quickly tainted and became a tool of greed, power and control.

The Goddess heard the pleas uttered in her name and helped where she could, imbuing a surge of knowledge, an idea, a moment of grace. Under her watchful gaze she came to know druids, and to know mankind, to understand their limits. Both had the power to master some of the magic left in the world after its creation, but each was so small in the scale of that creation, even those with great magical powers made no more than a ripple in the magical current that enveloped all creation. When mankind mastered magic, only An'dorna saw the great wars that raged. But quickly the magical conflicts ended, and druids, mankind, and all the other creatures on their world went back into the cycles of life designed for them.

An'dorna watched, unblinking, seeing everything. And so it was An'dorna who saw a vortex in the flow of power across the earth. Without thinking, she reached out from across the unfathomable distance of creation to smooth the ripple but was stopped by Xynel.

"What are you doing, sister," the formless voice hissed close to An'dorna. A sensation of heat ran up the giantess's enormous pointed finger.

"There." An'dorna pointed at the vortex.

Xynel leaned forward, staring at the point on the world, the point in time where An'dorna stared so keenly.

Xynel's intense gaze could see nothing beyond a swirl in the eddy of power.

"It's nothing."

"Look," An'dorna insisted.

Angered by the idea that her sister could see what she could not, Xynel focused the heat of her gaze across the ethereal plain and bore her sight into the world.

"I see a boy, nothing more. Just a little boy in a forest playing with sticks." She stared at the little boy. "He's humming to himself."

From across the chasm of time and creation, the little boy looked back at Xynel, held her gaze, and smiled.

The Goddess of fire, of rage, destruction, chaos and malice felt the little boy see her and felt a stab of cold cut through her formless body.

Xynel wrenched her gaze away and shouted to Shaa and Evram.

"Something has happened!"

By the time Evram and Shaa took their seats alongside their sisters, many years had passed. The Gods stared through the vortex and saw two young boys living with an older man.

"What are we seeing other than two young creatures?" Evram queried, intrigued. "Shaa, clear the image."

The God leaned his twisted misshapen body forward, one clawed hand resting on An'dorna's arm for support. The Goddess ponderously leaned down and put her arm around her brother's perpetually bent back, taking his weight. He bowed lower across time.

"L-Let's see what is happening," he stuttered.

Shaa blew softly at the vortex to clear the passage between worlds. As his breath moved across the chaos of the chasm of creation, sparks of raw magic ignited and coalesced, creating a sharper image.

"What do your eyes see, brother?" Xynel demanded harshly.

Evram heard a worrisome tone in her sister's harsh words and looked up.

"Why so curious, sister?" Her question was coloured with suspicion.

"Hush," Shaa whispered. They all quietened. Xynel stood up and took a step apart from her brother and sisters.

"The boy has your fire." Shaa turned to Xynel.

The formless Goddess took shape. Razor-sharp crystalline edges formed like silver-white knives along her skin.

"What of it?" she asserted. "There are always some on that world who are born with hints of our song."

"Not like this one," Shaa said, turning back to continue watching. The boys were now young men.

"What do you mean, brother?" Evram asked, but kept her gaze on Xynel.

Shaa was quiet for a breath. He closed his eyes.

"Hush," he repeated, "I have to listen to the breath of their lives and of those who breathe no more."

All the Gods were quiet.

While Shaa listened to the lives contained in every breath of every creature on their world, the boys grew older and set off on a sea voyage.

Xynel shifted where she stood. She thought back to the eyes of the little boy who saw her across the distance of forever. Restless, waiting for Shaa, Xynel's shape shifted into sharper edges, her hands and fingers became shards of icy glass that cut the air around them. Evram flew closer to Xynel's head and hummed into her ear.

"Why so nervous, sister?"

Xynel sneered in response.

At that moment Shaa fell out of An'dorna's arms and collapsed to the ground gasping. The hunchback who breathed life into the world couldn't catch his breath.

An'dorna bent down and effortlessly scooped him into her enormous arms.

Evram, on her tiny wings, raised herself to Xynel's gaze. Xynel twitched and moved to slap her hummingbird sister away but hit An'dorna's black marble body instead.

In the absolute stillness where the Gods existed, Xynel's glass hands shattered and the young boy on the boat had a dream about mirrors.

In complete shock, Xynel could do nothing but lean onto An'dorna and stare in horror at her body, heat and light oozing out of the stumps of her arms and cascading to the ground around her feet.

The Gods stared down at the chaos of countless shards of mirrors. In each, every life ever lived on their world stared back at them, and then one by one they disappeared until all they saw was a mosaic of a young boy crossing a lake.

"That is the lake of my first tears," Evram said, trembling, falling as her fluttering wings slowed, and she finally settled on Evram's shoulder.

They watched the boy sitting on an island in the middle of the lake.

An'dorna looked at Shaa, still holding him, holding up Xynel, supporting them all in the bind of her arms.

"That is the island I made for you." An'dorna's voice, once as loud as creation, was a whisper.

"They are sitting where I sat when I looked into the water, and with my song I brought unity to yours," Shaa moaned.

In the broken mirror of Xynel's body, the boy was on a boat with an old man who cared nothing for him. The young boy was tricked and gave up his life force on his journey.

A druidess followed the boy. She crossed the lake effortlessly. She crossed over to the boy.

"What is she doing?" An'dorna cried. An'dorna, instinctive and afraid for the life of a single cherished druid, sent a surge of power through the chaos to warn her. For a moment the Goddess was bound to the druid.

And the forsaken boy opened his eyes.

He saw the druidess bound to the Gods.

She touched the boy.

He took something from her.

He reached back and touched the Gods.

An'dorna, as strong as the weight of the universe, suddenly couldn't support herself. She collapsed, taking all the Gods with her. Xynel slipped away from her side, cold. Evram tumbled from An'dorna's shoulder and fell to the ground, the sting of tears in her eyes, but there were no tears to weep. And Shaa, who was always able to see to the end of time, when all the world would fall apart, could no longer see anything except the eyes of a small boy, and, behind him, his brother.

CHAPTER I

The small jackal leapt from boulder to boulder, bounding up the tor to claim her rocky throne and survey her kingdom. She sat on her haunches, settling down to run a pink tongue across her mottled fur, grooming out the knots and burrs that even a queen must endure in the harsh desert. Finally done, her jaws opened in a yawn, the top of her tongue sneaking out to lick her nose. Long white whiskers quivered from the touch of the hot wind blowing up from the south. She lay down, front paws crossed neatly, surveying her kingdom of sand and stone.

Her keen eyes spotted a long-tailed lizard basking in the sun; the brown scales shielding its body couldn't hide it from the huntress. She watched it intently, and it pleased her to allow it to live.

A sound captured by her large ears alerted her to a creature on the move, a small gazelle on unsteady legs, its hide still too wet, too white to blend against the muted browns and yellows of the rocks. The jackal observed the creature who had strayed too far from its mother in its first few minutes of life.

A yearning stirred in the jackal. The desire for prey. The desire to hunt, to attack, to sink long, sharp teeth into a soft, yielding neck, to feel the splash of warm blood against jaws clenched tight against a frantic straining body. To feel the fight for life, knowing it was hers to give or take simply by letting go.

The jackal rose from her seat, now standing on long powerful legs, her head hanging low, jaws open, eyes measuring the attack

She lifted a paw, about to leap, stopped.

Her wet black nose twitched. A new scent caught her attention; it smelled hot, angry. It smelled of rage and destruction. She took a step back, claws clipping on the stone, the sound stirring an innate memory of pebbles falling, becoming stones falling, becoming rocks sheering and shattering and tumbling, shaking the desert itself. A memory of danger.

The jackal turned and bolted from the castle of rock.

Desert creatures soon followed. Foxes left their holes to escape, mice and shrews jumped and scurried away, lizards and snakes and scorpions. If the small desert bushes could have walked on their thorns, they would have run away too.

Even the birds, who spent a lifetime on thermals never touching the land, followed her lead to fly away.

By the afternoon there was no creature within ten miles of the Ipcriss tower, where Orren was trying to murder Calem.

He leaned his full weight onto his chest, jamming his knees into his ribs. The boy on the floor thrashed wildly; already gasping for breath, and with burning lungs, he hit out at Orren's face, weakly slapping and punching him as his vision blurred. Orren pushed the small stone against Calem's closed mouth. Calem, squeezing his lips shut, tried to turn away. Orren gripped Calem's face in one hand and with the other jammed his fingers between his lips, forcing the stone through.

Like white hot steel quenched in a forge, the stone sizzled in his mouth. Calem tried to scream, tried to wrench himself free, but Orren had him pinned by the throat, forcing his head back. Reflexively, he swallowed the sea gem.

Bode saw his prince do the unthinkable to the young sorcerer.

He watched as Calem's body transformed into radiant white light. A detonation of energy and force erupted from him, slamming into Bode. He felt it burst against his chest and reverberate through his head and along his body, rattling his bones and scorching his skin. Curling into a ball, covering as much as he could with what was left of his tattered cloak, he thought of An'uek as he readied to die.

The first lick of hot flames kissed his arms, face and hands, and he thought, in a moment of clarity, of everything he had survived: battles, floods, vengeful husbands, trolls and inhuman creatures summoned from dirt. He remembered a conversation with Brennan when they were boys. Brennan was telling him about Calem and his flames. Bode remembered suggesting that Brennan drown the boy. Now he wished he'd done it himself.

The stinging pain moved across his body, and he breathed a sigh that he expected to be his last.

The pain abruptly changed from burning to stinging and he felt the cloak yanked from him. Surprised, he opened his eyes as he clenched his jaws, feeling a tightening across his chest and shoulders.

Mason was leaning over him, desperately flapping at him, attempting to put out the flames. He was speaking too fast and Bode wasn't catching anything he said.

The fallen soldier looked around the room slowly, his neck stiffening. He saw blackened stone walls liquifying into livid yellow lumps falling away from each other. Bodies on the floor were crisping and cooking in the heat, skin and spilled organs frying on the floor. Bode felt the tremors under him, and he noticed gaping cracks appearing between the stones in the walls around him and the domed ceiling overhead. He frowned. He knew what was happening but was ready to die and didn't want to move. And the pain; he put a hand on his chest.

Mason was frantically hitting him again, but not to put out any flames.

He saw Mason's face covered in dirt, ash and gore, one eye filled with blood.

In all the terror of what was happening, Bode noticed that Mason had lost his gloves, and he wondered where they were.

He felt Mason grab his head and force him to look straight into his face.

He was screaming something; spit flew from his lips, hitting Bode's gaping mouth.

He didn't hear his words. It didn't matter.

"Go," he said to Mason, "get Raef. Get out. Leave me." Bode clutched at his chest with one hand and with the other tried to push him away.

He didn't know if Mason had heard him, but he thought perhaps he understood.

From across the room, at the edge of his vision, Bode caught sight of Raef in a doorway, one hand at his mouth as he shouted, his other arm waving to get their attention.

Mason saw Bode look over his shoulder and turned. He raised his hand and waved back.

Bode watched Mason get to his feet and start across the hall. His friend got less than five feet before a burning piece of the ceiling fell and landed squarely on Mason's skull, sending him crashing to the floor so close to Bode that he could stretch and touch him, tell him to get up.

Mason didn't move.

Bode saw Raef's face, and he knew from the look that Mason would never move again.

Raef charged towards them.

Bode sat with his arms crossed, watching as Raef skidded across the floor littered with human detritus, and collapsed next to the body of his brother.

He watched him push the fallen stone away.

He couldn't hear Raef screaming Mason's name.

He saw Raef put his hand on Mason's head.

A new sensation of heaviness filled Bode's chest as he watched Raef scoop the bits of Mason's head, trying to put the pieces of Mason's skull back together.

Bode didn't hear Raef start begging the Gods. He was deaf to Raef pleading with Mason to wake up.

He didn't see Raef's eyes fill with tears that fell onto the face of his twin.

He didn't need to see or hear any of it to know.

And still he sat there, not dying.

Slowly, deliberately, Bode turned to the raised dais where he had last seen Calem.

Where he had been on the floor there was just a burnt outline of what his body had once been. In its place was a pillar of light, vaguely upright, nothing human and yet, Bode thought, it seemed to emit a feeling of unremitting sadness.

The pillar of sad bright white light moved purposefully across the room as the whole tower started to shake.

Bode waited, damaged and broken stone and mortar clattering down around him.

Bigger chunks of rock fell, the black smoke-filled air starting to swirl as it found a way to escape through the gaping holes in the collapsing dome.

The pillar moved across the hall until it came to Raef and Mason.

Bode had to squint to look at it; like looking at the sun his eyes started to water, he thought he saw it bend forward, looking down.

For a moment the incandescent light seemed to dim. Then it moved on.

Bode saw giant cracks appear in the floor, he felt the tremors and shudders and knew the entire building was breaking apart.

And still Raef sat cradling the pieces of his brother's skull trying to put him back together like a child with a puzzle in a lightning storm.

Orren was gone.

Tevez was gone.

Calem was gone.

Mason was gone.

Bode unwrapped his hands from his shoulders and braced himself against the shaking wall as he stood up. Slowly, orientating himself, he took careful steps over to Raef.

He hoped his young friend wasn't too heavy, knowing it didn't matter.

Bode bent down and pushed an arm under Raef's knees, put his other arm around his back, and gently he picked him up off the floor.

Raef didn't protest or struggle. He leaned against Bode and rested his face on the bigger man's chest.

Bode turned and headed for the doorway. With each step he felt the tower disintegrating behind him. He felt the vibration of Raef's cries against his body. He felt the heat as he walked them through the flames. He didn't look back at any of his dead friends he was leaving behind in the fire.

As Bode took each determined step calmly and consciously, the entire tower fell apart around them, until the only part of the whole structure still standing was the staircase. Each step he took down the winding spiral staircase was the last, each step collapsed and fell away behind him.

He stopped and looked around.

They were a hundred feet up in the air, on a stone step seemingly supported by nothing, the remains of the tower no more than rubble and stone scattered around the desert floor below them. The flames were far away now but the heat was still causing ash and soot to rise around them. Bode looked down. There at the bottom of the steps, waiting, was the pillar of light.

And somewhere, lost below, buried in the remains of the tower, were all the bodies.

Bode clutched Raef tighter to his chest and hoped his eyes were closed.

He took he next step down, sensing the stone falling away the instant his foot lifted off it, but there was no sound as it hit the earth so far below them.

He took another step.

When he reached the bottom, Bode walked away from the tower and didn't looked back. He carried Raef forward into the empty, endless desert. He didn't turn his head and didn't notice when the pillar of light that had kept pace behind them finally turned and went off in another direction. He didn't hear when Raef's voice finally broke and he couldn't cry anymore.

The sun. The burning desert sun. Bode walked on, oblivious to the heat that threatened to slowly cook his brain inside his skull. By the end of the first day his tanned skin was more a maroon colour. On day two the blisters burst as they continued; by the third day his body was numb and he was losing his mind. He'd started to see shapes in the haze on the sand and hear hushed voices telling him to turn around, to walk when he wanted to sleep, to strip out of his tunic that was unbearably heavy on his tired, sore body. He didn't really think of what he was doing anymore. He thought of Orren. He thought of Tevez. He thought of Mason. He thought of An'uek. He thought about them all, and he kept walking.

He didn't hear the way the wind whispered around him, whisking its message away, leaving the only sound in the emptiness the silent sibilance of the sand as step after step he walked into the waiting desert.

CHAPTER 2

Calem lay on the hard red sand, his arms clamped around his head over his ears. His dry broken voice could barely be heard above the scratching sound of the shifting sands as he tried to burrow into the ground with his knees and elbows.

He was under siege from a cacophony of piercing shrieks and howling screams that cleaved into his being and attacked his mind. His reality became the sensation of the land cracking and quaking apart, the heat of flames melting mountains, the misery of oceans rushing onto new lands like blood in a wound. After aeons, or hours, of exposure to the nascent raw magic of the deep desert, Calem sensed a pattern emerge in the chaos. There was an ebb to the pain, a flow into a moment of respite before looping back into the tempest.

It sparked an unexpected memory of shattered glass, countless shards splintering, spinning and glittering in the dark. Every fragment reflected his face. In the depths of the desert, outside the flow of time, Calem lay abused by the creation of the world. And there, as he looked, he saw himself reflected.

Bastion pressed himself against the cold black basalt, trying with all his might to dissolve his body into the rock face and save himself from witnessing the sight of the thing in the canyon below. He touched his fingertips to his eyes in a gesture of wiping tears and quickly offered a silent benediction of thanks that he had chosen to send his men back into the desert, back to the camp. They were safe from whatever was being born on the red sand.

As much as he wanted to look away, sneak away, run away, he couldn't stop staring. Nothing alive in the canyon could look away.

Bastion watched, captivated, alongside snakes, scorpions, lizards, and dragons, as the lump of man-shaped molten fire staggered into the canyon, collapsed and started to howl with the voices of all the living creatures of the world morphed into one.

Its light sparked brightly, then dimmed, until eventually, after minutes, or months, it was more man than magma. As it turned from bright white into red hot then angry yellow, Bastion heard the noises change from howls to hisses and spitting. Daring to turn his head just enough to see up to the highest ridges of the canyons, where the legendary beasts had been reborn, he saw dragons on every outcropping of rock unfurling their embryonic wings, still dripping in birthing juices, stretching them out to dry in the heat haze radiating from the man below them.

The heat didn't last; abruptly and without warning, a bolt of lightning speared down from the cloudless blue sky, striking the body in the canyon. On impact, an almighty clap of thunder reverberated up the rock faces, cracking and splitting rocks, sending enormous boulders and thumb-sized pebbles raining down the steep sides onto the man below. A single pebble struck him, and instantly his liquified fire-red body transmuted into diamond.

The sudden silence hit Bastion like a punch to the gut; his legs gave out and he fell forward onto his knees dangerously close to the edge of his rocky ledge.

The crystalline body didn't move, but Bastion felt, to his core, that it was looking at him.

The sensation of eyes moving across his body made him shake, and he pulled himself away from the edge and back up as far as he could go.

The man of brilliant rock started to cry out. A violent wail, shrill enough to shatter glass, echoed and filled the canyon. Bastion felt the pressure in his ears intensify.

Pain spread quickly around his eyes, like a rope wrapped around his head was being turned and tightened by someone that wanted to crack his head open like a boiled egg. He rolled onto his side, holding his knees and clenching his jaw so hard he cracked a tooth in the back of his mouth. His only coherent thought was to stay away from the edge as his ears started to pop and he lost all sense of balance.

But then, above all the other noise, there was a scratching and tapping against stone from something so heavy the vibrations moved through him to the very stone of his meagre shelter. He didn't need to look, he knew the dragons were starting to move, their talons scratching the rock with each tentative step on newly born legs. His most basic instincts flared, and he sensed a hunger growing in the canyon.

Without warning, the blue sky seemed to switch off and sounds became muted. Bastion was alone in absolute darkness with just the roaring echo of pain in his head and the flushing of blood around his body.

He was breathing too hard; he could feel his heart banging inside his chest; the fear was overwhelming.

He felt something shift in the canyon; something had noticed him.

His instinct flared again and he knew a simple fact. In the canyon, defenceless and unwelcome, alone and small, he was prey.

The clicking and scraping stopped and the canyon filled with ravenous predators who had found something weak.

Bastion waited.

The creatures waited.

The impossibly dark night seemed to darken. He chanced a glance at the man far below and was stunned to see his diamond body absorbing the darkness, it poured into him, an obsidian river. The sharp outlines of his crystalline body softened into a pool of thick black oil rippling out and back into itself. It absorbed the night, and with it, Bastion's fear and the dragon's attention. As it swallowed and ingested the peril of the false midnight, day returned.

Bastion watched as it swelled, engorged until it was more a cocoon than shaped like a man. It continued to fatten until the bulge distended and burst.

Throwing his hands over his face, he braced himself for whatever was coming next. Expecting a rain of ooze and muck, he wasn't prepared for an assault of wind pummelling into him so harshly that he could barely breathe against its force. It was like the whole power of a sandstorm focused into the canyon, pushing against him as the shapeless thing below exhaled its genesis. As it ejected all its consumed and metamorphosised power into the canyon, it shrank and collapsed into the body of a young man lying on the red sand.

Bastion was unable to withstand the rush of air that filled his lungs beyond bursting. As he lost consciousness, the last thing he saw was the sight of hundreds of dragons leaping into the air, circling on the tide of raw magic funnelling up the canyon, and then arching mid-air, diving towards the man lying on the red sand. He turned to see each monstrous creature rush down, and every one of them disintegrated into dust the very moment their giant talons extended to snatch him up.

When Bastion regained consciousness it was morning, a shy weak sun barely visible over the canyon wall. Its rays warmed his chilled skin quickly, heating the rock around him.

He lay in the warmth, on that edge of sleep and wakefulness, thinking about the strangest dreams he had ever experienced.

Rolling over, he felt the pain of a jagged edge dig into his thigh. His instincts recognised the dangerous rocky ledge before his mind did. His muscular body coiled, he carefully inched back away from the edge and got to his knees. He remembered his dreams again and looked around.

There were no dragons on the cliffs of the canyon.

He scratched at his head, rubbed his eyes, yawned and stretched out cramped arms and legs, feeling the bones in his back shift after a bad night's sleep.

Trusting himself, he stood up and let the sun warm his face. He felt at peace.

After a while he looked around. Sure enough, there was the rocky path that would take him back to the cave which would eventually lead him down to the canyon floor and then home to his people.

Without looking back, he headed into the open mouth of the dark cave.

He walked confidently through the long dark cave tunnels, thinking about the wild dreams he had had since he sent his men home. He tried to remember why he had done that, why he hadn't gone with them.

In the cold quiet halls of rock, he wondered if he had been affected by the desert madness, if just this once he had stayed out too long in the sun, too long without water, if even he, the Sand-Dancer, had reached his limits in the desert. A coldness crept through his body that had nothing to do with the deep cavern.

His worrisome thoughts clouded his mind and he forgot his footing, tripping over a stone. He fell forward in the darkness, landing on his hands and knees, scratching his open palms. Muttering to himself, he got up and carried on walking, sucking at his bloody hand, the rich salty tang like acid on his tongue. He dwelled on what his delusions meant.

The darkness slowly faded to grey and then to weak filtered light as he walked out from the safety of the cave and onto the canyon floor and stopped.

In front of him, less than fifty feet away, a young man lay curled up on a patch of red sand.

Scattered all around him, soot spread out like a dense blackened carpet. All around, but not touching him.

He touched the soot.

It was all real.

Bastion smiled and kneeled, felt a flush of relief that he wasn't desert mad; the pure terror had all been real. He pushed his fingers lovingly into the red sand, feeling the tiny grains against his flesh.

CHAPTER 3

In Kraner, in the throne room of the castle, the green silk banners hanging from the oak rafters fluttered as the palace guards charged across the floor towards A'taz and Troy, swords drawn, daggers out, ready to fight and die.

"Stop and be still." An'eris's command rose unnaturally above their shouts and cries. She twinned a spell into her words and a hush enveloped all the voices of rage echoing in the great grey stone throne room. Everything stopped; even a wooden chair hastily thrown aside stopped in mid-air, the seat cushion slipping but unable to fall off.

A'taz smiled and looked down at the druid queen seated demurely at his side.

"You have something to say, beloved?" He reached down and stroked her long brown hair, coiling the thick braid around his fingers. She looked up at him and nuzzled herself into his hand, preening at his gentle touch.

"Go on," he encouraged her, turning his head and staring, smiling. "You want to say something."

"Lock the doors," she ordered, her gaze still on A'taz.

"Happily, my Queen." Troy set off purposefully, striding past immobile palace guards. He went to the huge oak doors and chanted a short spell. The centuries-old rusted iron locks slid smoothly across the panels of hardwood, bolting themselves down. He went to each of the three remaining doors quickly incanting the same spell. As the last deadbolt slid into place, Troy clapped his hands. He rushed back over to his master, standing before him, rocking slightly on the balls of his feet.

Ignoring Troy, A'taz looked down at An'eris and leaned towards her. He unravelled her hair from the braid, playing with the long dark strands, twirling the tresses reverently, trailing his fingertips down her cheeks and under her chin. He stroked her arm down to her hand, entwining their fingers together for a moment before softly moving his hand to rest on her belly.

The utter stillness of the throne room was broken by a deafening gallop, the heartbeat of the baby growing in An'eris's belly.

A'taz looked over at Troy.

"Be quick."

Troy marched across the throne room tapping six of his men, breaking the spell; they fell into line behind him.

"Take them," he hissed, pointing at Homen. Pointing at Cotta. Pointing at Brennan.

The men moved and grabbed their frozen prey.

Troy stepped up to Homen. He reached forward and opened the buttons of his vest, untying the sheer scarf at his neck. He dropped the length of silk on the floor, his attention on Homen. Troy put his forefinger to Homen's throat, pushing his talon-like fingernail against the pale neck until he punctured his skin, drawing a single drop of red blood. Troy wiped the blood with his finger and raised it to his mouth. He touched it with his tongue, savouring it for a moment before licking it all away.

"Delicious," Troy said, grinning. He stepped away, took a handkerchief from his pocket and wiped his finger. Troy nodded to a henchman.

Homen didn't waste his last second on Troy. He looked at Cotta one last time. A nameless goon set his blade across Homen's throat. Without hesitation, he pulled it with practised ease and Homen was gone, just a body, face down on the blue and grey tiled floor of the throne room.

Cotta, still spellbound and motionless, screamed from her soul as Homen's body was released and dropped to the floor. The men holding her gripped tighter.

Troy pivoted on his heel and stepped over to her. He grabbed her face, pointing at Homen.

"You'll never forget that." He smiled, leaned down, and put his mutilated mouth against her own, snaking his split tongue between her wet lips, licking inside her mouth in a pantomime of intimacy.

When he was finished, he leaned into her ear.

"You'll never forget me either," he sneered, leaning back and kissing her cheek.

He gestured with his hand and the two men forced her to her knees. Then they raised her head up, facing Brennan.

"Hello, Brennan." Troy loomed over him. "I have something very special for you. For us."

Troy put his hand on the mercenary holding Brennan.

"Tip his head back," he said. "You, hold his eyes open wide," he said to the other.

There was a moment of shuffling, then Brennan was just where Troy wanted him.

"You see too much," Troy whispered. "I'll put a stop to that."

He stepped as close as he could and put his hands on his shoulders so he could look down on him.

Troy pursed his lips, moved his tongue around inside his mouth and then let a long white trail of spit ooze out between his lips to drop onto Brennan's eyeballs.

Brennan saw Troy's face hovering over his. His vision centred on the long drop of spit dripping off the ugly blackened lip.

He felt it hit his eyes, wanted to blink and pull back in an instinct of disgust, but he felt the spell, and the men, holding him down.

The burning started a moment later. A sharp sting, like a fleck of hot oil from a pan. He could hear his eyes sizzling, feel them bubble, and then there was a sensation he couldn't comprehend, and he felt something causing his eyelids to stick over his eyes. His vision became murky, colours faded to greys and then darker blues, and then there was nothing but blackness inside the darkest shadow. He felt the spell drag across his face, felt it infuse his skin, and then unfold in his body, magic inside him spreading like poison. On instinct, and out of his control, he reached for his power without any intention of controlling or directing himself. He cast it around himself, trying to block out the pain, suffocate the heat, strangle Troy's venom coursing through his body.

He felt his power grow, felt it rise up, and as it did so, he felt the rush of thoughts from everyone around him, the cacophony of words, images, sounds, smells, feelings and emotions, and it was an onslaught he couldn't process. So he reached again to that power he had never acknowledged and used it to push back.

He heard their voices, sensed their thoughts, reached into them all, to stop them, to stop it all coming towards him. In his blindness, he reached so far that he pushed past their thoughts, and without realising it, he pushed into their minds, his power seeking sight that Troy's spell had taken.

It was all too much. Brennan, blinded only seconds ago, was suddenly looking at the throne room through the eyes of every person there.

It was at that moment A'taz released everyone from the motionless confines of his power.

Brennan heard men roaring, charging, dying. He put his hands to his eyes and felt only skin. He started to shake, picturing what he could feel, but also seeing himself touching his face with trembling fingers. He was seeing himself but feeling Cotta's horror, and sadness, her rage and her confusion.

Brennan, overwhelmed and disorientated, collapsed onto the floor.

"Are you done?" A'taz called across the hall. "We need to move things along."

Troy stood.

"Almost, Master," he replied, his voice clear and light.

A'taz, ignoring Troy, looked down at An'eris.

He reached down and put his hand on her belly, searching for the tiny life growing inside her.

CHAPTER 4

Across the world, in a place that exists in secret, the druid lord
A'rrick sat naked, hunched over himself on a moss-covered stone.
His body was radiating heat in the freezing winter night; drops of
sweat turned to beads of ice across his pale olive skin, covering him
in a blanket of crystals so fine his body seemed dressed in stars.
White moths fluttered around in the moonlight, settling on his head,
shoulders, hands; some settling on the still body to rest for the night.

Though his body was still, A'rrick wasn't at rest. He frantically
cast his mind across the world until he found the heartbeat of the
baby in An'eris's womb.

"Granddaughter?" His contact was blunt and desperate. "I hear
your cries."

"He's here, grandfather." The words came to him with a lisp in
the silence between her heartbeats. She tried to send him what she
could, noises, voices, emotions and vague concepts cast in shadows.
A'rrick received impressions of men in different places, of violence,
death and terror.

"I'm coming for you," A'rrick called out to her.

"He's too strong," the baby in the womb wailed in anguish. "I
can't help her. I can't stop him."

"Wait for me," he begged. "Protect yourself, I'm coming."

"Help us," the baby screamed without a voice. And then was
gone.

"Wait!" A'rrick's terrified roar filled the glade and echoed off
the bamboo trunks standing silent sentinel around him.

He stood, his long supple muscular legs trembled, the second skin of ice cracked and fell off his body as he rose to his full imposing height.

"An'eris!" he cried into the dark, desperately casting his mind along the familiar paths of a lifetime that would lead to his beloved child.

Nothing.

"Granddaughter?" he tried.

"An'eris?" he tried again. The only response was the despair of his own words cascading back to him, each time fainter than the last.

A'rrick took a step back, reached out blindly and sat down on the moss-covered stone seat he'd used for centuries. His sense of terror was so strong he could taste it on his tongue, an unfamiliar bitter tang that made him gag. His mind conjured images and faces trying to make sense of the chaotic scene the baby had tried to convey from inside her mother's womb.

He knew a truth.

A'taz had taken An'eris. He pictured her, but not as she was. A'rrick's mind tortured him with images of An'eris as the brown-haired little girl with violet eyes who would wriggle out of his arms as often as she would leap into them. Now A'rrick imagined his little girl with A'taz, his decrepit fingers carding through her long hair, fondling her on his lap. His fear forced an image of A'taz's fingers transforming into talons digging into her flesh, piercing her tiny body as his mouth covered hers and the monster started to draw her breath out of her body.

A'rrick imagined all this happening on the throne of Barclan too many miles away from where he sat shaking in the dark.

At the thought of the throne, A'rrick's mind jumped to An'eris and saw her as she was. His heir, she would be the druid queen, but before that she was already a queen of man, with a simple ring marking her as Orren's bride, binding her to a people that were not her own. Orren. A'rrick felt a spark of anger flare up and burn away. He clenched his jaw at the thought of the boy who would be the man that stole his daughter from her birth right. Where was he?

A'rrick's anger turned to outrage and he flung his mind across the world looking for Orren.

From outside his body he saw the eddies and flows of primal power that coursed through the living earth. His practised mind's eye flickered across the world searching for the pattern he knew was uniquely him. After a few moments he found it lingering as a memory out in the desert almost at the end of the world. A'rrick grasped and pulled but was rebuffed.

Confused, A'rrick stopped and looked. And looked deeper. It took him a moment to understand what he saw, and as soon as he did, he broke contact and fled back to his body.

For a moment he forgot An'eris, he forgot the baby, he forgot A'taz. He ran from heat and bright white light.

A'rrick turned towards the tangle of bamboo that surrounded his seat in the mossy glade and picked out a path. The tight stems rose over sixty feet, pressing together so closely he had to move sideways between them, his body scratched and marked by the snags and splinters in the ever-growing forest. He walked without hesitation, intent on a place he alone knew existed. Finally, he reached it and stopped in front of a stem as thick as his own body. Not green but grey, the stem was more like stone than plant, hot and damp to the touch. In the cold of the early winter night the stone was steaming wet. A'rrick reached out and put his hands flat against it, closed his eyes and began a susurrant chant that was absorbed directly into the night. His words were not meant for his world.

"Shaa?" An unknown voice broke the silence of the Gods where they rested. The voice called one of them by name.

"Shaa?" The voice came again, not in supplication, but demanding attention. "I have called your true name using the words given to my kind by your sister, whose name still echoes in the earth. I stand in a place that is not one of you but is all of you, and I know you hear my call." The voice bellowed confidently into the eternity between his world and the Gods. "I have called, you must answer."

A'rrick stepped back. He focused on taking long slow breaths, the waiting as much a torture as the memory of the baby's heartbeat.

He had no doubt the hunchbacked God would answer his summons, but he had no idea how long he must wait. Would his child and her child be dead and the world irrevocably changed before his call was answered?

Dwelling on how a God measures time, he almost didn't notice the subtle change in the thick stem in front of him. At first, he thought it might be a trick of the few shafts of moonlight that managed to filter through the canopy of leaves above. Then he saw it again. A change in the patina of the stony bamboo stem, a shifting of the lines and cracks, moving until they held the vague misshapen outline of a misshapen man.

A'rrick felt a gentle breeze brush across his naked skin. A haze shimmered around the outline. In the moonlight it looked like the shape was breathing.

A'rrick stepped back, the empty air in the space where he had stood starting to thicken.

In the lazy moonlight, A'rrick blinked, and the hunchback trapped in the bamboo stepped forward into the world.

"You called my name." The hunchback sighed into the cold night. "Here I am."

"I learned the call. I know the lore, but…" A'rrick faltered, not quite believing a God stood before him.

"You, a druid, why do you not call my sister's name? An'dorna created you, your kin, it is she who likes to commune with your kind. Why do you call my name, using words to summon that have never been spoken before on this earth?"

"I need your help," he said simply, still shocked that his call had worked.

"Again, I ask, why me and not your own Goddess?"

"Our legends tell us you unified our world, brought order from the chaos."

"And what of it, Druid?"

"Something has happened. That order is broken. We are in chaos."

"And you assume I can reorder it, this chaos that you've seen?" Shaa looked around, spread his hands, shrugged his shoulders. "Everything looks fine to me." His words were cruel but, A'rrick also sensed, defensive.

"It is not here yet. The chaos is coming. It'll be everywhere soon."

"It must be a great thing, to dare, to assume I will come to your aid."

A'rrick licked his lips and steadied himself. Gathering his wits, he recalled an image of An'eris and his purpose.

"I have seen a great evil, a threat." He bowed his head in respect. "One perhaps you haven't seen."

"You think we are blind?" Shaa asked.

"No," A'rrick quickly answered.

"Then why am I here, A'rrick." Shaa surprised the druid, using his name. "Why did you call me to help you?"

"Because there is a sorcerer, an abomination."

"We know him," Shaa said, nodding.

"Then you know where he is."

Again Shaa nodded.

"We've seen what he has done, and for the first time in eternity, we know fear at the hands of a mortal."

"Why have you not done anything before now to stop him?" A'rrick demanded.

"Do not be so bold with your words to me, Druid," Shaa warned, and A'rrick felt a force push him back and a flash of heat across his cheek.

"I'm sorry, but please," he implored, "he has them." A'rrick stepped forward, the memory of An'eris and the baby giving him courage.

"And you want me to intervene?"

"Yes," A'rrick urged, "stop him, kill him."

"I am not death." Shaa shook his head. "He is elsewhere."

A'rrick didn't understand Shaa's words, and he didn't care to ask what he meant. He fumbled with his pleas.

"Save them," A'rrick begged.

"I can't interfere." Shaa sighed. "We can't interfere."

"But you do, all of you," A'rrick wailed. "I call on An'dorna and she heals through my hands. Evram brings rains when we sing for her, and even the cruel Goddess helps bring warmth and light in the cold dark when we beg for fire."

At the word "fire" Shaa recoiled.

"Do not speak to me of what we do or do not do. We cannot interfere, we cannot kill for you."

"But you said you were afraid; you must do something about him."

"We must do nothing." Shaa threw A'rrick's words back at him. "We are no longer of your world. Even now, I am here but I am not in your realm. When we stepped back from the world, we separated for all existence to spare you our rivalries."

"Then spare just my child, please," A'rrick cajoled, bringing the focus back to An'eris. "Protect her somehow, long enough for me to go to Barclan and find a way to save them myself."

"Barclan?" Shaa said, surprised.

A'rrick was confused by the God's response.

"Yes, of course Barclan," he said quickly. "An'eris is in Barclan. He's there too. I need to save them, to kill him."

Shaa drew himself up as tall as his contorted body allowed.

"Oh," he said, "you are speaking of A'taz."

"Yes of course," A'rrick shot back. "A'taz is in Barclan. He has An'eris. He must be killed. He is the one, he is the one you watched, the one you fear," A'rrick stated, a sense of doom and foreboding spreading through him.

"He is who you mean?" A'rrick asked quietly.

"No," Shaa said in a hush.

"Then who…"

A'rrick stopped. He looked at Shaa. The God reached out and put his fingertips to A'rrick's eyes.

"See what I've seen, there, in the desert."

A'rrick was struck with an image of a room, of men fighting, dying. He saw Orren and a young man struggling with each other, Orren forcing something into the boy's mouth. A'rrick felt the detonation of power before his mind comprehended the blast, and he felt the shock wave tremble through his body.

Shaa released his hold on A'rrick and the image faded.

"So you see, A'rrick, druid lord," Shaa turned away. "It is not for Barclan I answered your call. Or your daughter. Or your granddaughter."

"I understand," A'rrick whispered.

"If you wish to save them, you must do it yourself."

A'rrick nodded, saying nothing.

Shaa took a step towards the bamboo stem, then stopped.

"We cannot help you, not directly. And we cannot help ourselves," he rasped.

A'rrick frowned.

"This boy, this sorcerer, his fate is not known to us. We cannot influence what we do not know."

"Then what help are you?" A'rrick challenged.

Shaa stepped up to the bamboo and pushed his hands into it, returning to his realm.

"He has a brother."

"He does," A'rrick replied exasperated, "he is with my daughter. He was with her in the throne room when it happened."

"I know him," Shaa admitted.

A'rrick was stunned.

"How?"

"He has a touch of my power. Thoughts and words are two sides of the same thing. His power unifies those sides. It is my legacy."

"And he will help An'eris?"

"I hope so," Shaa pondered. "I hope he will help us all."

CHAPTER 5

Long arterial streaks of blood were splattered between the oak beams on the whitewashed ceiling of the throne room. Centuries-old hand-sewn banners had been ripped off the walls by men stumbling back desperate for something to grab onto, to hold them up; windows of beautiful, coloured glass were smashed to nothing. The long carpet would have to be burned.

A'taz ambled around the great hall, Troy obediently at his side. He was careful where he stepped, taking his time to find a path between all the bodies and blood to keep his boots clean.

He counted as he walked.

"There are too many bodies," he stated.

"I made sure all the Kraner men and all our mercenaries are dead, less to explain."

"You're sure they're all dead?"

"The spell was complete. Our men killed them all, then I killed all our men."

"I don't want problems."

"There are no witnesses."

A'taz pointed to the two viewing galleries on either side of the long hall.

"No one." Troy shrugged, not bothering to look. "They're only used for weddings and funerals anyway."

"And what about all this?" A'taz refocused on the bodies.

"Ah, I have an idea about that," Troy said, giddy with excitement from the killing.

As they walked, they talked, and Troy told A'taz the story he had concocted.

They stopped in front of Homen's corpse. A'taz stared down at the body, which was already showing the first signs of stiffening. Troy waited, careful to pick his moment to interrupt his master's thoughts.

"It would need to come directly from An'eris." Troy picked up the threads of the tale.

"The Queen," A'taz corrected.

"Yes, yes of course," Troy dipped his head and looked away for a second. "The Queen of course." As he spoke to himself, he tapped his fingers against his temple.

"Stop that." A'taz unexpectedly reached out and grabbed Troy's hand, pressing it against the side of his face so hard it made him stagger back.

Troy cowered at his master's touch.

"If the Queen explains it to the council, they will believe her. Treachery, murder, it's nothing new in a royal court, and Kraner is no exception."

A'taz considered his words, still looking down at Homen.

"No one will believe this man was a traitor."

"He died defending his Queen." Troy put his hands over his heart. "His last living breath, his last deed in service to the crown. What better end for him, and one everyone will believe."

"It's true." A'taz reached down and straightened the cuffs at Homen's wrists. "As much as possible, it must be the truth."

"Or we say he's gone away on an errand for the King. That way we don't have to hold a funeral."

"The Queen can see he's dead."

"We can take that from her mind."

He turned away and they walked towards the dais at the back of the hall, towards the thrones.

"And these two?"

A'taz stepped over to a huddle on the floor. Cotta sat slumped forward trying to cover Brennan's unconscious body.

"The woman is important to the Queen." Troy fingered the bloodied blade at his belt.

"And the man?" A'taz asked coolly.

"A liar. A conman. An old friend from Penrose." Troy kneeled and yanked Brennan's head up by his hair. "He thinks he's very clever." Troy's eyes swivelled at his handiwork and he licked his lips with his split tongue. Troy leaned in close as if to whisper, but his voice was loud. "I didn't like how he used to look at me when I was around the Queen, always suspicious." He looked over at Cotta. "Now he can't see either of his women."

A'taz watched disinterestedly as Troy played with the man's face. "Are you done?" he snapped.

Troy spun, his smile fading quickly under his master's malevolent gaze.

"Can I assume you've thought this through?" He stepped over to Troy, who immediately stepped back.

"A plot, to drive the King mad and seize power. The woman is known to be ambitious, devious even… and Orren, well, he was loved as a prince but not on the throne long enough to be loved as King. His reign was one of famine and starvation, so it's plausible that he's away somewhere. People accept a King away from his castle quite easily as long as there's bread on the table and no enemies at the gates."

A'taz turned to An'eris and beckoned her over.

The Queen picked up the hem of her skirt and came over to his side.

"What's happened here?" she asked, her words slurred and slow.

"There's been an attack," Troy said behind them all.

At his words, Cotta leapt up, trying to snatch at anyone she could reach, but her limbs didn't work properly and she tumbled forward. A'taz reacted instantly and slapped her face, sending her falling back onto Homen's corpse, she instinctively turned around, reaching blindly for Brennan.

"Yes," A'taz said, nodding, "it looks like treason."

Holding both of An'eris's hands together in one hand and then lightly placing the fingers of his other on the back of her head, Troy softly incanted a spell.

"No," An'eris said, shrugging and shaking her head, "not Homen." She glanced at Cotta, trying to say her own words. "I can't, I won't… believe it," she slurred, "not you."

An'eris shook her head from side to side, trying to dislodge A'taz's fingertips and his words. He held her firmly.

"Treason," he said again, "a clever plot to overthrow the crown, years in the making."

"Not Cotta," An'eris said, her voice starting to change, less shocked. "I won't believe you."

"Yes," A'taz said, "it must have been. Why else would she have attacked you? Why else would her lover have attacked you?"

"Not Cotta?" she said again, feeling sad.

"Yes," A'taz hissed, "you will believe me."

Troy stepped behind An'eris and leaned closer to her ear, whispering his incantation.

"Homen is dead." Her eyes filled with tears that flowed freely down her cheeks. A'taz released her hands to wipe her tears away.

"Loyal to the very last moment, he died trying to protect you."

She sobbed and put her hands over her eyes for a moment before looking at Cotta.

"She's my friend."

"She *was*. She probably still believes she *is*," A'taz said. "But the truth is lying dead all around you."

She looked up at him, turning around, oblivious to his hand on her head and the words Troy was putting into her mind.

An'eris saw Troy physically change into the body of her friend, dependable Lord Ravi, at her side, as he had been since he came to the royal courts. And with him, the stonemason who had come to rebuild Kraner and would help her, stay with her, support her to rule the kingdom—such kind, loyal men.

"I am so grateful to you both for being here to serve me, to save us from this clever plot to overthrow the kingdom."

A'taz smiled.

"How can we serve you, my Queen?" he asked dutifully.

An'eris surveyed the scene.

"I must call a full council and explain what's happened," she said, her voice firm.

"What do you want us to do with these two?" A'taz asked. "I suggest the dungeon until the council calls for their execution."

"Execution?" An'eris frowned a moment as she considered it. "Yes, that makes sense."

"And who else should we arrest? Who else do you think was involved?"

Again, An'eris frowned, and a thin band of sweat swelled across her forehead. Troy stepped closer, his whispering louder.

A'taz gripped her tightly.

"Surely there were more involved in this plot?"

"You think it was Travis?"

"Possibly," A'taz agreed. "I'm new to Kraner, I don't know these people, but if he was a friend of that woman then yes, he must be a traitor."

An'eris thought about his words, the unsettling feeling that they made sense cementing into her mind.

"Who else would this man and woman work with?"

"M-Marsha." An'eris stuttered out the name. "Travis and Marsha, and their own staff. But in the last few weeks they spent more time in the city, away from their duties it seemed."

"Then you must find them and uncover their role in the plot."

"And have them executed?" She finished his words.

A'taz smiled and released her from his grip. As he let her go, she fell forward against Troy, but it was Ravi who caught her, who scooped her up in his arms and carried her to the bolted wooden door behind the thrones that led to the private royal rooms.

"Troy," A'taz called clearly. "Do what you need to do, then find me when you are done. It's time to ensure the city is full of happy people who don't see anything and don't ask questions. I'll need you to augment with me. Bring me one of the gems, it must be done before nightfall."

With that, A'taz muttered some words, and the spell that had bound the room and kept all the doors shut was released.

Ravi ran from the throne room, shouting for help, for guards, for someone to help him save the Queen. In all the commotion, A'taz didn't notice a small body disentangle itself from a heap of lifeless limbs at the back of the hall and sneak away.

Denny burst into Marsha's bedchamber, bounced onto the bed and shook her awake.

Her eyes opened, a hand covering her mouth, soft urgent frenzied words begging her to be quiet.

"Denny?" she whispered, sitting up, her old bones moving stiffly. She was about to ask what he was doing but stopped when she saw the hysterical frenzy of his actions.

He threw open her wardrobe and pulled out the first cloak he could and grabbed her boots. Jumping back onto the bed he threw her covers off. He was struggling to breathe.

"Get up, get up, get this on," he gibbered, pulling her up and wrapping her in the cloak, one boot crammed on the wrong foot, the other forgotten.

"Denny, what's happening?" Marsha asked, panic blooming but still quiet.

"They're all dead. I have to get you out."

"Denny, stop," she cried out.

He grabbed her face.

"A'taz is in the castle. Ravi is one of his. They've slaughtered everyone and they're coming for you now."

Moments later he was leading her by the hand through corridors filled with distraught and frantic men and women crying or shouting or both. Everyone got out their way, assuming they were also rushing to help. But Denny didn't lead Marsha to the throne room, to An'eris, or to the healer's halls. He took the fastest route he could down to the lower levels, then lower still, and with each subsequent floor, they ran into fewer and fewer people, until, as they reached the lowest level, they finally came to deserted passageways.

He didn't slow his pace, physically dragging her along the cold dark empty hallways carpeted in dust undisturbed by footfall for decades.

"This way," he gasped. "There's a room full of old broken furniture and a way out."

Marsha couldn't reply. She was too old and weak for his speed and it was all she could do to get enough breath.

"I'll lower you down." He was talking more to himself. "I have to get you to Travis."

He found what he was looking for and with enormous effort raised an old trap door, peering into the darkness of the old sewer tunnel below.

He manhandled her over the opening despite her protests. She clung to him, still trying to catch her breath.

"Let go."

He dropped her through the trap door as carefully and gently as he could, but her old bones couldn't withstand the fall and her ankle shattered as she hit the stone floor fifteen feet below.

Her scream of pain echoed along the old chamber, and Denny was flooded with renewed panic at who might have heard her howl. Holding onto the latch, he jumped through the opening, slamming the trap door behind him as he fell, sealing them off from the bowels of the castle and consigning their fate to the sewer.

The room smelled of damp, the kind you can't find the source of because it's everywhere. He had shut the window against the wind blowing in off the sea knowing he wouldn't open it until spring, but it couldn't keep out the cold. Lately, icicles had formed inside the room, clinging to the edge of the windowsill and growing ever downward. Travis sat on the floor, his back against the wall facing the window.

He rubbed the oil into his gums and was rewarded seconds later with the rush of the poison through his blood, chasing the tiredness from his mind, sharpening his senses. He felt himself dribble as his lips numbed; it was always the same now. He looked down at his fingertips covered in spit and blood; he could taste it. He reached up to the desk, palm flat on the table top and moving around until he hit the sides of a bottle. He grabbed it and took a mouthful of strong brandy. He swished it round his mouth, feeling the sharp sting above his teeth, idly wondering if they really were as loose as they felt these days. He thought about spitting it out; booze and blood wasn't a tasty mix. But it was strong stuff, good stuff. He swallowed it, forcing it down his throat, then took another strong pull before getting to his feet, already feeling stronger, more himself than he had all morning. He held out his hands, licking the drops of blood and oil off his fingers and palms, waiting for the tremors to stop. Tucking the little vial of oil into his pocket, he went to the door, about to open it and head onto the docks when Denny burst through.

At first, he couldn't understand anything Denny was saying, and then he didn't want to. The boy was covered in what looked like dirt, and he smelled like shit and blood and was probably all those things. But it wasn't how he looked, or smelled, or his words that made Travis grab for his sword and immediately follow him down and out onto the streets, it was the madness in the boy's eyes.

Denny led him away from the main cobbled streets around the docks, and as they moved off, Travis heard guards calling for him from all around. He heard the voices of his own men meet the cries for his arrest, and as they rounded a corner and Denny pushed him into a dark alleyway, Travis heard the faint sounds of steel striking steel and voices raised in defiance as the melee began.

They found Marsha where Denny had left her, alone and cold in the dark.

Travis picked her up effortlessly, taking care on the uneven, slippery stones underfoot. He ordered Denny to leave them, to go back to the castle, to sneak back in and clean himself up and wait for his orders, promising to look after Marsha.

"I don't want to go back there," Denny begged. "Please, I can't go back."

"You have to," Travis ordered coldly. "You're the only man we have there now."

Travis picked his way through the alleyways where forgotten men and women lived until he found the well-lit street he was looking for. Squaring his shoulders and ignoring the cold sweat running down his spine and the sound of shouting and fighting all around him, he walked confidently to a locked door, banging it with the toe of his boot.

The door opened enough to let light flood through, illuminating his face and the obvious bundle in his arms.

"Kirin," he pushed past her, "close the door, we need to go upstairs."

Denny stood in front of An'eris.

"You don't have to hide your feelings." She held his hands, rubbing them with her own, trying to soothe him. "I'm as distraught by all this as you are."

"Yes, Your Majesty," he answered. He didn't know what else to say. Her words, her story of what had happened floated through his mind, and it felt so real, so absolute, that he almost believed it. With every image that his mind conjured to match her telling of the traitors in the hall, he remembered Troy dragging his finger across Homen's throat. He remembered the blade.

He remembered being in the hall, someone falling down on top of him, the sound of the blood bubbling out of the man's chest, his dead body weighing him down, hiding him. The feeling of the hot blood dripping down onto his cheek and not being able to wipe it away. He remembered watching it all, wanting to help, but not as much as he wanted to live. So he stayed as still as he could, buried under another body that fell across him.

He remembered it all and kept replaying it while his mind created images to match the story she was telling him.

He watched her, focused on the way her lips moved around the words she said, and thought about the people he loved, dead, or locked away in the dungeon who would soon be dead. He stopped hearing her words, and the urge to believe faded a little.

"Squire," she said louder.

"Yes, Majesty," he said to cover his lapse.

"I said… you are in my service now."

Denny bowed.

"And you are also to serve at the leisure of Stonemason Gavis of Aquam."

She stepped aside and A'taz stepped forward, his disguise of kind clear eyes, a broad wide smile, spindly arms and thinning hair devastatingly effective. He looked like someone anyone could trust.

Denny felt his whole body start to shake with fear, but a lifetime of duty and training forced him to bow.

"Master Gavis," he said respectfully, "I'm at your command."

"I understand you were squire and personal staff to one of the traitors?" the new master Gavis asked him.

"I was to Master Brennan all that… and more," Denny said defiantly.

"And more?"

"He loves him," An'eris said kindly, "don't you? You're loyal to him."

"I do." Denny let the tears fall honestly but saw a chance to do what Travis had begged of him. "I did, I was." He swallowed his sobs. "I loved my master." He clenched his jaw. "I don't love a traitor. I serve the crown."

A'taz, Gavis, put a hand on his shoulder, smiling.

"I know we can trust you," he said, the menace in his words barely discernible. "We must understand what plot was at play here. You were privy to much of your master's affairs. You must tell us everything you know. Everyone he spoke to, everyone he met, every bargain and deal he struck while working with your lawmaker."

"I will," Denny agreed, wondering if the thumping in his chest was his heart breaking apart as he prepared to betray his master.

An'eris presided over the full council and told them what had happened. As she spoke, the men and women watched as bodies were carried past the open doors of the council chamber.

"Traitors," An'eris said sadly. "I've sent Homen away to uncover more of the plot." Her anguish was clear for everyone to see even without understanding the lie she told herself. She was pale with dark circles around her eyes, and if anyone had dared step close to her they would have seen perspiration across her brow and the muscles of her neck stretched taut, as if she was trying to pull her head away from something.

"Perhaps the same plot that Orren himself uncovered in these same rooms?" someone suggested from the back.

"Show me a kingdom as vast as Barclan that doesn't have traitors waiting for an opportunity to strike," another called out. "I never did trust Cotta."

"Neither did I," a voice agreed.

"But how do we know there aren't more like them plotting right now."

"We don't," An'eris replied, "and so, as much as I think we should execute them straight away," she hesitated, flushed, struggling to speak. "I think we should hold them for questioning until the full extent of their plans are revealed to us."

Travis sat at the table in the tavern drinking another mug of ale, wiping the froth from his top lip on the back of his sleeve. It wasn't a drinking house where he expected to find any of the city guard. The stools and benches were filled with men and a few women he knew who had spent some time in the city cells; plenty he'd put there himself. He kept himself to himself, nothing more than a drunk looking to be a drunk on his own; people looked but no one saw him, the unwritten rule of certain places frequented by certain people. He listened.

"Heard the rumours coming out the castle?"

"What about?"

"Some of the higher-ups been done for treason."

"Anyone we know?"

"No, man and a woman. Few more, but they've disappeared, probably on the run or dead and they just not saying."

"Reward or anything for the ones they looking for?"

"Not so I know."

"Going to be a hanging?"

"Probably, don't know when though."

"Always good for a hanging."

And that was that. No purse at the end of the rumour; no interest from men and women who cut purses to stay alive.

Travis finished another mug, made sure he stumbled to the door as much as the other men he paced his drink with, and headed out into the night. He should have seen his patrols as he ambled through the centre of the city. He should have been asked what he was doing out on his own so late at night. He should have been told to take off his hood. There should have been someone.

CHAPTER 6

Cotta stood bound in rusty iron chains, defiant before An'eris in the very rooms she and Brennan had used as their offices only days before. The manacles were too small against her fine-boned wrists; slivers of flaking rusty metal cut into thin flesh, settling under her skin, her own blood making her hands sticky and warm. She refused to shift on her feet, to try to ease the pain shooting up her arms, to do anything other than stand straight and stare her accuser down.

"Tell me why," An'eris demanded, her face an inch away from Cotta.

"Where's the sorcerer whose words are behind your voice?" Cotta spat back.

"Tell me," An'eris ordered, her voice unnaturally high, her hands shaking at her sides, teeth clenched and the sinews of her neck stretched taut like a dog straining against a collar.

"There's nothing to tell," Cotta forced herself to be calm, "except that you're as much use as the dead they're dragging through the halls. You're betraying us all."

"You," An'eris shouted out of control, "are the traitor in my castle." She squeezed her eyes shut, forcing the words from her throat.

"Where is Ravi?" Cotta asked, looking around. "Where is Troy? Where is his master? Where is A'taz?"

"You speak lies and madness, Cotta," An'eris shrieked. "They've helped me uncover your treachery, and were it not for them, you would be on my throne wearing my crown."

"It was never your crown to wear," Cotta whispered, "and you know I've never wanted it."

"Tell me," An'eris said, almost pleading. "Tell me and I can make it a swift death, no pain."

"I won't lie to you," Cotta said, softening her voice, seeing how An'eris was physically crumbling under the weight of her words. "I am loyal to my King and my Queen and I always will be. But my King is not here, and you are not my Queen."

An'eris stepped away and turned her back to Cotta.

"You will be executed. I will order it."

"Will there be a trial?" Cotta asked, already sure of the answer.

"There's no need, I was witness to the attack. My word is enough the judgement will be mine."

"I'm sure it will," Cotta sighed, "those are our laws."

"Laws you passed," An'eris reminded her as her body visibly shook. "Laws that will see you hanged."

"Will you miss me, An'eris?" Cotta asked, coaxing her friend to turn and look at her.

The question took the Queen by surprise, and for a moment Cotta thought she saw A'taz's hold over An'eris break.

An'eris raised a hand and placed it to Cotta's cheek, A'taz's control firm.

"I don't know you anymore," she said, accusingly. "No, I won't miss you."

An'eris pulled her hand back and slapped Cotta across the face. The sound seemed to linger in the chamber. She turned to a guard.

"Take her away," An'eris ordered.

From across the room, A'taz waited until Cotta was led away before walking over to An'eris.

"I'm sorry, my Queen," he said, offering her a hand that she eagerly took, She let herself be led to a stool near the warm fire.

"I don't think I've ever known such grief." An'eris slumped forward and rested her head on her knees. "I've lost everything, and Orren is so far away." She let herself sob.

A'taz sank down beside her and put his arms around her shoulders. At his touch, her body slouched against his.

"I'm so glad you're here." She let herself relax into his embrace; the tears instantly abandoned.

"I'm only glad I arrived in time enough to serve you so thoroughly, my dear." He changed his affections as he started to stroke his fingers up her spine, letting them settle at the nape of her neck.

Her head lolled forward.

He waited for a few minutes, until she raised her head again.

"Are you listening, An'eris?" he asked her clearly.

"I am."

"Good, good girl," he said, grinning. "I want you to tell me a story."

"A story?"

"Yes." He nodded, holding her head firmly. "You see, I'm looking for something."

She frowned, and he felt her try to wriggle away. He tightened the pinch of his fingers.

"What are you looking for?" Her mouth formed the words but she glanced away from him for a second. He waited until she looked at him again, until he was sure she was under his command. Then he leaned in and whispered in her ear.

"I want you to tell me how to find the lake under this castle."

An'eris's head rolled to the side. She fixed her gaze on A'taz as she gritted her teeth. Through her clenched jaw, she broke through his control and spoke to him in her own words.

"Never."

A'taz, overtaken by fury at her resistance to his control, dug his fingers into the base of her skull and snapped her head forward, knocking her unconscious. She fell against him and collapsed across his lap.

As she was paraded through the castle on the end of a short iron chain, Cotta had no choice but to follow her captors. They didn't need to take the corridors that would lead her through her own halls, but they made sure they slowed down so she could watch as her maids and attendants, apprentices, deputies and servants were corralled. They made her stop and watch as, one by one, all the men and women who had served her faithfully, some since they were children, were killed just for knowing her.

She was walked past their corpses, and she recognised all their faces, young, old, scared.

One of the guards leading her abruptly stopped and turned to her.

"It's been a busy day." He pointed at the bodies on the floor with his sword.

Cotta wouldn't look; she kept her eyes on the man.

He yanked the chains, causing her to stumble forward, he grabbed her by the hair, forcing her gaze down. She wouldn't look.

"Cold bitch," he spat in her face. "This is all because of you and you don't even have a tear for them, not even the little ones." He kicked at a small dead foot.

Still she wouldn't look down. Instead she looked at him.

"I don't know you," she said to herself. "Is that his plan, kill all of us and fill the castle with his own monsters who are wearing men's faces?"

"I'm just the help, not the master." He dipped his head, ignoring the bodies littered around them, his gaze raking across her body. She knew exactly what he was thinking and held his lewd stare.

"Come on." He turned and yanked at the chains again. "I have orders I have to obey."

"I'm sure everyone does."

Without warning, the guard grabbed Cotta by the throat, squeezing as hard as he dared.

"Hold your tongue," he growled at her, "or I'll bite it out myself and be damned whatever the Queen thinks of that."

"Try it," Cotta croaked as he squeezed her harder. "I doubt you can."

He put his face right up to hers. She could feel the sharp prickling of his beard scratching her lips, and the snags of his bitten fingernails digging into the flesh of her neck. He bared his teeth against her mouth, and she could feel how much he wanted to bite into her.

Her fear spiked, and she lost control, suddenly reckless.

"Harder," she wheezed, as his hand crushed her throat.

She saw it in his face, how much he wanted it, but he couldn't do it.

"I didn't think so," she choked.

She wanted to pull away. Instead, she pushed her face against his, snarled and, twisting her head just a little, bit into the flesh of his bottom lip and pulled away.

He screamed, grabbed at his face, reeling away from her.

His cries brought more men. They saw the blood flowing down his mouth and streaming off his chin, saw the red smear across Cotta's lips and the flesh dangling from between her teeth.

"Enough!" A guard hit her from behind. Cotta fell forward from the impact, but the short iron chains at her wrist snapped taut and she spun around, suspended between the grey flagstones and the guard who had her at his mercy.

He dropped the chains and she fell to the floor, her head smacking into the stone. Her voice betrayed her and she yelled out. Overcome with dizziness, her vision darkened. As she lost consciousness, the last thing she saw was the open eyes of the dead.

Troy followed a step behind A'taz as they returned from casting their net across the city. They roamed the castle corridors smiling and greeting everyone that hurried past, offering words of comfort and condolence to the anguished men and women who were cleaning away the blood and the bodies.

Lord Ravi and the kind old stonemason were a balm to the sadness and grief of everyone they stopped to speak to. As the hours rolled on they found themselves walking alone.

"Why don't you just kill the baby," Troy asked. "She'll tell then."

A'taz slowed his steps and turned on Troy.

"Are you so stupid that after all the years under my care, my tutoring and mentoring, that you've learned nothing more than incantations and fancy dress." He gestured at the Ravi costume Troy still wore.

Troy looked away, ashamed. He quickly thought through what his master might have planned.

"An'eris is a druid," Troy stated, voicing his thoughts. "And if she loses the child, she'll die from the grief."

"And I need a Queen on the throne to maintain order around here so I can search in peace. I need Barclan functioning, I need people living lives, so I have no shortage of lives when I need them."

"Cotta then… slit her throat?"

"She's more valuable alive than dead. We can use her again and again until the Queen can't bear it anymore and she breaks rather than see her beloved suffer."

"What if she doesn't break?" Troy asked, thinking of what he knew of An'eris.

"She'll break," A'taz hissed.

Troy followed, quietly.

"What about the man?" A'taz eventually asked.

"Oh." Troy perked up. "Oh, I've made up a game."

"Do I want to know the game you're playing with him?"

"It's the best game." Troy's pace quickened. "I've bound his flesh and his bones, so no matter what I do, his body isn't damaged."

A'taz stopped and turned.

"And?" he asked.

"And he still feels whatever I do, but whatever I do doesn't linger."

Troy, wide-eyed and grinning, waited for his master's approval. When it didn't come, and the silence dragged on, he rushed to fill it.

"I had him taken to the dungeon earlier. The men beat him."

"Just beat him?"

Troy nodded. "Oh," he said, "They tried to beat him to death, but the spell is quite good. He's still good as new, I wouldn't say fresh, but he's holding together nicely, even after one of them stamped on his skull about a dozen times."

A'taz followed the tangled logic of Troy's fractured mind.

"So you have a plaything now?"

Troy nodded again.

As they continued, A'taz spared a thought for the man who followed so closely behind him. He quickened his pace just enough to put a longer step between them. Then he turned a corner into a corridor he didn't know, and the two men continued wandering around the castle, searching ever downwards into the dark.

CHAPTER 7

The thick velvet curtains had been pulled back, revealing a morning gloom. The insipid winter sun wasn't strong enough to cast shadows, so the maids had lit candles to mimic the day as they prepared the parlour for the Queen. Instead of waiting to serve her, they left as soon as the plates were laid and the food set on the table.

Troy had prepared An'eris's meal: oat cakes and dried apple. The food lay untouched on a slab of pressed pewter. Shards of shattered crystal lay across the table; some had landed in her food, some had lodged in her long plaits and fallen between her breasts. If she coughed, she thought she might cut herself. Evidence of Troy's anger. It didn't matter, she had no intention of moving, and if she could, she would will herself to stop breathing just for the satisfaction of seeing the frustration on the face of the creature sitting opposite her.

She wouldn't be fed and watered by him. Her refusal to succumb to his command alone, without being under the control of his master's spell, had enraged Troy.

Trying to regain his composure, he sat across from her, carefully picking the tiny bits of crystal from the lace ruffles of his cuffs. As he did, his disguise fell away.

He stared at her, his one black eye and malformed face constantly sneering.

As she stared back, she had to focus on imagining she was clenching her toes under the table. It soothed the torture of being forced to be so still.

Troy leaned forward on the small round dark oak-stained table.

"I will release you from the bondage spell if you agree to eat."

She moved her mouth, miming words.

Troy flexed his hand and she felt released enough to speak.

She immediately stopped.

Unable to stop himself, he leaned towards her.

She spat at him from across the table, then smiled as wide as she could.

Troy clenched his hand and the spell bound her movements again, her body cramping, the pain starting to flow in waves from her legs, up her body and settling in her back.

She felt her baby move, just a flutter, and the reassurance helped ease her mind, that his spell was not so absolute.

She realised, as she focused on the tiny movements in her belly, that he had been talking. She swallowed hard, her focus returning to the lunatic trying to have a pleasant breakfast with her.

Troy moved his hand and An'eris felt her words freed.

"Well?" he prompted.

"What," she replied, forcing disinterest into her voice, "I wasn't listening."

Troy leapt to his feet and bellowed in rage.

She didn't flinch, and her eyes never strayed from his.

Troy drummed his fists on the table, the plates and cups and knives and spoons bouncing around and crashing off the edge. A small ceramic bowl smashed near her feet.

"Oh dear." She sounded bored. "That was an heirloom, it belonged to Orren's grandmother."

"The old bitch is dead," Troy spat back. "I'll smash everything in this room and then I'll smash you against the wall and take the information we want right out of your head."

An'eris started to tut at him, like a mother waiting patiently for her child to finish his tantrum.

"And what would your master say to that, servant?"

Troy pushed his face against hers, leaning towards her, trying to force her back, but her body was held immovable by the spellcasting.

He couldn't push her over.

Troy's anger spiked to uncontrollable levels, and he grabbed handfuls of her hair and started to tug like he wanted to rip her head off her shoulders.

An'eris, bound in the spell, felt the pain but couldn't move away. Wanting nothing more than to help herself, she had no choice but to keep still and take it. Afraid that she would cry, that he would see her shed tears from his violence against her, and not willing to give him that, An'eris listened for the small mind of her tiny baby asking for help.

A small voice answered, and she felt the words unspoken, telling her to hold on, that all she had to do was hold on, help was coming.

In the dark of the dungeon beneath the castle, Brennan lay blind to the world.

Cotta leaned against him, holding a moist rag to his lips, a hand on his throat, trying to make him suck some of the liquid out of it. He wasn't sure it was water, but it was wet and he wanted it. A few more sips of the cloth was enough though; the rancid smell and taste too much.

"Don't spit it out," he heard her say, soothing fingers on his chest. "Keep it inside you, as disgusting as it is."

He was about to ask what it was but thought he probably didn't want to know.

"Help me sit up," he asked.

She shuffled round to kneel in front of him, put her hands under his shoulders and pulled him forward into a sitting position. His arms seemed like they had too many elbows and she felt him wincing in pain.

"I think I'm in bits," he sobbed.

"You don't look too bad." She took deep breaths before speaking to stop her voice quivering. She held him tightly, too scared to let go but afraid of hurting him by holding on.

"I can't see how I look." He started to cough and fell to his side. "Just need to rest a minute." He curled around himself, shivering so much she could hear his teeth rattle.

She eased herself down alongside his body, trying to share what little warmth she had left with his weakened gaunt frame.

He let her move his head under the crook of her chin, her knees behind his. Her fingertips danced across his face, avoiding his eyes.

They both fell silent; the only sound coming from the long corridor was the occasional thump of the warden moving around on his chair.

Brennan drifted off to sleep, or thought he did. The dark and the dreams had no boundaries because of his blindness and the beatings his body endured were his nightmares. He only knew he wasn't dreaming because of the little voice shattering the cold of the dark, and the surprised sounds of Cotta quickly getting up behind him.

"Brennan?" She pulled him up against her. "What is it?" There was no hiding the fear in her voice.

"It's An'eris," he wheezed. "I have to go."

Cotta felt his body go slack against her, his head fall to the side, the beat of his heart under her palm flutter weakly then slow, until she thought it had stopped.

Without thinking, and without knowing what to do, Cotta put her face against Brennan's, captured his thin split lips with her own and wrapped herself around him, gathering all her willpower and following after him.

She felt herself being pulled along, flashes of the castle flickering through her vision like grey reflections on water. Corridors, the council hall, more corridors, doorways, and then she was in An'eris's parlour and Troy had her, was trying to rip her to pieces.

Brennan stood behind the Queen.

Cotta saw him, his body strong and youthful, as it had been only weeks before. His beautiful green eyes, so like her own but more vibrant and hopeful, now clear and steady. His dirty blond hair wasn't stuck to his head with his own sweat and grime; she saw it short and thick, in the smart cut that he preferred; he looked like the person she knew he was.

She tore her gaze from him and looked at An'eris.

Her physical body was as grey as the world around her, as if someone had covered every living thing with ash from a cold dead fireplace. Around her, shimmering like a mirage, she could see the shape of phantom heavy metal chains wound around her legs, her body, her arms, undulating around her like a snake coiling around its prey. The thickest chains throttled her, and Cotta imagined the skin of her neck rubbing away under the bondage and torment of the impure metal. Troy's hands were in her hair, pulling her slowly apart, his rage out of control, all his focus on causing her pain. At the edges of it all, Cotta thought about every time a guard had yanked her hair or pulled her head back while they were abusing her, how much it had hurt and how she couldn't stop crying after. She remembered the pain and knew what An'eris was feeling; then she saw the way An'eris focused her eyes on Troy, how her gaze bore down on him, the look of defiance on her face, her eyes dry. She was fighting him in the only way left to her, and it was driving him mad with fury.

Cotta tried to step closer. She wanted to reach out, to call her friend's name, but in this place, between time and life, she had no voice and no body. All she could do was watch and wait and trust Brennan.

Brennan stood behind An'eris, all concepts of time gone as he thought how best to help her and the baby.

He didn't rush when he saw a small trickle of grey blood break across An'eris's forehead as a clump of hair was ripped from her scalp. He ignored the howl of triumph from Troy when the man's eyes lingered on the blood.

He saw the sorcerer's permanent grin widen impossibly, noticed the way his hands, still gripping her hair, start to shake from his excitement at her pain.

Brennan leaned forward over An'eris's shoulder, and he reached over her and grabbed Troy by the side of his head. He brought his sight to the man and looked into him.

Brennan saw nothing but pleasure, pain, and power. There was nothing in him that felt like the mind of a man. There would never be any way of reaching him, no path to reason.

Brennan, now with a glimmer of understanding of their enemy, put his spectral hands onto Troy's shoulders and pushed with all his power.

In the parlour, without warning, a burst of yellow light surged into Troy as his body was hurled across the room. He slammed into the wall head first, his body dropping to the cold stone floor unconscious.

Brennan's ghost crossed the room in a few long strides, kneeled next to him and leaned over him. Rubbing his hands together, a thin trail of smoke rose from between his palms. As it curled and rose in the air, Brennan reached out, pinching it between his fingers as if it was a fine thread. He took the thread of smoke, put it against Troy's forehead, and pushed it into his body.

"Now I can find you, and I can follow you."

Stepping away, he turned and rushed to An'eris.

Cotta watched as he went on both knees in front of her, bowing his head as he rubbed his fingers.

"My Queen."

An'eris reacted as she heard a voice she knew. "Help me," she sobbed.

"I am, I promise." His voice was sure, strong and steady as he created a thread and pushed it into her mind.

"Now I can protect you, and I can help you."

An'eris, her eyes locked on his, slumped forward, put to sleep under his hand.

Cotta watched Brennan get to his feet. Up until that moment, she had been an observer, an interloper on a scene. Then he turned to her and looked at her with eyes that she knew.

He crossed the room with one step, grabbed her in intangible arms and crushed his lips against hers. Impossibly, she felt the heat in his kiss and the fire of his embrace.

Just as suddenly, he let her go.

"Go back," he ordered, stepping away.

She instantly felt her form start to dissolve, saw the room fading away.

"I don't want to," she cried out.

Then she was gone, and Brennan was free in a place between worlds.

"This isn't how it was meant to be," he shouted into the grey nothingness around him. He looked at his body and thought of Cotta. "We were meant to have a chance," he whimpered. "This isn't fair."

CHAPTER 8

Brennan lay on the dungeon floor curled up like a newborn baby left to die in the dark. When the rats came, he didn't bother shooing them away. Their tiny claws dug into the exposed skin on his back scratching at his body, testing for the soft bits. One hooked onto him and scurried up his back, stopping on his face. He felt the rat's twitching snout ghost over his dry lips, nuzzle at his long whiskers, the needle-sharp claws gripping at his cheek, the long tail flicking and curling under his chin as it moved off him and down onto the floor. At the edges of his consciousness he could feel it, hear the rat, smell it. If he stuck his tongue out he'd taste it. After a quick click of claws on cobbles, it settled on a spot. Brennan felt the tug and slice of sharp teeth and claws as it brazenly began to gnaw the flaps of skin at his elbow. He heard excited clicks of more teeth and the scratch of more claws on the floor. More rats. Coming out from the corners, they moved around, braver still, two, three, four, more rats. They set on him, some at a foot, another behind a knee, all starting to nibble, eating him alive.

Brennan lay still, oblivious. His mind wasn't on his body, or in his body. Brennan's mind was with Cotta, wrapped around her thoughts, shielding her from what Troy's men were doing to her in the corner of their cell.

Later, when the dungeon guards had finished and made enough noise buckling their belts to scare off the rats, Brennan lay on the dirty floor with his head in Cotta's lap, her fingers gently combing through his hair and scratching at his beard. He could feel her gaze, and if he focused, he could see himself through her eyes, but it was too much, it took energy he didn't have anymore. Brennan shifted just enough to keep the weight of his head off her thighs. He hoped she didn't notice, but even in her condition, she noticed everything.

"You don't have to do that for me you know," she murmured.

"There isn't much else I can do, I may as well do that," Brennan mumbled back.

Cotta turned her face away.

"Slipping into my mind I mean, taking the pain for me while they're… I can take it."

He didn't see her nod to herself, the way she clenched her teeth together and widened her eyes to refuse the tears a chance to form.

"You can't do it again. The next time they come in, you can't. It weakens you too much, and An'eris needs you more."

"I can't just lie here and listen to them raping you," he said softly, not moving.

"Enough," she said gently as her fingers moved over his lips, stopping his words. "Let's not talk of this."

"Can we talk of something though?" His voice was quiet. "The dark is so…" He couldn't find any more words.

"Of course we can, my love." Cotta made herself smile, hoping he could hear it.

"Where are we?" he asked.

Cotta looked around the dungeon. The oil lamp in the corner threw up just enough light for her to see they were locked away, surrounded by their own filth in one of the cells deep in the bowels of the castle. For all that they were alive, they might as well have been dead.

Cotta shifted slightly, refusing to release the shudder of pain radiating from her lap. She moved enough to settle Brennan more comfortably and wipe some of the sweat from his fevered brow. She rolled her hands at the wrist, hearing the bones click as they shifted, felt the sting of the shards of metal still buried in the flesh where the manacles had cut into her.

"Where are we? We're at Falconfall. I've taken you home." She offered him a lie. "It's late afternoon. We've spent all day at the edge of my family's land. It's the most beautiful place you could ever hope to see. The hills aren't so high here and the sky is enormous. It's a gentle place with space to walk or run, but if you don't look where you're going, you'll trip over small loose stones and twist your ankle. There are boulders small enough to leap over, and some so big you could build a house on them." She moved her hands languidly over his face, across his dry lips, feeling where the blood had dried in the cracks. She licked her fingers and then traced them over his lips, hoping it helped a little. She let her fingertips trace patterns across his cheeks and over his forehead, avoiding where his eyes should have been. Cotta's head fell back to rest on the clammy damp stone wall behind her. She chased her memories for Brennan. "The tracks onto our lands, to the house, come off the roads to the west of Crestwood Lake. From the first posting that marks our boundary, it takes all day and some of the night on horseback to reach the stream alongside the house. The stream isn't very wide but it's deep. If you try to wade it or cross it with a mount, you and the horse will be swept away and your brains bashed out of your head on the rocks on the banks. It starts in the mountains to the west and flows through our lands; it's fast. It never freezes even in a harsh winter, but on the coldest days there's ice around the banks and all the tufts of grass are frozen white and stiff. It tastes like the air in a blacksmith's forge when he's finished quenching fresh steel. My father used to say it's because there's iron in the water, iron in the land, iron in the animals." Her voiced faded away for a moment.

"There's a stone bridge over the stream. It's old stone, covered in moss, and sometimes during a storm, lightning hits the bridge. The crack and boom is the loudest thing you'll ever hear, and for a second the lightning makes all the colours in the world turn inside out. If there was ever a low parapet it's been worn away. The bridge is slippery, and you have to know where to place your feet."

Brennan twitched under her hands and Cotta started to feel the tell-tale sensations of Brennan at the edges of her mind. Her memories, dulled from so many years, started to feel more substantial in her mind's eye, and she could recall the images in sharper colour. Cotta mentally released her hold, letting Brennan into her thoughts. She carried on talking, wanting to share it all with him so he could taste the experiences of her memory.

"The house, at least the one I grew up in, was once a crofter's cottage, I think, before my father had it rebuilt into a suitable home with the space he wanted for his books and his music and all the little things he and mother liked to do with their time. There's a tree behind the house with a swing and a table. We'd eat lunch there sometimes; I'd play all day when the sun was lazy. I would hear my father singing from inside; my mother would be lying on a blanket reading a book in the shade of the tree. I loved living in that house. It's nestled between the stream and the steep hills about half a league away from the family manor. That house is so big and has too many staircases and long corridors leading to empty rooms. It's always cold, always feels barren, like an enormous tomb. Like this place." She stopped, eyes roving over their dark dungeon. Brennan, entwined in her memories, waited. "Built for ghosts," she whispered. A dark sense of loss and hopelessness washed through her, and Cotta realised she was projecting her emotions onto Brennan, who was quivering in her lap. She mentally roused herself and forced her mind onto other memories.

"Falconfall is beautiful. In summer, cattle graze on green grass, the crops grow tall and strong, turning yellow and heavy with ripe grain seeds that are harvested by men and women swinging scythes as they sing all day. We get two crops a season, but when it's time to let the land lie fallow, wildflowers invade and the land becomes a sea of small bright flowers, purple like an amethyst, scarlet, and yellow like freshly churned butter."

Brennan started to relax, the terror of a moment ago forgotten as his mind followed Cotta to a brighter place. Cotta sensed he needed more to keep the darkness back.

"In autumn on a cloudless day it's warm until the very second the sun dips behind the lowest hills. Then the shadows grow long and the wind chills you just enough to make you wish you had a shawl and you remember how far it is back to the house."

"Do you have your shawl?" he asked.

"I do," she told him.

"Show it to me?"

"It's old, tattered. It used to be my maid's when she was a young woman. I think she used it more often as a makeshift bed in the long grass with her lover before they were married." A genuine smile crossed Cotta's face. "It was blue once, pale blue like winter ice that reflects the sky. By the time she was old enough to wrap it around me and tell me to keep it close, it was as white as her hair. And now it's around my shoulders and we're walking back home, the shadows are behind us. You're holding my hand telling me something, but I'm not listening to the words, I just like hearing your voice. I'm smiling now, and you've stopped talking. Instead you're humming a silly tune and I want to laugh and hum it with you. We're warm. We're safe."

"Tell me what I see," Brennan whispered, lost in her lie. Cotta's fingers paused for a moment at his words. In the squalid gloom she squeezed her eyes shut and willed her voice not to break.

"The red flowers that stand on tall strong stalks on the hills all summer are gone but you can still smell their scent. It's heavy in the air, a thick sweetness that gets into your nose until you can taste it. Everything smells of that flower. There are crickets clicking and chirping away. They blend into the background, but we don't notice them. You have dirt all over your boots and bits of dried grass have wound their way into the stitching at the bottom of your cloak. You rolled up the sleeves of your tunic earlier in the day, and your arms are tanned from the sun and there's dirt under your nails instead of ink. You're smiling."

"We're happy?" Brennan asked.

"Yes, love," she said gently, her fingers pausing.

"I can see it," he sighed. "Cotta, I'm so tired."

"I know. Enjoy it," she crooned. "Stay in the dream, rest. Sleep." Cotta bit her lip until she tasted blood, her fingers hovering over his empty eye sockets.

Brennan held onto the threads of Cotta's mind for as long as he could. His strength faltered, and he fell away to sleep.

As his conscious mind succumbed to exhaustion, his self-control weakened, and the tendrils of his mental powers unfurled like a mist seeping out from his core. His powers strengthened with each moment unbound from his self.

His mind pulled out of his body and saw with his different eyes.

He saw his weakened body. He saw Cotta. He couldn't look at her. He turned away and pushed out through their cell. A lone guard he didn't recognise slept on a stool in a corner of the corridor. The other cells were empty of any living souls. Just bodies. Some still rigid, some bloated, some already starting to rot, the flesh already mostly gone into the bellies of the bold fat rats asleep on top of each other in the middle of the floor.

Brennan reached out and touched the edges of the guard's mind. He found the simple mind of a man who enjoyed violence. A cruel, weak-willed nasty mind easily swayed and controlled by glittery coins.

Brennan pushed into his mind and forced a vision into his slumber that would terrify him awake, denying him any restful sleep. Leaving a nightmare was an unsatisfying act of vengeance, but with this new facet of his power in such an embryonic state, it was all he could do. It left him a little depleted, but he knew, like any muscle, the more he pushed the stronger his mind would become.

Forcing himself to ignore his unsatiated wrath, he moved through the maze of unfamiliar illusory hallways until he found dark stairs that took him upwards. He kept moving up until his ghost breached a doorway and his mind exited up a steep set of stairs near the very limits of the castle boundary. He let himself take a moment to get his bearings. He wasn't very far from the barracks, and across the open ground he would find a doorway that would take him back into the castle.

A midnight stroll wasn't his purpose.

Moving out across the ground, his mind, like a spectre, saw traces of the people who had recently moved through the area. A faint trail, an insubstantial ribbon, the essence of the person. Trails he could follow if he wanted, but he didn't. He didn't care about them. There was only one trail he was hunting, one person he was looking for.

Moving into the castle, Brennan headed for the royal apartments and stopped.

He felt his mind start to rewind; he was being pulled back to his own body.

That could mean only one thing.

Snapping into himself, he woke to the sound of grunting and a flood of physical pain cascading across his senses.

He tried to push into Cotta's mind to use her eyes, but her mind was clamped shut like a vice.

Desperate to know, desperate to understand what was happening, to see, Brennan coiled his mind's spectre tighter and tighter and contorted his power until it came under his sway in his self. With ghost eyes, he looked out.

He saw the sleeping guard, asleep no more.

He saw Cotta.

She was on her stomach, the guard's body covering hers, one hand clenching her hair at the back of her head. Her arms were crossed in front of her face, taking the brunt every time he shoved into her and banged her face on the stone floor.

To stop herself from screaming, begging, she bit into her arm until bright red blood flowed out across the floor.

Brennan stared at the ribbon of blood slowly seeping from her. It looked grey to his spectral sight.

Everything looked grey. But he remembered the colours of her life.

He tried to go to her but she had shut him out. He turned to the man whose mind was open in his single-minded pursuit of pain and pleasure. He should have been able to snare his mind, to crush it in his grasp, but he didn't have the strength. The effort to go into a mind was nothing to him, but to push so hard, to gain control of a human mind, so infinitely complex and layered, after exerting himself on his earlier journey, was just beyond his reach.

Brennan looked around, desperate for anything he could use as a weapon, tried flexing his stiff immovable fingers and body, but there was nothing. All he saw was a line of curious rats attracted by the smell of bodies and blood.

Brennan paused. Then he sighed, the sound like a hush aimed at the rats.

Cotta lay on her side, her hands clamped over her ears, her face pushed into Brennan's chest. She tried to bury herself in him, to get as far away from the shrieks and squeaking, the unnatural frantic chattering and thrashing as every single rat in the castle descended on the guard, attacking as one, single-minded, eating him alive.

Brennan kept Cotta from the horror as much as he could, while gorging on the knowledge of the rats devouring her torturer. He felt his bloodlust and desire for vengeance dissipating, the frenzied pile growing bigger and bigger as more rats scurried into the dungeon and joined the feast.

Eventually there was only the sound of the rats' teeth cutting through flesh and sinew, snapping the small bones and gnawing on the larger ones. And then, after a while, there was no sound from the rats, and they scampered away back where they had come from or collapsed on their small legs, unable to bear the weight of their engorged bellies.

And then there was silence. Cotta had finally fallen asleep, her tears and blood a temporary amber stain on Brennan's dirty porcelain skin.

The rise and fall of her chest, and what little warmth was left to seep out of her body warmed them both on the cold dark floor of the dungeon.

Brennan didn't notice, he didn't feel cold, or wet from her tears or sick from the sight he had seen. Even though he had relinquished his control, he knew if he wanted he could do it again. And that it would be easier a second time, then a third.

CHAPTER 9

Raef woke up gasping for breath and desperately thirsty. His eyes wouldn't open. He reached up, rubbed his eyelids to try and dislodge the hard-dried gunk that had glued them shut. His tongue felt too big for his mouth and he couldn't find any spit to help him swallow. His fingers felt sticky on his face, like he was smearing something on himself. He tried to open his eyes again, having no choice but to delicately use his fingers to pull his eyelids apart. The sting made him hiss, brought precious tears to his eyes and finally greasing them enough to open. Pulling his hands away, he looked down and for a second thought he was wearing gloves. His skin looked as black as coal dust and was covered in clotted grime. Fine sand had stuck to whatever he was covered with, turning his skin to sandpaper when he rubbed his hands together; it hurt. Everything hurt. He moved to stand but couldn't work out where his feet were as they slid unsteadily beneath him. Stumbling forward, he fell onto sand, his hands disappearing under the surface as easily as if he'd fallen in a puddle. Carefully, he stood up and looked around.

In front, stretching for eternity, was the rise and fall of shimmering yellow sand dunes touching the cloudless azure blue sky. Nothing else seemed to exist.

This is death, he thought to himself, eternal nothing. A moment of peace pierced his thoughts, and all words, feelings and sensations scattered from his mind as if blown away on a desert breeze.

He closed his eyes and fell to his knees, content to be dead.

And then he heard his name, and he wondered in his capitulation why death sounded like Bode and not like Mason.

Mason.

Raef's mind filled with memory. Already on his knees in the sand, bent forward like a penitent man praying for absolution from a vengeful God, Raef realised he wasn't dead.

Bode, resting a few feet away, had watched over Raef through the cold desert night. He hadn't roused him when the pale yellow sun peaked over the crest of the sand bowl they'd fallen into, and he chose to wait as Raef slept through noon, dusk, and well into the second night. By the time he thought he should wake him, his voice was too dry to speak and he was just too tired to try. Instead, he sat and waited, increasingly oblivious to the heat and the sun, thirst and hunger just a memory now. And so he sat, unnoticed, as Raef woke up, remembered, and faced life.

The two men sat together but apart in the desert, staring into another night unlike any they had seen before. The sky above, usually as black as spilled oil and dotted with shining stars, was awash with falling ribbons of light that pulsed and danced above them. Vivid blues and greens, sometimes deep purple and bright pinks. The night sky throbbed with colours they'd never seen and couldn't name.

Neither turned round and pointed up, calling to the other to look. They saw and they watched, utterly spent, with no energy left even for awe.

As the sun rose on them again, whatever water they had in their bodies was gone, sucked out by their three days in the desert. They sat in what shade the high dunes offered from the ferocious heat, the shadow only there if the sun was behind them, which wasn't for long.

Raef couldn't bring himself to look at Bode. He spent his waking time rubbing his hands in the sand trying to get them clean. His skin reddened then cracked and bled, mixing the stain of his brother's blood with his own.

As the sun rose on the fourth day, Bode drifted between nightmares and hallucinations in the few minutes he was conscious. He felt his heart beating in his dry throat and was in constant agony from cramped muscles. By noon he realised he must have somehow rolled out of the dune shadow that had been sheltering him. The bright sun brought the memory of Calem, of the pillar of fire and all the death he had seen all through his life into the forefront of his mind, and a great sadness filled his empty soul.

He conjured the images of the dead, and those he hoped were living, saving himself the final pleasure of recalling the smiling face of An'uek.

He imagined the sound of her laughing and was finally ready to die.

The sounds seemed to echo around in his skull, hammering at him, refusing him the final peace of silence. He thought he heard her call his name.

The sensation of hearing a sound jarred him from his sombre thoughts, and he sat up, the small movement causing his heart to slam into his chest.

He looked at the horizon, and in the hazy air he thought he saw dark shimmering shapes hurrying towards them.

He felt heat rising inside his body and couldn't catch his breath.

Pain radiated from his heart, across his chest and into his shoulders. Bode raised a hand to wave but fell face down into the burning hot sand.

"Run," An'uek shouted, as she sped forward, ordering the men behind her to quicken their pace.

She could see him standing at the bottom of the monstrously high sand dune only a few hundred feet away. Her light nimble feet fairly flew across the loose sand, but as fast as she was on the shifting desert floor, she wasn't fast enough and watched him collapse.

"Bode!" she shrieked. He didn't rise.

Out of breath but filled with a desperation she had never known in her life, An'uek flung her mind out ahead of herself and into Bode's consciousness.

She felt the last of his strength give way and met the touch of his death with her mind.

The shock ricocheted her back into herself, and she screamed in pain, her legs giving out from under her. Falling forward, she felt herself caught up in strong arms and hauled onto a broad back. She wrapped her arms around the runner, clinging to him as he raced ahead on long legs. She kept her eyes looking forward, oblivious to the fact she was still shouting Bode's name. Still too far away, An'uek watched Raef rise next to Bode, roll him onto his back and start to pound on his chest.

By the time she reached the two men, Raef was jabbering nonsensical sounds as he beat his fists against Bode's chest, barely able to keep himself upright.

An'uek threw herself off the tall dark man who had carried her the final leg of the way and lunged for Raef and Bode. She unhooked a waterskin from a cord at her waist and shoved it at Raef, pushing him over in her fervour to help. The man who had carried her collapsed next to Raef and caught him as he fell over, pulling him into his lap, cradling his weak body against his own and taking up the waterskin.

"Save him," she ordered, pointing at Raef, then she turned her attention to Bode.

Another man dropped to Bode's side and cradled the man's head, tipping it forward an inch, opened his mouth, and put another skin of water to his lips.

He dribbled in a few drops of water as another man took up the motions of his heartbeat, and yet another appeared beside him to force breath into his lungs. They forced her to take a step away.

An'uek watched them tend Bode, her body cold and numb even as she sat fully exposed to the desert sun. Desperate for contact, her hand reached out and found his. She wound her fingers through his and closed her fist around them. With her other hand she reached out for Raef, and after a moment she felt his fingers weakly touch hers. Her eyes never left Bode but she was aware of the sounds of Raef greedily guzzling sips of water. She heard them muttering at him, telling him not to take too much too soon. She picked up a sweet scent that filled the sterile air and knew it was honey from the combs of the desert bee. She heard Raef smacking his lips and knew they were smearing dabs of honey on his tongue and then chasing it with more water.

All this while a man was Bode's breath and another was his heartbeat. Every time they pushed on his chest An'uek felt herself grow impossibly colder.

"Please don't die," she said softly. "Please don't leave me."

He didn't answer.

As her eyes filled with tears, she felt movement beside her, and Raef pushed himself forward against the men who were trying to save him.

Raef's head lolled back and he fell sideways, fainting away.

A man leaned down and scooped him up off the sand.

The men working on Bode started to talk; An'uek didn't understand their language but she understood the gestures and the looks they shared with each other.

They were giving up.

"No, please," she begged, wrapping her arms around the body of the man next to her. "Keep trying."

She grabbed at his hands and put them onto Bode, staring up at him, pleading.

More words, and the men started again.

An'uek held her breath; she thought, for some reason, it might help. She squeezed her hand around his, her thumb rubbing circles over his.

They breathed for him. They kept his heart beating. They breathed again.

After another few minutes, An'uek felt a hand gently touch her back and gesture at her to look down.

On the sand at their feet, Bode was breathing.

An'uek, in shock and flooded with relief, covered her face with her free hand and lay down next to him, stretching her body alongside his, utterly silent, listening to him breathe, counting every breath. The desert men got to their feet and stood around the two of them, their bodies blocking the sun, casting a lifegiving shadow across them as they lay in the sand together. But they could only offer a moment.

Soon one of the men knelt, nudging her, bringing her back to sitting.

"Little sister, we must make up the litter and get on our way as quickly as we can."

She nodded and moved aside an inch, starting to unwind the thin gauze shawl that covered her head and was draped down over her shoulders.

One of the men leaned down, placing his hand on hers, stopping her movements.

"You don't need to do that," he gently chided. "We have what we need."

"I was going to hold it over them, keep them from the heat." She gestured to the blazing noonday sun above them.

"We have what we need," he repeated softly.

The men behind them retrieved bundles of stout strong sticks from rolls of cloth slung across their backs. It was too quick to follow, and An'uek lost track of what they were winding together, watching with confusion as some of them hooked strips of cloth over their shoulders and tied them across their chests. It was only when four of them stood up in pairs that she realised they had created two harnesses and the men were going to carry her friends. The unconscious Raef and Bode were lifted, laid out and covered over with a delicately thin woollen weave that kept them in shadow.

Without a word, the men set off in a direction only they knew, carrying Raef and Bode across the barren dunes.

An'uek watched as they headed off.

"Will they live?" she asked the man at her side.

"I don't know," he said, kneeling in front of her. He held his hand out to her, palm up, waiting for her to take it. "We'll take them to Sona perhaps she can heal them. When we reach the camp, I'll send some men to the tower to discover whatever there is to see."

An'uek took his hand.

"Thank you, Miqa," she said, as her eyes shone with tears quickly drawn away by the heat.

He bowed, smiling at her, and gestured at his knee.

She lowered her head and took his offer.

The tall man stood, sweeping her up and placing the druidess on his shoulders as he set off across the desert following his men.

He handed a small skin of water up to her.

"When the Sand-Dancer returns you must tell him the story you told me. He will decide what to do."

From her perch on his shoulders she took a deep drink of the cool sweetened water. She stared off at the horizon thinking on his words. After a while, and another long drink, she rewrapped her shawl around her head to protect herself from the sun's glare.

She handed the water pouch back to Miqa, who clipped it to his belt.

They walked through the desert into the night and through the next day and night, stopping only to force honey-sweetened water into Raef and Bode, and to give An'uek a rest from sitting on Miqa's shoulders.

As they set off on the final leg of their journey to the camp, following directions and signs only they knew, An'uek tried to decline his offer of carrying her.

"You and your men haven't slept since we set off to find them. The least I can do is walk for myself."

"Your legs are much shorter than ours, and we must walk slower to not leave you behind."

His logical insistence won over and she climbed up to her perch on his shoulders.

"Don't your men need sleep? Don't you need sleep?"

"We will rest when the time is right. We are desert people. This is our way when it must be," was all the explanation he offered.

"Thank you again," An'uek said, putting her hands together on his head to rest, her gaze steady and alert, searching, hardly blinking in the harsh sunlight. As they walked, the empty landscape of sand dunes started to change. On the horizon, hazy at first, the dunes started to change colour. Swooping, curving shadows became edges and ridges, and the rolling dunes flattened out into hard-packed ground covered in stone, boulders and outcroppings of desert rock. Barren ground gave way to clumps of long thin-stemmed dry desert grass, spindly low-lying brush covered in thorns, and the occasional bright blue flower, green or purple desert cactus, standing alone, out of place, looking like the only thing alive in a dead world. At dawn, as the sun rose, the sky was momentarily red, orange, pink and purple, colours matching the magnificence of the light displays An'uek had watched from her seat as the men kept walking through the night.

"I don't remember ever seeing this before," she said to Miqa in the quiet hours before dawn.

"That's because it's never been like this."

"When did it start?"

"On the day of the second sun. During the day," Miqa said, "you can sometimes see the blue sky split with black lightning. It is unnatural. Even here, in this place, where we live, where we tend the wild magic, even here, it is not right what we see now."

An'uek didn't know what to say.

Chapter 10

Kraner was alive. The crammed streets and alleys were pulsing with the slow meander of people making their way through the city on a rest day. The smells of meat slow roasting over coals banked with bushels of wet rosemary and thyme competed with the aroma of freshly baked cinnamon buns and fruit breads. There were trays of pies oozing beef gravy or bursting their pastry seams with roasted carrot and parsnips in thick buttery sauces. Children tucked into pasties dripping with fat as mothers sipped cups of warm spiced wine and fathers downed deep draughts of strong ale. The thieves gave up their easy pickings by mid-morning, their own pockets filled with so much pilfered coin they soon found themselves the target of their own kind. Dogs slept instead of sniffed for scraps, hindlegs twitching in their sleep as they dreamed of chasing rabbits. Even the gentle first falls of snow had stopped long enough for the people of Kraner to fill the streets.

Denny walked out the castle gates at mid-morning with a group of wardens. He kept his sweating hands in his pockets, lingering at the back of the small group, thankful for the slow pace. He was so tired all the time but couldn't seem to stay asleep. He didn't want to shut his eyes, he was afraid to sleep, awake sometimes for days, until his body, utterly exhausted, would shut down and he would pass out for a couple of hours. Then the nightmares would start, the memories. He kept imagining what might happen, turning everything anyone said or did into a scenario that left him shaking and terrified. He yawned as he trailed the wardens, focusing on what they were saying instead of his memories. His gaze kept shifting, looking everywhere and at everyone, wondering if any of them were looking too intently. He didn't know who was loyal to A'taz and who wasn't. It didn't matter; everyone seemed either to love him or see him as just another royal guest and not care.

None of them had been in the throne room when it happened.

They ambled down the slopes and through the streets into the city crowds.

"Feels like old times again around here," an older man remarked. "Like when Lenard was on the throne before all the troubles began." As he walked, he rolled dried leaves into a short sheaf of thin paper.

"Smoke?" he said, and he offered it around. A few of them accepted. Denny nodded, appreciating not having to roll his own, waiting to light his tip of someone else's.

"Orren's been away longer than he was ever here as King," the older man continued.

"Too long," another agreed.

"The Queen's done the right thing though, bringing that stonemason here from Aquam. He's brought gold… and men."

Denny tripped over his feet, falling forward, catching himself on his hands. One of the men helped him up. He mumbled his thanks and wiped his palms down his cloak. He bent forward and picked his smoke up off the floor, glad it wasn't damp or too dirty.

"More money in the city, more men to work, everyone is eating again."

"Good times," another said, nodding.

"It's been, what, a couple of weeks, and already there's work started on that new temple in the square."

"Be up before winter's end with the number of men coming in to work on the build."

They stopped near an oil-powered street lamp and the man reached up to touch the end of his smoke to the wick, catching it alight. Taking a long drag, he slowed the pace and passed round the wick to the others. "I hear that the stonemason is nice enough. Queen's given him some rooms in the castle. My girl's one of his servants now, and she says he always makes time for anyone who wants to pray with him. Says it perks him up quite a bit."

"Maybe the Gods like him, eh?" One elbowed the other. "Things have certainly got better round here since he arrived."

"What do you think, Denny," they asked him, speaking directly to him for the first time.

He couldn't hide. He wished he could swallow his tongue. Instead, he cleared his throat, hoped his voice wouldn't break, and answered as casually as he could after taking a deep drag on the mangy stub.

"I've only been in the Queen's service a couple of weeks," he shrugged his shoulders harder than he needed, "there's not much difference I suppose."

The men turned left. Denny made a point of telling them he had errands to run. He turned right, kept a slow amble to the end of the street he was on, took another corner and then picked up his pace, finding a shortcut in an empty twisted alleyway. As he walked, he started to feel hot despite the cold winter air. He dropped the smoke, not bothering to step on it.

A surge of dizziness came over him and he had to stop. He shrugged out of the short cloak he'd pulled on earlier, scratching his already grazed palm on the open-handed brooch he still wore pinned to his tunic. Yelping, he put his palm to his lips and sucked at the small spot of blood. The taste reminded him of what he had seen, and he turned against a wall, vomiting the scant breakfast he had forced down earlier. A bit of egg, some bread, and… as had started happening recently, some fresh blood.

He puked, and he cried.

His hot salty tears splashed down onto his lips and tongue, mingling with the blood, making him gag. He tried to breathe between heaves but couldn't catch his breath, and when he did he felt like he had too much air in his lungs. His heart thumped harder; he could feel it throbbing at his temples and in his neck. He squeezed his eyes shut, tried to keep his mouth closed. It didn't work. More bloody vomit surged from him.

He slid down the wall, falling to sit next to his shame. The open-handed brooch on his tunic suddenly felt too heavy. Sobbing, he grabbed at the thing and yanked hard, tearing his tunic open as he wrenched it off. He threw it away over his shoulder across the alleyway, not caring where it landed. But it didn't land anywhere. Turning to look behind him, Denny was surprised to see that a tall slender man, his face hidden in a cloak, had caught the brooch in a gloved hand and was turning it over, carefully studying the design. Denny got to his feet quickly, wiping the snot and spittle from his lips. This man didn't look like anyone from the castle.

"This yours?" the stranger asked him, motioning with the brooch.

Denny nodded.

"You work at the castle?"

Denny nodded again. He had the strange sensation someone was stroking his hair. The man tucked the brooch into a pocket inside his cloak. He crossed the alley and came to stand a foot away from the boy.

Denny was a mess. His hair was too long and falling in his eyes, a patchy first beard covered a face that hadn't been properly cleaned in days. His fingernails were bitten down, scabbing at the edges from where they'd been gnawed.

"You work in the stables? The smith?"

"Royal court," he answered quickly, the dampened flare of a squire's dignity momentarily reignited.

"You smell like a street beggar."

Denny refused to look at the vomit on his boots.

"I ate a bad oyster this morning."

"Did you?" the stranger asked rhetorically.

Denny started to feel nervous. As his anxiety rose, he felt that sensation of having his hair stroked again, and he felt calmer.

"It must be a very fine place to spend your days. Have you been in the royal court long?"

The stroking feeling intensified and Denny started to feel warm; he had the urge to smile, to talk.

"All my life. I'm a squire. I *was* a squire," he corrected himself. "My master was the Master Trader. But he's gone now," he said, smiling, feeling good for the first time in weeks, forgetting to feel anything other than happy.

"And who do you attend now in the castle?" the stranger asked pleasantly.

"The Queen."

"Oh."

The stranger lifted his hands and slowly pulled the hood of his cloak back. Denny watched as he revealed a long angular face, skin the colour of pale olives, and violet eyes. Eyes the same as those Denny had been staring at for weeks.

The stroking sensation stopped.

"Oh," Denny yelped. "Oh, thank the Gods."

The fishmonger behind the white stone countertop stopped gutting a fish just long enough to look at him, her gaze resting on his boots for a moment before slowly coming back to his face. Her gaze flicked to the man beside him. She cleared her throat loudly.

"What will it be, boy?"

"Castle cook asks if you have any trout?"

"Trout's a river fish boy." She dropped her knife on the cutting board and came towards him, wiping scales off her hands. "You see a river nearby?"

"Right…" He scratched the scruff of new beard growing on his flushed cheeks. "That's what I said to her. May as well be asking for a mermaid in these parts at this time of year."

"Does your cook want a nice flatfish? Had some in just last week, been on ice since then."

"No." Denny shook his head. "We had the flatfish two days ago, we want something new."

The woman regarded him, inclined her head as she considered all the code words he'd spoken.

"This is a friend," Denny said in response to her silent question.

"Close the door, boy." She flicked a cloth at him. "The door is always closed, best not to cause anyone to wonder why it's open."

A'rrick kicked the door closed and followed the woman into a back room and up some stairs. The smell of fish turned from fresh to rancid to putrid with each step up the staircase.

She reached the top flight and opened the only door on the floor, which led to a small windowless room.

"Travis," she said to a cloaked figure at the back of the room, "your boy is here with news… and someone else."

"Denny…" Travis crossed the room and deliberately drew his sword from its stiff leather scabbard.

"No, wait." Denny stepped forward in front of the man and put his hands up against Travis's sword. "This is A'rrick. This is the Queen's father; he's here to help."

Travis stopped. From behind him, hidden in the shadows, Marsha's voice called out.

"Is that really you, A'rrick?"

"Marsha?" A'rrick stepped boldly forward, eyes levelled at Travis. He tried to step round him but was blocked as Travis stepped towards him.

The sounded of old bones creaking accompanied Marsha as she shuffled forward, leaning heavily on a stout stick, her ankle wrapped tightly in bandages.

"Show me your eyes, show Travis," she commanded.

A'rrick obeyed. Taking the hood down, as he had earlier with Denny, he showed himself.

Travis stepped back, quickly sliding his sword away, making space for Marsha to come forward and grasp A'rrick's hands.

"You know then," she stated, her voice quivering.

"I do," A'rrick answered. He took her weight as she leaned into him and then walked her back to her place in the shadows. It was less a seat and more a mound of cold pillows and blankets shaped to give her as much comfort as possible.

"We must make plans…" Travis began, but was shushed by A'rrick.

"We must do something about this first." A'rrick kneeled at Marsha's feet and held out his hands.

Slowly, and with a wince, she let him run his hands over her ankle and start to gently unwind the wrappings.

"This can wait," Travis snapped. "There are more important things that need our attention."

"Right now," A'rrick replied calmly, "in this moment, this is important." He took off the final loop of bandage. "This needs my attention."

Marsha's ankle was swollen as thick as her leg, the skin blackened from bruising, little bleeds in the cracks of the dry flesh hot to the touch.

"I've crossed hundreds of miles to get here, it's taken all my magic and the blessing of my Goddess to travel so far so fast. I've been in Kraner for three days now," A'rrick said to Travis over his shoulder as his hands deftly traced over Marsha's skin. "I've been gathering what information I could, even found a way into the castle last night, but for all my power, I couldn't get anywhere near An'eris without the risk of exposing myself."

Marsha started to feel sleepy.

"It's remarkable," A'rrick muttered as his hands closed softly around the deformed joint, his eyes finding Marsha's, unblinking, captivating her attention with his stare. "There's no sign of A'taz overthrowing the crown."

"Because he didn't," Travis replied.

Denny went over to the wall and slid down, his head in his hands.

A'rrick took a firm hold of Marsha's ankle as her head lolled back and she fell into an unnatural stupor.

"I don't know very much. I was at the docks when it happened. The only attack as far as I know was in the throne room."

A'rrick twisted hard and Marsha's bones moved.

"Troy... he killed everyone with steel, but he used magic to make it possible."

Travis got A'rrick's attention and motioned for him to look at the boy.

Denny balled his hands into fists and pushed them against his closed eyes.

Still looking at Denny, A'rrick twisted Marsha's ankle again, setting the bones and forcing them to heal.

"He killed all the guards." Travis lowered his voice.

Denny started shaking.

"And where were you, Denny?" A'rrick asked softly, winding him in a spell.

"I was at the back with two of the guards." He tried to curl up. "One of them took a crossbow to the chest, another got a sword in the chest at the same time. They fell on me. I fell forward and hit my head and they bled all over me. I didn't know what to do. I couldn't move. I tried, but I was still, like a dead thing."

"It was spellcasting," A'rrick said kindly. "There was no way you could fight against it. It sounds like they thought you were dead too. That saved you." He started to soothe Denny, stroking his mind just as he had earlier in the alleyway, as the spell loosened his tongue.

Denny jumped to his feet, angry and defiant. He balled up his fists but didn't move.

"It's her fault," he shouted as the words spilled out "The Queen, she should have known but instead she welcomed him in. And he killed them and she didn't even care, she just kept smiling and letting him kiss her and touch her. There was blood everywhere and she didn't even see it. I wanted to die I was so scared. I had to step over my people and walk through bits of them. I slipped and I fell, and when I stood up there was bits of them on me. I got to my rooms and I don't know what I did after that. Then I got called to her chambers. And then she said I was in her service, in his service, and they told me a story and I believed it, but I don't believe it, and it's in my head and I can't get it out, but I know what I saw and it's like they put something in my head and it hurts all the time. They don't trust me. I can see it when they look at me. They're looking for a reason to kill me, but the Queen won't let them. She keeps needing me to do things, keeps me busy in the castle for her." He was screaming now, screaming at them all.

"I don't want to do it. I don't want to do any of it. But I can't stop myself. They make me do whatever they tell me to do."

"What do they make you do, Denny?" A'rrick pressed him for more. "What do you see when no one is looking at you?"

"The two of them go to the high towers sometimes... they go up like themselves but come down like old people, like they're empty of something, but then the next day they're full again. A'taz, he wanders the halls, exploring the castle. He's looking for something, but I don't know what. I hear him sometimes, trying to make the Queen tell him stories. She refuses and he gets so angry. Whatever he's looking for, he hasn't found it."

"An'eris?"

"She sleeps a lot. She smiles a lot. She's always around when he is. They're like old friends, and she pretends he's wise counsel and people listen to him. But when he asks her to tell him stories about Kraner, and she won't, it's like… it's like something in her is still her, but then it's gone and she's nothing more than his servant again. It makes me want to kill her, even though sometimes I can see this way she looks at me and I know she's in her head somewhere and she's trying… she's trying so hard to get out. But I still hate her," he admitted without any shame.

"What else have you seen, boy," Travis asked from his place in the dark.

"Master Brennan, Mistress Cotta."

"They're alive?" Travis asked incredulously, stepping forward. Denny nodded.

"But not for long. Master Brennan, he just lies on the floor. They kick him, hit him. One of them ran a sword through his guts, but when he pulled it out, there wasn't a wound."

"Who? The castle guards?"

"No, Troy sometimes, or A'taz's men. They're everywhere now in the castle. An'eris told some lie about Homen taking a trip. Everyone believes it. No one knows Master Brennan is still there in a tiny cell, blind and just lying there."

"Cotta?" Travis asked, almost too afraid to hear what was happening to her.

"She's alive. The guards, they take her away to another cell with more space, so they can use her sometimes." Denny went visibly paler and A'rrick shuddered as Denny's horror transferred to him through the spell between them.

"Last I saw them was this morning. One of the guards, I think he was trying to snap her in half. He was getting so angry. It doesn't matter what they do to her, she never cries out anymore. Brennan used to, sometimes. I heard him screaming in the cell once while the guards were having her. She doesn't make a sound now. It drives them crazy."

"Enough," Marsha said, surprising the men out of their heartless interrogation.

"No, Marsha." Travis shook his head and gently pushed her back. "We need to know."

"He's a boy, Travis."

"He's our only way into the castle and the only chance we have."

Denny ignored them and carried on with his spellbound confession.

"I snuck in."

His revelation caught their attention.

"I made up a story, to take them some clean water."

"Brave boy," Marsha said kindly.

He nodded.

"I saw what they were doing to them."

The look Marsha saw in Denny's eyes was one she hoped never to see again.

"They want them alive. I'm not sure why," he said, his voice breaking. "I think they'd be better off dead." Denny looked away.

"It doesn't matter how much I sneak to them. Nothing matters now." He turned his head and stared off into nothing in the dark shadows of the room. "No one knows it's all wrong. No one knows what's happened. That we've lost the kingdom already."

"We've not lost, Denny."

"But we have, Master Travis," he argued. "And we didn't even see it happening. Our King went to fight a war, but A'taz was never waging a war. It was a sham and we let him walk right in."

"We're still here to fight," Travis stated.

"No, we're not." Denny countered with unusual confidence. "We're in a fish shop, and it's us against the kingdom that thinks everything is fine now. The court carries on. Foreign dignitaries are still making plans to come to the city because of the deals struck at the Tradefair. Everyone has accepted Homen is off doing something, that Lady Cotta and my master is a traitor, and the changes in the city aren't really affecting anyone so much that they care to take any real notice. Food and water, something to drink, smoke, a warm bed with someone in it. People are happy. No one thinks anything is wrong." He whispered those final words before turning to Travis.

"How do you go to war to rescue everyone from peace and a full belly?"

"We don't." Travis grabbed Denny and shook him. "We lost. For right now, we lost."

"We have to get An'eris," A'rrick interrupted, but Travis cut him off.

"She's safer where she is right now, so we leave her there," Travis stated. "But Cotta and Brennan are alive. We focus on them." He turned back to Denny. "That means you get back to the castle, and you do whatever you have to do to get something, anything, we can use to get them out."

A'taz slowly tore the ancient fragile pages from the timeworn tome cradled in the crook of his arm. He watched An'eris's face as he let each page fall into the crackling flames in the fireplace.

"Wonderful views from here," he said pleasantly. "I can see why he chose this place. It's quiet, not a lot of people passing by outside."

Taking the edge of the page, he pulled down, the ripping filling the quiet. To An'eris, it sounded like a scream.

She looked away, away from A'taz, away from the fireplace, away from the oak desk still covered with Homen's scribbled notes, his books stacked on top of each other, always on the verge of tumbling over. She recognised his favourite quill sitting in an open inkwell; he must have left in a hurry, intending to come back and finish whatever he was writing. His favourite crystal goblet was on his desk; she could imagine him holding it up to the sunlight, turning it lovingly in his gentle grasp.

She closed her eyes as A'taz moved towards it, preparing herself for the crash and shatter as he knocked it off the desk.

She looked away, refusing to see the scattered trinkets that he'd saved from all the people who had passed through the castle, passed through the city. He would've known the story of every one of them. Now he was gone, and they were just things, destroyed and smashed to bits, like everything in his rooms. A'taz had destroyed it all, and now, bit by bit, he was making An'eris watch as he burned it all away, one piece at a time, patiently erasing all trace of him from the castle.

"This one," he drew her attention as he ran a fingertip down the length of the page, "is in a language I don't recognise. Could be Reven, it looks like their script, all swirls and dots."
He ripped it out. "But who knows." He dropped it into the flames, the dry brittle paper consumed in fire almost instantly. "Who knows what just burned away, gone from history forever."

An'eris turned to look into the flames, wishing with all her being that she could move the flame, engulf him in fire and burn him to death.

As if sensing her thoughts, or just reading the hatred in her eyes, he smiled, slamming the heavy book closed without warning, making her jump.

She cursed herself for reacting as she heard him laugh at her skittish response.

"Not so brave as you pretend." He walked to stand behind her. "Stubborn, yes. Angry, definitely. But weak." He stood close enough for her to feel his breath tickle the hairs on her neck. "Ultimately… feeble. You'll tell me what I want to know." He walked away over to Homen's desk, moved around it, and sat in the red leather chair, sighing contentedly.

"Good taste in furniture too."

A'taz started to inspect the desk, pulling open the drawers.

"What's this?" He seemed genuinely curious. He pulled on drawer after drawer until they were all open.

"Empty?" An'eris guessed.

A'taz looked up, his eyes narrowed, his brow pulled into a frown.

"Homen was a man of secrets," she said, smirking. "Did you think you'd find a nicely drawn map, some pretty words, perhaps an arrow, showing you what you want?"

A'taz flicked his hands and the drawers slammed shut; An'eris was prepared and didn't startle at the sudden noise.

"Nice try," she snarled. "But your tricks are getting old, and in case you hadn't noticed, we people of Kraner, we take our secrets to the grave."

"You're not from here though, are you," he snarled.

She paused, contemplating his words.

"This is my home." Her simple statement was the last straw.

Her defiance, intolerable, angered A'taz, who pushed away from the desk and started to pace the edge of the circular room.

"So it is," he growled. Raising his arms, he murmured a short wave of words, the language piercingly familiar to An'eris. She knew what was coming next, stepped over to the nearest bare space near a wall and braced herself.

She felt the vibration a second before she heard the air start to whine. Her hair started to flick across her face as if caught in a storm. Loose papers stirred off Homen's desk, quickly fluttering up and blowing across the room. Books flipped open, pages turning, tearing out. The inkwell started to wobble, buffeted until it tipped over, the dark ink spilling over everything, running across the wood, staining it black. An'eris clamped her hands over her ears, squeezed her eyes shut and dropped down to hide her face against the wall.

Stools started to skid across the hard stone floor, and everything in the room started to shake as A'taz called forth his maelstrom. Furniture tipped over, smashed into other pieces, tapestries tore off their wall hooks, even the scattered rugs started to lift under the onslaught of the turbulent wind.

His words changed, and An'eris felt the abrasion against her skin and turned away to protect herself. By the time the wind stopped, and the shriek and screams that filled the air abated, there was nothing left in the room except heaps of sawdust on worn-out threads that were once thick carpets. Bare walls, the smell of charred paper and sparkling clusters of crystal and glass shards; whatever there once was… now, there was nothing.

A'taz, his gaze not leaving An'eris, was revelling in the surging aftermath of his spellcasting. He reached down and picked up a handful of sawdust from around his feet, walked over to her, still trying to hide herself against the wall, and let the dust trickle through his fingers to fall on her.

He leaned down, and with his other hand he snatched at her face, gripping her jaw and turning her to look up at him. The dust falling from his fingers covered her face. He forced his words into her mind. "You will tell me what I want to know, and then I'll show mercy and let you die." He blew the last of it into her face, forcing her to breathe it in. "Here is your dust, keep it with you. My promise is that you'll know your grave at my hand."

A'taz walked for hours through the castle. He turned corners he didn't recognise, went down every staircase he could find and conjured spells intended to illuminate hidden passageways, secret entrances or false doors. There was nothing. Eventually, he headed upstairs, trying to find space to consider the infuriating folly of his search and the searing defiance of the Queen. His feet led him to the small library in a tower he had come to think of as his own.

A'taz drummed his fingertips lightly on the windowpane, tapping out the melody playing through his mind. He gazed through the glass, past the tiny smudges of his fingerprints, across the castle ground and over the city that spread out from its walls. He imagined the tune in his mind, saw it as ribbons of colour that wove through each other, giving it texture and depth, and his fingers, tapping it out, hurling it across all the people sleeping in their beds, skulking in shadows or working through the night at jobs that kept food on the table and coats on their backs in winter. He didn't need to hear the constant chanting of his clerics as they murmured their incantations day and night, the force of their resonance was enough to feed him, the power now as thick as the fog that clogged the streets and alleyways of the city.

He kept tapping out his tune, a simple one that made people smile, made them amenable. As he tapped it out, he thought to himself, looking down at the city he had conquered so easily, at his city, how savage it was, full of the life of men and women, bound in the disease of humanity. Dirty, like rats.

As the tune ended and he felt the last of the power move through him, through the glass, spread out and over the city, he pulled back and drew the curtains to hide his sight from the rooftops, chimney smoke and dark windows as the night clung to Kraner.

He turned and went over to the small table and chess set, choosing the seat opposite the one he had sat at the night before.

He put his elbows on the table, leaning forward, his chin in his hand.

"What would you have done against me, boy, if you'd been here, if you'd lived?" he mused.

Swirling his fingers over the wooden king chess piece, he watched as it transformed into a tiny statue of a man with Orren's face. A death mask. He placed a finger on the tiny ornate crown on its head. The wooden piece blackened, the features charring away to nothing. Under his touch, it turned to ash, blown away with a quick breath from the man studying the board.

"Irrelevant," he answered himself, turning his gaze to the Queen. "But this one..." He touched the wooden chess piece and it altered into a tall woman wearing an ornate crown. "What do I do with you?"

He picked up the piece, held it gently in his hand, rubbing his thumb slowly over the statue's face.

He sighed and ran his free hand through his wispy hair, resting it against the back of his neck, massaging his strained muscles. He leaned back in the chair, crossing one leg over the other. Still rubbing the statue, he let his gaze cast around.

Books lined the walls, were stacked on the floor, on shelves, on stools. Books... everywhere.

"Did you read all these?" he asked no one. He moved, spying a low table covered in parchments, the rolled edge held open with weights that might have been put there fifty years ago, a hundred even. The only fresh thing in the room was the oldest layer of dust and the chess board. Yellowed pages covered in ink too faded to read, old maps, sketches of parts of the castle A'taz didn't recognise... everything so very old.

Still toying with the chess piece, A'taz stood up and went over to the low desk. He was reminded of Homen's tower and thought about the man who had once sat opposite Homen, the two of them playing at the chess board. Opponents, he thought to himself. Equals even? he wondered.

Gazing down at the detritus of scrawled history covering the tabletop, he summoned a searching spell. Closing his eyes, bringing it forth in his mind and casting it across the table and around the room, he felt the familiar surge of anger and frustration when he opened his eyes and saw... nothing. The spell had failed. That which he was seeking was not written down or recorded in any way, anywhere.

He clenched the statue in his hand, squeezing it until it broke in half in his palm, the wooden edges digging into his flesh, drawing blood.

He dropped the pieces to the floor, bringing his hand to his mouth to lick away the red.

Turning to walk out, he stamped his foot on the two halves of the figure of the queen, the force of his contained rage slamming down, cracking the stone floor under each step as he walked out, the door of Lenard's library slamming shut with such force it smashed the frame to pieces, leaving an empty door, a gaping wound into the empty room.

As he made his way down the tower, he cast his mind and summoned Troy.

The body and face of Ravi caught up with him in the hallway heading to the council chambers.

"Send word to our men on the borders and tell them to increase the attacks. Kill everyone with the King's mark. I want a report of the King's death to be here in two days. I don't care how you do it, it needs to come with evidence that the King is dead. Make it a border raid, something easily believed." A'taz turned on Troy, grabbing his arms, squeezing tight. "Do not embellish the death," he ordered. "I know what you're like. We just need him dead, not a story to go with it."

"Yes, Master." Troy said it like a promise. "The Queen?"

"I can't force her. I can't kill her child. I'll break her heart instead and get what I want from her grief."

"Can I be there…" Troy asked, "when you tell her?"

CHAPTER 11

The encampment in the desert was an oasis of life. Men and women raised girls and boys, trained hunting dogs, strong horses and kept hardy desert goats. They wove baskets made from tough desert grass and dyed their clothes bright purples, deep reds and deeper blues using the petals of the cactus flowers. The grandfathers taught the children the stories of how the world came to be, and the grandmothers taught them prayers.

Some of the boys and girls grew to be warriors trained to cross the endless desert, to listen to the sounds of the animals, to find water in dry places. They practised the arts of holy warfare, honing their bodies and minds so they needn't carry weapons, their fists more powerful than a mace. They trained for battle in a place at the end of the world where, if battle came, it would not be fought with sword or shield.

Other boys and girls became parents themselves, goat herders, cloth makers, desert beekeepers. Everyone had a purpose for their life in the desert, but there was only one Sand-Dancer, who was their prince, and one healer, who was their leader.

And so it was that Miqa brought the little druid and her dying friends to the large tent in the middle of the encampment and laid them at the feet of the dark-skinned woman with the long red hair and large luminous blue eyes.

"Can you heal them?" An'uek begged.

"The healing will only work if they want to live," Sona replied as she moved between them. "There is work for you to do before I can help them."

An'uek understood. Without hesitation she held her hands out and rested her palms on their foreheads.

She closed her eyes and went into their darkness.

Raef's grief was immediately apparent; she felt his pain like a hand around her throat squeezing too tightly.

She wanted to pull away but stayed still as he unconsciously lashed out and wrapped himself around anything solid and stable in the maelstrom of his despair. She waited until they were entangled and she was sure he couldn't easily pull away from her, then grasped onto his misery and used it to pull herself into his mind and follow the beckoning of his heartbreak.

She saw herself wading through water to reach a small island of sharp rock. Raef sat alone on the island at the edge of the water, his reflection staring back at him, hazy and shimmering as the ripples distorted the image. He sat with a rock in his hand bashing himself in the face.

An'uek rushed to stop him, but he held his hand above his head out of her reach. It took all her strength to bring his arm down and force his hand open. The rock dropped out of his fingers, stained in his blood, and landed next to him within easy reach.

He looked at her, his face mangled and broken, his dislocated jaw hanging down, held to his face by sinew.

The face in the water looked back at Raef; it had half its skull missing.

An'uek shuffled around and settled behind him. She leaned against his back, running her hands up and down his arms, resting her chin on his shoulder. She stared down at the pool with him, but only his face was reflected.

His body was cold, lifeless. She began drawing the cold into herself, fusing them together.

She started a chant, her voice unsteady, the words stuttering.

Again she tried to start the incantation that would give his mind some chance of healing. But again she felt his loss, felt her own loss, and the sadness was too much.

She felt Raef's tears drip onto her hands.

Realising there was no druid spell that could heal him, she stopped trying. Instead, An'uek stood firmly behind him as he slumped against her. She bore his weight, a sentinel as he wept, while the face in the water, his own face, but not himself, waited for him to finally open his eyes.

After some time, he reached out and put his fingertips into the water to touch the reflection.

The face in the water began shedding its own tears. With each tear that fell, a little of the face healed until the image that gazed back at the two of them was whole.

"I'm sorry I can't keep my promise to stay with you," a voice said from the water.

"Do you have to go?" Raef asked.

"I've already gone."

"I miss you so much."

"I miss you too."

"I'll never let you go."

"You must," Mason replied. "Please, you have to."

"I want to follow you," Raef said.

"I don't want you to." Mason smiled at his brother. "I want you to live."

"I don't," Raef whispered, as the face in the water slowly disappeared.

"You will." Mason's voice filled the chamber. "I promise you will."

The bloody stone on the sharp rock beside them disintegrated and was gone.

An'uek held Raef as all around them turned to darkness and the dream ended.

She let him go, and he drifted away from her, but the young druid was trapped.

The sorrow that she had submerged herself in to reach him was overwhelming, and she felt desolation consume her. Alone in the cold, afraid she would be too lost to despair, too late and too weak to help him, her dreaming turned to Bode.

Instead of looking outwards for the thread that would take her to him, she turned inward into herself. Deeper into her mind she journeyed, to the bond they shared.

In the dark, the young druid called and Bode answered.

She went to him.

An'uek saw Bode as he saw himself. The sight was enough to break her.

He came to her not as a proud, strong soldier in dented well-worn armour, but a man on his hands and knees, naked skin torn and burned, his body pierced with brutally sharp swords and thick wooden spears. As he crawled towards her on broken knees, his skin morphed, and An'uek saw the faces of all the friends they had lost and so many more she didn't recognise. He wore their deaths upon him. A short sword had cleaved through his skull, puncturing through his mouth, rendering him as mute as the grave.

His misery touched her, and she went to him determined to take his anguish and bear his torture, to lose herself in an eternity of pain and go to her own death if it meant giving him a moment of peace. She reached out a hand... and hesitated, a final spark of intuition giving her pause to wonder if her death would be his salvation. What would he want her to do for him? Instead of reaching into him, to soothe him, she wrapped her small hand around the bloody hilt of the sword in his skull and yanked it out.

She freed his voice.

Stepping back and creating a space between then, a void for him to fill, she raised her hand, and with a look, she demanded his obedience.

His crippled body went still, waiting for her command.

"It's not your fault," she stated. "Free yourself."

In the darkness, Bode opened his mouth and unleashed a primal scream. He howled into the darkness between them.

His wail became a cry of loss, of loneliness and regret. An'uek heard his screams turn to anger, rage and defiance. As he released himself from the weight of his guilt, the faces of the corpses dried away to dust and the swords and spears shattered into splinters that pierced him, leaving gaping holes in his body that slowly closed until, as his lament ended, he breathed deeply and his wounds healed.

Spent, his ethereal body collapsed at An'uek's feet. Reaching down, she touched her ghostly hand to his palm and breathed the very last of her energy into his being.

She felt herself grow thin and start to waste away. Accepting the fate she had cast herself, she turned her face away from Bode and looked into the dark abyss.

But instead of tumbling away, strong hands reached around her and pulled her from the edge. They felt warm and solid, alive and real.

She felt ready to wake.

She lay covered only by her own thin shawl on a pile of soft cushions. A small earthenware bowl of water was within reach, and next to it was a delicate clay plate with small purple fruits already cut in half, exposing delicious ripe flesh that begged to be tasted. But she turned away, the site of the food too much.

Beside the fruit, her clothes lay neatly folded.

She raised her eyes to look beyond and noticed dim lights hung high that flickered on dirty fern-coloured canvas walls that tapered upwards. Taking deep breaths, she recognised the aroma of dried herbs, a unique mix of sharp rich smells that reminded her of drinking bitter tea and talking all night with friends.

She felt safe in this familiar place, her memories recalling images of the last time she was in the desert so many years ago. She let herself relax a little more, ran her fingers over the threads of her shawl, wriggled her toes and her feet and turned her face into the cushions. It didn't concern her that she didn't remember anything of what had happened after sitting with Raef and Bode; she assumed Sona had carried her and put her to rest. A lazy smile crossed her face and she indulged herself in closing her eyes for a few minutes more.

Bode and Raef would live.

As she lay still, eyes closed, fingers still moving, touching, she came fully awake and began listening intently.

There was a shuffling very close by, and the soft rustle of someone trying to be quiet. She purposefully sniffed the air, recognising a subtle perfume. It made her nose twitch enough that she had to move her hand to cover a sneeze.

The noise stopped and An'uek sensed someone come close. She felt a hand lightly brush a fingertip across her cheek, pushing her hair away from her face, and heard a familiar voice mumble her name.

"I'm here, Sona," she answered as she sat up.

"Slowly." Sona's tender hand reached out and gently held her by her shoulder. "You have some burns from the sun, and you have sacrificed much of your own water in salvaging the life of these men. Drink before you try to move too much."

"You're my healer too now?" An'uek asked.

"Anyone stupid enough to rush into the desert eventually comes to my tent." Sona feigned a lecture. "But if it's what it takes to get a visit from my friend then let all my friends be so stupid," she said, chuckling.

Sona reached down, picked up the water, and handed it to An'uek.

"Please drink."

"Thank you, Sona." An'uek lowered herself back to the cushions. "Bode? And Raef?"

Sona nodded across the tent.

An'uek looked where directed, and what she had thought were shadows were the two men laid out naked on leather pallets on the floor. Both were breathing, alive, asleep.

An'uek felt herself momentarily weaken as relief overwhelmed her, then strengthened by it. She sat up again, taking the bowl of water that Sona offered. She drained the bowl until there wasn't a drop left.

"I'm so tired," she said.

"The dreams you took part in were not the kind that bring rest. Your body is weary."

"There's too much to do to rest though."

Sona frowned but didn't push.

"I've done the healing rituals on them both twice already since Miqa brought you all to me," Sona explained. "The younger one's body is healing very quickly. I sense wounds in him, though, that are not of the body, that I can't heal."

"I know," An'uek said. "I did what I can, but it'll never be enough."

Sona pushed the water bowl at An'uek.

She looked down, seeing it full of water. Confused, she thought she had already emptied it, but she was so thirsty she drank deeply, finishing it again.

Sona smiled.

"The older one is badly burned. He lost his mind from the heat no doubt. I can think of no other reason he would remove his tunic, expose himself to the sun like he did. Everywhere the sun touched his body he is deeply burned." She softened her words. "He will have many scars."

"Scars will be a small thing to him." An'uek let her eyes rest on Bode, ignoring the implications of Sona's words.

"We had to cut away his boots. His feet were swollen and fat inside them like he'd walked over coals and cooked them inside. The tissue under his skin had burst. We cut what we had to. He's lost toes."

"But he's alive."

Sona opened her mouth to speak, then paused.

"Say it, Sona, whatever it is you don't want to say."

"His heart is very weak. It flutters, sometimes strong, sometimes fast, too often slow and is not steady."

An'uek put the bowl down, not trusting herself not to drop it.

"We have to wait," Sona said. "When the heart is damaged like that, often there is no strength left in the body, or if there is, it does not last long."

Her back to Sona, An'uek nodded as she wiped the back of a hand across her face and tried to hide a shudder.

"Then we wait."

Sona sat down next to her, picked up the bowl, and handed it to An'uek, full of water.

An'uek took the bowl, staring at the water, and then at Sona.

A man coughed behind them. An'uek recognised Miqa and offered him a soft smile.

"Forgive me," he said, his hand touching his heart as his head dipped. "I didn't mean to startle you."

He carried a flat basket woven from long strands of plaited grass. In the basket was a mix of dried herbs and wood chips. Without instruction he went to the small red clay brazier in the centre of the room and threw the herbs and bark onto the low flames. After a few minutes the tent was filled with sweet smoke.

"It will make them cough, clear their lungs," Sona explained.

"The men returned from what is left of the tower," Miqa said, staring at the flames. "There is nothing there but blackened stone and rubble. The fire burned so hot the stone is still hissing and popping."

"Wait," An'uek said, frowning, "how can they be back already?"

"You've been asleep," he said.

"How long?" An'uek demanded.

"Almost six days," Sona explained. "The young one thrashed in his sleep, sweated out a fever and tore at his skin in his dreams. The older one made noises unlike anything I've heard from a man. It chilled my waters." Sona looked at Bode with caution. "Whatever burden he bore," she looked at An'uek, "whatever it cost you to save these two, I hope they're worth it."

"They are." An'uek shuddered, thinking on what she had heard. "Six days of dreaming. It felt like moments."

She got to her feet with the help of a hand from Sona and walked over to Raef. Bending over him, she dropped a light kiss on his forehead.

"I'll miss him too, forever," she said just to him. She stroked his hair and then rose to her knees and shuffled over to Bode.

"Time to wake up soon," she softly commanded. "And remember, when you do, don't be cross that I disobeyed you and came back." She lightly kissed each eye before sitting up.

"Miqa," Sona called over to the man hovering nearby. "Help our sister with her clothes then take her outside. She needs fresh air and something to eat."

"I want to stay," An'uek began, but Sona shushed her.

"I need to perform the healing ritual a final time to put water back into their bodies. It's a ritual not for any eyes, and certainly not a druid."

Annoyed, but accepting Sona's insistence, An'uek let herself out.

An'uek walked with Miqa through the camp. His steps were short and slow to match her tired pace, his arm firm and strong, taking her weight as she held herself to him to keep steady and upright.

"It's been so long since I was last here, but it feels like yesterday."

"Time doesn't move here like it does in the world beyond the sands." Miqa manoeuvred her steps through corridors of ropes staked to the ground. "The last time you were here, we were across the desert far to the east. You were here with others of your kind." He stopped to let a group of children rush by. "You brought us news of the world, new songs to sing as we weave, new games for the children to play, and stories of the rise and fall of kings and queens in lands far away."

"I remember." She clung to him tightly. "Do you still watch over the creatures that live in the heart of the desert?"

"We do," he said, nodding. "We still hold the words of the first songs. We watch, and we keep, and we bear it all."

They continued in silence, An'uek barely noticing the camp, content to be led around to stretch tired limbs. Eventually they found their way back to Sona's tent. She sat outside with Miqa on a low bench as dusk fell, transforming white clouds into billowing towers of red and orange that contrasted with the streaks of green and blue lights that fell out of the darkening sky.

Around them, small children with wide eyes and silent feet lit lanterns that hung from knots in ropes, poles jammed into the hard, dry ground or scattered on upturned baskets, wicker boxes or simply left on the ground. As night settled in, the chaotic camp was transformed into subtle shadows split by corridors of gentle welcoming, flickering flame.

Miqa sat plaiting long strands of desert grass into single thicker threads that he plaited again. A long coil of rope slowly grew at his feet as he kept her company through the lonely hours.

"It's hard to believe it's been so many days." She was speaking to herself.

"It's like that sometimes with the healing."

An'uek shuffled closer to Miqa.

"Are you learning the healing ways?" she asked.

"I am," he said, and smiled. "But what Sona is doing now," he nodded behind them, "that can't be learned."

"Have any of you seen it? Been with her when she does it, I mean?"

Miqa stopped twisting the strands and looked down at the druid girl at his side who he knew was already older than any desert born had ever lived and would live so long his people would know her for generations.

"It's private," he stated.

"Of course," An'uek said apologetically. "I didn't mean to offend. It's just, I know someone... I knew someone," she corrected herself, "who had similar powers, but different, and he wasn't so shy about using them."

A shadow passed behind her eyes and the night grew cold.

From one of the alleyways between the chaos of tents a young man appeared carrying a small bowl of goat's meat and root stew and two hand-carved wooden ladles.

Miqa thanked him and took the meal but An'uek declined.

"I don't think I can handle that right now," she explained, putting a hand across her mouth to emphasise her words.

"More for me," he joshed, but instead of eating, he put the bowl aside.

The desert breeze had turned cool quickly and An'uek pulled her shawl tightly around her shoulders. She stared at her bare feet, desperately trying to keep her mind from what was going on behind her.

"When will it be done?" she whispered.

"Soon," Miqa replied, and he started twisting the grasses again.

An'uek closed her darkened eyes as the wind came up again and whipped a few loose strands of pale silver hair across her sunken cheeks. She shuffled in her seat, turning her head to look at the closed entrance to the tent.

Miqa followed her gaze and An'uek felt him stiffen.

"Are you keeping me company or keeping me from going inside?" she asked suspiciously.

"I am keeping you out," he admitted with an open smile.

She was about to respond when a faraway shrill whistle split the quiet of the night. Miqa's head snapped to attention.

Again the whistle, but closer, and a different tone, pitch and cadence.

The whistle faded into the desert silence until, a moment later, the original whistler responded.

And then, from within the camp, another whistle response.

An'uek looked in the direction of the sounds as more and more whistles filled the night one after each other, realising they were passing messages. In the desert, she knew, the whistles carried for miles.

Snapping her out of her reflection, Miqa stood quickly, dropping the rope he was creating. The camp came to life as the last whistle died away. People rushed between the corridors of ropes calling to each other, the sudden noise brutal in the quiet.

"The Sand-Dancer is returning." Miqa quickly but gently lifted An'uek to her feet, turned and hurried away.

An'uek wanted to call out, to ask him what he meant, but she was left alone, unguarded, outside the tent where Sona was healing Raef and Bode.

An'uek didn't hesitate. Taking a few swift steps, she pushed past the heavy canvas entrance into the tent and looked around for Sona.

The tent was bathed in darkness, no lamps were lit, and no light came in from the stars shining outside. It took a minute for An'uek's eyes to adjust, and when they did, she had to cover her mouth with her hands to muffle her screams.

Sona stood between Raef and Bode. Instead of flesh, her body had transformed into something like thick black oil. Her face was featureless, just a flat surface that rippled out and down through her liquified body.

Where her arms should have ended in hands, they stretched down into thick streams pouring onto Bode and Raef, completely cocooning their bodies in her own liquified black flesh.

An'uek watched, unable to close her eyes, barely able to breathe behind her hands.

The power emanating from Sona was a physical force that touched the druid, breaking across her like thousands of tiny needles being dragged under her skin.

An'uek fell backwards, crashing against the entrance and falling half through it. She hit her head on the ground as she fell just outside.

Overcome with the sensation of being wet, she started to gasp for air. Too close to the healer's powers, An'uek started to feel water seep through her body. Taking deeper and deeper breaths and filling her lungs with water, An'uek started to drown in the desert.

Chapter 12

An'uek coughed violently and water spurted from her lungs, a damp patch of sand quickly spreading near her mouth.

A pair of heavy hands rapidly beat her back.

"Stop," she gasped.

The hands paused, gently traced up her back and over her shoulders enough to support her and turn her round.

"Take a breath," a familiar voice said, soothing her, "there's plenty to breathe here."

She gulped at the air.

"Slower," he commanded.

"I'm all right," she groaned, rolling her head to spit up mouthfuls of water.

The stranger sat her upright, holding her against his broad chest.

She felt strong slender arms encircling her weakened body as she sat on his lap. Deliberately slowing her breathing, she twisted to look at him. His mahogany skin contrasted against her own pale flesh in the desert night. His dark russet eyes shone like oiled wood, a short fresh beard covered most of his face, and she could see the dark swirls and lines across his cheeks. Her gaze travelled down his neck to his chest and she could clearly see the patterns of circles and loops of ink made from charcoal ash scratched into his skin with the tip of a scorpion's tail. Her hand rose to trace one of the patterns from his shoulder down across his chest, round the loops and then down across his sculpted torso to his naval.

She flattened her hand against his bare chest and glided her palm up the smooth expanse of his skin. He wore a simple braided leather circlet at his neck. She looked at him for a moment. The shape of his mouth, the colour of his eyes. She remembered such happy times with him.

"Bastion," she whispered, and pulled herself up into the arms that took her into an embrace. She melted into his strength. "I didn't know how much I missed you until this moment."

"It's been too long," he said affectionately, his voice muffled as he hugged her tightly.

"I wish I was here for better reasons." She choked on a sob, letting herself be held a moment longer before pulling away and putting her hands on his face.

"So do I," he replied.

An'uek reached round and hugged him again.

"You're here because of the day of fire?" Bastion asked. "And because of the man who burns."

An'uek sat up so quickly her head hit him under the chin.

"What man?" she demanded.

"The man who walked away from the tower," Bastion explained. "The one who is bleeding magic all over my sands."

"You've seen him?"

"Yes." Bastion's voice was solemn.

"His name is Calem."

"Is that so?" Bastion sounded bemused. "When I asked him, he wouldn't tell me."

An'uek froze. Her face didn't move, her body didn't react, but her mind reeled at his words.

Bastion watched her reaction and waited a moment before continuing.

"I found him in the deep desert. It feels like only days ago, but I understand we've been gone for much longer. It's like that in that place, and now here too."

An'uek put her finger to his lips, and Bastion stopped.

It took her a moment to speak, and when she did, it was barely a whisper, barely controlled anger.

"You've spoken to him?" she hissed.

"Spoken to him, yes," Bastion confirmed, "and convinced him to come here with me…"

An'uek leapt up in Bastion's lap, levering herself against him, covering his mouth with her hands to silence him, pushing him back.

"Where is he?"

Bastion sat up a little straighter and pushed her away, his hands gently taking her wrists and lowering her trembling fingers from his mouth.

"He's in a safe place, not so near that he will affect Sona, but far away from the deep desert."

"Why?" It was all An'uek could think to ask.

"I couldn't leave him there," he said, his words a half-truth. "What he has done, he must undo."

"And what is that?"

"You know, little sister," Bastion said affectionately. "You can sense it."

An'uek sat back on her haunches, her hands still trapped by Bastion.

"I can feel it, it's like a taste on the edge of my senses that I can't quite grasp."

"Yes." Bastion nodded. "It's raw magic, violent, it's world-making power, and it's leaking out of him."

"Leaking?"

Bastion nodded. "Yes, leaking. He's hurt." Bastion let go of her wrist and, with one finger, pointed up.

An'uek looked up to the lights dancing in the night sky.

"What is that?" she asked.

"Wild magic." Bastion looked up, following her gaze.

"He did this?"

"He did something. This is what we see of what he did."

"What did he unleash?" she asked.

Bastion looked away.

"I don't know how to say what he did."

"You won't tell me?"

"I can't."

"Can't… or won't?"

"So curious, little sister." He smoothed her hair on her head. "Not all knowledge is for you. What has happened in the deep desert, in my domain, is for me."

She didn't push.

"Is he dying?" she asked.

"No, I don't think so. And I don't think we want him to die."

"Why not?" An'uek challenged, wrenching her hands out of Bastion's grasp. "So what if he bleeds and dies."

"If he dies, everything dies." Bastion stated it so simply it caught An'uek off guard. "I understand that what has happened has cost many lives." He tucked strands of silver hair behind her ears. "Like I know that to be a druid, and around so much despair and hatred, is changing you."

An'uek tried to pull away but Bastion held her firm.

"Tell me," he started smoothing her hair again. "How have you been tainted?"

"I was sent to help them months ago by A'rrick. I didn't want to, but I obeyed. I wasn't one of them. I didn't think I'd ever feel anything for them."

"And now?"

"Now, I never want to leave them. I don't think I could, even if I tried."

"Yes, but what is it doing to you?"

"Nothing anyone can stop."

An'uek thought of Jedda, and Bode, and Mason, and she thought of Calem.

She turned sad eyes to Bastion.

"We got it all so wrong," her voice broke, "and so many died."

Sona dipped long strips of new finely woven cloth into a small bowl of water that sat boiling on the brazier in the middle of her tent. The steam carried the odour of an oil drawn from a cactus flower. Moving the strips of cloth around with a thin ceramic rod, she eventually decided they were ready and lifted them out, hanging them over some open coals to dry.

As they dried, Sona took her time grinding dried herbs and flowers together with an oil until they formed a thick paste.

Bode sat talking softly with An'uek. Neither looked happy.

Raef and Bastion sat apart, sharing a plate of meat and trying to ignore them.

"I understand why he's so angry, but if she hadn't come back you would be dead."

"Some of us are dead anyway," Raef replied, moving bits of meat around on his plate.

Bastion chewed slowly. He didn't know this man sharing his meal enough to ask about his grief.

He ate another mouthful.

Bode and An'uek stopped arguing, her small hand gripping his.

After enough time had passed, Sona tested the paste. She touched the strips of cloth and, deciding everything was ready, motioned for Bode to come over to where she sat beside two stools.

Bode took his time getting up, unsteady on his damaged feet. An'uek stood up beside him but was careful not to reach out when his legs trembled and his first few steps were weak.

He crossed the short distance and sank down onto the stool, sweating. He looked at Sona, his face expressionless under the thick stubble and mangled hair that hid his eyes.

Sona looked over his shoulder at An'uek.

The druid came over and took the stool next to him.

"This will hurt very much." Sona looked at Bode, who in turn looked down at his bare blistered arms, and raised them up, holding them out.

"Get it over with."

Sona held back a sigh and picked up the small bowl with the paste. Scooping it into her palm as gently as she could, she started to rub it into Bode's burnt skin.

He hissed, his face scrunched, and he tried to pull away. She held his arms.

Bode trembled uncontrollably as Sona wrapped the long strips of cloth around his palms, over his wrists and up his arms. She secured each one over and around his shoulders. The smell of the plant oils surrounded him, making him remember a time he sat with a friend in a field tent while a medic sawed off the man's leg. The man died.

Sona, watching his reactions, reached down and picked up an empty clay mug. By the time he took it from her, mumbling barely coherent thanks, it was full of cool water.

He slurped it down, holding it clumsily in bandaged hands.

"I have to do your chest and your back."

"Make it quick," he begged.

When Sona was done with his body, she rubbed the remaining paste across his face and into his beard, the back of his neck, around his ears and into his scalp, slicking it through his hair.

His ordeal over, she helped him to stand and then walk to a mound of blankets and scattered pillows.

"Thank you."

"Do you want to rest?" Sona asked him.

"No," Raef answered quickly from across the room. "No, none of us want any more rest. We want to hear about Calem." He looked at Bastion. "And then we want to go find him."

"And kill him," An'uek declared. "Enough is enough. If he is alive, he can only ever do more harm. He has to die."

"No," Bastion replied firmly. "I can't allow it, blood on my sands is poison."

"He's poison all right," Raef mused.

"I'll take you to him," Bastion offered, "but only if you promise to take him away, he must undo what he has done. Then, kill him when it's all over. I don't really care as long as it doesn't happen here."

"Agreed," Raef answered straight away. "We'll take him and kill him."

"No." Bode's deep, low voice caught their attention. He was sitting leaning forward, elbows on his knees and head on his hands.

"What did you say?" Raef asked, his voice shaking, eyes wide in disbelief and challenge.

"We can't kill him," Bode said softly.

Raef got to his feet and stepped towards Bode. He stopped in front of him and kneeled.

"And just how do you think you'll stop me?" The voice was Raef's but the words were an echo of someone else.

Bode looked away and then back at Raef.

"I remember it too," he said.

Raef's eyes widened.

"I remember when the stone fell on him."

"Shut up."

"I remember the sound of it hitting him."

"Shut up." Raef involuntarily went for his belt, but there was no belt. There was no blade.

"I remember how still he was afterwards."

Raef said nothing.

"But it's not the boy's fault," Bode said sadly.

"I'll kill him."

"It would be easier."

"He should be dead instead of everyone else…" Raef's voice fell to a whisper.

"I know. But it's not his fault. Is it?"

"I don't care."

And killing him… well, we can't, can we."

"No." An'uek scuttled over to Bode's side. "He's too powerful now."

"And besides…" Bode didn't take his eyes off of Raef, who finally looked at him.

"It's not his fault," Raef said sadly.

"No," Bode shook his head, "it's not."

"It's Orren's fault," Raef said, "and he's already dead."

"But A'taz isn't." Bode kept Raef's attention. "And as far as I know, he's on the throne."

"He won." Raef shrugged and moved away.

"No." Bode shook his head again. "No, I don't believe that."

"We're on the other side of the world to him. What can we possibly do, even if we wanted to?"

"I honestly don't know," Bode confessed. "But if we find the boy…" he looked at An'uek, "it's like you said. Calem is so powerful now, maybe he's powerful enough to destroy A'taz."

"And then what?" Raef scuttled over to Bode. "Can he raise the dead?"

"I don't know," Bode said honestly. "Maybe."

"No…" An'uek stepped into the conversation. "Don't even think about such things, don't speak them."

"Then what's in it for me?" Raef sneered. "I followed a lunatic out of loyalty to a man who served a crown, and for what?"

"A usurper sits on the throne of your kingdom," Bastion reminded them all.

"So what?" Raef scoffed. "Kings, queens, princelings, lords, ladies, they rise and fall, and today's usurper will be someone's legacy in two hundred years."

"Someone is still sending raiding parties into your villages. Mercenaries are still riding through your border towns killing everyone who doesn't join them and burning everything else to the ground."

"All the borders now?" Bode asked, curious.

"Yes," Bastion confirmed. "My people gather news, and the early winter covering your kingdom has not stopped the ferocious attacks that are spreading. At first they were on the borders, now they are encroaching deeper into the interior. Day by day, these armies are reaching into your land."

"Like a net," Bode mumbled.

"What?" Raef couldn't help himself.

"We always wondered about the randomness of the border attacks. Before we got to Ustred, Orren and I were looking for a pattern."

He was silent until prompted.

"And?"

"And it makes sense now. If A'taz is in Kraner, we don't know what he wants but we know it's there. And we know that if his armies of mercenaries are raiding along the borders, and now coming into the kingdom…"

"People will start to leave. They'll be trying to escape the coming raids."

"And where do you head when you're afraid?"

"They'll try to get to the cities… Penrose in the south."

"Most will make a run for Kraner."

"A'taz is in Kraner."

"And he gets his power, his life fuel, from the living."

"Those mercenaries, they're herding our people to A'taz… to feed him."

"The garrisons will be emptied and everyone who can lift a sword will be sent to fight, so there won't be anyone left inside the kingdom if they're all on the borders."

Bode sat on the high dune ridge looking out across the endless desert.

"It's funny how all this sand reminds me of the sea," he said to An'uek. "This all started for me when Brennan asked me to go with him to Penrose."

"It must seem like a lifetime ago."

"It was," he mused. "I met Brennan when we were boys. I wasn't one for books, he was. I was always going to end up a soldier, he had business and responsibility to inherit." Bode looked up at the stars glinting in the dark night. "This was before I was anything, just a soldier. Before the trolls. Before Penrose. Before I was a knight. Before Orren, and gems, and magic and a thief and a murderer and a dead paladin. Before now." He looked at his bandaged hands. "Raef will come with us. He'll want to murder the boy, but he won't."

"You keep calling Calem a boy." She followed his gaze. "He's nothing like a boy."

"He'll always be a boy to me," Bode mused. "When Brennan and I were learning to shave and trying to get girls to let us under their skirts, I told him once it wouldn't be a bad idea if we drowned Calem."

An'uek pulled back, looking at Bode in surprise. He ignored her.

"I was only joking, Brennan knew that. We never talked about it, but I wonder, if we had done it, what would we have been doing now?"

"You'd be a murderer. Once you start taking lives, it's all you end up knowing."

"But would we be here?"

She hugged his arm.

"Why did you come back?" he asked. "I know we talked about it earlier, but... why?"

"I told you why."

"You told me you couldn't leave us there."

"I told you I couldn't leave you there," she corrected him.

He pulled her closer.

"Why?"

"Because…" she looked wistfully across the dunes, "it's not time for us yet."

Bode moved to put his arm around her, and she sensed more than heard him wince.

"Is it very bad?" she asked, her small hands tracing over the soft woollen tunic covering the wrappings covering so much of his body.

"Have you ever broken a bone, a leg or an arm?"

"No," she answered.

"Well, it's a lot like that, a deep throb, an ache that you can't reach." He tapped his chest. "When I lie down, it hurts more, and I can feel my heart beating. Sometimes I feel like I need to gasp, like I'm running but I'm sitting still…" He lost his words and looked away.

"I'm so sorry." She held herself still.

"It's not your fault," Bode replied.

An'uek wanted to take his face between her palms and make him believe the pain would go away, but she wasn't sure it would, or that she should.

She sighed and lightly hugged his arm.

"Have you been here before?" He changed the subject.

"Many, many years ago, when Sona and Bastion were young children, and again maybe ten years ago."

"They seem to remember you fondly."

"This is a quiet, restful place." She smiled up at him. "Only the very sure or the very foolish make the journey to the desert to seek Bastion's camp. And you only find it if he wants you to find it."

"This place is full of magic?"

"Old magic," she agreed. "Have you had a chance to see much of the camp?"

"Been too tired." He fiddled with the bandages around his fingers. "Maybe tomorrow."

"Bastion's people are amazing, so kind, so much life in them. They do so much more here than just survive the sun and the sand."

"I'll take a look," he promised. "I still need to find where they stored my weapons. They're bound to be here somewhere."

He noticed An'uek stiffen.

"What?" he asked, looking down at her sombre face.

"Miqa found you, and Raef, but he didn't find anything else."

"My sword?" Bode asked, his voice rising. "My daggers?"

"Nothing," she answered. "I'm sorry."

Bode put his head in his hands, wincing, and put his hands down, letting them hang between his knees.

"Damn. I loved that sword," he muttered. Taking a deep breath, he chewed his dry lip. "I'll have to get a new one," he said, nodding to himself. "Once I get my strength back."

An'uek looked away at the desert dunes unfolding around them. She didn't say anything about his sword, or his strength.

"Take a walk tomorrow around the camp," she suggested again. "See how you feel after."

"I'll do that," he said, and followed her gaze. "It's nice to be out of that stuffy tent. All those herbs Sona keeps burning make my eyes sting."

"They're good for you."

"This is good for me." He breathed deeply and was abruptly overcome with a cough. Instinctively he hit himself on the chest, taking ragged deep breaths. "It's okay," he said, puffing. "I'm okay." But what strength he had was gone, and he slumped against her.

She reached up and ran her fingers through his hair, seeing the streaks of grey shining brightly in the moonlight changing from silver to indigo.

Looking up, she saw the lights come out, brilliant blue ribbons unfolding above them.

"They're beautiful…" She felt sad but couldn't help but smile.

Bode watched her, seeing her absorbed in the lights.

Her small body felt like a deadweight against him and he struggled not to topple over. He thought, as she looked up, of all the times he had picked her up, carried her, how light she was, already wiser and older than he would ever be. Lighter than his sword but strong enough to catch him and hold him if he fell… now, so heavy, or was he truly so weak? He tried to clench his hands but was barely able to hold his fists shut for more than a second. Looking down, he wondered how he would lift a sword if he couldn't even hold himself up.

CHAPTER 13

He did as she said; the next morning Bode roused himself and went out into the camp before the morning meal.

It felt as chaotic as it looked, tents of different sizes pitched haphazardly all over the place seemingly without order. A few men, women and children walked past, nodding and smiling and greeting him in a language he didn't know, but most were still waking up and starting their day in their own way. He was careful not to trip over ropes staked deep into the hard ground, wondering how close he was to someone's front door when he walked between stretches of material almost touching. He walked quietly, hearing snippets of soft conversations, wondering if mothers were waking their children, husbands talking to their wives about what needed to be done that day or what was for breakfast. He blushed and walked quicker when he heard sounds of lovers enthusiastically greeting each other. But he couldn't see anyone, and he was sure none of the voices were from inside the tents.

So much was familiar that it didn't feel that different to the way he had set camp in his army days, but there was something missing that he wasn't seeing.

It wasn't until he'd been drifting through the canvas corridors for almost an hour and stepped between a sudden gap that he saw the pattern and realised the design. The tents were only big enough for storage, they weren't for living in. Bastion's people truly lived in the desert itself.

The tents, he realised, were staked together in a circle. They formed a small enclosure, an almost intimate garden space shared only by those in the round. Stepping into one of them, Bode saw dozens of finely woven blankets and carpets thrown across each other in all sorts of ways, strewn with cushions and pillows all set out around a central firepit. Around the edges a few children slept soundly in soft blankets as men and women knelt washing their faces in buckets of water or dressing. One of the women finished wrapping a skirt around her hips and shrugged into a loose-fitting sleeveless vest and started to make the rounds of the sleepers, gently prodding them awake. She noticed Bode and beckoned him forward. He looked around, self-conscious, but stepped over to her.

In words he didn't understand, she greeted him.

Not knowing what to say, he raised a hand and waved.

She waved back and then pointed to the centre of their small family courtyard. He saw low tables placed around the central firepit, set with clay bowls and cups neatly stacked for the morning meal. Round flatbreads were cooling on one of the tables, chunks of meat slowly roasting on a low heat over the coals. He looked over but didn't catch on, so the woman gently pushed him towards a table and put her hand to her mouth.

"No," he said, shaking his head, putting his hands out, palms upwards. "I'm not here to intrude."

Whether she understood him or not, she didn't take no for an answer.

Taking his hand, she tugged him forward over to a table and pushed him to sit down, indicating that he needed to wait.

Some men and women woke up the children, dressing the youngest ones and haranguing older ones to dress themselves and hurry up about it. Young women checked that the food was ready, and young men carried clay jugs of cool water and filled cups, and Bode sat and ate breakfast with the family.

He listened without speaking, tearing off small handfuls of the bread, dipping it in the bowls of meat drippings, savouring the rich flavour that he washed down with the cold water that tasted better than any drink he'd ever had. He didn't eat much, but he ate slowly, making sure he wasn't the first to finish, and at the end of the meal he carried his plate and some of the cups over to a young man who refused to let him tend to his own mess.

He wandered back and sat down again, stomach full, content, feeling alone but not lost.

A little while later some older men came over and sat with him. They talked animatedly using gestures, and he felt he understood what they were asking.

He stood up and pointed at himself. Then, taking a slow step back, he raised his hands as if holding a sword and pretended to swing it through the air.

The men looked at each other and shrugged.

Bode wasn't a mime, but he did his best and tried again.

He crouched down as far as his sore legs would let him and pretended to be peering around a corner holding his imaginary sword. Then, acting as if he had seen something, he jumped around and pretended to fight.

He heard the children burst out laughing and added a little flair to his performance, pretending to stab someone, be stabbed, and then he slowly pretended to stumble down dead.

It was the best he could do to convey that he was a soldier.

The men slapped their hands on their thighs in delight, and the children all jumped up and started to mimic his performance, engaging in mock warfare and naturally dividing up to play against each other, all taking turns to attack and dramatically die on the sand.

Bode put his hands out to get himself up but winced as his shoulders jarred from the pain of lifting his own weight. He sagged back into his heels and noticed a hand reach down to help him.

"Thanks," he said, taking Bastion's hand and letting him haul him to his feet.

"What was that?" Bastion asked, grinning, keeping Bode's hand in his.

"I was trying to explain that I'm a soldier." He put a hand on his hip.

"We don't have a word for that in our language."

"Well in that case, they probably think I'm a bandit."

Bastion laughed, and quickly translated to the men standing with him, who started to chuckle.

"Yes, that they understand."

"Fantastic," Bode muttered.

He was about to ask Bastion about his camp, but a group of children surrounded them, chattering and jumping for his attention.

"They want to know if you'll play a game with them?" Bastion explained.

"A game?" Bode repeated, surprised. "Are you sure?"

"They want you to play with them, they think you're very funny."

"I was actually planning on seeing if I could find where you keep weapons. I wanted to speak to someone about arming myself."

"Later," Bastion said, and he smiled but stood firm. "Play first, the children will tell you what you need to know after."

Raef had also escaped the confines of the healer's tent and made his way through the camp. He crept past tents, taking his time to loiter and listen to the sounds of life coming from them, and beyond them. He kept out the way, avoiding being seen as much out of habit as for the comfort of not wanting to see anyone, desperately trying to escape the press of his own thoughts.

He stumbled upon, rather than found, the centre of the encampment, not realising where he was until he noticed he was surrounded by dozens of people of all ages filling bowls and buckets and waterskins from a clear spring bubbling out of the rocky ground.

Raef stood and stared, bemused, at the water gurgling up, knowing instinctively it wasn't natural.

An old woman shuffled past him, her arm grazing his, and he recoiled from the touch, stepping back so quickly he fell against a man and lost his footing, ending up on his backside on the ground surrounded by a sea of dark legs.

The press of people around him, all looking down at him, as one, extending their hands to pull him back to his feet, felt like a wall around him, and for a moment he felt panicked. But as quickly as it started, it disappeared, as he was yanked to his feet and everyone stepped away and went back to their own business.

His eyes wide, back straight, Raef looked around for a space between anyone and darted away from the group as fast as he could. He reached the first blind corner and turned to run between the rows and circles and loops of tents. Moving too fast, he tripped over a rope and fell forward, barely catching himself on his hands to avoid impaling himself on a wooden stake.

"That was close."

He heard Bastion before he saw the hand extended down to help him up. "A hand to the right and you'd have smashed your face."

Raef said nothing.

He didn't take Bastion's hand, getting to his feet himself.

"I guess I'm lucky then."

"Maybe." Bastion withdrew his hand, hooking his thumbs into the belt that hung loosely around his waist.

"Are you looking for something?" Bastion asked.

"Not really." Raef couldn't meet his gaze. "I just needed some air."

"Plenty of air in the desert."

"Air and sand," Raef muttered quietly. But Bastion heard him.

"Yes," he agreed, "air and earth."

The silence between them escalated from uncomfortable to unbearable straight away.

"What are you looking for?" Bastion asked, not unkindly.

Raef felt compelled to answer truthfully.

"I don't know." It felt like a confession. "I'm trying to get lost." Raef gestured around him.

"Lose yourself… from who?"

"From myself." Raef finally looked at Bastion.

The thief felt the desert prince look past him, into him, and shuddered that the man might truly understand what he had said.

"I have a job for you," Bastion said, surprising Raef. "Come with me."

Raef followed the revered Sand-Dancer through the labyrinth of tents, content to be led, stepping into the man's sandal prints in the sand. He stopped counting paces and memorising left and right, stopping when Bastion stopped in a clearing that looked like the backyard of a group of small flax awnings strung over wooden poles. A group of old women sat weaving baskets and humming a low tune, a choir of singers, not quite singing, but filling the air with music.

"They need your help." Bastion motioned over to the women, one of whom looked up and patted at the space near her on the carpet.

"Are you joking?" Raef replied, sniggering. "You want me to make those?" He pointed at the baskets next to the women.

"No." Bastion shook his head, clearly amused. "You don't have enough skill to weave with desert grass." He patted Raef on the back and pushed him towards the old woman. "I want you to hand her the stems, it'll save her having to bend down."

"Bend down? She's on the floor, how much further does she have to reach?" Raef crossed his arms over his chest. "This is ridiculous. I'm not a weaver."

"What are you then?" Bastion asked.

"I'm a…" Raef stopped. He didn't know what to say.

Bastion stepped a little closer and reached to Raef, putting his hands on his shoulders.

"What are you?" he asked again.

Raef looked away to his left. But there was no one next to him.

Bastion, following Raef's every movement, pushed, just once more.

"I know what you were," he said, his voice low. "But that was when you were two. Now you are one."

Tears filled Raef's eyes, rolling down his cheeks.

"I know why you want to get lost." He squeezed Raef's shoulders.

"I don't know what I am if I'm not a thief, if I'm not his brother, if I'm not in service to Homen, or the crown, or doing something for someone else. I've got no one."

"Come, sit down, for today I'll tell you who to be. Be a man helping old women weave baskets."

Raef turned and walked over to the old woman, who settled him down next to her.

"Who are these women?" Raef asked.

"These are the mothers of those who have died on the sand."

"We never had a mother." He stated his words as fact.

"Everyone has a mother."

"Not us."

"Then let her be your mother for today, let her sing for your brother, let him have a mother who mourns him. Let yourself have a mother who, just for today, loves you more than anything else she has ever known."

Raef put his head into his hands. The woman at his side, without turning to see him, put her arm around his shoulders and pulled him against her. He fell into her side, his arms circling her, clinging to her as she rocked him slowly, softly singing to him as she stroked his head.

An'uek had been awake through the night, so when Bode crept out, and Raef scurried after him a little while later, she didn't have the energy or desire to follow either of them.

Her exhaustion went bone deep; her hip started to ache from lying on it too much, but it hurt to roll onto her other side. The bones in her back cracked as she turned, and the throbbing pain in the base of her neck spread up and over her skull until it hammered at her temples and forced her to keep her eyes closed.

She curled up, lying as if under a blanket woven of fatigue heavy enough to push her into the earth for ever.

Her hands gripped her blanket, a silken shawl, for all it was worth. Her knuckles white, she pushed her forehead against her knees.

She knew she was being irrational, that she was just tired and it would pass; the earth wasn't pulling her down into a living grave. But at the same time maybe it was; she was so tired.

Eventually An'uek sensed someone nearby.

"Sona?" she asked, surprised by the slurring of her words.

"It's me," Bastion replied.

She knew he would settle next to her so she didn't move. She wasn't surprised when she felt his slender fingers start to comb through her long, thick hair.

"Sona tells me that you don't sleep anymore?"

"I sleep," she disagreed, aware that her tongue felt like it was sticking to her mouth.

"Collapsing is not sleeping," he argued. "And if it were, you are not collapsing enough to get proper rest."

His fingers stroked the base of her neck, following subtle ridges up over her head and down across her forehead to circle her eyes and trace her cheeks down to her chin. Looping back, he slowly caressed and massaged her, shifting her head until it lay in his lap.

"Sona has seen you," his fingers kept moving, "sitting up watching over your men every night."

"Raef wakes up some nights and sneaks out," she said slowly. "He thinks I don't know where he's going."

"You followed him?" Bastion asked, surprise in his voice.

"Once," An'uek replied, her eyes heavy. "He didn't go far. He just wanted to get away from us."

"Get some air?"

"Get some darkness," she replied.

Bastion frowned, giving her space to fill the silence.

"I heard him talking to his brother."

"The one who died?"

She nodded under his hand.

"He's trying to come to terms with what happened."

"And you?"

"I'm here if he needs me," she said, sighing.

"Haven't you helped them both enough already?" He started to draw circles on the skin around her eyes with the tips of his fingers.

She sighed again and leaned her head a little more against him as some of the tension left her muscles.

"They're mine to help." She unclenched her hands.

"They're not yours," he disagreed, widening the circles, starting to smooth the frowns in her forehead.

"We belong to each other now." Her voice was low and slow.

"Is that a good thing?"

"I don't know." She opened her eyes, just enough to see him. "But what I did for them, with them, I can't undo it. I wouldn't even if I could."

"Why?"

"I love them."

"You shouldn't," Bastion reminded her.

"I know." A smile ghosted over her face.

"You have to find a way to be apart from them when you're with them so you can sleep." He covered her eyes with his hands, her eyelashes fluttering against his palm.

"I want to sleep," she said, her voice starting to fade. "Would you stay with me?"

"Nothing will move me from your side, little sister. Trust me to watch over you while you rest."

Bode and Raef found their way to the same spot as the sun was setting. Standing with his hands in his pockets, the thief kicked at the large stones set around the bubbling spring.

"This is about as unnatural as a pink dog with four eyes and two legs." Raef put the toe of his boot into the water, flicking it away as the soft brown leather darkened to the colour of mud.

"I think it's the woman, Sona."

Raef put his other toe in the water, trying to even up the stains on his boot.

"Must be nice," he muttered.

"What, the water trick?"

"Being able to keep them all alive."

Bode stretched his arms out as far as he could. It caught Raef's attention. He stepped away from the water and mooched over to Bode's side. Slowly, he reached up to take Bode's outstretched arms in his own. Bode frowned.

"I don't want to dance," he scoffed, as Raef stepped closer to him.

"Shut up," the younger man said gently, a crooked smile on his face. He put his hands on Bode's biceps and pushed, forcing his friend to stretch further than he could manage on his own. Bode grunted with the effort and it brought beads of sweat to his forehead.

"Again," Raef said, pushing Bode's arms up higher and further back. "Sore?" he asked, as Bode hissed.

"Stings." He clenched his jaw but let Raef move him.

"Sit down," Raef ordered.

"Really, a massage?"

"If I did, you'd love it," Raef joked.

"Are we flirting now?" Bode laughed a little, wincing as Raef lowered his arms to his sides and pointed to where he wanted him to sit.

"If we were flirting, you'd know, and you'd already be saying yes please."

Bode laughed loudly, sitting down.

"But no," Raef said, sighing and moving to kneel behind him, "and this isn't going to feel good."

Raef grabbed Bode from behind and squeezed his arms against his body, compressing the muscles in his back.

Bode yelped at the pain, and then sighed as a second later the bones in his spine all popped and he felt the tension disappear from his back.

"I didn't even know I needed that," he said as he felt his body relax.

Raef smiled behind him.

"You have a dirty remark on the tip of your tongue, don't you?" Bode asked. He could feel Raef chuckling behind him. "Do that again."

He could practically hear Raef smirking.

He did it again, and again Bode felt pain just before the relief of his aching bones.

"You're good at that." Bode shrugged his shoulders, delighting in how loose they felt and the way they moved. His skin still stung, but it was a bit more bearable.

Raef patted his shoulder and shuffled behind him. He put both his hands to Bode's neck and started to press and pull the sinews ad tendons under the skin with skilful fingers.

"Mason use to get terrible cramps and pains sometimes, from the things he'd do with his body if the job needed it."

"The first year in the army all I did was moan about stiff and sore arms and aching muscles."

"Swords are heavy."

"They are if you're the biggest man and get the biggest sword."

"Did you find yours?" Raef asked as he worked his fingers from Bode's neck across his shoulders and down, kneading the muscles of his upper arms.

"No, they're gone. I was hoping to get my hands on some weapons, but I ended up playing with some children for most of the day."

"I spent all day singing sad songs with a bunch of old women."

Bode turned to look at Raef over his shoulder, one eyebrow arched.

"You also had a visit with Bastion then?"

"Let's just say," Raef replied, nodding, "today did not go as expected."

"I'd drink to that if there was any beer in the camp."

"Or wine. Or something to smoke."

"They live a very pure life, don't they?"

"Too pure for me," Raef admitted conspiratorially.

They both laughed.

Raef moved down Bode's arm to his wrist, clicking and creaking the small bones of his hands and fingers through the bandages. There was a slight tremor as he held Bode's fingers, closing his hands around them. Bode went still for a moment, the muscles so recently relaxed tense again.

"Don't," Bode whispered, looking away.

Raef held his hand a moment longer.

"I knew a man once…" Raef started to talk above him, releasing his fingers and moving back up to his neck to start again.

"We've all known men," Bode joked.

"Well this one was a giant."

"Really, a giant man?"

"Yes." Raef pressed into the hard muscles of his other shoulder. "Nine feet tall, he was a farmer with a tiny wife and four beautiful daughters."

"What was his name?"

"His name isn't part of the story."

"Really, that's convenient," Bode muttered.

"Are you going to shut up and listen or do you want me to go find some children for you to entertain?"

"I'll shut up."

"The giant was a farmer, and all his life he ploughed his own fields. He was so big he didn't need to use oxen to pull the plough, he could drag the chisel through frozen ground in winter as easily as loose earth in summer." Raef moved to his arms and felt Bode flinch and start to draw away; he held him still and kept up his story.

"He grew crops, and every year he made lots of gold and his family ate well. He was the best farmer in the land, and soon everyone knew about him and he started to plough other people's fields as well."

Bode's bunched muscles started to give way.

"But one year, he was ploughing his fields, and he tripped over a lose stone and fell down and broke his back."

Bode stiffened, but Raef ignored him and started to massage his forearm. He moved to sit beside him.

"He spent a year in his house, his small wife tending him, his daughters bringing him food and water, and eventually he learned to sit up and to walk again. One day in summer he tried to plough his fields, but he couldn't bend down to pick up the beam, let alone actually pull the damn thing."

"Get to the point," Bode muttered.

Raef spent time on Bode's wrist, and it was stiff and unyielding, again with the sensation of tremors under his fingertips.

"The giant was sad, angry, and thought about throwing himself down the well, because if he wasn't a farmer, what was he?"

For a moment, Raef paused, and he thought he heard Bastion's voice echoing in his own words. He shook off a shudder and carried on, as he felt Bode waiting on his story.

"But the farmer's wife, she wasn't the type to sit there and let him feel sorry for himself. She slapped him a few times and reminded him there are many ways to be a farmer. The next day she sold the plough, and with the gold she bought a herd of sheep that the giant could watch over, and he became a sheep farmer."

Raef held Bode's hands in his own, and again they trembled.

"That's a terrible story," Bode grumbled.

"You kept interrupting, it's your fault." Raef didn't let go, but neither man looked at one another.

"I know what you're saying," Bode admitted. "I'm just not ready to let it be true."

"We don't have time though." Raef denied him his self-pity. "We need you too much and you have to get past this."

"I'm really good with a sword." Bode tried to pull his hands away, but Raef held on as tight as he dared.

"You're just as good without it, probably better if you give yourself a chance."

"And you," Bode asked, finally looking at him. "If I'm the giant, what are you in the story?"

"I'm the storyteller. I'm not in my own story."

"That's lucky," he snorted.

"I had my lesson earlier. It stung a little, but I learned it, and you can now have the benefits of my vaunted newfound wisdom without the embarrassment of weeping like a baby for most of the day."

Raef squeezed Bode's trembling hands one last time then let them go.

"Thanks for the terrible story," Bode muttered, feeling a little better despite himself.

"Maybe, when all this is over, I'll become a bard, travel the world telling stories."

"You heard the part where I said your story was terrible?"

"It could have been worse," Raef declared, helping them both to stand up.

"I did wonder why you threw in the four daughters."

"That was instinct." Raef shrugged as they walked away. "If I'm telling a story about ploughing a field, I'm going to add some girls."

"You're terrible."

"Believe me, my friend, if we ever get out of this place, I plan to be very terrible."

Bode and the young druid sat together in a quiet space outside Sona's tent.

"I don't want to do this," An'uek said to Bode, but she looked at the stars.

"I need to know," he insisted.

"What if they're all dead? I don't want to find that out on a shaft of starlight," she implored.

"That's why I need you to try," he urged.

"I wish you wouldn't ask me to do this."

"Who else is there?" He got to his feet and held out his arms as high as he could raise them. "I need to know, An'uek." He sat down again. "Please."

She looked away, angry and sad and tired.

"Fine," she snarled.

She got to her feet quickly, too quickly, and her vision tilted for a moment. Grinding her jaws as tightly as she could bear, she waited for it to pass then stepped into the starlight.

"There's so much magic in this place it shouldn't be difficult to cross the distance." She looked at him over her shoulder, her eyes as cold as her voice. "Unless they're dead, even I can't cross that distance."

An'uek closed her eyes, drew her senses forward to feel the starlight on her face, to infuse them into her body, then threw her mind out into the void, searching for others like herself.

Her mind flew over Barclan, across mountains, rivers, meadows, forests, towns, cemeteries. It raced through the great void, crying out to the other young druids that she knew were with the men under Bode's command, that had set out with them at the start of their journey a lifetime ago. Six minds she sought. Four minds she found.

As dawn approached, An'uek returned to herself.

Bode saw it in the way her shoulders slumped. She fell forward, collapsing onto her knees and back onto her heels, toppling over to lie prone in the sand.

He took a step forward, his fists clenched at his side, his breathing fast and shallow, ragged in his chest as his heart hammered behind his ribs.

But he didn't reach for her or pull her into his arms. He waited for her to rouse herself, knowing any touch would be torturous until she had her mind under control.

She regained consciousness on the sand and rolled onto her side, sliding her knees beneath her, keeping her head low, letting it rest on her hands. She stayed like that, only turning enough for Bode to be able to hear her strained words.

"I've found four."

"They're alive?" Bode couldn't keep the delight out of his voice.

"Yes," she drawled.

"The others?"

She looked up at him, her eyes hard.

"I don't know. I couldn't find them."

"It doesn't mean they're not alive."

"It doesn't mean they're not dead." Her voice was flat.

"That's not what I meant," he started, but she interrupted him with a glance.

"The fighting along the borders is relentless."

"The forces?"

"Worn down." She relayed the gist of the messages. "Every day there are skirmishes, small raids, larger attacks on the bigger towns. The squads are losing men. They're calling up reinforcements from the garrisons, but most are depleted."

"It's as we thought."

She nodded.

"It seems like it's a plot to empty all the bigger towns, empty Kraner."

"Destroy the army without a full-scale battle."

"Smart," An'uek said, coughing. "And ultimately it'll work."

"I can't tell them to stop calling for more soldiers."

"If you do, the towns along the borders will be wiped out."

"Thousands of people will die," Bode said, frowning.

"Thousands of people are already dying… your soldiers. But if you pull them away, it'll be tens of thousands more," she cruelly corrected him. "And then they'll get to Kraner."

"Barclan will be lost."

Bode and An'uek regarded each other in silence.

"No one is going to help us," she said.

"Not true," Bode countered.

She looked at him, raising an eyebrow and frowning before realising what he meant.

"Dammit," she said.

"It's time to go get Calem."

"Yes." She clenched her fists, lifting herself and sitting upright.

Bode kneeled and shuffled over to her, offering her a hand. She took it, letting him help her to her feet.

As she stood and shook her head, Bode saw An'uek stiffen and felt her warm skin turn ice-cold in his hand.

"An'uek," he gasped, instinctively dropping her and stepping away.

But she was gone; her eyes looked through him and he could see the silver light of the stars dancing in her gaze.

He had to wait, barely breathing as he watched her.

And then it was over and she fell forward again, her face hitting the sand before he could catch her.

"An'uek," he gasped, as he rolled her over and saw blood flowing from her nose.

He slapped her face, calling for help, and was rewarded with her eyes fluttering open.

"Bode…" She sat up, oblivious to her injury, eyes wide. Grabbing his face in her hands, she pulled him close. "We must go back to Kraner."

"An'uek, what are you talking about?"

She pulled herself against him, her head on his shoulder, letting him wrap her in his arms and pick her up.

"I saw An'eris." She was shaking. "It's this place, there's so much power here, I saw something, some sort of echo of minds. We have to hurry, we have to bring Calem."

"Who, An'uek?" Bode held her tighter. "What are you talking about, what did you see?"

"I don't know. There was a face behind An'eris, it reminded me of Calem."

"Who are you talking about?"

She pulled away from him, speaking low, her words only for him.

"Bode…" She turned to him. "I think it was Calem's brother."

CHAPTER 14

Marsha handed Travis a small wooden bowl of watery mussel soup thickened with grains. He took the bowl in both hands, sniffed it reluctantly, and put it down.

"Choosing not to eat is a habit of mothers with hungry babes and bare cupboards," she gently scolded him.

Her words echoed through his memories.

"Every babe in Kraner has a full belly these days."

She picked up the bowl and pushed it back into his hands.

"You need to eat."

"I can't keep anything down yet." He fidgeted on his stool, rubbing his hands across his lips and against his teeth. His fingertips came away bloody. "Too soon."

She waited, watching as his nervous energy started to subside and he visibly calmed down and focused. She imagined the poison running through his veins, concentrating his mind even as it sped to his heart, chased by the oil that would keep it from killing him.

"I could do with a smoke though." He started to pat his pockets.

Marsha frowned.

"Maybe later, outside."

As the minutes passed and Travis calmed, she watched his gaze turn to the blank wooden panels on the walls as he tapped his hands on his thighs. She waited as he absorbed himself in his thoughts.

"Every day that we sit here, more of the old buildings are coming down. At first it was the wooden ones, but now it's stone ones too. He's clearing parts of the city. He must have a design."

Marsha let him brood. She ate her own bowl of soup quietly, enjoying the salty flavour and the feel of warmth in her belly.

"I wish I had a small draught of ale to go with this," she said wistfully.

Travis smiled, but the silence grew deeper. In the dim light she knew what to watch for and saw his eyes glancing around the room as if each object was a new thought he was sewing together. It wasn't long before his gaze came to her and stopped.

"I would ask what's on your mind, but I'm afraid you'll tell me the truth," she said eventually.

Travis waited until she had finished her soup. He got up and took her bowl from her, at the same time filling a wooden cup with water from a jug in the corner.

"It's not ale, but it washes it down well enough."

Marsha thanked him, sipping the lukewarm water.

"I have to get you out of Kraner," Travis announced.

Marsha put the cup down.

"So that's it."

"It?"

"The thing that's suddenly bothering you?"

Travis looked around the bare room they were hiding in.

"One of the current things preoccupying me, yes."

"I'm not leaving." It was a statement of fact.

"You must, especially now we know Orren is dead." Travis leaned towards her. "We don't know much, but we know more and more mercenaries loyal to A'taz are entering the city every day calling themselves scholars and builders from Aquam. They're hunting us. And if they find us, they'll murder us."

"Then they mustn't find us."

Marsha reached over and put her hand on his.

"Travis?"

He raised his head and looked at her.

"I am a very old woman. Too old to leave the city."

"You'll be safer if you leave."

"In winter, in the snow and the cold, I think I'm safer in the castle than I am on a horse."

"I can get you out safely."

"Travis, I don't want to go," she said wistfully. "This is my home. I want to stay and help defend my city. In the last year I've lost my son, and now my grandson is dead. No, I want to stay no matter what happens. An'eris is here, I want to help her."

"Right now I have to think about what happens if we can't save An'eris, knowing Orren won't be back."

"I am too old to wear that crown again." Marsha denied Travis the truth behind his words.

"That might not be your choice, and I can't protect you forever here."

"Travis," she said his name softly, "has it occurred to you that you're not supposed to?"

He was about to ask what she meant, when the door opened and A'rrick came in.

The druid lord closed the door softly and unfurled himself from the oiled cloak he wore as protection in a city of metal and men.

"What news?" Travis asked immediately.

"None that can't wait a moment for me to take off my soggy boots," A'rrick moaned as he pulled at his leather shoes, throwing them into a corner with enough force that they bounced back and landed almost at his feet. He kicked them across the room.

Marsha put her hand out to Travis, silently indicating for him to wait.

The druid lord hung his cloak on a bent nail near the brazier to dry.

"This city is filthy, even in mourning for the King. Nothing but people shouting. There's dirt everywhere and it stinks."

Still they waited.

"I don't know why An'eris loves it here so much. I should have never let her leave our home. I should have kept her with me. Coming here, even once, was a mistake. This whole place is rotten."

He hooked a stool with his foot and pulled it towards him to sit down, taking his long gloves off as he stretched his slender legs out.

"I should never have let her come here." He stared at the fire. "If I can't get her out, if this place kills her, if his death is what kills her…" His words faltered. He turned to Travis and Marsha as if seeing them for the first time.

"Everything is affected by A'taz's touch. It's like a sickness spreading through the city. I can sense it."

He put his head in his hands, his jaw clenched, his body rigid.

Marsha and Travis watched as he willed his anger to dissipate; there was no point asking if he had found An'eris. Eventually, Marsha could wait no longer.

"Tell us what you learned in the city."

A'rrick moved over to where Marsha and Travis were sitting on a long low bench. "I snuck into the castle," he began, "using a mix of lies when there wasn't a shadow big enough to hide in."

"Did you go to my halls?" Marsha interrupted.

"I did," A'rrick nodded. "Empty."

"What do you mean?"

"The halls are empty. No healers, no one being healed, no students. No one."

"Impossible. There were many injured, many sick in my care."

"All gone," he said, frowning. "I suspect they didn't miraculously heal and walk out themselves."

"No healers?" She repeated his words.

"Empty. Not even a lonely ghost to haunt the halls."

"Ghost. You think he's killed them?"

"I've no idea, but it's a guess." A'rrick shrugged. "There's so much magic being cast in that castle I'm surprised the stray cats haven't grown wings and are chasing mice across the ceilings."

"Is A'taz so powerful he spellcasts all day?"

"It's him, it's Troy, it's the rooms full of clerics that constantly chant his name in their incantations all day long and through every night. Whatever he's doing, he's drawing power from all the sources he can and using as much power as he's getting."

"Why?" Travis asked, confused. "He has the city, he has An'eris and virtually the kingdom now we know Orren is dead. What does he want?"

"I don't know, but we can assume he wasn't after the kingdom. There's something he wants in Kraner, and he hasn't got it yet."

"What does that mean?" Marsha asked, still upset.

"It means we have a chance," Travis exclaimed.

A'rrick nodded.

"After the halls I made my way around the castle edges until I could sense An'eris. I found the nearest turret across from where I sensed her. I tried to make contact, but the sunlight was too weak behind the storm clouds building, and whatever connection we have from being so close is lost in her stupor to him."

"Did she sense you?"

"No." Travis shook his head. "I tried all our ways to call to her mind, to call to the baby, but I was throwing myself at a wall. Whether it's his wall, hers, or my granddaughter's, I don't know. But she's sealed from me."

He looked away, his eyes turned down and his lips pulled tight.

"What did you see, A'rrick?" she asked.

He looked up.

"The windows in her room. It looks like a tree has been blown through them." He scrunched his face as he tried to explain. "I don't know, I didn't see it happen, but it's damaged."

He stopped.

"And? Travis prompted.

"It's like it's blown out, but neither of them paid any attention to it. I could see them both inside."

Marsha and Travis, shocked, stared at A'rrick.

"I wanted her to see me." A'rrick stepped forward, towards Travis. "I wanted her to see me, to break free from the spell, but I couldn't get through."

Marsha stepped forward between the two of them.

"A'rrick, the way you say that, was A'taz in her room?"

A'rrick nodded.

No one asked A'rrick anything else for a long time.

The three of them sat in silence, each subconsciously moving as far away from each other as they could.

Marsha sat wrapped in blankets, her back against the cold hard wooden wall. Travis was perched on a stool wrapped in his own thoughts, oblivious to the cold in the room or the rain beating against the roof inches from his head. A'rrick paced a few short steps, back and forth, to keep the warmth in his limbs.

Denny stood quietly in line with the other squires waiting to be inspected by the House Master. They boys chatted quietly amongst themselves while they waited.

"Can't believe it about the King, it's awful," one of the boys said quietly to the group.

"Happens though, doesn't it."

"My brothers and my uncle died a few weeks ago," another responded.

"My cousin died last week," another replied.

A quiet settled on the group as the boys looked at each other, then anywhere other than each other.

"Has anyone heard who the new House Master will be?" one boy asked.

Denny felt his stomach knot. The all too familiar feeling of nausea started to rise in his throat at the memory of Homen lying dead with his blood staining his long white hair. Now he pictured Orren lying dead with him. The dead kept piling up.

He didn't want to be in the room with the other squires. He didn't want to be in the castle. But Travis had ordered him back.

"I heard word Homen's ridden off to help win the battles with the mercenaries raiding into the kingdom," someone said.

"Can't see that being true. Travis maybe, but not Master Homen, he's not a fighter."

"No one's seen Master Travis for a few weeks now, come to mention it."

Denny remembered the back room in the fishmonger's. He forced himself to remember Travis and Marsha. And A'rrick. He kept still.

"Word from the stewards is Lord Homen's off on some errand for the Queen, and Master Travis has gone with him."

"That doesn't make sense. Why would we need a new House Master if he's off on an errand?"

"And why's there not a new Sword Master then if Travis is off with Homen?"

"I don't know, do I, that's why it's gossip."

Denny felt trapped in the small room in the gatehouse where they'd gathered. He stared at the door and thought about running away. Leaving the gatehouse, leaving the castle. Leaving Kraner. Would it be so bad, he wondered, to just leave? He wondered if they'd understand. His fingers started to prickle, as if he'd been sitting on his hands for too long. He started tapping them against his thigh to bring the feeling back.

"I heard the Queen's banished them. It's been done quietly so no one knows."

"Why'd she do that?"

"I heard from my sister in the kitchens that there's word around the docks that Travis has taken to drink and that's why he's not around anymore. As for Homen, it's something to do with Mistress Cotta and her father."

"He's been dead for ages though."

Denny's throat felt like it was closing. He wanted to pull at his collar but kept still. Silent.

"Lord Brennan's gone too."

Denny felt a bead of sweat run between his shoulder blades inside his embroidered tunic.

"He's gone off to Orania to work on some trade deals. He left the day the stonemason arrived in the city," the boy next to Denny said confidently.

"That's right, I saw him leaving," another confirmed.

"Did you?" Denny challenged, a flare of anger momentarily overtaking him.

"Yeah, course I did. I said so, didn't I?"

"And you know it was him, saw his face, did you?"

"All right, mate," one of the other boys said, "no need to get so worked up."

"Worked up?" Denny countered.

"Your hands are shaking," the boy pointed at Denny's quivering hands, "and you're covered in sweat. Are you sick?"

"No. Maybe." Denny looked at his shaking hands. "I don't know."

"Best get off," the boy said kindly. "I'll tell the new master."

"Doesn't matter if you miss inspection anyway," someone said from the line. "You're in the Queen's service now, you don't get duty assignments with us anymore."

"I suppose not." Denny put his shaking hands into his pockets and stepped out of line. "I think I'm sick," he mumbled, and headed for the door. Without another word he walked out and started down the spiral stone staircase. His legs felt unsteady and the steps seemed to be trying to move from under his feet. He stretched his arms out either side of him, both palms bracing against the walls of the stairwell as he walked, head down, focused on each step.

He walked straight into a man walking up the stairs.

Denny froze.

"Lord Ravi," he said as he dipped his head in respect, "I'm sorry, my lord, I didn't see you."

Denny saw Troy.

"I'm sorry, my lord," he repeated.

"You're going the wrong way, squire, inspection is upstairs."

Troy blocked his path.

"I think I'm going to be sick."

Ravi, Troy, inched closer and peered at Denny. He leaned his head near and sniffed him.

"Go," Troy commanded, stepping aside so Denny could squeeze past.

The boy wanted to run down the stairs but was afraid he'd fall and break his neck. By the time he reached the bottom of the spiral stairwell he was dizzy and struggling to get enough air in his lungs. He pushed himself until he was outside. The cold autumn air hit him like a fist in the face and he fell down. On his hands and knees, his face barely an inch away from the frozen grass under his palms, he scrambled quickly out of sight into a small recess behind the thick stone walls. He pulled his knees in and tried to hide until the pain in his chest went away.

He closed his eyes, losing track of time until the bell in the tower struck the quarter on the hour and he remembered he was due to attend his Queen.

"Damn it!" He jumped to his feet, almost falling over himself as muscles stiffened from the cold made it hard to move. He emerged from his hiding place and raced awkwardly across the inner courtyard. His blood was soon pumping and his earlier faltering feet now felt nimble and back under his control. He darted past porters and servants and all the others working in the castle. A shortcut through the gardens would get him to his room quickly, so he turned and headed around the outer wall. It would mean staying outside in the freezing cold, but it was better than being in the castle.

He ran through the herb gardens and the orchards. The trees were dormant, the garden soil covered by straw, everything asleep and waiting for spring.

He leapt a low wall into the moon garden, ignored all the deadheaded roses and the gardeners working to put the flowers to bed.

After another few minutes he dashed through a doorway, up some stairs and back into the castle, heading for his room. He barged through the door, ignoring the hefty bang as it hit the wall. No candles flickered, no fire burned in the grate; old uneaten plates of food were stacked on the only small table in the room, covered in fine white mould. He ignored it all. Knowing he had only minutes to spare, he stripped out of his duty uniform, throwing it into a corner with all the other soiled clothes he hadn't taken to the housekeeper. He pulled on his last clean pair of trousers and his formal tunic marking him to the Queen's personal service. He found clean enough boots and dragged a finely whittled wooden comb through his tangled hair. A splash of freezing water across his face, some mint leaves crushed between his teeth quickly spat out the window, and he was ready.

Denny made his way through the corridors to the Queen's chamber. He kept his gaze level, made sure he greeted everyone with a smile.

He got to An'eris's parlour and spared himself a moment to rest his forehead against the dark wooden door. Immediately he pulled himself back; the wood was icy cold. He knocked and waited. A moment later the door creaked open as a handmaid curtseyed in a daze and ushered him in before leaving the room.

As he stepped into the parlour he saw his breath turn to mist in front of his face. He walked across the room with as much confidence as he could rally. He saw his Queen, stopped, and bowed as low as he could. Before he could straighten up, he heard scratchings from the corner of the room. Turning his head, he saw A'taz seated at the small cherrywood writing desk in her parlour, the quill moving rapidly across new parchment.

Denny stood slowly, transfixed by the man at the desk.

A'taz didn't move to look at him but raised his voice to be heard.

"The Queen has reacted badly to the news of her husband's death," he said as if in explanation.

"My Queen..." Denny heard his voice and surprised himself back to attention. "I am at your service." His voice trailed off as his gaze fell on An'eris.

All the windows in the parlour had been smashed, the shards of glass scattered around the wrought-iron frames. An'eris stood at one of the empty windows, shivering.

She turned to Denny.

The sun was hidden behind heavy clouds, and in the dim, dismal autumnal light, everything about An'eris was grey.

A blustery wind kicked up outside, sending fallen leaves up into the air, carried through the gaping hole into her room.

Her long hair whipped around her face in the gust and she looked dirty.

Denny felt tears fill his eyes as he stared at his Queen. He didn't move. She didn't move. Their eyes locked for a second and he saw hers go wide in shock, but then her gaze slipped to the man scribbling behind him, and Denny watched as An'eris looked at A'taz... and she smiled.

A'taz finished the message on the parchment and reached into the desk for a handful of fine sand. He blew on the wet ink and sieved the sand through his fingers across the writing before tipping it off and rolling the parchment up.

Ignoring them, A'taz took out another parchment and began another message.

An'eris stared at him, shivering, waiting.

Another gust of wind blew through the room, stinging Denny's eyes and making his tears run. It carried with it the smell of a storm.

He turned to look at A'taz and then back at An'eris. He wanted to swallow his tongue, but instead he coughed to get A'taz's attention.

"My lord," he bowed as he addressed the man he detested, "do I have your leave to make arrangements to have the window repaired?"

A'taz ignored him.

Denny waited, trying to ignore the rapid patter of rain that was inside instead of out. He didn't need to imagine the ice-cold drops falling on An'eris.

The wind blew into the room guttering out all the candles, except those on the writing desk, which burned steadily and too brightly for such small wicks.

"My lord," he said again, about to continue when he felt cold wet fingers grasp his hand.

He jumped and wrenched his hand away.

An'eris had crept up and was less than a foot behind him.

Denny stepped back, avoiding looking into her eyes, once bright, now darkened by their own inner shadow.

He wanted to grab her hand and run. Anywhere. Nowhere. Just grab her and run. But he didn't.

"My Queen," he said, bowing again.

"Squire, your lord is busy, best not to disturb him." Her voice was steady.

"Of course." He tipped his head. "If you would permit, I can arrange to have this repaired."

An'eris frowned.

"What repaired?"

At her question, Denny felt physically ill.

"My Queen..." He dared to take a step towards her and to the side, forcing her to move so he was between her and the wall, between her and the rain. "The window, it needs replacing. It's broken."

He spoke slowly, a pause between each word.

"Do it," A'taz ordered from his seat, not raising his head or slowing his scrawl.

"Of course," An'eris said without hesitation. "Yes, get it repaired. In my grief, I think I did that."

An'eris said nothing more, simply standing in the room.

Denny felt pressure building in his chest as he moved to the centre of the parlour.

He wondered whether if he screamed would either of them do anything? If he kicked over a stool or ripped up the rugs, would An'eris even blink?

He looked around the room at the tapestries hanging from the walls. One made him stop. He knew it to be centuries old and had walked past it many times.

As if seeing it for the first time, Denny felt himself pulled towards the image carefully stitched by nimble fingers so long ago.

It was a simple scene of two women, one old, bent low, one younger with long black hair and wearing a green gown. Denny couldn't be sure what was stitched around them, but he felt like it was a dark mountain, or more possibly, as his mind offered up an image of memories from the Tradefair not so long ago, of two women standing in a pavilion.

"Cotta?" Denny muttered to himself, eyes wide as he stared at the figure in the green gown.

"What did you say?" An'eris stepped over to him.

Denny ignored her.

He shifted his gaze to the old woman, whose hand-stitched eyes seemed peculiarly alive.

He stepped closer and reached out to touch the tapestry.

An'eris stepped closer to him.

"What did you say about Cotta?" she asked again, more softly.

He ignored her.

Denny touched the cloth, still staring at the eyes of the old woman.

The eyes stared back.

Denny didn't feel the wind whip up and blast into the room, blowing cushions off chairs and sending candlesticks crashing off the mantlepiece above the large fireplace. He didn't hear the clatter of the broken windowpanes banging against the stone walls or the thumping and snapping of heavy velvet curtains that billowed in the gusts and pushed over the small window stools nearby.

Denny heard a story spoken over every thread stitched into the old tapestry. He heard the words and knew what to do.

He turned to An'eris, emboldened by a sense of confidence not of his own. He gently reached out and took her hands.

"My Queen, let me help you."

"What did you say about Cotta?" she asked again, softly, her gaze locked not on Denny, but on A'taz.

Denny was about to answer when he sensed movement behind him. He turned as A'taz was crossing the few feet between them. He had rolls of parchment in his hands, which he thrust at Denny.

"Squire, take these to the clerks. Tell them the Queen is calling the council to meet at daybreak tomorrow to discuss the traitors. They'll be hanged before noon."

"Of course," he said calmly. "One more thing, my lord?"

A'taz reached out and grabbed Denny by the collar. He pulled the boy towards him, away from An'eris.

"What?" A'taz said, his face barely an inch away.

"Please," he looked down respectfully, "allow me to attend to my Queen."

He dared to look around the room, to gesture around him.

A'taz looked around the room, taking inventory of all the damage as if he had only just noticed the destruction. He turned to An'eris and gently lifted her face to look down on her. Her wet hair clung to her sunken cheeks and hung in ragged knots over her shoulders. The thin fabric of her nightdress stuck to her cold skin, showing the stark contours of her ribs and her slightly swollen belly.

"This won't do at all," he said quickly. "We have visitors in the castle, dignitaries, noblemen and women. I can't have you looking like this. They are expecting to see a Queen after all."

"What would you have me do?" she asked dutifully.

A'taz turned to Denny, grabbed his face and forced his words into his mind, as if erasing what he'd seen, leaving only what A'taz wanted there.

"Take care of this," he stated, and without another word to An'eris or even a glance, he left the room.

As soon as the door closed behind him, An'eris let out a sound like a scared animal and seemed to become alert to her surroundings.

She started to shiver and looked panicky.

Denny stepped over to her and gently held her arms.

"Hold on, just for a minute," he said, and when he was sure she wouldn't drop if he let her go, he quickly darted through the door off to the side that led into her dressing room and moments later reappeared carrying her heavy woollen clay-coloured cape and slippers.

He pulled the cape tenderly over her shoulders and knotted it closed. Bending down, he eased her bare cold feet into the slippers, stopping to remove as many glass shards as he could. He winced for her as he stood up and made sure she was covered.

He held her hand and moved her away from the broken window, then he directed her through her bedroom doors and settled her down onto a settee against the wall. He piled pillows up behind her back, rummaged in her wardrobe for a shawl and pulled it across her stooped shoulders.

She was still shivering.

He moved in front of her and knelt down, bringing his face level to her own.

"My Queen," he said softly, surprised and pleased when she looked up straight away.

Her hands crossed instinctively across her belly.

"Squire..." Her voice sounded strained, like she was fighting to speak. Denny could barely hear her words, so he leaned in closer, put his head near to her face so she could whisper. She raised a hand, grabbed him by the collar of his tunic, as much to keep him close as to hold on to something. He held her other hand in both of his and waited as she drew a long breath through clenched teeth. Her eyes focused, and for just a moment he thought she looked like herself again.

"Squire," she pleaded, "what did you say... about Cotta?"

CHAPTER 15

Denny held the parchments in his hand and took slow deliberate steps along corridors, down stone stairs, through doorways and across empty halls. He was able to change his route but the compulsion to walk was beyond his control. He tried to will himself to put the parchments down, to let them drop to the floor, but he couldn't make himself do it. The most he could do was slow his steps until he was barely more than ambling, but to do so took all his will and he was physically exhausted from the effort, sweat staining the armpits and sides of his tunic. He knew where he was going, A'taz's words echoing through his thoughts, loud and clear, but not so loud or so clear that they overruled another compelling order that had cemented itself only moments before the sorcerer's command. The more Denny focused on the voice of the old woman in his mind, the fainter were A'taz's words.

Denny veered through the throne room into a seldom used corridor that eventually ended in a spiral staircase that only led down. The walls were smooth under his fingers as he steadied himself. He noticed that each stone step looked older than the one before it, and he thought of the thousands of steps taken before his own.

The castle was old, and as he walked downwards it felt older than anything else, except, he thought, perhaps himself at that very moment.

At the base of the cold grey stone steps he found himself in a narrow passageway where the air tasted of secrets. The passageway ended in a thick wooden door with well-oiled iron hinges. Two heavyset men wearing dented armour stood either side of the door. They recognised him and frowned.

"Why are you here, Den?" one asked. "This is no place for a stroll."

"Orders from the Queen." Denny's teeth clenched around the lie. "She has a council meeting in the morning and has business with a new law."

"And what of it?" asked the other guard, his back straight, shoulders set as if he was on parade in front of the whole city, not guarding a single room.

"She needs her crown. Come on," he implored them. "Normally Homen does this but he's away. If I don't get it done the Queen won't be happy, and I really want to stay in her service."

"You really want to impress her, don't you?" the guard asked, a wide grin on his face. "Hoping for a well done pat on the head?"

Denny spotted a chance and had the wherewithal to let his mouth fall open and to shift on his feet.

"No, no, not like that, I just want to carry out my orders, it's nothing," he replied.

The two guards pretended to confer.

"What do you think, Kris?"

"I think that ever since he figured he could grow a scruffy beard his head's been in the men's game and he's got eyes for our Queen."

They laughed and gently squeezed his shoulder.

"All right, if it's the Queen's order," the guard called Kris agreed. "You'll have to wait here with Rolo while I get it."

He opened the door just enough to let himself in, then closed it behind himself and left Denny alone with the other guard.

"Have you heard anything about all the changes around here?" Rolo asked curiously.

"What changes do you mean?" Denny kept his tone light.

"All the new faces coming in, a lot of the old faces disappearing."

Denny locked his gaze with Rolo's, looking for signs of deceit.

"All I know is that Homen and Travis have gone away. There's rumours they've called up a lot of the men, gone to help at the borders."

"I've heard something like that. Word comes to us through the walls." There was no conviction in his words. "But then you'd know what's going on, wouldn't you? You seem to be everywhere anyways, seeing everything."

A feeling of being trapped in a small room overtook Denny; a bead of sweat rolled down his back between his shoulder blades.

"I just do as I'm told."

Rolo stepped towards him and put a hand on his shoulder. He seemed to be thinking through his words.

"If something is ever amiss in the castle, we're always here." His voice was quiet. "These corridors, this place, we're forgotten, like no one's memory reaches this far on purpose, until someone needs something from the vault, and then they can only remember us for as long as it takes to come and get it."

"Everything is fine," Denny said slowly and clearly.

"All right." Rolo released him.

They lapsed into silence until Kris came back with a large heavy box sealed with an iron lock on each side.

"Not that one." Denny was genuinely annoyed.

"What?"

"She didn't mean that one." He pointed at the box. "She wants the smaller one, for official business. The one in that box is the fancy one with all the jewels."

"You said crown," Kris muttered, taking it back.

"Remember us if you ever need help." Rolo surprised Denny with his final words. "Not where we are, that never works, just our faces."

He turned away and didn't look at Denny again.

When Kris came out again, he held a much smaller, slimmer dark wooden box with a single lock on one side.

"It's half the size but just as heavy." Kris hefted it over to Denny. "Bring it back as soon as the business is done. If you don't, we'll know… we'll come for it." Kris held it a second longer than he needed to.

"Don't make us come for it."

"I understand."

Denny walked back up the spiral staircase, forgetting the guards and their conversation with every step that led him upwards. His feet carried him, as if subconsciously, into the recesses of the castle where no one went of their own accord: the ugly, dark secret of Kraner.

He hated this place.

He passed through a low doorway into a small room lit with wax candles hanging from creaking ironworks bolted into the low ceiling. The air was wet and hot, and in some places, little drops of moisture dripped down from the ceiling as if the place had tears.

Denny coughed to get the new dungeon warden's attention.

He was terrified of the man.

"What do you want, squire?" the warden asked without looking at him.

"The Queen wants these signed by the lady." The half-lie was suffocating.

"Why did she send you, why not one of the guards?"

"Why don't you go ask her that?" Denny shot back.

He detested the man.

The guard swore, annoyed, as he stood up and fingered a heavy iron ring of keys on his belt. He worked out which one he needed and then pointed for Denny to follow.

Denny complied; his feet wanted to move even though he didn't want to head through the unlocked iron door into the dungeons beyond.

"You know which one it is?"

Denny nodded and the guard followed a few steps behind him.

The smell hit Denny first, the suffocating reek of the dead, the rotting.

All the cells were full of corpses, but he didn't look at them. He was sure he would recognise the bloated blue faces of the men and women within.

The guard saw him start to gag and laughed. "You get used to it."

He kept walking, trying to hold his breath, pretending he couldn't see through the iron bars.

Denny marched slowly to the end of the line of cells through circles of weak light cast from small torches that burned high up out of reach. Finally, he stopped.

He didn't turn to look through the bars immediately. He felt the guard step up too close behind him and bend closer until the man's whiskers tickled his ear.

"Talk to me like I'm beneath you, boy…" His breath was sour. "I don't think so."

Denny wasn't prepared for the kick that came next, and it sent him head first into the roughly hewn rock wall that marked the end of the passageway. His face hit the stone, light flashed behind his eyes and he felt his nose break. His legs gave out and he slumped and slid down to the flagstone, grabbing at his face. His mouth filled with hot blood, and he spat out as much as he swallowed.

He could hear the guard laughing behind him, loud and cruel.

"What do you say now?" the guard called over loudly to him, exaggerating his question with his hand to his ear.

He loathed this man.

As he swallowed, he realised his fear had gone, it had left his body, carried out in the stream of his blood.

Unexpected energy filled his veins. He mumbled something at the guard.

"What's that?" he shouted at Denny. "Can't speak?"

"I said…" Denny spat on the man's boot. "I still need these signed."

He held out the parchments, bloody and stained, for the guard to see.

The guard bent down and snatched the sheets from his hand. He unrolled them, looked at them, then turned them the other way round and looked over them again.

Denny grinned.

"What's that?" he said to the guard, mania in his voice. "Can't read?"

The guard roared in anger and lunged at Denny, who at the last second hoisted the wooden lockbox in front of his face. The guard's fist smashed into it, breaking bones as his fist splintered the wood.

The Queen's crown fell from the confines of the shattered box, landing with a heavy dull thud on the stone floor.

Shrieking in pain, the guard fell back, clutching his broken hand.

Denny scrambled to his feet. He could smell the fear, but, finally, it wasn't his own. He bent down low and picked up the crown, feeling its solid weight in his hands.

He turned to look into the cell behind him and saw Cotta.

He turned back.

Denny waited a second, to make sure the guard was looking at him, and then lunged.

Cotta sat in the dungeon, waiting patiently while Denny beat the guard to death with the crown. She watched impassively, noting that he only aimed for the head and face. It wasn't long at all until the sound of cracking bone was replaced with the moist squelch of flesh and gore. And then the only sound was Denny's laboured breathing and the sound of scuffling as he fell against the blood-splattered wall, his rage spent.

He rolled onto his side, curled into a ball, clutching the crown to his body, eyes fixated on what was left of the man beside him. The once silver crown was a mess of bits of hair, skin and blood.

Cotta saw Denny start to shake until he couldn't hold the crown anymore and it slipped from his grasp. It fell beside him and rolled across the narrow passageway, clanking against the latticework of iron bars that held her captive.

She reached out and grabbed the crown, pulling it through the small space between the bars.

Denny, startled by the noise, sat up and looked over.

He saw Cotta, an approving smile on a face that was a mosaic of bruises of blues, purples, yellows. Her lips were split, and there were cuts across her forehead, infected scratches from dirty fingernails down her once flawless cheeks. Her hair was knotted and wild and she had barely a scrap of clothing to cover her beaten and tortured body. He could see her bruised ribs, her bloodied thighs, and what he knew were handprints across so much of her.

He couldn't believe it was her. Not this woman, not this damaged thing clutching a bloody crown. He looked away.

Cotta looked down at the crown, gripping it tightly enough for it to cut into her hands.

"Denny," she called out clearly.

He felt his stomach lurch. If he closed his eyes, he could believe she was calling him from across a hall, or as he passed her rooms, or anywhere else. Not in this place.

It was her voice. Her strong, calm, beautiful voice.

He squeezed his eyes shut.

"Denny," she said again.

He put his hands over his ears.

"Don't," he choked. "Don't call me."

"Denny, please?"

"No!" he shouted, covering his eyes. "Don't ask me to look, don't make me see you like this."

"Like what?" her voice said kindly. "Alive?"

He shook his head.

"It's too much," he said, shuddering.

"Denny," she called again. "It's all right to look at us. To look at me like this."

"No," he whispered. "Please, I can't anymore, I can't do it anymore."

"You've already done too much," she said kindly, trying to keep her own desperation from her voice. "But just this one last thing, and then, I promise, I'll make sure you never see this place again."

Denny heard her voice and remembered every time she had called his name, every time she picked him over another squire, the way he felt taller every time she looked at him. He wondered if she knew he was the one who gave her maids fresh-cut flowers for her parlour every morning. He thought she probably did.

"Do you remember a few years ago, when you were a little boy?" Her question caught him off guard and he turned at the sound of her voice. "It was spring, and the ground was soft from all the rain, but it was unusually warm, and Homen and I wanted to get out of the castle for the day. We decided to take the horses out after the long winter. It was just after your birthday, you were nine."

"You chose me as part of the riding party."

"For such a young boy you sat a horse better than some of the guards."

She saw him smile a little smile.

"We went north of the city."

"That's right, we did. We were out all day and we rode up into the pastures, do you remember? We stopped at Jeri's bee yard and she showed us all the hives. We listened to the sound of the bees waking up for spring. Homen got stung on the hand and you played with the dogs while we had our lunch."

Denny looked at his bloody hands and started trying to clean them on his filthy trousers.

"We left there after lunch and carried on. And do you remember, in the afternoon, I kicked my horse into a gallop along the riverside?"

He nodded.

"And do you remember how muddy the ground was?"

He nodded.

"And what happened?"

He swallowed. "The horse stumbled. She threw you clean off and you landed on some rocks."

"That's right," she said softly, seeing him start to shiver at the memory. She quickly pulled him back. "And do you remember who was the first person to my side?"

"Me."

"And do you remember how I looked, thrown from my horse, landing on the rocks?"

He opened his eyes.

"You were bleeding. And your face had scratches and blood and you were cut up."

She nodded.

"And I helped you up," he said as he leaned forward and shuffled over to the iron bars. "And they said you'd broken an arm, and that you weren't to move."

"And what did I say?"

"You told them all to shut up, to ride to the castle and alert Marsha."

"And what else?"

"To stop fussing, that you weren't dead, just a little broken."

"And what do I look like now," she asked, putting her hand out to gently stroke his face.

"Just a little broken," he said sadly.

She nodded.

"Denny," she said slowly, "I want you to turn around and take the keys off his belt. Don't look at him, just get the keys and pass them to me."

"Does it hurt?" he asked, still looking at her.

She bit the inside of her cheek to stop the tears and shook her head.

"Not anymore."

Cotta held Denny's gaze for a moment longer then inclined her head towards the guard's body.

"The keys, Denny," she commanded.

When she saw him straighten his shoulders and turn to the man he had just murdered, she felt joy. She watched him take a single step and kneel and carefully, almost respectfully, untie the dead man's belt.

With trembling hands and clumsy fingers, he pulled the heavy ring of iron keys off the leather belt and brought them over to show Cotta. She kneeled against the cell bars, hands clinging on to them, her face inches away from the lock.

"Which one?" he whispered.

"I don't know." She had to hide the irrational annoyance at his question. "You'll have to try each one and see which works."

Nodding, he stood to do as he was told.

Denny strained to turn the key, his slippery fingers struggling to grasp it properly, sliding on the cold metal shaft.

Cotta wanted to grab the key, grab the boy and yell at him to hurry. She stepped back, giving him space, and rubbed her hands across her face, trying to rub away her frown.

"Try another key."

Denny nodded frantically.

"Yes, Mistress Cotta," he stuttered.

In the quiet of the dungeon that was fast becoming their tomb, the sound of the iron key trying to turn in the stubborn lock echoed like the boots of angry men coming down the stairs, like heavy mailed fists banging on the doors, like swords being drawn, like a man being beaten to death with cold metal.

His trembling hands could barely hold the ring of keys. He had to lean onto his knees to keep his grip; it wasn't enough and he dropped them.

At the sound of the heavy metal hitting the floor, Denny yelled, overcome for a second. He felt dizzy, disorientated, and started to fall backwards.

His backside hit the floor, and Cotta dropped to her knees against the bars, calling to him, an arm reaching out as far as she could, but he was out of reach.

Denny sat wide-eyed, leaning back on his hands, staring at her. He was breathing in fast gasps and was covered in sweat.

Where she had hoped, Cotta now felt familiar fear.

She wanted to call to him, to tell him to get up and pick up the keys and give them to her, to get himself together and stand up, to help them.

She decided she would tell him to go, to tell him to turn around, run away, and never come back.

She reached her hand out again, but as she was about to call his name one last time and tell him he had done enough, she heard Brennan shuffle up behind her and felt his cool hand close gently over her shoulder and ease her back.

"He's just a boy," Brennan said softly, only for Cotta. "We can't ask anymore of him."

"I wasn't going to ask him to do more," she said sadly.

She waited.

Brennan didn't answer. He lowered his head and looked up using his sight.

Denny was as grey as the stone behind his head. Brennan could make out the shimmering monochrome of his sweat-stained skin under the pallid white light seeping from the oil lamps. His breathing was erratic, the pulse in his neck beating a jerking staccato as frenzied as his eyes, which were darting everywhere and nowhere.

Brennan looked past Denny and looked into him.

He felt the boy's sadness and fear; he was about to reach out, to soothe those feelings, pat them down to give him a reprieve, just for a minute, but stopped.

"Someone else has been in his mind," Brennan stated.

"What?" Cotta jerked forward. "Who?"

"I don't know, I don't recognise who. There's only a faint trace, but it reminds me of An'eris."

"That's not possible," Cotta said, sitting back.

Brennan shook his head as if to clear it.

"Wait," he ordered.

Cotta turned and looked at Denny, who sat as if in a trance, staring at his bloody hands.

Brennan reached out again and gently brushed across Denny's mind.

"I don't know," he said again, "but I'm sure of it. And more than one mind. He's been spell cast, I know that for certain. I can see many hands on him. It must be a terrible weight for him to bear. Some are forcing him to do things, Troy, A'taz. This other one isn't."

"What is it doing?"

"I think the same thing I was about to do, calm him down, give him a little distance, give him a little push." Brennan put his face closer to hers. "He's seen so much; he's had to do so much."

"Who, Brennan?"

He frowned and went back for a third time.

"I don't know. I see… faces, but they're vague, indistinct touches…" Brennan stopped. "A'taz. But I don't know what he made him do."

"Can we trust him?" she asked coldly.

"We can. He's here to help us, aren't you, Den?"

"Master Brennan?"

Denny's voice cut through the whispered quiet of the cells, silencing Cotta and Brennan.

"Yes," Brennan replied gently.

"I'm alone here doing this. I don't have a plan to get you out," he confessed. "I'm half on orders from the Queen, from the stonemason, but I don't know what I'm doing."

Silence.

"I just…" Denny shrugged. "I don't know. I just knew I had to get to you and the crown, that if I didn't… The Queen is going to have Mistress Cotta executed tomorrow."

Cotta turned and reached to Brennan.

"We have to help ourselves."

He heard the words she didn't say.

"I'm not strong enough to do what you're thinking," he replied. "Too many minds, too many people, even if I could hold one for a second, I'd lose it as fast and we'd have a sword in us the next."

"Can you send them away?"

He shook his head.

"No, too many. I can barely stand, Cotta. I don't know if I can even make it out of this cell. If I was stronger, if I'd had more time to get it under control, maybe. But no. And what about An'eris… the baby?"

Still holding Brennan, she turned to Denny.

"Denny, go find the men who gave you the crown. Go now," she commanded.

"They'll be very angry," he replied.

"No they won't." She tried to sound encouraging. "Please, Denny, go find them, go in secret, but go now. Tell them what happened, what you did. Make sure you tell them what you did. Tell them I have the crown, make them come here."

"Why? They'll have me hanged for murder."

"Trust me, Denny, please, trust me, and then, I promise, you're done here."

CHAPTER 16

"How did you do this?"

The two guards stared at the body on the floor.

"Honestly, Kris, I don't even remember doing it."

"You must've, look at you."

"I know." Denny looked down at his hands and tried to wipe them on his blood-soaked clothes.

"Why were you even down here?"

"I don't know. I made a mess."

"A mess! You've killed him."

"But only him." Denny shouted back, stabbing his finger towards the warden's body, finally able to lose control. "You walked past those other cells," he yelled. "Who do you think are all those bodies piled up on each other?"

"He's right." Kris grabbed at Rolo and pulled him aside. "We've got to do something about this."

"I don't even know what this is." Rolo put his gloved hand to his head. "Where did all those bodies come from? Some of them looked like the lads from the city patrols. Why are they all dead?"

"We're under attack," Denny said. "And it's crazy, because we've got no enemy at the walls because they've somehow already got in, and everyone who hasn't gone away, they're dead—you just walked past them."

"That's insane. Who are we under attack from? Vaden hasn't moved against us in decades, and we've no real enemies."

"Then why did the King have to leave? Why is he dead and why have almost all our soldiers headed to the borders? It's someone new," Denny explained. He had nothing left to lose. "The stonemason… and everyone he's brought with him."

"Aquam are not our enemy."

"He's not from Aquam." Denny was almost screaming.

"All the new people in the castle? His?"

"They're taking over. They walked straight in and they've taken over and we're maybe all that's left."

"But the Queen? She must know."

"She doesn't," Denny shouted. "She's under some sort of spell. The people who came here, they aren't who they say they are."

Kris and Rolo thought about his words.

"You're saying it's magic?"

"Don't pretend you don't believe me." Denny heard new words enter his mind. "You stand guard over a vault that no one remembers even exists unless they need something from it. This whole place could be overrun and no one would even turn right into your corridor. It's magic and you know it, you're part of it."

"Den—"

"No." He reached out and punched Kris's breastplate, the hollow bang echoing in the dark. "Stop talking and listen," he hit him again, "and help me."

The two guards heard Denny's words.

"Believe me," Denny begged.

"We've got to sort this out." Kris turned to Rolo.

"I'm going to be hanged for this," Denny said.

"Yes, you will. If they find out."

A'taz stood motionless in the dim light staring down at the corpses. Troy and several of his personal guards waited a few feet behind him.

"You did this."

Troy, his whole body shaking, crossed his arms and hugged himself as tightly as he could.

A'taz turned and deliberately stepped slowly towards the quivering man.

Troy's guards, as one, turned and walked away, leaving the two men together.

Troy wanted to call out, to demand they stay, but he couldn't move.

A'taz licked his lips.

"You told me you had got rid of the bodies."

A'taz put his hands against Troy's chest and started to slowly untie the laces at the throat of his tunic.

"You told me the men were careful."

A'taz pulled Troy's tunic open and started to stroke the smooth tanned skin of his chest, up his neck, resting his fingertips on his throat.

"You told me there would be nothing to arouse suspicion. I told you what I wanted you to do."

He pushed harder as he stroked, red scratches forming under his fingers.

"I wanted the woman kept alive. I needed her."

He stopped his hand, his thumb over the pulse in Troy's neck.

"I wanted the man killed early on, but you wanted a toy."

A'taz pushed hard on the pulse; Troy felt a pressure in his chest. He tried to struggle away from A'taz's grip, his mouth closed, eyes wide, sweat starting to run off his body.

"I wanted this to be handled while I handled the Queen. But now I must handle you."

Troy felt the pain building in his chest, deep inside, behind his ribs, between his lungs, which couldn't get enough air.

"I wanted time to work on the Queen, to find my prize."

Troy felt something cold in his chest, like claws of ice wrapping around his heart.

"I'm sick of you," A'taz muttered.

Troy's body went limp but stayed upright.

"Your vile pursuit of pain for pleasure." A'taz relaxed his fingers, Troy's eyes trembled, and the corners of his self-mutilated mouth twitched.

"Your incompetence." He squeezed again and Troy let out a barely audible moan of agony.

"I gave you everything." With his free hand, he grabbed Troy by the back of the neck.

"Do I need to take it away?"

Troy couldn't shake his head. He couldn't speak.

He didn't need to.

"I warned you once what would happen if you disobeyed me again."

A'taz spell cast over Troy, magic unleashed with just a thought; he ripped Troy's heart from his chest through his throat.

Troy died, upright, on his feet, at his master's hand.

A'taz dropped the heart, his lips pursed, a frown creasing his forehead.

"But I need you. You'll live because I have work for you to do." A'taz put his hand on Troy's empty chest and pushed. Troy felt the rush of life surge through him again.

And he wasn't dead.

A'taz stepped away from Troy, making sure he was watching, and he stepped on his heart, grinding the tough sinewy organ into the floor under the heel of his boot.

Troy felt the pain deep inside himself.

He looked up at his master in awe.

"I'll fix this," he gasped weakly. "I'll make arrangements, get rid of the bodies. We'll find them."

A'taz turned and walked away. As he walked past the bodies into the small office and then out and up the winding staircase, A'taz thought about the incredible pain that he was inflicting on Troy. There was no doubt in his mind that the constant agony would remind the rabid goon of his master's power and bring him into line. But as he reached the top of the stairs and prepared to once again become the benevolent stonemason, A'taz remembered something about Troy and pain.

An'eris sat on her throne in front of the gathered council.

"And so you see, we believe the squire had a hand in their escape." An'eris's words reached to the back of the great hall, the sadness in her voice there for everyone to hear.

"I've ordered the patrols in the city to be on alert and they are preparing to send search parties out. We'll find them." Her voice faltered for a moment. "They won't have got far, and although they were treated with dignity and respect while held captive, they will have weakened, and there's no escaping Kraner."

"The squire…" a voice called out from the back, "how was that allowed to happen?"

"We believe he was coerced."

"Is it not more likely he was a traitor too?"

"No," An'eris said clearly. "No, he was in my service. I trusted him."

"Then how?"

"Perhaps threatened." Lord Ravi stepped forward and turned to address the crowd. "We don't know, but when we have recaptured them all, we will find out the truth."

The bodies were carried out of the dungeon and piled onto a wagon behind the castle's north wall. No one knew how many bodies there were, or how many there were supposed to be. No one counted. No one looked at the faces. No one checked that the dead were dead.

Brennan's spectre watched impassively as his body was loaded onto a wagon by the driver and his partner. He watched until he was sure Denny and Cotta were there too.

He held their mind's asleep, under his control, the only mercy that they would never remember being taken out under the corpses of the men and women they knew so well.

He followed the wagon as it was pulled away from the castle along quiet streets that led out the city.

At a sharp turn, the wagon hit a protruding stone and broke a wheel. The wagon tipped and a few of the bodies slid off. A small parcel wrapped in old cloth rolled off the side and into a ditch.

The driver, not uttering a word, quickly scooped up the bodies and put them back onto the wagon—all but three.

Brennan waited, and watched, and when it was time, he let go.

Cotta opened her eyes, waking as if from a deep sleep.

Denny woke too, from dreamless, restful slumber.

Brennan sat up, his eyes unseeing, but seeing nonetheless.

He reached over to Cotta and Denny, all three helping each other.

Slowly, they all got to their feet.

"This is as much as we can do for you," Kris whispered, taking three full-length cloaks from under his seat and handing them down to Rolo, who wrapped them around cold hunched shoulders.

"Please live."

Without another word, the two disguised guards took up their seats on the wagon and drove it out the city, away to burn the bodies.

CHAPTER 17

An'uek held onto Raef, her small slight frame hiding tremendous strength focused on keeping him from rushing out of the camp to get to Calem.

"Let me go," he demanded, his jaw tight, fists clenched, the taste of fury on his tongue.

"If I do, and you go for him, I may as well kill you myself."

She kept her gaze steady as she exerted more pressure on his forearms, forcing him down until eventually he was on his knees before her, shaking with the futile effort to free himself.

"You can't hold on like this, keep me from him forever." Raef grinned, his face red, the tendons in his neck as tight as a bowstring.

"Yes I can." Her voice went straight into his mind. "Raef," she spoke only to him, "this is not how you avenge your brother."

Raef closed his eyes, ground his teeth, but forced his fists to open.

Like a burst bellows, he gave in to her control and deflated against her. She let him fall, his weight bearing down on her much smaller body, solid and unmoving against him.

He wished she would wrap her arms around him; instead, she stayed still.

After a minute, he pushed himself back onto his heels and raised his eyes just enough to look at her.

"I'm sorry," he mumbled. "I thought I had come to terms with what happened. I don't know where this came from."

She wanted to put her hands on his face, kiss his cheeks and tell him it was all right. Instead, she moved her hands from his forearms, up to his shoulders and applied pressure.

"Raef…" She said his name, her tone flat.

He waited.

"You will not go to him with feelings of anger." Her statement cut through him, her hands tightening.

Raef, on his knees in supplication to the druidess, could only nod.

"Give me your word," she insisted.

Raef felt the sting of her demand.

"The last man who aligned himself to that fiend burned to death right next to him. You'd consign me to that fate?"

An'uek didn't react to the taunt.

"I'm not asking you to promise him anything. I'm commanding you to obey me."

"And what if the day comes when he needs to be killed and there's no one left but me."

"If that day comes, and we've lost whatever battle is left to us and Barclan is gone and all the kingdoms are in ruins and the world has ended," she listed off exaggerated terms, "then, yes, I'll release you from your bond, and if you want to kill yourself trying to get to him, I won't stand in your way."

"Then you have my word."

An'uek let him go.

He didn't move.

She looked at him and saw some of her own sadness reflected in his gaze.

"How did it come to this?" she wondered aloud.

He shrugged, eyes downcast, shoulders slumped.

"Let me go," he pleaded.

"I already did." She raised her hands to show him.

A shudder moved through his body, and he turned away from her; he didn't want her to look at him.

An'uek sensed the shift in his emotions, his shame tangible between them.

She put her hands on his shoulders again, squeezing them gently, kindly; her dominance gone.

"I'm sorry," he muttered.

"Don't be, I understand," she said, and she started rubbing small circles across his shoulders and up his neck.

"I want it all to be his fault. I want to kill him and kill this ache that's inside me."

She carried on consoling him.

"What if it never goes away?" he asked her, his voice coloured with bitterness. "What if I live the rest of my life with this urge, and all I think about, all day, every day, is killing."

An'uek looked at his face and wondered who she was seeing behind those words.

"If that happens…" she put her hands under his chin and raised his face to hers, "I want you to tell me."

"And you'll stop me? You can't."

"I can."

"Give me your word," he begged.

An'uek put her hand to his cheek, her thumb stroking slowly.

"I give you my word," she promised. "You won't become a killer."

She held him tight against her, comforting him in her strong embrace.

Bode had to wait until nightfall to make the journey, when the sun was gone and the heat of the day had dissipated. There was enough moonlight for him to see his steps. It took Bode an hour to make his way to the edge of the encampment and another hour to follow the path to the slab of rock where Calem was waiting.

Bode saw him first, stopping for a moment to check. He had spent all his time wondering what he might see but hadn't considered that the boy might not have changed at all. His white hair hadn't burned away, he didn't have scorch marks on his body, and his skin hadn't melted off his bones. His eyes still shimmered with their own curious radiance and he still looked thin and nervous. Someone must have given him some clothes; he was dressed for the desert: tan leather trousers laced at the sides, a light linen tunic with sleeves that hung over his hands, the cuffs already frayed.

"Hello, Calem." Bode was cautious not to sneak up on him.

"Hello, Bode." Calem sounded scared. He didn't look like a man who could incinerate someone with a hiccup.

They looked everywhere but at each other, both seeming intent on studying the bands of colour in the rocks that surrounded them.

Calem shifted on his feet.

"Did you come alone, or—"

"I came alone," Bode confirmed. It took him a second to realise what Calem was asking. "Raef survived."

He didn't mention any other names. He didn't need to; he saw Calem swallow and look away, his mind turning. He looked sad.

"An'uek is alive too." He picked at the bandages wrapped around his fingers, creating a loose thread he could tug. "She found us. She brought us here, helped us."

"I'm glad," Calem muttered. "I didn't know how far it reached, or who it might have touched."

Bode flexed his fingers and tried to make a fist.

Calem started to rub his fingertips together.

Bode saw the nervous gesture, so familiar, and frowned. He looked up at the boy and stepped forward.

"Don't touch me." Calem immediately took two steps back and held out his hands as a shield. "Bad things happen."

Bode stopped and raised his hands, palms up, open.

"Easy," he said gently. "Don't scare off, boy."

"I'm not scared," Calem said.

"Yes, you are," Bode stated.

"Should I be?"

"Of me?" Bode asked.

"Maybe?"

"No." Bode held up his arms, the clean white bandages disappearing beneath his clothes above his collar. "Look at me. I'm no threat to you. It's all right."

"Is it?" Calem said, coughing.

"Yes," Bode replied. "It's just me. The others thought it best if I came alone."

"Why?"

"In case… I don't know, to see how you are I suppose."

"Not how I am," Calem said bitterly, "you mean, to see what I am."

"Maybe," Bode agreed. "I don't know."

"You blame me."

Bode was silent.

"Yes," he admitted. "And no. It's difficult. We're all still making sense of everything."

"It wasn't my fault," Calem whined. "I didn't know he wasn't at the tower. I didn't know about Kraner. I didn't know any of it."

"I know." Bode shuffled forward, lowering his voice and speaking slowly.

"It hurt," Calem confessed, raising a hand to his throat and dragging it down his chest to his belly. "It burned me inside out."

"I saw." Bode kept talking softly. "I was there. I saw what Orren did."

Calem started to shuffle, his eyes flickering as he started to cast his own shadow behind himself.

Bode kept still, his voice low.

"It shouldn't have happened."

"But it did happen." Calem's voice quivered.

"It's not your fault."

"Everyone thinks it is. You all hate me. You want me dead." Calem's agitation was rising quickly, making Bode worry he would lose control. He moved back and tried to make his large frame smaller; he put his arms down, kept his hands loose.

"It's not like that…"

"You're afraid of me."

"Calem, stop it."

"I'm afraid of me," he shouted, his voice echoing off the rocks.

Bode instinctively put his hands in front of his face, expecting to feel the heat of flames break out across his body. He stood motionless but for the gasping breaths that slowly deepened as his panic receded. When the flames didn't come, and the spark of terror finally went out, Bode lowered his hands and looked at Calem. He put a hand to where he had once worn his sword.

"Sorry," he said, looking away.

Calem was looking at Bode unconsciously fidgeting with the pommel of a blade that wasn't there.

"You can't kill me you know," Calem uttered.

"We don't want to," Bode said as he tried to get his breathing back under control.

"Now who's lying?" Calem asked.

"There's all the time in the world for lying, if that's what you want to do."

"There's not enough time in the world for all the lies we can tell each other."

"Then let's skip to the end, shall we?" Bode took a step closer. Calem took a step back.

"What happened?" Bode asked.

Calem seemed unprepared for such a direct question, couldn't answer. His slender frame seemed to shrink.

"I can't think straight." He put a hand up and touched his forehead. "I don't know anymore." He took a step forward. "It's like my head is bleeding it out."

"What?" Bode asked softly. "What's bleeding out?"

"Everything that was in the gem."

"The one Orren made you…"

"Yes." Calem clutched at his throat. "I took it inside me and I unmade it, and I took what it was and it bound itself to what's in me."

"And what is it now, what's in you now?"

"Everything." Calem looked down at his hands. The centres of his palms started to bubble and writhe and transform into a small perfectly formed scorpion made from his flesh. The creature was ashen, the colour of his skin, but within seconds it darkened until it was as black as the night. Calem breathed over it and it sprang to life, jumping from his hand and skittering away across the rocks for a few seconds before it stopped, quivered, and burst into a tiny fireball that burned itself out to nothing.

Bode stepped back.

"Everything," Calem said again, staring at his hand.

Bode, dumbfounded, turned his back to Calem to give himself a moment to reconcile what he had just seen.

"Was that a trick?" he asked of the man behind him.

"I wish it was."

"You made that thing alive?"

"For a brief moment, yes."

"And you can do that sort of thing now?"

"I didn't know I could until I just did it."

"And that's what's in you?" Bode gasped in disbelief.

"I don't know." Calem coughed again. "Whatever it is, I don't want it. I have to get rid of it before it finds a way out."

"You say it like it's a wild thing with a mind."

"It feels like it is." Calem clenched his fist loosely. "I feel like it's this thing in me that's pushing at me, from the inside, trying to get out of me, to get itself out into the world."

Bode looked at him, his eyes wide, his mouth open.

"If it's inside you, why don't you kill yourself?" Bode asked.

"I tried," Calem stated. "After that day, I went to a place. I had these memories, ageless visions of a place when the world was forming, full of creatures that I was sure would rip me apart, feed off me, end me and then go back to their slumber."

"They obviously didn't."

"No." Calem looked away, guilt clear on his face.

"What did you do?" Bode asked.

Calem shook his head.

"It doesn't matter now," he wheezed.

"Oh, but it does matter," Bode stepped back towards him. "I have to decide if I bring you back with me. I have to choose if we help you or if we cast you aside."

Calem, his back to Bode, looked at him from over his shoulder.

"If you do that, I'll destroy the world."

Bode stood still, overcome with helplessness.

"Then what?" he asked. "What can we do to hinder or help you when you're as strong as a God?"

"Take me to Kraner." Calem stepped up to Bode. "Take me to Brennan. He'll know what to do."

Bode put his hands on his hips and raised his face to the sky, a long sigh escaping him.

"What?" Calem asked.

"Kraner," Bode muttered.

Calem shuffled closer, his head low, his voice lower. "What's happened in Kraner?"

An'uek sat with Bode on a scattering of boulders.

"See these..." Bode pointed to where they sat. "And that big one?"

"It's like a table and chairs," An'uek said, smiling.

"For giants maybe." Bode scratched at his face. "This place looks like giants made it, like they took a mountain and tossed it around like a toy, letting it break apart and fall to pieces wherever they dropped it."

"That's a nice way to imagine it." An'uek leaned back on her hands, looking around at the boulders and stones all around them. "Or maybe once the world was upside down, and the blue sky was the sea and the mountains were clouds and it rained these stones. Then the world flipped over, and here we are."

"Sitting on clouds of rock with an ocean above us?"

"Maybe." She shrugged, her gaze turning from the sky to the stones, to Raef and Calem.

They watched them, too far away to hear what they said to each other, close enough to see Calem shifting on his feet and Raef pinch the bridge of his nose and squeeze his eyes.

"How are you doing?" she asked, slipping her hand around his, careful of his fingers. She felt the tremors as she put her fingertips to his, exerting just enough pressure and warmth to stop them for a little while.

Shocked, Bode looked at his hand in hers, then up to her face.

"They've not been still since I woke up. How...?"

She lifted her fingertips and the tremors returned.

"I can't take it away, I can only ease it when we're close."

Bode sighed, releasing the breath he hadn't realised he'd been holding.

He looked down at the bandages.

"I won't lift a sword again or hold a shield, will I?" It wasn't a question. "So much for the kingdom's great Knight Protector."

"So much for kings and murderers, sorcerers and druids." She squeezed his hand and felt him squeeze back. "We don't need those titles anymore."

"What are we then?" He let her fingers dance over the bandages, checking their bindings.

"A little bit lost right now." Her voice lifted, and he raised an eyebrow. "But not for long."

An'uek stood, stretched, and turned, hand out, pulling Bode to his feet. She couldn't help grinning as he made a show of bending his back and stretching aching muscles.

"It's time to go," she told him, gazing up as he towered over her.

He sighed and looked around, as if mulling it over.

"Time to buy some sheep," he said to himself remembering Raef's story. "And none too soon either. I'll never get the sand out of my boots, and I'm a bit sick of goat meat if I'm being honest. Plus, these dunes…" He gestured around them. "A bit monotonous and boring."

An'uek laughed softly.

Bode turned to look at her.

"What?" she asked, self-conscious.

"I haven't heard you laugh, even a tiny laugh, since before Jedda died."

"It's been that long?"

"It has."

An'uek thought on his words.

"That was so long ago," she exclaimed. She looked at Bode, then looked down at her hands, turning them over.

"Sadness. Violence. It can change us, my kind." She put her hands together. "Make us more like you I suppose."

Bode lowered his head a little and pursed his lips.

"Can it be undone?"

"I don't know," An'uek confessed, "but like you, I'm done being sad."

She turned away, standing a little straighter.

"Come on," she called loudly, and she was rewarded with Raef and Calem turning immediately. "This melancholy can't go on. We all lost too much getting here to find it was for nothing. But we're here, and the world is changed." She looked at Calem, who had the decency to look away. "We have to decide what we're going to do about it."

"A'taz is in Kraner," Bode stated. "My friend is there too. I'd like to go back."

"Homen sent us here with you all," Raef mused. "I suppose I'm still on the job, so if it's to Kraner, I'll follow." He stepped over and stood with Bode.

An'uek turned to Calem.

"What about you?" she asked, no hint of warmth in her voice. "What do you want?"

"I want to go to Kraner."

"To get there you need us?"

"I think so," Calem agreed. He raised his hands, swished them through the air, and a little trail of flame followed his fingers, gone before they were sure they saw it. "I don't know what to do about this. I need help."

"I can't help you."

"You have to," he implored. "Who else have I got?"

An'uek felt Bode and Raef watching her, waiting for her decision. Calem was waiting too. Waiting for her to tell them all what to do.

"All right," she said, pretending to herself that she ever had a choice. "We go to Kraner."

Sona helped An'uek with the supplies while Bastion and Bode sat in quiet conversation.

"That one is very dangerous." Sona didn't need to say his name.

"Yes he is," An'uek agreed vehemently.

"The quicker he's gone, the better I'll feel."

An'uek stopped. She reached out and touched Sona gently.

"Is it very bad?"

Sona rolled her neck, the bones popping under her skin.

"It's like being out of breath all the time, and my water feels thick like cold oil."

"Even though he's nowhere near the camp?"

"Can someone like him ever be far enough away?"

"No," An'uek agreed, "not even if he was dead."

Sona continued wrapping dried food in small bundles for their packs. She watched An'uek, saw the way the druid frowned, how her hands stuffed things into the bags a little quicker, a little more forcefully.

"You've spent a lot of yourself on these men." Sona gestured vaguely off over her shoulder. "They can sleep at night because you no longer do."

"What's your point?" An'uek snapped.

"Make sure you don't give them everything. Don't spend too much time among them. Just remember you're a druid. Remember what that means, what can happen if you give too much of yourself away."

"Have you and Bastion spoken?" An'uek couldn't keep the accusation from her voice.

"No, perhaps we've just seen the same shadow."

An'uek packed the last of the food rations, pulled the drawstring tight and knotted it. She hefted it off the table and put it on the ground with the others.

"Please tell the Sand-Dancer we're ready to leave."

"An'uek, wait," Sona called.

She stopped and turned.

"I don't think I've ever heard you use my name." She couldn't keep the worry from her voice.

Sona came over, kneeled in front of her, and pulled the smaller woman into her arms.

"I feel like this is the last time I'll ever see you again."

An'uek let herself be wrapped in the embrace. She pushed her face into Sona's neck, her hands reaching up to circle her and hold her tight.

"I hope you're wrong," he forced herself to breathe slowly, "but I think you might be right."

Sona held her tighter.

Bode crossed his arms over his chest, shoving his fists into his armpits.

"You're saying it's enchanted somehow?" Bode asked.

"Not enchanted." Bastion shook his head. "The gap in the mountains is a doorway of sorts. Few come through as far as you did."

"And going back?" Bode didn't like where the conversation was leading.

"Going back, they must take a harder path." Bastion gestured above his head. "The desert is a wild place, things here are raw. You eat our food, you drink our water, you walk the sands, you take in some of the wild. When you get to the pass, the wild in you comes out."

"What do we do?"

"There's nothing you can do except keep moving forward, or you'll never leave, you'll spend forever trying to find your way out the corridor."

Bode thought about Raef and Calem. He let his thoughts turn to An'uek, who was both weakening and hardening before his eyes, and a deep frown creased his features.

"Can you guide us?"

"I'll get you through the pass, but I can't guide you."

Bode looked around, and not for the first time he wished he'd never set foot in the desert.

"It looks empty," he said to Bastion. "Until you really look, and even then you can't see it, but you can feel it."

"My sands are so full... compared to the desert, the rest of your world is barren and dry."

Chapter 18

Cotta walked through Kraner, dirty, beaten, barefoot like all the common whores heading to wherever they slept off the day after a night's work.

The sun was forcing its way between thinning clouds, a rare respite from the early winter rain; it lit the early morning streets with a welcome glow but did nothing to erase the heart-clutching cold that gripped her.

Her teeth chattered, her body shook, and she kept fumbling her steps as she tried to avoid all the muck and detritus that littered the dank alleyways and rubbish-festered back streets. Somewhere on her journey one of her feet started bleeding, but she dared not stop to fish out the shard of glass that was stuck somewhere in her heel. By the time she reckoned she was halfway there, a limp was slowing her down enough that she'd become fair game for the city.

She hobbled straight into a man whom she hadn't noticed stepping out of a doorway and who had put himself in her way.

"Hello lovely," he said, grinning, his breath as sour as his sweat. "Looking for a customer?"

"Heading home," she snapped back in a voice playing the part. "If you're looking, there's men and women enough for you just waking up. Leave me be."

"Are you sure? I'll be quick. You're already here and I've got the coin?" He put his hand on her shoulder. It felt heavy. It felt like the warden's hand. It felt like all the hands she had tolerated for weeks.

It felt like the last hand that would ever touch her without permission.

Raising her head slowly, Cotta motioned to take the man's hand in her own. He smiled as she brought it to her mouth, and then he screamed as she kicked as hard as she could into his knee, the satisfying crack of the bone her reward for enduring his touch.

She flung him away from her and he doubled over, clutching his leg. By the time he gathered his wits and shouted for a guard, she was already a street away, running for her life.

"Here, lean on me a bit more." Denny pushed himself closer into Brennan and took his weight. "Pretend like you can't barely walk."

"I can't walk." Brennan couldn't keep the scorn from his voice.

"Just let me do it for you then." Denny said. "You're so cold."

They pulled their cloaks around them and set off, Denny dragging Brennan through the streets.

With any luck, Denny thought, they'd slip through most of the city between patrol shifts. He knew where most of the men changed over, he just didn't know most of the men anymore. He hoped that meant they wouldn't know him. All their haste depended on him being just another poor city boy trying to get his falling-over drunk father off the streets to sleep the drink off.

Brennan felt the strain of his own diminished weight on Denny as the boy sagged under him and stumbled every few feet.

He hated feeling so useless. Brennan tried but struggled to use his legs; they burned as if full of shattered bones and torn flesh.

Denny kept him upright, kept his crushed re-formed ribs tight into his body.

"Slow down," Brennan wheezed, "I feel like I'm running." He had to stop and catch his breath, the agony of each lungful of air making him dizzy.

Denny only let him rest a minute, then lifted him up and kept going.

"We can't take too long," he huffed. "Once the stalls and offices open there'll be too many people to avoid and someone will ask questions."

Brennan nodded, unable to speak. Too tired, too spent, he couldn't even bring his other sight to bear. He was blind and useless.

"Do you think Mistress Cotta's there by now?" Denny asked no one as he hurried them down a side street full of opaque windows showing silhouettes of men and women getting ready for the day. "She should be…" He was talking to himself. He could hear voices floating on the morning air. "It was safer, wasn't it, to split up?" He didn't expect an answer. It was harder to hold onto Brennan, his own sweat greasing his palms.

"Travis is there." He dipped and shoved his shoulder under Brennan's armpit to keep him up as they passed a shopfront. "And Lady Marsha too." Brennan stumbled and started to fall.

Denny let him fall into the doorway, realising he was unconscious as his head hit the wooden frame.

"And a druid." Denny knocked out a random staccato on the wooden door.

It opened just a crack, enough for a familiar face to stare out suspiciously.

"Delivery," he said to himself, as his legs gave out and he crumbled onto the cobblestones beside his master. Denny reached out and patted him twice on the shoulder.

"All done now, Master Brennan, all done."

The door opened and Denny and Brennan both fell backwards into the shop. Strong hands grabbed them under the arms and dragged them in, the door closing as soon as their feet were over the threshold.

A'rrick picked up Brennan and rushed upstairs. Travis was a step behind, and hauling Denny over his shoulder, he took the stairs two at a time.

Marsha urged them both into the upstairs room and slammed the door, all sense of secrecy forgotten for the urgency of haste.

Denny lifted his head, his eyes searching for Cotta. He saw her, wrapped in blankets in the corner, her face peering out at him like a scared child hiding in her bed. Travis put him down on the floor and Denny let himself crumple over, pulling his knees in to his chest. He lay there, staring at Cotta staring back at him.

Marsha bent over Brennan, her hands running swiftly and purposefully across his body. A'rrick settled across from her, kneeling at Brennan's shoulders, his hands going to the tangle of hair plastered across his face. He started to smooth it out, pulling the strands back, then quickly pulling it down and across the stretched skin where his eyes had been.

"Impossible," Marsha said as she ran her hand up his arm. "There's not a mark on him save for filth, but I can feel that he's been broken again and again."

"He should have died from these injuries alone." A'rrick put his palms where Brennan once had eyes. "This was done first."

Marsha looked up at A'rrick, moving back when he motioned her away with his hand.

She did so without question, holding her tongue as he leaned over Brennan and uttered long strings of words her mind forgot as soon as she heard them.

Marsha noticed a subtle shift in the light played across his prone body as A'rrick used his power to understand the enchantment.

"It's an old druid spell," A'rrick said, frowning as he delved deeper. "It's been augmented to heal him instantly. They wanted to keep him alive as long as they could." His head tipped to the side as he gazed at the eddies of power visible only to his sight. "It can be broken," he said, looking at Marsha.

"Do it."

"Not yet, he's too weak. He has to be part of it to break it."

"Then we have to leave him as he is for now."

Marsha let A'rrick pick him up and move towards the bundle of blankets in the corner, where Cotta was hiding.

She lay in the scratchy wool, her eyes shifting to watch Marsha and a stranger who carried Brennan over to her. She hadn't heard their words, her hands tightly covering her ears. A hand reached down and touched her cheek.

She flinched and wheeled around, recoiling into the blankets. It was Travis. He kneeled next to her, his fingers on her cheek, his eyes on hers.

He felt Cotta start to shudder against his hand. He expected to see her weeping, but there were no tears.

"A'rrick," Travis called out, without taking his eyes off her, "put him here, with Cotta. Put them together while we get things sorted."

A'rrick held Brennan in his arms as he stood looking down at Cotta; she reminded him of a mouse caught in a corner by a cat. He waited as Travis eased some of the blankets out from under her, then tucked Brennan under the blankets against her, hiding the two of them away together.

Travis nodded and stepped back. Cotta looked at him, gave a nod of her head so slight he only saw it because he was looking for it.

"Can you put them to sleep?" he asked.

On the cold wooden floor of a fish shop on the docks, A'rrick gave them both dreamless rest, the only good thing he felt he had done since he got to the forsaken city of Kraner.

CHAPTER 19

Marsha moved quickly around the small space, thanking Travis and A'rrick every time they trudged up the stairs with another bucket of hot water.

Travis was sweating and shaking, but not from the effort of filling the small high-sided wooden bathtub.

"I need a minute," he said, putting the bucket in the corner of the room and dropping to his knees.

Marsha went over to him and put her hands on his face, her thumbs on his eyelids and pulled them up. The whites of his eyes were grey.

"Kirin knows where she can get some," he said, as if reading her mind.

"It has to be soon, or you'll get sicker," she remarked.

He nodded.

"I know, she knows too."

A'rrick appeared in the room a moment later. He poured the hot water over the edge of the bathtub and dropped his bucket, sitting down on a nearby stool, out of breath.

"Last one," he said, panting.

"Come on, old man." Travis hauled himself up, pulling A'rrick up with him. "Let's go wait downstairs until they're done, then you can see to Brennan."

"Old man…" A'rrick accepted Travis's hand with a grin, but his eyes roamed over him. "I brought up twice as many buckets as you did."

"Mine were heavier."

"Is that why you're whiter than snow and sweating like a man introducing his wife to his mistress?"

"Lord A'rrick," Travis said, laughing, "as if that would ever happen to you."

"Or you," he shot back. "Old man indeed."

"You're only about four hundred years older than me." Travis bumped into him as he walked past. "Still time enough for me to have a wedding day at least."

Marsha heard them bicker as they left the room, closing the door as they went. She was about to go over to the corner, to rouse Cotta from the tomb of blankets she'd wrapped around herself but was interrupted by Kirin's discreet cough outside the door.

"Soap…" She crept in and offered a small knob of hardened paste to Marsha. "It's not gentle on the skin like she's used to up in the castle, but it gets the smell of scales and guts off me at the end of every day. It'll get rid of the dirt and the scent of whatever they've left on her."

"Thank you, Kirin." Marsha accepted the small dish. "You're taking such a risk for us already, this kindness is more than we could ask for."

Kirin handed over a brush, a small cloth, a blade and finally a large needle and fishing line. "There's a smell on her. Some of her skin is starting to dry out and redden around the wounds," she said to Marsha, who nodded in understanding. "I'll help her into the water before it starts to cool and then see to getting things so everyone can eat after dark. I'll be back with something for her to wear."

Cotta heard a familiar voice, and for a moment, as she wakened from a deep sleep, she felt warm and thought she might be in her bed. It only took a moment to know the smell was wrong, the blankets felt rough, and her body ached in a way she wished she didn't know. Before she opened her eyes and slowly pushed her head out from under the shroud of blankets where she had buried herself earlier, she felt for Brennan.

Behind her, cold and curled around her, clinging to her, under the same mound of protective covers, Brennan slept soundly. She leaned into him and let herself have a moment pretending they were all alone. She had a sense of deep peace as her thoughts strayed into his. Content that he was so far into his slumber that nightmares couldn't reach him, she moved enough to indicate to the voices that she was awake.

An unfamiliar face greeted her, made safe by the sight of Marsha over her shoulder. The woman held out a coaxing hand. Cotta put her own hand out to take the offer, stunned at how her arm shook with the effort of simply reaching.

"Cotta," Marsha said her name. "This is Kirin. We're in her home, above her shop near the docks. You're going to let her help you."

Cotta could only do as she was told

"Slowly," the women said, luring her out. "It's only a few feet to the bath and we'll get this muck off you."

Cotta had to let Kirin take her hands to help her to stand, help her to take the few steps across the small room.

Marsha held Cotta close to her body as Kirin pulled the tattered cloak from her shoulders and cut the rags off her body with her knife. Cotta kept herself upright refusing to even shudder as Kirin dug into her foot with the blade, and she couldn't look when she pulled something out and tossed it into the open brazier in the corner of the room. Kirin collected up the rags and the cloak, wrapped them up, and put them into the fire, letting them burn along with the extra logs she put on the flames before closing the small hinged grate. Then she was gone.

Marsha settled Cotta onto the lip of the tub, steadying her before helping her lift her legs over the edge one at a time.

The hot water burned. Cotta couldn't hold in a hiss as Marsha lowered her down. Finally seated, she instinctively hunched forward over her knees.

Sleeves rolled up over her elbows, Marsha swished the cloth around in the hot water then lathered up the bitter soap, wringing it out before gently easing it across Cotta's back. As she washed, Marsha struggled to find any spot on her body that hadn't been touched by violence. Cotta shifted and stiffened as Marsha rubbed across open wounds or tore at festering ones. She twitched and jerked as the cloth washed across her neck, down her throat and over her breasts to her narrow waist and further still. She didn't try to cover herself, but her hands were tight fists under the water, trembling at the effort of sitting still even under such loving and gentle touches. Marsha washed down her arms, but when she washed over her wrists Cotta yelled at her touch.

Putting the cloth down, Marsha held her hands out, waiting for Cotta to show her. Embedded under the delicate flesh, flecks of iron could be seen. Marsha ran her thumbs across the skin, feeling where they were lodged.

"I can't dig these out," she said, and she sighed, soothing the skin with her touch. "If I cut too deep, you'll bleed to death."

"Leave them then." Cotta turned her wrists, pulling her hands away. "They seem a small thing anyway." Marsha didn't miss the way she grimaced for a second as she rolled her wrists, the sharp-edged shrapnel moving just under the skin.

"A small thing indeed," she murmured.

Marsha was steady in her care, her experiences over the years made into fresh horrors, unable to distance herself from the body of someone she loved so much.

As the cloth wiped away the first layer of dirt, Cotta's head came up a little higher of its own volition. After a while her shoulders started to relax and she moved with the motion of the cloth not against it.

"The water's already filthy," Marsha said, starting again at her shoulders.

"I don't care, it's hot and I'm not cold," Cotta replied, wincing as the soft cloth moved over scabs shaped like teeth on her shoulder.

Marsha dipped it again, wrung it out, and went back to the same spot. Cotta could feel the bruised skin, swollen and sore.

"You can't wash them away," Cotta chided.

"I can try."

"You sound like him when you say things like that." Her voice was distant even in the small room. Cotta closed her eyes and let Marsha try. It hurt.

Marsha tried to ignore the trickles of blood snaking down Cotta's back as she cleaned her, and how, no matter where she scrubbed, Cotta still looked dirty.

She kept washing.

"We need to get the facts of what's happened." Cotta grimaced over a particularly fresh wound.

"There's time for that later," Marsha said, rebuking her.

"We need to know who's been turned."

"Travis and Kirin are gathering the names of people we can trust. You need to eat," Marsha reminded her.

"Who's for us?"

"You need to sleep." Marsha's voice softened.

"We need to figure out what A'taz is here for."

"You have to recover."

Marsha knew she wasn't listening.

Cotta winced and jerked forward as Marsha rubbed over a deep gash. She pressed a little harder and yellow pus oozed out, dribbling down her wet skin.

Marsha reached down and picked up the small sharp blade.

"This one is infected."

"Damn," Cotta groaned, letting her head fall into her hands.

"I can't wash the infection out." Marsha tried to offer some comfort. "I'll be as fast as I can."

She saw Cotta swallow, take a deep breath, then nod as she moved to grip the sides of the bathtub.

She counted aloud to three, then dug the blade in, excising the infected flesh in four swift strokes.

Cotta cried out, uttered every filthy word she could manage between gasps, and would have collapsed forward if there was enough space in the small wooden bath.

She let her head fall onto the edge, her fingers digging into the wood, trying to break it, knuckles white even under the bruises.

"Last bit now," Marsha said, as she picked up the needle, already threaded, and began to sew.

Cotta ground her jaw shut, moaned low and long with every stitch but kept still.

"Done," Marsha said, gently wiping the closed wound.

She waited until Cotta relaxed, her shoulders slumping forward, hanging her head. Bending over the side of the half barrel, she grabbed a small clay jug.

"Look up," she said, as she placed a hand to Cotta's forehead and gently guided her to lean back.

Cotta let Marsha move her, and she shifted, ever so slightly, trying to find a way to sit that didn't hurt.

Marsha filled the jug and poured it over Cotta's tangled hair.

She poured again and then took up the soap between her hands. She worked it into a lather and began gently washing Cotta's hair, rubbing her fingertips into her scalp, pulling gently through the long strands of black hair. The hot soapy water washing across Cotta's face and through her hair cleansed more than her body.

"I remember you doing this for me when I was a girl when you came to visit." Cotta allowed a small smile to break through. "The water was always scented with the oil from the wildflowers that grew on the hills around the house."

"You always loved bathing, especially if you'd been riding with Homen and your mother all day."

Cotta paused, and Marsha regretted mentioning his name before her words vanished from the air between them.

She held the jug, empty, uncharacteristically unsure what to do next.

Without turning to face her, Cotta snaked a hand over her shoulder and reached for Marsha, who twined their fingers together, holding her tightly.

"Don't stop," she begged. "I can pretend the water is my tears. I can hide my shame at having no more left to cry."

Marsha refilled the jug.

"You don't need to hide when the tears run out," she said sadly as she poured the hot water and saw how Cotta turned her face into it.

"I remember you saying that to my father, when my mother died."

"Yes," Marsha said. "And I said it to Homen when your mother died."

"I want to cry and properly mourn him, mourn all of them," Cotta admitted, looking at the dirty brown water that felt so pure. "But all I feel is anger, so much rage I can't find space for anything else. I can't feel grief, or maybe it's all I can feel. I don't know anymore."

Marsha doused her in the water and waited.

"Did you cry?" Cotta asked Marsha.

"I wept for days for them all," Marsha said, as if proud of her ability to grieve. "And I'll be weeping for my last boy for the rest of my days."

Cotta turned in the bath, clearly confused.

Marsha, seeing that Cotta didn't know, braced herself on the edge of the tub and told her about Orren.

Cotta stared at Marsha as she listened to the news. Her face was a mask of calm.

"I wish I didn't believe you," Cotta whispered.

"I got to bury my son, but I can't bury my grandson," Marsha said, tears falling, and she smiled sadly. "But at least I can cry, it helps."

Cotta reached up, and with a shaking finger she touched Marsha's tears and brought the wetness to her own cheek.

"Do you have enough tears for me too?" Cotta turned, her eyes wide open in her bruised face.

Marsha bent down and kissed her softly.

Cotta turned back to face the wall, her back to Marsha, who refilled the jug. From somewhere on the floor, she found and lifted a hairbrush.

"Hold still, my girl," she said, as she started to pull the bristles through all the tangles.

When they were done, the brown bathwater was covered with a grey soapy scum and Cotta was clean. Marsha left her in the small room, exiting as Kirin came in.

The fishmonger helped her into a pair of plain woollen hose followed by a creamy homespun long-sleeved smock that reached to her thighs. She eased her feet into a pair of well-worn black boots that went to the knee, a little too big, but with tight laces to pull them in, snug enough. The kind woman insisted Cotta take a tightly woven brown woollen surcoat that belted at the waist.

"Space on there for a few blades," she suggested, as she knotted the belt through the buckle and tightened it to the last hole.

"Space for an army?" Cotta asked cynically.

The fishmonger chuckled and reached for the cape lying across the stool.

She stretched round Cotta's shoulders and fastened it at her neck with a silver pin.

"Don't mind about the clothes," she said, as she smoothed the cape, "but make sure you take care of that pin. Give it back to me personally when all this is over."

Cotta thanked her as she pressed a pair of warm soft gloves into her hands.

"There," she said, and she finished fussing.

"Thank you so much for all this," she said. "I feel... new."

"It's as much as I can do without drawing any attention," the woman said as she manoeuvred Cotta to the stool.

For the second time that day, Cotta let herself be moved as someone started to brush her hair.

She let out an unexpected sigh, long, low, content.

"What do you want done with your hair?"

Cotta answered straight away.

"Cut if off."

Travis and A'rrick sat on the floor of the locked-up shop front, their backs against the counter, as good as invisible to anyone looking in. Denny sat across from them near the back watching the door.

"It's late," Travis said to him. "No one buys fish after noon anyway, you can relax."

Denny didn't reply.

A'rrick let his head fall to the side and caught Travis's attention. He shrugged in reply.

"Anyone want a smoke?" Denny said, surprising them. He shifted onto one hip and started feeling for something in his pocket. After a moment, he pulled out a small pouch; opening it, a familiar rich smell floated across to Travis.

"When did this start?" Travis asked, amused.

"Who cares?" Denny muttered. He was patting his other pockets but came up empty.

Travis smiled; his hand went into his own pocket and came out with a small roll of paper. He threw it at Denny.

"Got a light?" Travis asked.

"No," he replied, and set to rolling.

"I'll get one."

Travis looked around the shop floor, there were no lit candles, but in the back room there was a fireplace with a few banked coals. When Denny was done, he tossed the smoke over to Travis, who caught it in one hand. On hands and knees, Travis crawled into the other room and lowered his face over the narrow hearth into the coals.

Denny looked at A'rrick, who raised a hand and shook his head in reply.

He rolled another.

Travis crawled back, the glowing red tip like a tiny star in the dark room.

A'rrick saw how deeply he pulled the smoke into his lungs, and how, after only a second, Travis seemed steadier.

"It's warmer in the other room," Travis suggested, as Denny lit his own smoke off Travis's tip. "We could go in there and still sit and stare at the door but not freeze while we're doing it?" He breathed deeply, a pleasant sigh escaping his lips as he exhaled circles of white smoke into the air.

"It's up to the boy." A'rrick pointed a gloved finger at Denny.

"It's not safe." Denny's hand shook as he held the roll-up to his lips. "Need to keep watch."

A'rrick and Travis looked at each other, Travis's concerns mirrored in A'rrick's eyes.

"No one's coming tonight," Travis tried to assure him. "I've still got people on the streets, in the patrols. We're safe for now. They think Cotta and Brennan are dead and you've run away. They're not searching the streets. They're looking past the city gates in the north."

"You can't trust anyone." Denny inhaled deeply, letting the smoke hang off his lip as he started to roll another, his hands a little steadier than minutes before. "I need to be sure."

Travis and A'rrick shared another look and lapsed into silence.

A'rrick muttered under his breath and flicked a hand at Denny, who abruptly fell asleep. Travis darted over to him and caught the smoke as it fell from his lips, easing him down onto his side. Unhooking his own cloak, Travis laid it across the slumbering young man, absentmindedly tucking it tightly around him.

"Here…" A'rrick scooted over, rolling his cloak into a ball and shoving it under Denny's head. As they settled him, A'rrick reached out and touched his fingertips to his forehead.

"Are you doing what you did for the other two?"

"Yes," A'rrick affirmed. "No dreams, just sleep."

"Thank you." Travis settled back to sit, but stayed close, a hand resting on the squire.

Just over an hour later they heard familiar steps coming down the narrow stairs. Kirin reached the bottom and looked into the side room. Surprised to see it empty, she turned into the shop front.

"It's freezing in here, why aren't you in the other room?"

"We've been fine here," Travis lied.

"They're ready for you upstairs." Kirin looked down at Denny. "Are you going to wake him?"

"I can get him upstairs," A'rrick replied.

"Go upstairs one at a time. There's food enough for everyone and you can settle him in there while you see to the blind man."

A'rrick moved forward on his knees, scooping Denny into his arms as if he was nothing more than a baby in a blanket. Bent absurdly low, he scuttled to the stairs and moved carefully, soundlessly up in the dark.

"He moves like a crab," Kirin said, watching him ascend before turning to Travis.

"Did you get what I need?" he asked pointedly.

Kirin reached into a pocket in the fold of her pleated skirt and pulled out a small vial with a cork stopper.

"This stuff will kill you," she said, handing it to him.

"Something will eventually kill me, that's true." He took it from her, holding it tightly.

"Have you any word from the streets?" he asked Kirin.

"It's bad." Her voice was low as she set about her regular routine of preparing the shop for the next day. "It's as you suspected, his people are replacing ours. It's not clear if they're all being killed or run out the city, but they're disappearing. It's as if they were never there."

"He can't disappear everyone without raising suspicion."

"It's like no one is seeing or saying what they're seeing. Apparently, the castle is full of clerics now."

"So is the city. More and more of his people come in every day."

"It's an invasion," Kirin agreed, "of that there's no doubt. Just not one we've seen before."

"We need to let our people know to be ready."

"Ready for when, for what?"

"I have no idea, not yet. Just tell them I'm still here. I'll think of something."

"I'll get word out."

"And one more thing," he said, as he prepared to head for the stairs.

"Yes, Master Travis?" she addressed him formally.

"I don't want anyone knowing about Cotta and Brennan. Let everyone believe they're dead."

"My lord," she asked, "wouldn't it be better to give them something?"

"No." Travis shook his head. "I need something to tie them together. Those of us that are left are seeing An'eris giving the kingdom to this murderer. Their loyalty won't be to her, and it'll fracture them. I need them focused on something that can bind them, and for now, all I've got is their anger, so we stoke that."

Kirin didn't acknowledge him as she started sharpening her knives on the block.

Travis crept towards the stairs on his knees, stopping as a group of strangers wandered past her door on their way to somewhere else.

"It's a busy street night and day," Kirin said, not looking up. "Best go up now. The food won't stay warm, and cold fish stew is worse than being hungry."

Travis knew a dismissal when he heard one.

CHAPTER 20

Travis moved silently upstairs, opened the door carefully and eased himself into the cramped room. Marsha sat on the floor, her back to the wall, Denny's head resting on her lap. Travis recognised his coat still wrapped around the boy. Marsha raised her eyes to Travis and smiled. She looked down at Denny, her hand on his chest, and Travis could see the slow and steady rise and fall of his breathing. Tight-lipped, he let his gaze linger a while. It had been so long since he had seen anyone look so peaceful. He wanted to leave them both there, but his heart was beating fast and hard in his chest and he was starting to struggle to breathe.

"M-Marsha," he stuttered, his teeth chattering, "would you help me a moment with something?"

He tapped his chest and saw understanding flicker in her face.

Across the room, A'rrick saw Marsha cradle Denny's head in her arms before easing him down onto the floor. Surprised, he was about to ask her why she was moving him when earlier she had insisted on holding him, until he noticed the way Travis was standing, shifting from foot to foot, scratching at his skin, looking furtively around the room. A'rrick looked at Travis, looked beyond him, and saw a subtle shift of colour coursing around his body, brown and sluggish.

He felt a slow sadness seep into his heart as he understood what he was seeing.

"Can I help?" he offered.

Travis didn't turn in response, but Marsha did.

With a false smile and a quick gesture, she said no.

"He's fine," she lied, "just needs something for his stomach, probably an undercooked oyster."

"Are you sure?" A'rrick asked, remembering Denny using the same excuse. "Seems oysters in Kraner aren't good for anyone."

"He's fine, thank you."

A'rrick let it go. He turned back to focus on the bowl of soup in his hand and the man next to him. He sat with Brennan, helping him eat.

"Go slowly," A'rrick said softly, as Brennan tried to grip the spoon.

"I can't hold it." Brennan's words were slurred. His fingers slipped along the thin wooden handle. The spoon fell into the bowl; as Brennan's fingers fumbled for it, it flicked out, landing on the floor, slopping food over his hand.

The sound of it striking the floor was the only noise in the room Brennan heard.

He licked his lips. And then, very slowly, he reached down with his free hand to the floor, patting around until he found the spoon near his feet.

It took a few attempts before he could wrap his fingers around it and bring it back up to the bowl of food.

"Try again," A'rrick urged gently. "Think of where your other hand is, think about the bowl. Go easy."

"Why this first?"

"I won't try to break the spell over you unless I know you have half a chance of living through it."

"Please," Brennan pleaded. "This is torture."

"You have to eat." Cotta came over to his side, one hand on his trembling thigh to ground him, the other taking the spoon from his fingers. "The bread was too much. This is easier to swallow."

His hands dropped between his knees and his head fell forward, causing him to fall off the stool.

"None of that." A'rrick bent down to kneel on the other side of Brennan, catching him as he fell. He put his arms around his skeletal frame and settled him against his chest, both on the floor. It was like cradling death.

A'rrick had to turn Brennan's head with his hands so Cotta could bring the spoon to his limp lips.

"It isn't hot," she said, soothing him, "just swallow."

Brennan gulped it down, took in too much air as he swallowed and started to cough.

"A'rrick," Cotta hissed.

"Keep going," he replied. "Get it in him."

Cotta's hands started to shake as she tried to ladle another spoonful up to him, but she spilled it before she could get it to his lips.

"Here…" A'rrick reached out and took the bowl. He brought the whole thing up to Brennan's lips and tipped it gently.

"Sip," he ordered.

Slowly, like a sick child, Brennan drank the soup as he leaned against A'rrick, the bones of his bare chest heaving with every desperate breath.

He fell asleep like that as soon as the last savoury drop was past his lips.

"When will you do it?" Cotta asked.

"As soon as I can." A'rrick put his palms over the smooth stretched skin where Brennan's eyes once were. "The longer it's like this, the less help I can be."

"Can you restore his eyes?"

"I'll try," A'rrick answered. "I can't heal him myself. I can only remind his body of what it was when it was whole and see if his body can restore itself." He didn't sound confident. "Honestly, Cotta, I can barely fathom the magic used for this…" He couldn't find the word.

"Torture," she said it for him, echoing Brennan's own words. "Troy did this to torture him."

A'rrick ran his fingers through the tatters of Brennan's hair, absently pulling the strands down, hiding his disfigured nightmarish face. Clumps of hair came away tangled in his fingers, fine like a spider's web.

Cotta moved away quickly to the back of the room, coming back just as quickly with a washcloth and a small bowl of water.

Dipping the edge in, she ran the damp cloth over his lips, wetting and cleaning him.

"How bad were the beatings?"

She wiped his forehead, running the cloth down and over his ears, around the back and down his neck.

"He should have died from every one of them."

There was a coldness to her reply that made A'rrick shiver.

"You watched them, each one?"

She didn't reply. Dipping the cloth again, she washed his throat and the back of his neck, wiping over his shoulders and across his chest, across invisible bruises, wounds and fractures that she knew, in some way, were there, even though they weren't.

Putting the bowl down, she leaned forward and moved Brennan's sleeping head a little to the left, in her eyes making him more comfortable. Her fingertips on Brennan's jaw, she looked up at A'rrick.

"I think we're done talking about that place, I'm perversely grateful for whatever Troy did. Brennan's here because of it. This needs to end." She reached up and touched A'rrick's hand, bringing it down towards Brennan's face.

"I don't know what I can do about that," he admitted.

"Just start with his eyes," she said wistfully, looking away, as if ashamed. "I want to see them again."

She glanced around the room. A'rrick sensed she was searching for words and gave her the space to find what she needed to say.

"A'rrick, can I ask you something? Can I tell you something?"

The druid lord looked at Cotta.

"I've known you all your life and you've never asked me that before." His voice was so quiet she barely heard it as he reached for but didn't quite touch her hand.

"We've always had a bond since…" She stopped, a slight blush creeping over her face at an intimate memory. A'rrick read her body.

"Since you became lovers?"

"Yes," she said softly. "It's like a feeling… on the edge of my skin. After the first time, if I cleared my mind and thought of him, I could feel him, like a memory of a feeling in a dream."

"And now?" he prompted.

"When he lost his sight," her voice was quiet, "something changed in Brennan." She looked at A'rrick. "Now he can enter my mind, and it's so much stronger than before. In that place, in the dark, sometimes I could feel him in me, looking out through my eyes. He could take me away from myself, and I could take him into my memories."

She quietened, her body going still before she continued.

"One night, or maybe day, I don't know, it was always dark there, he told me he could leave his body, roam around like a ghost. Not very far at first, but each time he did it, it was a little bit more."

"His power?"

"Never before, not like this, not so strong, or so... so dislocated from his body. He said he could see patterns, like smoke, faint trails of magic in places where A'taz or Troy might have been."

Cotta looked up at A'rrick.

"Each time he left himself, he got stronger but his body got weaker. The beatings happened all the time and there was hardly any food, barely enough to drink. He was protecting both of us."

"Both of you?"

"Me and An'eris."

A'rrick shuddered at her words, the shock moving through him.

"Brennan was in her mind?" A'rrick asked.

"At the edges." She kept looking at her lover. "Some days he didn't feel a call, other days he would be out of his body for hours. I stopped asking, but I knew where he was."

"How is she, what was he doing, why didn't he free her?"

Cotta, ignoring his questions, moved her gaze to the ceiling as she forced herself not to cry.

"I told him to stop helping me, to only help An'eris. I was sure it would kill him if he kept trying to save us both, but he wouldn't stop. He's stubborn..." she looked back at his cadaverous eyeless face, "wilful."

"Powerful." A'rrick mulled her words, stunned.

"More than I think he ever imagined he could be. He can do more than read someone's thoughts. He's able to go into someone now, affect them. He was practising. He thought if he was strong enough he could go in, take control."

"That's incredible." A'rrick gasped. And then he understood what Cotta wasn't saying.

As he stroked Brennan's face, A'rrick looked down at him.

"You want to know if his power changed because of what Troy did. You want to know what will happen to his power if I try to heal him?"

She shook her head.

"I want to know how to strengthen his power." She swallowed a lump in her throat, not taking her gaze from Brennan. "If it means leaving him as he is, then so be it."

"Cotta?" A'rrick looked at her in disbelief.

"We need him." She looked up at A'rrick. "I need him, and what he can do now." She clenched her fists between her knees. "He might be the only weapon we have against Troy and A'taz and the only chance of freeing An'eris."

A'rrick's hand paused, his fingertips resting on Brennan's brow.

"That is not your choice to make." His voice shook, his eyes wide. "And as much as I want him to, for the sake of my child, my grandchild, I can't ask that of him."

"It's the only choice," Brennan said, surprising them both. A'rrick put his hands across Brennan's chest, infusing his cold body with his own warmth.

"Do as she says," Brennan said, coughing, his breathing too fast, his body shivering. "Do it quickly," he uttered.

A'rrick didn't move.

"You're still too weak," he cautioned. "If I do it, you might die."

"I'm dying anyway," Brennan growled.

"I can't… If I try this and I kill you…"

"If you don't try I will absolutely die."

"I can't."

"Think of it like this…" Cotta grabbed A'rrick's strong arms. "Do it… or your daughter and her baby die, and it'll be your fault."

A'rrick shrugged her off him and swore at her in words she couldn't understand, but she knew what he meant.

"I don't care," she replied. "You have to do it, whatever it costs us."

"I can't create the energy to get you through it," A'rrick protested to Brennan. "You don't know what this will take from you."

"Take it from me," Cotta interrupted them, her soft voice cutting across them both. She looked at A'rrick, imploring him.

"Brennan did it once… he joined us." She moved forward and picked up one of his hands, putting their palms together. With the other hand she reached out to touch his face. "Do it again, put yourself in my mind and draw on what you need." She ran her fingers across his cheek to touch his thin dry lips, but she looked at A'rrick.

"Hurry," she ordered.

A'rrick was stunned. Brennan lay dying against him, Cotta resting alongside, offering her own life in exchange for something he didn't even know how to do. He looked over towards the far corner of the room and saw Marsha huddled over Travis as they did something that he couldn't quite see. He looked down at Denny, asleep on the floor, not a child but barely a man, already a thief, murderer, liar, traitor.

He looked at Brennan.

He thought about An'eris and her child, alone in that place, trapped, only safe until the moment A'taz didn't need them.

"All right," he acquiesced.

Cotta wasn't sure what to expect. Would Brennan appear in her mind, an image of the man, or would it be a feeling, a sense of everything in him that she knew so well, that she loved so intimately? She felt the cold skin of his hand in hers, the hard floorboards that pressed so harshly into her tired bones, the pressing weight of fear inside her chest. What if he dies, she thought to herself, what if we both die?

We won't.

His voice resonated in her mind and Cotta felt herself turn to greet him.

Travis and Cotta sat on the stairs alone, facing each other in the dark, leaning back against wooden walls with no space between them. They were wrapped in their thick cloaks, warm in a rare moment of tranquillity. She sat one step above Travis, his arm looped under her leg.

"You look like a beggar," she teased as she sipped hot bitter tea.

Travis scratched his beard and ruffled his hair into a dishevelled mop, making it worse.

"Beggar still, or scoundrel, gambler, conman?"

She nudged him with her knee, leaned forward and pushed it back off his face, combing his hair with her fingers.

"Don't hide your eyes," she said softly, unable to keep an edge of command out of her voice.

"Yes, my lady." He held her gaze, letting her do what she wanted.

They lapsed into a comfortable silence, both sipping their drinks on the cramped narrow stairwell.

"You always do as I say, don't you?"

"Not always," he countered. "I only do what you say when you ask nicely."

"And I'm known for asking nicely, aren't I?"

He had the decency to hide his snort of laughter at her words.

She made a point of ignoring him, changing the subject.

"There's a lot to do, isn't there?" Travis mused.

"I've swapped nice comfy halls with fireplaces and cushions for cold floorboards, a perfume of vinegar, and fish scales turning up in places you don't want them," Cotta replied.

"Don't let Kirin hear you say that, she keeps this place cleaner than anywhere I think I've ever been."

"I'll keep that in mind," Cotta said, grinning. "Was she always one of yours?"

Travis shook his head as he swallowed.

"Not mine exactly." He didn't say anymore and Cotta let it go.

"Where do we start?" she asked.

"With a crown."

"An'eris?"

"No."

"I don't follow." She sipped her drink, waiting for him to explain.

"Do you remember when we were in the guildhall?" His question surprised her.

"Which year?"

"Final year."

Cotta looked past his shoulder.

"A lot happened that year." She brought the mug to her cracked lips to hide her smile.

"Mid-summer," he reminded her. "The week before you joined the full council and immediately left for Orania after…"

Cotta groaned.

"Are you going to ask me about the brandy?"

"No, not exactly."

"Then what?"

"Well…" he took an exaggerated sip, "I was going to ask you about what happened because of the brandy."

Cotta instantly knew where his mind was going.

"You know what happened, you found us… remember?"

"Found isn't the word I'd choose, you were hardly hiding."

"I'm not loving this little game." Cotta leaned forward and poked him in his chest. She settled back, a smirk across her face.

"You want to ask me about Bris."

"I want to ask you if Bris still remembers you so fondly?"

"She should do," Cotta said smugly. "It was a long summer after all."

"And you worked hard all summer on those treaties between Barclan and Orania."

"I certainly worked hard that summer, yes." Cotta grinned. "Best treaties of her life, if I remember her words correctly."

Travis let himself grin, resting his head on the wall behind him.

"You want to send Marsha to Orania don't you, into Bris's care?" Cotta guessed.

"Right now, she might not be in the castle, but Marsha's our true Queen until we get An'eris out from under A'taz's control."

A heavy silence settled between them as Cotta thought through the implications of what he wanted to do. She thought of An'eris, the look in her eyes the last time they were together. She felt her thoughts threaten to unravel at the idea of her friend alone in the castle.

The minutes flowed on as they finished their tea together.

Travis got up, stretched his back and cracked his knuckles. Bending down, he took Cotta's mug and went back up the stairs, disappearing behind the closed door.

A little while later, he came back down and took his seat below her, two fresh mugs steaming in the cold air.

Cotta took it, thanking him with a slight smile. She rolled her wrists, keeping them from stiffening.

"Where did you go while I was upstairs?" he asked.

She shook her head.

"Nowhere I want to share right now."

"Well?" he asked.

"I want Denny to go with her," Cotta replied, bringing herself back to the conversation. "I'm sure by now the stories about my treason are across the kingdom and over our borders. But I can write a letter. There are phrases I can use so she'll know it's from me. It might be enough." Cotta clenched her jaw. "It might not be. Do we take that chance?"

"We can't send her north into Vaden. She won't survive the trip in winter and I don't trust them not to use her as a hostage. We've got one war on our hands; I'd rather not start another."

"The quickest road to Orania is across the Silverstone Plains."

"Kirin and I talked about how we can get her out the city, and I have some people I can ask."

"We can't protect her here, can we?"

Travis shook his head.

"I won't risk her. Asylum is the only safe option we have."

"You didn't answer me about Denny."

"We need him here. We need everyone who can hold a sword when the time comes."

"He needs to leave, if not Barclan then definitely Kraner." Cotta leaned forward into Travis's space. "He's done enough."

"There's more to do."

"He can't do anymore." She put a hand on his arm, squeezing gently. "He's a boy."

"He's been man enough so far."

"No, Travis, he's done. Let him go with Marsha." She squeezed his arm a little harder. "Denny will protect her. Let that be his last duty and then let him be free of service to the crown."

"He won't go."

"He'll do as I say."

Travis thought a moment before nodding.

"All right," he agreed. "Write your letter tonight. I'll have Kirin make arrangements."

"I want them gone within three days," she stated.

"I'll see what can be done. It's not as easy as walking to the nearest city guard and ordering up a carriage you know."

"You're telling me you can't do it?" She raised an eyebrow in mock challenge.

"I'm saying I was going to put my feet up and let the rebellion start itself, but as usual with you there's something you want done so…" He threw his hands up dramatically, eyes wide, lips tight.

"That's right, I'm back and I'm in charge of everything," she said and grinned.

"And everyone."

"A rebellion you say?" she said, as if tasting the word. "That sounds like something I'd like to try."

"Well, it's just a small one." He put this thumb and forefinger together.

"Small isn't like you."

"I've been busy," he said, and chortled, "but it'll get bigger when I get some more people involved. Enlarge the ranks, so to speak."

They both started to laugh, doubling forward and leaning on each other. Cotta snaked her arms around Travis's neck as they both let the laughter roll through them. It felt good. Travis pulled her close, holding her as tightly as he could without hurting her. After the laughter died away, they sat for a while in comfortable silence.

"I missed you," Travis admitted, pushing a loose strand of short hair behind her ear.

"I'm here now," she said, a hand at his neck, keeping his head against hers as if to ground herself.

"I thought you were dead. If I'd known, I'd have come for you. When I found out you were alive I…"

He felt Cotta put her finger against his lips, silencing his words.

"I need to go write that letter and I need to speak to Kirin. I left a parcel of sorts near the castle, can you have her send someone to retrieve it for me?"

"I can get that done for you." He pulled back, but she held him in her grip. "And then we need to send them away and deal with whatever happens next."

"Travis…" She said his name, capturing his gaze from barely an inch away. "We have so much to do and no time, but if there's anything you need me to do for you…" She let go of his neck and pushed her hand against his chest. "If there's anything you can't do yourself once Marsha is gone, something you need someone to do for you…you come to me."

Travis pulled back. He looked away, unable to meet her gaze.

"Homen told me," she said, answering his unasked question.

Travis sucked in a deep breath and hunched forward on the step, putting his back to her.

"Please don't do that," she asked softly, reaching out to move beside him, her legs either side of his body. "Don't turn away from me, not now, not when we're going to need each other more than we ever have. You can trust me with everything, you must know that?"

"I do," he confessed. "But I'm not ready for you to know, that. Can you understand?"

Cotta pulled him into a rough embrace, his back to her chest, her chin resting on the top of his head.

"Who else is there to help you if not me?" she asked.

"No one," he agreed sadly.

"When this is all over, and we've won, or burned the castle to the ground and all those monsters inside it, I'm taking Brennan home." She kissed his head. "Will you come with us?"

"To Falconfall?"

"Yes," she slipped both her arms around him, "to Falconfall. We'll be lazy all day, sip wine, eat cheese, get too fat to ride even the sturdiest horses. Get old, sleep in the afternoon, and reminisce about all the people we've known, wars we've fought, dances we've danced and lips we kissed in dark corners on hot nights."

His arms came around hers as he clung to her.

"I'd like that." He closed his eyes. "How long would it be before we're both bored?"

"A month," she said, sighing, "and then we'd be heading back here as fast as a strong horse could carry our fat backsides."

"I can't picture you fat," he teased.

"I could get fat." She let herself lean into him, feeling warmth spread through her again.

"How is Brennan?" Travis asked cautiously, his long fingers playing with her short hair.

"Alive. Eating as if he's never seen food before." She rubbed her face into his arm. "I can't explain what A'rrick did."

"Can you try?"

She nodded and abruptly pushed Travis back, sliding down to sit next to him.

"I heard Brennan in my mind." Her voice sounded far away. "I was seeing him, but it was his vision, through my eyes like when you stare at the sun and then suddenly look at something dark, all the colours are backwards and blurred, that's how it is now. I could see the magic around him." She looked at Travis. "It was like he was encased in a cage of crystal that was growing over him like scales. And his eyes…" She looked down at her hands for a minute, thinking of the words. "Black oil, bubbling, melting his eyes in his head over and over again."

Travis felt her body stiffen and held her tighter.

"Brennan was barely there anymore. In the vision, his body had wasted away to bone and dust inside the crystal body cast."

"Dying?"

She nodded.

"A'rrick was there, in the vision, like a reflection of himself if a mirror was underwater. I was so scared." Her voice quivered. "And then I remembered a dream I had once, of a dagger with a white pommel and grey blade, like smoke trapped in a mirror. I looked down, and the blade was there, in my hand. I looked up, A'rrick saw it, and he nodded."

Cotta looked down at her hands.

"So I took the blade and dragged it across my palm, let my blood drip onto the blade, and I set the tip against the crystal scales on Brennan's thigh and I moved it upwards, splitting the scales open and up across his belly. The blood from my hand ran along the blade, seeping into his body like it was filling him up. I cut through the spell, dragging the blade up over his chest, along his throat, over his head, and then I dropped it. It fell point down and the blade shattered, and a red mist filled the air between us. Brennan breathed it all in, his body getting stronger until the crystal scales shattered off his body and fell to nothing around him. His eyes, though, were still, a boiling darkness. I stepped forward and held my hand over him, letting my blood drip into his eyes, putting out the boiling mess."

She stopped.

"And then?" he prompted.

"And then I was back in the room." She shrugged her shoulders. "And A'rrick was holding Brennan, and it was like no time had passed at all."

"It was hours," he told her.

"It felt like seconds."

"Is it done?"

"I don't know." She leaned forward. "I looked at his eyes but couldn't see much. They looked like the eyes of a fish that's been on the counter for too many days. I don't know if he can see yet. A'rrick says it's too soon to tell. I hope we did the right thing."

Travis heard something in her words. He pulled her close.

"How can trying to save him ever be anything other than the right thing?"

Cotta thought of what else she'd seen in the vision. The sight of Brennan, encased in the crystal scales, slowly being suffocated by Troy's spell. But, behind him, the embodiment of his powers, a dazzling, brilliant column of blue light coiling and shifting around and into itself, like a beast waiting to be unleashed. As she broke Brennan free of Troy's spell, she'd watched as the blue light infused his body, lifting him off the ground, surging into him. She remembered looking away, unable to keep looking into the light, searching for a shadow to hide in. She had turned around and seen someone else behind her. A young man with white hair who reminded her of Brennan. In her vision, the boy had walked over to Brennan and reached out, taking his hand, pulling his body towards himself. Brennan had opened his eyes, the blue radiance spilling from them, striking the white-haired boy, who let it pass through him.

In her vision, she heard Brennan's voice.

"Hello, little brother."

"Hello, Brennan."

They stood looking at each other.

"Are you coming back?" Brennan asked.

"I am," the white-haired boy replied.

"You need to hurry. He's growing stronger every day."

"So are you." The boy raised his hand and trailed his fingers through the blue haze surrounding Brennan.

"I don't know how to control it," Brennan conceded. "I don't even know what it really is."

The boy raised a hand, an orange haze rising to mirror the blue around Brennan.

"Neither do I. All I know is you need to keep An'eris safe. She's the key to all of this."

"Why?"

"Just keep her safe, and when I get to the city, I'll find you. She must stay on the throne, there must always be a guardian in the castle."

"Guarding what? Dammit, Calem, enough riddles."

"Orren is dead."

Calem's words hit Brennan like a fist and he took a step backwards, stumbling at the pain of sudden loss.

"Did we cause all this?" Brennan asked Calem, tears in his eyes. "By coming here?"

"No." Calem shook his head. "I don't think so. I hope not."

"Hurry back. Let's get this done and then be done ourselves."

Brennan looked past Calem, his eyes falling on Cotta.

In her vision, Calem followed Brennan's gaze, turned around, seeing her for the first time. He took a step over to her, his head cocked, looking at her as if through her.

"Oh," he said, reaching out to her. "Oh, I wasn't expecting this."

"Calem," Brennan took a step forward, his voice stern, "leave her. She's not part of this."

Calem turned to Brennan but stepped towards Cotta, his head close to her ear.

"You know?"

Cotta stepped back, but he reached out and grabbed the hand she had cut with the dagger. Opening her palm, she saw the wound was gone.

"Let her go." Brennan was suddenly behind her, the sensation of his form pressed against her. She was caught between the brothers.

"You don't know?" Calem asked.

"Know what?" Brennan replied.

Cotta snatched her hand back and tried to move from between them, but she was stuck.

"Know what?" Brennan demanded.

But Calem faded away; the last thing he did was reach out to touch Brennan's face, but his eyes never left Cotta.

CHAPTER 21

Exiled to the sands, forbidden from coming near Bastion's people, near Sona, Calem had gone to sleep wrapped in his cloak and shrouded in the shadows of the high dunes. He dreamed of Brennan and a woman he barely knew with such vivid urgency it pulled him out of his slumber and infused him with an energy he couldn't remember ever feeling.

He moved quickly to the edge of the encampment and stamped his foot on the earth, forcing shockwaves through the jumble of tents to the ground under the bedrolls of his companions.

He wanted them to awaken; he wanted to get moving. Kraner was calling. His brother was calling.

As the day broke, they readied to leave.

"For some reason, I thought he'd be better at sitting on a horse by now."

Raef and Bode sat comfortably in their saddles watching Bastion try to settle Calem on his dun-coloured colt.

"He's going to slip off the other side." Raef leaned forward over his pommel and tapped Bode. "Want to place a wager?"

"No bet, it's a sure thing," Bode replied, his attention fixated on the pantomime of Calem trying to slip his boots into the stirrups but instead kicking at his horse, which as a result was getting agitated.

"There he goes!" Raef cheered and started to clap the moment the horse flicked its head enough to scare Calem and pitch him backwards.

He landed with a thud on the hard earth, instinctively rolling away from the lethal hooves that were near his head. He shuffled away on his hands and knees, falling onto his back, breathless, covering his eyes with his sleeve.

"What's wrong with this horse?" he wailed.

"Nothing," Raef countered. "It's what's wrong with the rider."

"I used to be able to ride," Calem retaliated.

"No, you didn't, you had an old fat horse that couldn't be bothered to throw you off."

"I got here, didn't I?" Calem replied to Raef's teasing.

"Enough," An'uek called out as she crested the sand dune riding a pure white mare that dazzled in the light of daybreak.

"I see you got the pretty one." Bode dipped his head respectfully as he leaned forward across his own horse to grip her reins and pull her closer to his side. He regarded her in her saddle.

"Sona?" he asked, looking at her new clothes.

"It seems while we've been here she's had the measure of me."

"Of all of us," Bode replied.

An'uek sat in her saddle in clothes fit for the desert. Thin-spun stockings clung to her legs, loosely enclosed in soft grey leather chaps that tucked into boots laced to her knees. A matching sleeveless leather vest covered her body from neck to navel, fitted over a gossamer-thin white cotton tunic that hid her skin from the sun and an errant touch. A long wide shawl wound around her neck and looped over her head to cascade off her shoulders and drape across her body. Darker grey gloves, expertly cut to her hands, covered her long slender fingers.

Bode looked over at Bastion, his thanks conveyed in the tilt of his head and set of his eyes. Unconsciously he lowered his hand to run his fingers across the chainmail he would never wear again. He caught himself in the gesture, clenched his fist against his chest and let his hand fall.

An'uek looked away, unwilling to see his thoughts so clear to her in his deep brown eyes.

Bastion sensed a moment of unease and so moved between the four horses, bending down to offer his hand to Calem, hauling him back to his feet.

"There's a bedroll for each of you behind the saddle. You each have a satchel on a panel hook. Inside there's food, and some clothing to help you through your journey out of my sands. There's a little coin to buy you a meal when you get into your lands, but no more than that, we don't have need for your coin here. I would like to do more but we don't have what you need to endure the winter of your lands. What we've given you is to keep you cool and keep the sun off your skin."

Raef looked down, tapped the satchel in recognition of it, and touched his hand to his forehead.

"Thank you," he said on behalf of them all.

"Your waterskins will always be full while you're on my sand." Bastion didn't add an explanation. "Drink as much as you can every day, then remember the sun, and drink twice as much as you can again. Keep yourself covered even if you get hot, the sun will kill you before you notice your skin is red. Water my horses, feed them and they will treat you well. When you've gone as far as you need to go, release them from their bindings and they will come back to me."

He held Calem's foot in one hand and the stirrup in the other. Ramming his boot in, he forced him into the saddle and held him while he steadied himself.

"I want my horses back," Bastion insisted, looking at Calem. "Don't change them."

Calem reached for the reins slowly, trying to move his hands without moving his body.

"You each have a saddlebag." Bastion checked all the lines and buckles on each of their saddles as he spoke. "You came here to us without the means to defend yourselves." He cinched the billet on An'uek's mare another notch. "Little sister, stay wrapped in the clothes Sona has given you. They'll never tear, and you'll never need to fear the touch of metal on your skin as long as you wear them. They will grow with you and be a thickened skin, an armour. Wash them only with water and Sona's gift will last you even a druid's lifetime. I know your kind don't take with weapons, but you're in the world now and the choice isn't yours anymore. I've provided you with a blade."

An'uek reached down, opened her saddlebag and pulled it out. A white hilt and grey crystal.

"The blade was cut from our sacred caves deep underground. It's safe for you to handle. It's strong. Strike along the edge and it'll never break, but pierce true on the point and it will shatter." Bastion took her hand in his and put her fingers through the small holes along the hilt. "Your thumb here, grip like this." He placed her hand. "Hold tight, and no one will be able to take it from you unless you choose to give it away. Choose wisely, it can't be taken back once it's given."

"It's beautiful, weightless." She hefted it in her hand, admired the intricate script etched into the fine white handle.

"It will remain that way until it takes first blood. After that, it will weigh as much as you can bear."

Her eyes met his as she digested his meaning.

She slipped the blade back into the saddlebag, tying it tightly.

Satisfied, Bastion moved to Raef.

"A small dirk for you, in obsidian, the strongest rock the desert offers with the sharpest edge for a clean kill. A short blade for a man who does his work up close."

"How many?" Raef asked, his fingers on the bag, curious.

"As many as you need, but never enough as you want."

Raef looked away.

"One?"

Bastion nodded.

He moved to Bode.

"Your days at war are done. Your heart couldn't bear the weight of it again, even if your arms could."

Flexing his fingers around the reins, Bode tried not to think about the bandages covering so much of his body.

"We'll see," Bode said thoughtfully. "I'm not ready to turn away from the only thing I've ever known."

"I understand," Bastion replied. "But things change. Tactics and songs, not the sword or shield, will win out now."

"We'll still need a lot of swords and shields," Bode countered. "But I won't be holding them." He held up his trembling hands.

"You've held enough weapons," Bastion said.

Bode reached down to shake his hand.

"We may never be able to repay you for all this."

"I don't give you these things for payment." Bastion's words were warm. "I'm doing it because I can."

"Thank you." Bode stressed the words, hoping they conveyed his gratitude. Bastion tugged on Bode's arm and pulled him lower to whisper in his ear. On hearing his words, Bode frowned but nodded.

"And now…" Bastion stepped over to Calem, "now for you."

Calem, who had finally settled into his saddle, was eager and curious.

"What could I possibly have for you?"

"I don't need a weapon," he said.

"You are a weapon," Bastion agreed, "a blade doesn't want a blade."

"Then what?" Calem asked, puzzled by Bastion's riddles.

The dark-skinned desert prince reached out and opened the bag buckled to Calem's saddle. He gestured for Calem to look inside.

Calem flinched.

"What do you expect me to do with that?"

Bastion pulled Calem down to whisper into his ear.

"If you can't hold it in, if you feel it under your skin, trying to break out, hold this." Bastion put the lump of raw metal mixed in with heavy red-speckled rock in his hand. "It was always what it is now, and it always will be. You can't undo this, so use it because you can't change it."

"I understand," he whispered back.

Bastion let him go and steadied him in his seat.

"Are you ready?" Bastion turned to An'uek.

"No," she replied, "but we're leaving anyway."

She clicked her tongue and her mare took a step back; touching her heels to the top of its flanks and tugging gently on the reins, she turned around.

"If I ask you to point us in the direction we need to go, will you be insulted?"

Bastion laughed and slapped the backside of her horse, sending them all on their journey.

"Stay in the saddle, the horses know the way."

He watched them leave. They fell into a single line behind An'uek, the druidess relaxing in the saddle, Raef riding a few feet back. Bode settled his stallion into a steady walk, letting Calem's colt keep pace, keeping him close. As they rode away, becoming smaller on the horizon, eventually disappearing over the crest of a distant dune, Bastion finally let himself turn away and head back to his people. He made his way slowly through the ropes, stopping to chat to anyone who called out to him, accepting a drink of cool water, stopping to play a round of chase with a small group of children.

He smiled. He laughed.

He sought out Sona, knowing she would be waiting for him in the solitude of his canvas home.

"They're gone?"

"They are," he replied, going straight to the basin to wash his face, his neck, his broad shoulders and dusty chest.

Sona stepped up behind him, snaking her arms around him, taking the washcloth from his hands. She didn't dip it back into the basin, but as she held it and wrung it out, water spilled from it.

"I've seen you do that thousands of times, it still amazes me," Bastion said as his eyes drifted closed at the first gentle touch as she started to wash his arms.

"Now that boy is gone, my water is my own again."

"He has no idea, does he?"

"None."

Bastion stood still as she washed the rest of his body.

"I told An'uek," Sona said quietly, running the washcloth down his back.

"What did you tell her? Exactly?" Bastion asked.

"That the boy has to die."

Bastion nodded.

"I think she already knew that."

"She did," Sona agreed.

As they rode through the long hot day, Raef emptied his waterskin over a dozen times. From the time the last drop fell on his tongue to when he hooked it onto his satchel it was full again. The horses' hooves hardly kicked up any dust as they crossed the dry hard earth and mile after endless mile of yellow sand and brown rock under a monotonous brilliant blue sky.

He thought of moving up alongside An'uek, to ask her about the water, but the sight of the druidess, resplendent in pearl white and soft grey leather sitting cross-legged on her snowy mare, seemingly floating on the saddle, made her seem unworldly, and he thought twice about disturbing her musings with idle discussion.

He pulled at the collar of his tunic, sweat pooling in the hollow of his throat, trickling down his back. He rerolled the large square of cloth like he'd been shown, placing it on his head, tying it at the back. Keeping safe from the sun was everything.

He turned and glanced behind. Bode had fallen back and was travelling alongside Calem. As he had done with An'uek earlier, the once great knight had taken both reins and was guiding the other mount. All Calem had to do was keep on his saddle. Bode seemed relaxed next to the boy; they talked quietly enough that Raef's keen ears could pick up their mumbles, but not so sharp as to hear their words.

He did notice when Calem's shoulders shook—laughing, he realised.

The realisation that they were in easy conversation sparked a flare of resentment in Raef. He forced himself to stare straight ahead. He wouldn't let his mind wander to the emptiness next to him, to the absence of a rider at his left.

Bode, hanging back and talking with Calem, was aware of Raef at the edge of his sight. He saw the way the man flinched as Calem laughed, and a sense of unease settled in his mind. He would need to watch him. But for now he turned his attention to Calem's questions.

"How long will it take us to get to Kraner?"

"A week out in the desert on these horses according to Bastion." Bode moved his gaze to the horizon. "Then the fastest route is straight up across the plains, maybe ten days if we keep out of the way, but I say we stick to the roads and make straight for Penrose. We could be there in six."

"And then the sea crossing?"

"It's four days at sea or another two weeks across the Crestwood Lake system, and at this time of year it'll be all bogs, frozen ground and winter floods. Best stick to sea."

"Yes," Calem groaned, "I suppose that's what we have to do."

Bode scratched at the skin starting to heal under the bandages around his hands. He let go of Calem's reins, not at all surprised when his horse stepped a foot away but kept pace.

"Would you live here if you could?" Bode gestured to the sand. "The desert?"

"Seems like a good fit for you, doesn't it?"

"You'd think so," Calem rasped. "Not so much to burn, but still enough life that I'd be a danger, you just don't see it."

Bode looked around. All he saw was sand. Endless desert. He was about to reply, but as he opened his mouth a shadow moved across their path. He raised his head. High above, a bird of prey circled them, rising and falling on the thermals.

"It's a hunter," Calem said without raising his face to the harsh sky. "If it's hunting…"

"Then there's something to hunt."

"Something other than us."

Bode looked again. Sand, monotonous dunes that went on forever, became dunes peppered with clumps of pin-thin grasses, bristled bushes covered in long thin thorns tipped with tiny vibrant purple flowers. Amongst that hard low-lying brown scrub, the occasional tall thick-stemmed purple cactus emerged like a king from the loose sand. Topped with succulent vivid yellow petals, that, if he squinted, he was sure gave rest and sweet nectar to the smallest delicate butterflies he had ever seen.

He looked ahead at their path, seeing for the first time the way the sand had been disturbed. Tracks that if he was in his homeland he would swear were from a small hare.

"Nothing here is as it seems," Calem said after a while. "It's really quite beautiful." He was looking around, his voice wistful.

As they rode on and passed a thin-stemmed bush, Bode leaned down and picked a bright flower. A few yards later he pulled some grass. Then more small flowers. He started to braid the grasses as the horses followed their path. After a while he twined the bright flowers into the grass braid.

"Are you making a bracelet?" Calem asked, curious.

"My mother used to make them for my sisters," Bode replied. "I used to help her. Necklaces too sometimes."

His fingers weren't so nimble, and the bracelet fell apart as soon as he handed it to Calem.

Bode laughed.

"Never mind."

The words died on his lips, replaced with a sharp yell.

Bode stared at the grass and flowers in Calem's hand, which had started to grow and uncurl as soon as he touched them.

"An'uek," Bode called out, not taking his eyes off Calem.

The long, thin, dry grass started to thicken, to fatten, and it changed to a verdant rich green. The strand split into two, into four, kept splitting until Calem was holding a tuft of fresh new grass that was growing long pale yellow roots that lengthened and curled and spilled over the side of his hand desperately seeking the ground.

"Calem, stop it," An'uek ordered.

"I can't," he squealed, throwing the grass as far away from him as he could.

It fell to the ground, immediately taking root and starting to grow rapidly into a thick blanket of tall lush grass that seemed to spread like spilled green ink on the dry desert floor.

"Is this because of you?" hissed Raef.

"I'm not doing anything," Calem shouted, his horse stepping around and flicking its head.

"What the Gods is happening?" Raef pointed at Calem.

A flower had stuck to his other hand, and like the grass, at the touch of his skin, it started to change.

Its petals grew bigger, the short stub of its stem where it had been picked grew downwards, and from nothing a whole plant started to regrow.

Calem threw it away.

"I can't stop it!" He rubbed his palms on the arms of his robe, trying to wipe them clean, but the flower kept growing, and seconds later it was a bush of stunning petalled flowers that smelled of rich earth.

They all backed away as fast as they could from what was growing around Calem's feet.

"Calem," An'uek lunged forward, grabbed at his arm. "Calem, you have to stop this."

"I'm trying."

"Try harder!" she shouted.

Calem, locked in panic, did the only thing he could do.

He put his hand out and instinctively called forth his flame.

But the flames didn't answer.

He expected a blaze to engulf the unnatural growth. Instead, the grass and flowers stopped growing. They stopped spreading and they stopped moving. And then, as quickly as they had come from nothing, the travellers watched as the grasses and flowers shrivelled and died on their stems and aged in an instant into dust on the ground around their horses' hooves.

The horses quickly calmed down and stopped raking the ground.

The silence of the desert surrounded them again.

None of them knew what to say. None of them could look at Calem. None of them knew what to do until Raef clicked his tongue and his horse walked around to face Calem.

Raef urged his horse closer. Bode tensed in his seat, wishing he had his sword. He looked at An'uek. She flinched but shook her head, urging him to wait.

Raef, unaware of the silent exchange behind him, was focused on Calem, and he slowly leaned towards the boy in the saddle. He raised his hands, dropping his reins, and bent forward.

"Easy," Raef muttered to Calem, who hadn't moved and looked like he might have stopped breathing.

"Don't touch me," he pleaded.

"I won't." Raef moved as slowly as he dared, keenly aware that Calem scared easily and was rubbing his fingertips together. "I'm reaching into the saddlebag," he explained with soft, slow, gentle words.

Having no idea what to expect, Raef closed his hand around whatever it was Bastion had given the boy, and just as slowly he pulled his hand back up.

He reached out to Calem, offering him the lump of raw metal and rock.

"Take it," Raef suggested.

"And do what?" Calem said, sceptical.

"Hold it." Raef did his best to sound encouraging. "Bastion gave this to you for a reason."

Calem sat still, and then, unexpectedly, he reached out and grabbed it from Raef's hand as quickly as a striking viper. He made sure he didn't touch Raef's skin, but still, just from the closeness, Raef felt a sharp tingle move through his hand and up his arm.

Calem grabbed it, held it close to his chest, and squeezed.

An'uek watched as the boy snatched the lump of metal and hid it away, cradling it against his body. There was nothing for the eyes of a man to see, but to her druid sight she watched as a wave of energy swelled around him, red and hot and angry, and as he squeezed the lump, it started to seep into it and dissipate around him.

Bode saw Calem struggling as his breathing got faster and lighter, and then he started to settle as he held the lump of metal and rock.

"It's grounding him," An'uek said as she pulled her mount closer to his. "Whatever it is, it's working."

"How?" Bode asked.

"I've no idea, and I don't think he does either, but let's just be glad for it. We need to move on before nightfall."

With that, she steered her mare round and touched her heels gently to get them going.

It was the horses that moved them on. One by one they turned, fell into line and walked away, carrying their stunned riders.

The steady rhythmic movement of their gait acted like a meditation, and after a time Bode fell in beside Calem.

"If I ask what happened, could you tell me?"

"A little bit leaked out," Calem said, shuddering.

"That's awful," Bode replied. He didn't know what else to say.

"When we get to Kraner, Brennan will help me." Calem nodded, more to himself than Bode. Bode thought he sounded a lot younger than a moment ago, struck by memories of the powerful sorcerer at his side, once a small boy who couldn't take his own dog for a walk without getting lost.

"When we get to Kraner," Raef surprised them both, "the first thing I want is a bath and a shave." He scratched at his beard with ragged dirty fingernails, acting as if recent events hadn't happened. "Then I want to dress up in fine clothes, go to a rich man's house for dinner, steal everything I can fit into my pockets, win at dice, find some laughing women and wake up the next morning not sure which warm body belongs to which set of long legs, then sneak out before any of the ladies wake up and ask me my name." He sighed dramatically. "What about you?" he asked Bode, letting his horse move to the outside of Calem's so he was to the boy's right, Bode on his left.

"I can't follow a night like that."

"No one can," Raef said, chuckling. "That's why it's my night. What will you do?"

"Take off these boots for a start." Bode tensed his feet in the fitted leather. "If I spent the rest of my life in soft woollen hose and sandals, I think I'd be all right with that."

Calem chuckled and turned. "What colour?"

Bode turned and grinned at Calem's question.

"Well, brown of course, to go with the sandals."

The absurd image of Bode in sandals and hosiery made Calem laugh; Bode noticed a genuine smile appear on Raef's face at the sound of the boy's glee.

"They'll make an awful noise in the corridors of the castle."

"I'll have to take them off then if I'm sneaking around the kitchen at night hunting leftover ham and a bit of pastry and ale."

"Ale enough to share with the rest of us I hope," Raef cut in.

"I thought you were going out."

"Well I was, but if you're putting on a small feast I might stick around for that."

"I wouldn't say no to cake," Calem joined in.

"So, ham, pastry, ale, cake… anything else you want while I'm running around after you all night."

"Are you planning a party?" An'uek stalled her mare enough to settle between Raef and Calem and join in.

"We are," Calem replied. "Bode is supplying the food and drink."

"I'll bring the card tricks," Raef said with a flourish of his hand.

"I'll keep my hands to myself. Seems the least I can do," Calem said forlornly.

For a moment no one said a word, then An'uek, despite herself, started to chuckle.

"Best you do," she said gently to him. He tipped his head, his white hair slipping from the confines of the hood of the light cloak he wore.

"If it's a party, we need music for dancing and songs for singing."

"Brennan sings," Calem offered.

"He does," Bode confirmed. "Not very well, but not so badly that I'd throw something at him."

"Homen plays the fiddle," Raef added.

"Does he?" Bode leaned forward to look at Raef. "Well he has to come to the party, that's for sure."

"And when in Kraner, where Homen goes, Lady Cotta is never far behind. The last time I saw her I was dropping off a letter I had acquired for her that she needed to bribe some statesman. I never did get my reward. Maybe I can convince her to dance with me."

"Well, it's a daydream after all, so dream big my friend." Bode smirked, thinking of the last time he had seen Brennan, and the looks he had shared with the woman in Raef's vision.

They rode for another hour oblivious to the real speed and distance being covered by the desert horses. All four indulged in planning the party for their return to Kraner. By the time the sun was closer to the western horizon than its midday peak, there were performers, dancers, a fountain of sweet wine and all the food and drink they could imagine. None of them mentioned what Calem had done.

CHAPTER 22

Their horses took them as far as a towering finger of solitary rock that changed colour in the rays of the setting sun. Sand piled up in waves around dark rock shot through with streaks of red and darker brown. The sky deepened from cerulean blue to deep cobalt as the sun started to slip towards the horizon, becoming a fireball on the edge of the world. The sun's rays hit a few lingering distant clouds, blazing gold across the darkening sky.

Bode helped An'uek out of her saddle, wincing on her behalf as she stretched her arms above her head and rolled her neck on stiff shoulders. The rapidly cooling air chilled her skin as the shadow from the rock swallowed their camp.

Bode took her mare along with the three other horses. He walked them away and set to caring for them.

Raef had been collecting wood for a fire, enough to last the night, and after hauling armfuls back to their camp he finally settled down and put his tinder and flint to some dry grass to get it going. The dry grass caught quicker than a handful of hair in a fireplace, filling the air with a pungent scent that reminded him of the perfume sticks burned by monks in prayer schools in Orania. The cheerful ruddy glow of the flames warmed his hands and his mood. He emptied his waterskin into the small bronze pot he hung over the fire and tossed a handful of vegetables and strips of dried meat in to slowly stew.

"Raef," Bode called over. "She can't eat anything from that it's metal, it'll poison her." Bode stared at the pot.

"Yes, I do remember, you know, you don't have to remind me."

"Sorry." Bode's gruff voice didn't sound apologetic.

"I've no intention of poisoning her," Raef muttered, making a show of moving to a separate pouch and pulling out a small clay pot and equally small clay kettle. He made an exaggerated display of filling the clay pot with water and food, and the small kettle with water and leaves and putting both onto the burning logs in the fire.

"Happy?" he asked, with his hands up.

"Sorry," Bode said again, more sincerely.

About to reply, Raef looked over at Bode, and then around the camp.

"Where is she?" he asked.

Bode stopped grooming the horses, took a step away from his stallion, the currycomb falling from his bandaged hand.

"Where's Calem?"

An'uek had slipped away as soon as Bode had turned his back. She sent her voice specifically to Calem, bidding him to follow as she walked away from the camp.

He followed, creeping behind her in the shadows as she walked to the rock that rose up like a wall behind them.

"Tell me what you want of me," she demanded.

"Just like that? No soft words to make us comfortable."

"I'm comfortable," she replied.

"You have the same look on your face as Bode does when he lies."

"Don't test me with mock audacity," she warned. "I can choose to help you or not. Right now, I'm still deciding."

"I'm sorry." He held up his hands. "I'm just scared," he admitted, "and it makes me wary."

"Fear makes everyone wary. It's a trait of mankind, and one I'm glad to hear you still possess."

"You're glad I'm afraid?"

"Let's say I'm glad you're still you."

"You thought I wasn't?"

She let him think.

"Maybe I was, maybe I'm not anymore," he said softly, the pitch and tone of his voice changing from someone much older to someone much younger, but still broken and rasped. "On the way to the tower I had Isaac's lifetime in my mind. It consumed whatever was me, and I couldn't tell the difference in the end."

"You had to accept it?"

"I did," he said, shrugging.

"You don't seem like the man I got to know on the road to the tower."

"You didn't really know me." He looked at her. "No one does. Maybe Bode, a little, but even then he always looks at me like he's meeting me for the first time. I thought Isaac knew me, and I trusted him because I didn't know myself, so I let it happen. And now I'm split," he tapped his head, "in here, and there's a chasm that's been filled with all this knowledge and power, and it's too much."

"It must hurt."

"No…" his voice raised a little as he lied, "maybe. But it's starting to ease, like I'm finally getting used to it, gluing myself together a bit at a time."

An'uek let herself lean a little closer to him.

"What do you want to tell me…" she coaxed, "that you're too afraid to tell anyone else?"

"That day in the tower, A'taz would have won if he had been there." Calem looked away as he made his confession.

An'uek frowned. It wasn't what she had expected.

"I was already so worried before we even got to the top of the tower, scared for all the lives I knew were in my hands. I already knew what it would've taken to kill him, and it would have killed all of us. I didn't want to. He wouldn't have cared, would have detonated the world to get to me and get that gem, and in that, he was stronger and would have killed us all. But that wasn't what he wanted, and I don't know why."

"It was all a trap, a masterplan none of us can see yet."

"It feels like my fault. Like I should have known because I'm like him."

"And you think you have to atone for it?" Her question made him turn to look at her.

"Of course."

"All roads lead to Kraner," she mused.

"Isn't that what's written in stone over each of the four gates into the city?"

She nodded.

"I need to kill A'taz."

"Will killing him redeem you?"

"It might." He picked up some twigs and started to roll them between his fingers.

An'uek reached over anxiously, and with her hands safe in her gloves, delicately put her fingertips on his, pausing their movement and making him drop the twigs.

He looked away for a long minute, then reached into his pocket and pulled out the lump of metal, turning it over and over, safely, in his hands.

"There's a narrative in my mind, perhaps it's Isaac, or some memory of his from his travels, maybe to your kingdom, I don't know. But the narrative is about fate or free will."

"My people don't hold with fate."

"I don't think my kind do either, but I feel like I was… made," he stressed his words, "and what if I was made to do all this just so I would end up strong enough to wipe him out."

"If that is true, then he was made with a purpose too?"

Calem weighed the metal, passing it from hand to hand.

An'uek thought she could hear a faint hum resonating from the lump each time he moved it.

"Now, I'm so powerful, the struggle won't be to kill A'taz, it's going to be not wiping out all of Barclan when I do."

An'uek had to stop herself from physically recoiling.

"I need you to teach me to control it."

"What?" she asked, shocked. "I'm no teacher, no sorcerer, I'm a druid, I—"

"A'taz was once a druid," Calem said, cutting her off. "An'eris is a druid. Isaac learned from the druids. I have some of those memories. I have the knowledge but not the teachings."

"Calem, I can't teach you. Your power is unfathomable to me. I can't begin to teach you to wield it."

"You don't need to teach me to use it… just control it, control myself." Calem got onto his knees; he reached for her but didn't touch her. "Don't see me as all these things I am because of what everyone else made me to be. Just start at the beginning, like you would any child."

"Calem—" She stressed his name, but again he interrupted her.

"I'll learn." He sat back on his haunches.

"And what if I do something wrong?" She got to her feet, wrapped the long shawl around her body as a deep chill settled in her bones. "What if I damage you, what if I teach you something and it all comes pouring out? What if I teach you control, and you grasp it, and—"

"And I become the next A'taz?"

His words silenced her.

"Isn't that what you're afraid of? He's the shame of all druids, isn't he? The ugly truth of what could happen?"

"Yes," she said, defiant at his words. "Yes, he is. But we both know he can die. What if I teach you and you become something far, far worse?"

"You once said I was something like an abomination." He shuffled over to her on his knees.

"Yes, I did."

"You're right." He turned sad young eyes on her, finally capturing her gaze. "I'm that and more. I'm lost at the edge of a dark waterfall, and I'm so close to going over the edge. This power is an anchor trying to pull me into the same space that A'taz fell into so that I'll give up and let it free from inside me. But I'm not over the brink yet. You can save me."

"What if I can't?"

"What if you can?"

She turned and walked away.

"Does he know?" she asked.

"A'taz, about me?"

"Yes."

"He must sense it. Why he hasn't struck out, sent some form of attack, I don't know."

"Could he do, for himself, what was done to you?"

"No." Calem shook his head. "But he has three gems. His power is unlike mine, but it's still world-breaking."

"But you believe you have the upper hand?"

"I do, for now, but only because he hasn't found what he's looking for in Kraner. If he finds it, and he has those gems, then for all I am, I don't know what it'll take to stop him."

She walked back to him.

"You mean the lake?"

Calem remembered his journey across with Isaac, in the boat, in the dark. It seemed so long ago he wondered if it was someone else's life.

He remembered An'eris.

"Yes." He nodded. "The lake under Kraner, formed from the first tears of Evram's song."

"The start of all life on our world."

"The very same."

"He's looking for it?"

"He is."

"How do you know?"

"Because it's what I would do if I was him."

"Why?"

"To harness the power of the Gods, to remake the world. To have the Gods bow to me."

"Oh, Calem." An'uek buried her face in her hands. "Only one druid in a lifetime is born with the knowledge of how to find it under the city. An'eris is the only one who knows where it is, and she would die before revealing it."

"I know where it is."

An'uek covered her mouth in horror.

"So did Isaac," Calem confessed. "She must have told him. It's where he took me when he poured his lifetime into me."

"She wouldn't."

"She did."

"She wouldn't." An'uek glared at him.

"She must have."

"Why would she do that, betray our people, betray the Gods, doom our world?"

"Can't you imagine why?" Calem asked, his voice calm, mature. "It's the same reason you've made some of the decisions you have."

An'uek wanted to weep but bit the inside of her lip instead.

"Too much time with your kind." An'uek turned cold eyes on him.

"It changes you," Calem said, unconsciously reaching for her.

"Get away from me." An'uek stepped back from him until she was standing against the rock wall and could go no further.

"I'm sorry," Calem said, his voice quieter. "I'm sorry for all of this. For Orren, for Jedda, for all the dead. For A'taz, the fires, for Isaac and Brennan and everyone else I'll touch along the way."

He collapsed at her feet, dropping the block of metal between his knees.

"I'm sorry." He reached for her again. "I'm so sorry." His voice echoed unnaturally off the rock behind him, filling the still night. "But please," he begged, "don't leave me like this. Help me. Give me a chance of setting all this right."

He leaned so close, staring up at her from beneath her gaze. Her tears fell from her cheeks onto his upturned face below, sizzling and burning his skin. He flinched at its touch, little scars blossoming on his cheeks where her tears fell.

An'uek saw the way he reacted to her tears, the way she marked him.

"Impossible," she mumbled, her eyes wide in shock.

He put his fingertips to his face, feeling the pockmarks on his once smooth skin.

"You can hurt me," he told her. "Surely that's fate."

Bode ate his meal in silence sitting across from Calem and An'uek. He refused to look at her. The campfire flickered between them, casting their shadows like dark figures fighting in the night.

When he was finished, he sat quietly until everyone else was done, then gathered up their wooden bowls to clean them and pack everything away into the saddlebags.

He set himself into his bedroll, put his back to the fire, and pretended to sleep.

The only sound was the whinnying of the horses and the crackle of the dry sticks on the coals.

Raef poked the fire, added another four stout logs and built the flames up.

"I'll keep first watch," he said, rising to his feet.

"You don't need to," An'uek said to him. "Nothing will hurt us here."

Raef looked at Calem, then at Bode.

"All the same, I'll keep watch."

He walked away into the night. The others could only just make out his shape as he found somewhere to sit and turned his face away, to stare into the night.

Bode lay motionless. Too still, breathing too evenly.

"I'll also go to sleep." Calem turned to An'uek. "I think I'm tired."

He got up carefully and shuffled to the bedroll set out for him earlier. He burrowed into it, making himself as small as he could. An'uek sat and listened, expecting to hear him fidget, but within minutes he was dozing.

She let herself smile as her gaze rested on the jumbled heap of blankets and robes that hid the most powerful being she had ever encountered.

She turned her gaze to the perfectly still sleeping form of Bode. She was sure he was holding his breath. Getting up, on silent feet, she padded across the hard ground, coming to sit on her haunches just beside him. She shifted onto her backside, leaning her back against his, eventually lying down, still pressed against him back to back, facing the fire where he faced the night.

"Why are you so angry with me?" she asked. "I don't like arguing with you like we did earlier."

He didn't answer. She didn't expect him to.

"Is it because I scared you? You turned around and I was gone?"

She felt his back arch.

"Is it because I said yes to Calem?"

Bode twitched.

"Is it because you think Calem will hurt me?"

She noticed how cold he felt even through his blanket.

"He won't."

He went still again.

"You have to trust me."

"I have to keep you safe," Bode finally replied. "If you sneak away, I can't do that."

She thought about his words, the hurt conveyed in his voice.

"We start tomorrow."

"And what will happen?"

"Whatever happens will happen."

They were silent for a while.

"It's because I care for you," he said softly.

"I know." She rolled over and shuffled up enough to snake an arm around his neck and hold him tight. She lay on the hard earth, waiting for him to fall asleep, her fingers combing through his hair.

"Will you always care for me?" she asked the sleeping man in the dark night. "No matter what happens?"

She kissed the back of his head.

An'uek didn't go to sleep; she lay gazing at the fire, her thoughts wandering along the moonlight, unconsciously reaching out for the minds of other druid far-criers. She sensed them: some in their homes in their perpetually hidden land, some wandering in solitude in kingdoms beyond Barclan's borders, some in their aging slumber. She didn't call out to them, and any who sensed her voice only felt it like a whisper of breath in a storm.

As her mind wandered, the stars sparkled overhead and gossamer ribbons of violet light appeared above her in the night sky. An'uek turned her gaze upwards to watch the dazzling clouds of falling luminescence flow across her vision as if she was lying on the bottom of a river seeing neon colours in the water flowing over her still body.

She tried not to blink in case she missed a second of the magnificent show, the colours reflected in her amethyst eyes. A warmth infused her skin, and finally looking away, she looked down at her body bathed in glimmering splendour.

She jumped to her knees, feeling the sudden press of time against her.

Bode was asleep. Raef was sitting at his self-imposed guard post, his back straight. Calem, dreaming, had kicked his way out of his blanket and was lying with his limbs everywhere on the other side of the fire.

An'uek glanced upwards once more, the violent radiance above her undulating faster, the colour stronger.

"Forgive me." She leaned forward and put her hand on Bode's forehead, pushing him into deep sleep. "I wish I didn't have to do this without you, but I know you won't understand."

An'uek snuck up to Raef, her steps so light there was barely a footprint to mark her footfall. But still he turned towards her just as she reached him a second too late.

Touching him as she had Bode, she saw his eyes widen in surprise just as they closed into unconsciousness. Falling forward, she caught him easily, laying him gently on the ground before turning back to the camp, to the fire, and beyond that to where Calem lay sleeping.

Each step was slow and measured as she thought through what she was about to do.

She removed one glove.

Moving around the fire, she knelt next to him.

She removed the other glove.

On her knees, she settled next to him.

His cloak had come loose in his sleep, and the hood usually pulled low had fallen back, exposing his pale skin and white hair.

She could see the subtle ever-present aura of orange flames flickering across his skin even as he slept. Like a baby holding a blanket, in one hand he gripped the lump of metal.

She took a steadying breath, keenly aware of how fast her heart was beating and how her hands had started to shake.

She unwrapped the long white shawl from her head and shoulders, flinging it behind her. Her long silvery hair hung down her back in a thick braid reflecting the colours shining above, like a waterfall of light cascading over her, surrounding her. Silhouetted by the brilliance of the light show, her eyes were in dark shadow, only the sharp outline of her features faintly visible on her hidden face.

"Wake up," she commanded to his mind.

His eyes snapped open.

Calem lay on the hard, cold ground. He awoke instantly to a glowing creature of another world hovering over him, the whole of existence transformed into a radiant river flowing around her.

"Touch me," she ordered.

He obeyed.

When Bode woke up, the first thing he did was roll over and call for An'uek.

"I'm over here."

He heard her voice a little way off, towards where Raef had gone to sit the night before, but something about her sounded off. Rubbing his hand across his face, he peeled himself out of his bedroll, yawned, and had to stretch to get his legs to work. His eyelids felt so heavy he was having trouble waking up.

"Bode?" He heard Raef call him.

"In a second," he replied gruffly.

"Stay here a moment please." He heard An'uek talking to Raef, and then heard the shuffle of boots crossing the dirt.

He yawned again and a familiar hand squeezed his shoulder. Still rubbing his eyes, he covered her hand with his own, patting it gently.

Holding it still under his own.

His instinct told him something was different a moment before his hand registered the difference.

The small hand on his shoulder was bigger.

He flicked his head round, his eyes finally opening properly, and saw An'uek, standing before him, a grown woman.

On his knees, for the first time staring up at her standing over him, Bode opened his mouth, closed it, opened it again.

He reached out towards her then stopped, his brow creasing as he started to sit back and move away.

An'uek reached for his hand, capturing it and holding it in both of her own.

"It's me," she promised.

"Who are you?" he muttered.

"Bode, it's me." She stepped closer to him, leaned down until they were sharing the same space, breathing the same air.

"It's me," she said again. Releasing one of his hands, she slowly lifted her fingertips to his forehead, rubbing her thumb across his brow, smoothing the lines of worry and shock, running her fingers through his hair.

Leaning over him, as she did the first day she'd met him, she pressed her forehead against his, and he knew it was her.

Gasping, almost falling back but held in her strong grasp, Bode looked at her.

She gently released him.

"How?" It was all he could say.

"There's magic here." She looked out across the landscape, over at Calem. "We threw a stone into the flow of time." She paused, leaned down to pick a blade of grass growing near where Bode kneeled. She presented it to him.

He held the stem in his fingers, staring down.

"I don't understand."

"I know."

Still holding one hand, she carried on running long fingers through his beard and up into his hair, holding his head. She sensed his confusion, felt it shifting in his mind, felt it turning to distrust.

Acting on impulse, she let herself fall to her knees in front of him, surprising herself for a second when she didn't have to crane her neck up to look at him.

As she had done time and time again when he had carried her, sat with her nestled in his lap, held her in his arms throughout their journey, she tried to burrow against him.

"I don't know you like this," he said coldly, carefully holding her at arm's length and leaning away.

He shuffled back, got stiffly to his feet, and walked away.

She turned to follow him but was stopped by a strong hand holding her arm.

"Leave him," Raef said softly.

"He's upset."

"Of course he is." Raef didn't keep the scorn from colouring his words. "Look at you. We wake up and you're someone else telling us to just accept it and be okay? It's insane."

"It's not," An'uek shot back.

"You should have told him what you were going to do."

"I wasn't so sure myself until I knew I had to do it."

"And this was your only option?" He gestured up and down. "What, being taller, older, somehow now you can do more than you could yesterday."

"Yes. You don't understand."

"Of course we don't!" he yelled. "We don't understand any of this." He raised his arms, gesturing to the emptiness of the endless desert.

"My people age differently. Who we are, what we are in our youth, is not who we are or what we are in our later years."

"I don't care," he snapped at her. "Really, I don't. I know you're still you, you have that same arrogance to you that you had yesterday," he pointed at her, "but you should have told us. After everything that's happened," he shouted, "you chose to do this now, to break all trust now?"

Raef stepped away from her.

"I didn't plan this." Her voice was calm but her hands shook.

"You put us to sleep." The words hit her like an accusation. "You knew what you were going to do, don't play the innocent little girl."

"I was never a little girl." She turned on him, staring him in the eyes. "I've already lived longer than any of you ever will, and what I chose to do to get this thing done is my choice."

"If you believed that, you wouldn't be so heartbroken over Bode walking away from you."

"I'm heartbroken because I love him and he just looked at me like I'm a stranger," she shouted at Raef.

"You are a stranger," Raef shouted back, the two squaring up to each other. "I know you're not," he said a little softer, "I just don't know why you didn't trust him enough to tell him."

"Because I had seconds to decide." She wanted to screech at him but held her calm.

"And if you'd had time?"

"Then he would have convinced me to let him stand by me when it happened."

"And would that have been so bad?"

"Yes." She balled up her fists, her voice breaking.

"Why?" Raef asked, his voice lower.

"Because I might have killed him."

"You, or that horror?" Raef said softly, just for her ears, but he pointed at Calem.

"He had nothing to do with this." An'uek stood up to Raef, stepped closer, pulling herself to her new height to loom over him. "I used him."

"What?" Bode's deep voice, full of sorrow and distrust interrupted them both.

Startled, An'uek turned and reached for him, grabbing the cloth of his tunic before he could pull away from her.

"I didn't know if it would work." The sob broke through her mask of control and her features softened. "I guessed it would after seeing what happened to the grass and the flowers, but I didn't know. Last night, I felt the pull of the aging sleep come over me. If I was in my lands, I'd have felt it as a gentle tug, nothing more than a fleeting thought, and I'd have years to prepare and I'd have gone to sleep for decades and grown surrounded by song. But here, in this place, around him, it was an onslaught. I had barely minutes to prepare, and it was like a wild urge swelling in me. I hardly knew what I was doing myself..." Her words faded away. She looked at Bode, to Raef, and over to Calem, who was still sitting with his back to all of them.

"I didn't give him a choice. I made him do it. I was compelled by something beyond my control."

"And just like that, it happened?"

"Years... in a few seconds," she said solemnly. "The aging slumber of the druids, when we grow into ourselves and emerge renewed. It's meant to be beautiful, a time of pure peace and rest when our thoughts and our lives mix with the world and we come undone as we were and are remade into who we are, finally connected to each other and to our lands."

She let him go, stepped back and looked down at herself, in the clothes Sona had dressed her in, stretched over longer arms and legs, tight against her body.

"And now what?" Bode asked, his voice flat from behind them.

"Now we carry on," she proffered.

Raef, furious, slapped his thigh, about to speak, but Bode threw a glance that silenced him.

"Calem." Bode called to the boy without turning to look at him. "Get yourself together, get your things tied onto your saddle. We're mounting up in half an hour."

Calem immediately did as he was told.

"Raef," Bode directed, "prepare the horses."

"Right," the thief replied, the set of his jaw so tight Bode thought he'd crack his own teeth.

"And me?" An'uek asked.

Bode turned his head, his eyes searching the horizon, scanning the skies, looking any way he could other than at her.

Eventually, he turned to face her.

"I feel like this is harder than it should be." He frowned. "I know it's you." He touched his hand to his forehead.

"But?"

"But?" he said incredulously. "But, look at you, you're a different person. I can barely believe this."

She waited, the silence growing.

"But," he said eventually, "but it is you, isn't it?"

She nodded.

"It is me." She stepped closer. "I'm still the same woman I was yesterday, but I know I look different. And in many ways, I am. I know more now. When we age, when we wake up, we have parts of the ancient knowledge of our people open to us. That part of me has awakened now, and I need it to be able to help the boy."

Bode chuckled, which seemed to surprise An'uek, changing the mood for a second.

"What?" she asked him, the corner of her lips curling.

"It's funny to hear you say boy when yesterday you were so like a little girl who couldn't put her own foot in her stirrups."

She took his hands in hers.

"I was never a little girl," she said to him. "Are we going to get past this?" she asked and Bode heard genuine fear in the question.

He squeezed her hands.

"I don't know," he said honestly, warmth returning to his eyes as he spoke to her. "I feel like a part of me should be grieving."

An'uek pulled on his hands and brought him to her, wrapping her arms gently around his bandage-covered body.

"I know," she said sadly, her mouth close to his ear. "But please, please," she begged, as she put her hands on his face and kissed his eyelids. "Please remember I came back for you. No one else. I chose them because of you," she said, straight into his mind. "We can still be a family, if that's what you still want."

He looked to Raef, to Calem, and back to her. Then he hugged her more tightly.

A'taz walked through the streets of Kraner, taking his time to buy small things, stop for a warm mug of spiced tea or a finger of strong brandy. He found ways to introduce himself to as many people as he could reasonably stop for aimless banter, making men and women laugh, young children grin and the old and frail feel warmed to their bones.

The people felt good, really good, after speaking to him. They couldn't quite remember what they'd talked about, but they were sure he was getting things done. They couldn't say what things, but they felt really good about life on that cold early winter day.

He found his way to one of the demolition sites, pleased to see the buildings had already been torn down and the foundations were being laid for the first of the chapels on the land the Queen had granted him.

"Master Gavis?" One of the workmen stepped towards him.

"Yes," A'taz replied, plastering a benevolent smile across his carefully crafted features.

"Are you here for the blessings before we lay the first stone?"

"Indeed I am." His smile widened into genuine pleasure.

"Are you a cleric then?" the man asked.

"I was ordained as a younger man." A'taz rolled out a response to the workman. "I am a servant of the Gods and they will bless this land through me."

"Well, as you're a stonemason then, do you want to lay the first stone yourself?"

A'taz, genuinely surprised at the idea, reached out and grabbed the man's shoulder.

"What a splendid idea," he said, delighted. "I hadn't thought of that."

"Happy to be of service then." The workman dipped his head respectfully. "I'll get the men to clear off the site. If you give us half an hour, we'll be ready for you."

"Good, see to it."

"Will you be needing anything from us for the benediction then?"

A'taz cocked his head to the side.

"What do you mean?"

"Well, Master, we've none of us been around one of these ceremonies before. Here in Kraner the crown doesn't hold with blessing land, we just build or rebuild as needs be. Quick and fast and stable is our way. So we've no idea if there's anything to be done or if you'll just be saying some prayers and then we'll get straight back to it."

A'taz put a finger to his lips and regarded the man for a moment.

"There's usually a few clerics singing prayers, and although there are some that came here with me from Aquam, they are at their midday prayers and I wouldn't dare break their liturgy."

"We could help?" The man seemed compelled to offer, the feeling of A'taz's hand on his shoulder prodding his words.

"Could you?"

"Maybe, if you tell us what to sing... to say, or whatever. I'm sure we can do it."

"It's a simple chant, only a few lines. The key is repetition, to really believe in what you're saying, to put as much of yourself into it as you can so I can draw the power from it and strengthen the blessing, strengthen the presence here. Give yourself to me, through the song, so to speak."

"Me and the lads can do that," the man said, nodding and raising his hand to point at the other men working on the site. "I'll get them over here. Tell us what to practise and we can get whatever you want in our heads while we tidy the site."

"That," A'taz said, licking his lips, "would be ever so special."

An hour later A'taz felt like a man twenty years younger; he had to focus on maintaining his old appearance and not let the life he had siphoned from the group of workmen give him away. It wouldn't do for the old stonemason from Aquam to sprint through the city back uphill to the castle.

He chose streets jammed with people, making his walk back naturally slower and putting himself in people's way. As he turned into a side street his keen hearing picked up the soft murmurs of snuffles and sobs.

Sensing distress and fear, he looked around and pinpointed a little girl near the end of the street close to an alley. He made his way over, approaching her carefully so not to frighten her. She was sitting on a low bench outside a cobbler's store.

He sat down on the bench as far away as was possible. The girl didn't look at him but he could see her eyes were red from crying and her nose was runny.

"What's the matter?" he asked gently.

She looked at him, wiped her nose on her sleeve, but didn't reply.

"Are you lost?"

She turned to look into the doorway of the shop, her eyes resting on a woman at the counter in conversation with the cobbler.

"Your mother?"

The girl regarded him then shook her head.

"Your sister?"

The girl nodded.

"Why are you crying?" he asked again, scooting up a tiny amount. "Are you in trouble?"

"I lost a bag," she replied, her tiny voice escaping between sobs.

"What was in the bag?"

"New boots for winter."

A'taz reached over and, slowly, the little girl let him wipe a tear from her cheek.

"Are you in trouble for losing them?"

She nodded.

"I bet they cost lots of coins."

"They did." Her face crumpled as she started to cry. "Maisie says if I don't find them, I'll get a beating, but I don't know where I lost them."

"What are you doing here then?"

"Maisie is asking Mister Thom if anyone brought them back to the shop." She started to hiccup as she cried, unable to say anymore.

Just then, the woman who must have been her sister stepped outside.

"What are you doing?" she asked suspiciously, stepping into the small space between her sister and the strange man sitting far too close to her.

"I was asking if she was all right." A'taz stood up slowly, offering his hand to the older girl. "My name is Gavis. I'm from the castle."

"Come on, Cilla." The older sister reached behind and grabbed her sister, hauling her to her feet. Without a word, she turned and marched them away up the street.

"I hope you find your shoes," A'taz called after them, raising his hand to wave before looking at the thumb he had used to wipe the tear and putting it to his mouth to lick the salty taste of her sadness off his skin.

High-spirited, and feeling bloated on life, A'taz turned sharply and stepped straight into a man walking past him in the street.

They side-stepped around each other, both mumbling apologies and turning to carry on their way. A'taz stopped in the street to straighten the collar on his tunic, listening to the idle chatter of people passing by, revelling in how good he felt. The city was so full of life and he planned to enjoy it.

Clasping his hands behind his back, he turned in the general direction of the castle and was about to set off when he was overcome with a sudden weight pressing down on him.

He staggered forward and fell to his knees in the street, barely able to lift his head.

Shaking, and on his hands and knees, he choked up mouthfuls of spit that dribbled out of his parted lips, a sheen of sweat breaking out across his body. Dampness seeped into his clothes and within moments he was sodden, his tunic clinging to his body like he'd just got out of a tub of water fully dressed.

"Are you all right?" Someone passing by stopped and knelt next to him.

"Help me," he gasped, starting to cough up water.

Strong arms grabbed him and tried to pull him up.

"What the—?" The person abruptly let him go and stepped away as A'taz started to retch in the street, small clumps of mud spewing from his lips.

A'taz heard voices around him but couldn't make out any words. He was only vaguely aware of people hurrying away from him.

Disorientated, he finally stopped bringing up the mud, stopped spitting out mouthfuls of water, and collapsed down to lie in the street.

He rolled onto his back, opened his eyes and watched in a surreal stupor as the cerulean blue sky seemed to briefly flicker to amethyst and lilac.

The old man who had fallen down and been sick in the street howled up at the sky, his shrieking screams so loud and angry it shook the roof tiles of the buildings near where he lay, and all the dogs in the city cowered and found somewhere to hide for the rest of the day.

CHAPTER 23

An'eris ran as fast as she could through the slippery sewers under the streets of Kraner. She was fifty yards from the secret hatch that would take her into the cold light of day and the safety of strangers who would surely save her from the group of men chasing her down like starving dogs smelling fresh meat.

Thirty yards.

She could see the light coming through the breaks in the wooden slats illuminating the ladder she needed to reach.

She heard men's voices shouting her name.

Twenty yards.

She put her hands across her stomach, breathing as hard as she could as she forced her legs to move forward.

Ten yards.

She heard the whipping sound a second before she felt the sting across the back of her legs, then her vision was tipping forward and the light streaming down fell sideways as she lost her footing and crashed head first, skidding along the dirty cobblestones.

Five yards.

She screamed in anger and pain, her sight turning red with her own blood flowing freely across her face, but she got to her feet and raced to the hatch.

She reached forward, a foot away from grabbing the wall and being able to haul herself forward; again she heard the crack of the whip and knew that pain was coming.

This time the whip fell across her back and she screamed for all the world to hear; as she fell forward, hands grabbed at her arms and legs.

Immediately she kicked, tried to twist and throw herself away from them. A hand in her hair gripped as hard as it dared and pulled her body down onto the floor, other hands and knees pinning her under their weight.

"Where's he?" one of them shouted to another.

"He was behind us," someone replied.

"He's coming."

An'eris thrashed at them, trying to break free, straining to bite and scratch until a huge hand grabbed her throat and started to squeeze.

"Careful, don't snap her neck."

"Just choke her a bit."

"If she can't breathe, she'll settle down."

"Where is he?" someone raged.

An'eris moved from rage to smothering fear in as many moments as it took her to realise she couldn't draw breath and the baby inside her was starting to flutter and move in response to her mother's suffocation.

She lowered her hands from a nameless face and put them over her belly.

"Ease up a bit," she heard someone say, but the words sounded far away as the roaring drumming of her heartbeat muted everything else.

She could breath, but only barely.

Giving up, she lay still on the cold stone sewer floor, held down by Troy's men.

Behind the panic and the frenzied anger, a small quiet voice reminded her she had to focus on breathing, on being still, or the desire to fight, to try and break free, would be the thing that killed them both.

An'eris squeezed her eyes shut, her mouth open, gasping for air, fists clenched as she fought her own instinct to keep trying to break free.

As she forced her lungs to expand under the weight of the knees leaning on her chest, she willed her mind to calm. She kept thinking of her baby, breathing for the baby. It was the only thing left to do.

It was easier to breathe out. The pressure from the man kneeling on her forced her lungs to decompress so quickly she started to feel warm as her head felt heavy and she lost the feeling in her body.

Breathing in, breathing out, she barely noticed the echoing sound of wooden-heeled boots clipping along until Troy was there.

He kneeled next to her. The man holding her down moved out the way. Troy braced his hands on either side of her head and moved over her, straddling her chest, pinning her under his body. He sat up, content she couldn't move, staring straight down over her face so the only place she could look was up at him.

"That was a good chase," he said, dramatically wiping his brow with the lace cuff of his finely embroidered velvet tunic. "I didn't think you'd get this far."

"I'll always run," she said between gasps.

"Is that so." Troy leaned down, his deformed mouth grinning at her, as if his face was splitting apart.

"Always," she mouthed, struggling to breathe.

"Not if I kill you first."

"Go ahead." An'eris grinned back as her lips started to discolour from red to blue. Trying to lift her head, she made sure he heard her. "Do it. I dare you."

Troy stared down at the druid, the woman, this Queen utterly helpless under him, dying on her back in a sewer, who refused to look anywhere but straight at him.

He wanted nothing more than to drag his nails down her and tear the skin off her pretty face, and jab his thumbs into her eyes to make her stop staring.

He knew his master would not be pleased if he did that.

He had no choice. He lifted his weight off her body, just a little, and then stood up, kicking her as he moved away.

She choked, gulping in as much air as she could as quickly as she could, rolling onto her side to curl around her belly and aching ribs.

"Bitch, I'll make sure you die," he said, but in the long sewer tunnels, his hollow words echoed back, and for a moment Troy heard voices in the dark repeating "you'll die" and he felt a shiver run through his body.

"Carry her back," Troy said to whoever was nearest. "Bring her to my master's chamber. He needs her prepared for a dinner with the council tonight."

Across the city, A'rrick and Travis kept their heads down and their hoods up as they walked through the main streets towards the castle. Travis resisted the urge to scratch his freshly shaven chin. He went to run his hand through his hair, then stopped, remembering it was gone. Cut as close to his head as he could without going bald, the simple change meant he was a different man. He took a pull from the small flask hidden in the pocket of his thick brown woollen cloak. He offered it to A'rrick, who thanked him but declined as he fiddled with the cuffs of his sleeves.

Tucking it away again, Travis started to casually roll a smoke as they made their way, through the city.

"I didn't expect Kris to agree, but I'm glad he did," Travis said as he licked the paper to stick the edges down. He stopped to ask a passer-by for a light, thanked him and they continued.

"He's one of yours?"

Travis sort of shrugged.

"Yes and no. Most of the time I forget about him and Rolo." Travis looked at A'rrick from under his hood. "But then, that's part of the magic of the castle, isn't it?"

"I think so," A'rrick agreed, pulling the laces of his leather vest tighter across his chest.

"You think?"

"I know I'm old, but even I'm not old enough to have been around when the druids and your kin built this place, but it feels like that's the reason."

"I don't much care for magic today or any day. I just need to get this done, and if we're doing something with the crown, then Kris and Rolo have to do it."

Travis took another deep pull on his smoke and uncapped the flask, emptying it.

"I'm surprised you could pull all this together so soon," A'rrick commented, stepping aside to let a man and woman move past him up the street, careful to avoid any accidental contact.

"Cotta demands it." Travis assumed that was explanation enough.

A'rrick chuckled, understanding.

"That she does," he agreed. "Still, it must have taken all night and most of yesterday."

"That doesn't matter. The castle is never asleep, and I can keep going when I need to." They turned a corner into Bakers Row and immediately had to slow down because of the press of people.

"Still," A'rrick continued, "it's quite the risk you took. I know you've been moving around the city a bit, but heading back to the castle to find your people not knowing which ones even are still your people. That takes something else."

"Kirin was busy. There's no one else but me to do my dirty work."

Travis mused on A'rrick's words as they stepped around men, women, children, dogs, and more children.

"Is the city always like this?" A'rrick asked, irritation at the edge of his words as, again, he had to step around a group of people standing and eating in the street.

"Everyone is getting ready for the winter festival in a few days. People come to the city from everywhere else. Hot bread, a warm drink, people are enjoying the day if they aren't working."

"It's busy." A'rrick pulled his cloak a little tighter.

The simple gesture and his understatement spoke volumes to Travis, and without saying anything he led them towards a crossroads that would take them off the main streets and through relatively quieter parts of the city but still heading up to the castle.

"Kris, Rolo, they're not my people exactly," Travis said thoughtfully. "They belong to the crown."

"Can they do what we need?"

"I trust them." Travis flicked the butt of his smoke against a brick wall, stamping it out with the heel of his boot. "They helped Denny when they didn't have to. They got Brennan and Cotta out."

"But you don't actually know them that well?"

"My old master knew them when they were boys, knew their families. I knew them briefly, but like I said, they're always forgotten."

"Is that enough?" A'rrick asked thoughtfully, his voice noticeably less strained as the crowds thinned out.

"It's going to have to be." Travis stepped closer, lowering his voice. "Homen would have known them too."

"Would have?"

"Homen knew everyone." Travis had to look away for a minute. "Besides, we're committed now."

They continued walking.

"Where do you think Cotta has got to?"

"She'll be at the castle by now with Marsha."

There was no sharp wind, but Travis felt colder and hugged himself inside his cloak.

"And the squire?"

"He'll be at the western gates by the time we get her there." Travis sounded more hopeful than sure.

"Let's pick up the pace then," A'rrick suggested.

"No," Travis said, sniffing. "Best not to be loitering around the castle if we get there too early."

"Right."

As they continued, A'rrick slowed until he stopped.

"What is it, friend?" Travis asked.

A soft snowfall had begun from a few heavy clouds moving across the sky above them. The white flecks settled on the two men, who came to a stop under a narrow balcony above them and a few feet away from a grated wooden hatch in the street.

"It's An'eris."

Travis watched as the almost supernaturally calm and unshakeable druid lord started to fidget and shift on his feet.

Travis waited.

"I just have this sense." A'rrick spoke to his hands. "I feel like she's near."

"Near now?"

"Yes." A'rrick looked around, up and down the street, at the people nearby and far away as if searching for her. His eyes widened and he dashed over to the nearest woman, grabbing her and turning her to face him.

"Get off me," the woman shrieked, pushing A'rrick away.

"Sorry." Travis stepped in. "My friend thought you were someone else." Travis apologised and grabbed A'rrick before he could rush off to the next woman.

"She's not here," he hissed, holding the slender strong druid by the shoulders. "Do you hear me, A'rrick? An'eris is not on the street."

"She's near," he argued, frantically looking around. "I can feel her. I can feel the baby."

Without warning, A'rrick fell.

"She can't breathe," he gasped. "She's dying. They're dying."

Travis forced a laugh and waved at the people stopping and staring at them in the street.

"Just a bit too much brandy at lunch," he said, chuckling. "Come on, up on your feet."

Travis bent down and grabbed A'rrick's cloak, pulling his face to his own but hiding them from sight.

"You can't do this here, not now."

A'rrick wasn't listening, his sight was elsewhere.

"They're choking her."

Travis felt the shadow before he heard the voices, as two men appeared behind them.

"What's going on here?" a man wearing the tunic and armour of Travis's own city guard called over to him.

Travis didn't recognise his face but didn't dare challenge the imposter.

"Nothing," he reiterated, "just drunk."

"Bit early to be falling over in the streets."

"He doesn't hold his liquor well."

"Then get him home."

"I will." Travis thanked them and waited for them to leave. As he raised his hand to wave them on, his cloak fell back, exposing his face.

Travis froze.

The man looked down at him but didn't recognise him.

"Be on your way then," the new city guard said, hitching up his belt under his ill-fitting breastplate, and he turned and walked away.

Travis let out the breath he didn't know he was holding and reached down, grabbing A'rrick and pulling him up.

"They're leaving," Travis said, getting him to his feet.

"I can't feel her anymore," A'rrick murmured, back to himself again as if he had momentarily had a bad daydream.

"You can't do that," Travis insisted, gripping A'rrick's cloak in his fists. "You can't just... whatever that was, you can't."

"I can't not," A'rrick said. "She was near, I know she was."

"We're nowhere near the castle," Travis protested, breathing so hard from the stress of moments ago that his cheeks were red and puffed out as he took quick shallow breaths.

"It was her," he repeated. "She's trying to escape."

Travis thought that through, his mind, honed on military strategy, working through what that would mean.

"Then we've run out of time." He let A'rrick go, smoothing over the creases from where he'd grabbed him. "If she's trying to escape, if A'taz's control of her is slipping, or if she's fighting it, he won't linger, and we don't have time to figure out his plan and work out what our play is. We thought we had time, we were wrong."

"She's fighting him, they both are, her and the baby. But she's tired, she can't carry on for much longer."

"We have to get her help then, get someone into the castle to protect her until we have our own plan."

"I can't go in," A'rrick contested.

"I wasn't thinking of you."

"Then who?" A'rrick stopped speaking as Travis raised his finger to silence him.

"I need to come up with something," Travis said to himself, putting his hand on A'rrick's shoulder. "Let's get Marsha and Denny out of the city, then get back to the shop. I need something to help me think."

A'rrick waited a heartbeat.

"What do you mean, help you think?"

Travis squeezed his shoulder.

"Don't worry about me. I'm the man that brought food back to Kraner, aren't I? I'll think of something."

Marsha and Cotta huddled together talking quietly just outside the western gatehouse of the outer bailey.

"This is utter madness," Marsha pointed out.

"No," Cotta disagreed. "Right now, the best place to hide is in plain sight. No one is looking for us here, and the people looking for us aren't here."

"You might have changed how you look, but I'll be recognised."

"That's why I need you to keep you hood up and your voice low," Cotta chided, fussing with Marsha's cloak, retying it more times than needed.

"Remind me," Marsha raised her eyebrows, "who is the Queen here?"

"Is it me if I'm holding the crown?" Cotta joked.

Marsha didn't smile. The look she gave Cotta made the younger woman wish she hadn't said anything.

"Never mind," Cotta mumbled, clutching the heavy leather satchel in her arms a little tighter. "They'll be here any minute."

"Let's keep looking like we belong here then," Marsha suggested, her eyes on the satchel.

Her words hit Cotta in the gut and she raised herself up, her back straight.

"I do belong here," she declared.

"I know." Reaching out to put her arms around Cotta, Marsha drew her in, holding her as close as she dared. "There's more of this place in your blood than there ever was from Falconfall."

Cotta was about to respond when a man wearing a black tunic embroidered with the royal mark stepped up to them.

Cotta looked into his face and recognised him. Her body went rigid.

Marsha, feeling Cotta stiffen at the sight of the man, sensed it was nothing to do with fright. She could feel the warmth draining out of Cotta's body as she looked at him.

"What are you ladies doing here?" he asked, his voice thick with suspicion.

"Waiting for my brother," Cotta replied. "We're taking our mother home for winter."

"Are you now?" The man stepped closer and moved the shawl back from her face. It fell to her shoulders, freeing her short black hair, exposing her still-bruised face.

"Not had a good time of things recently?" he asked, his gaze running down her body.

"No," she answered, her voice flat.

Marsha, her arms still round Cotta, felt her twitch and her hand go to her belt.

"The lads will be here soon," she said gently to Cotta, trying to take hold of her hands, but her words were aimed at the man starting to loom over them. "We won't be much longer, and then we'll be on our way."

"Do I know you?" The man took a step closer, inspecting Cotta's face.

Marsha looked away.

"Yes," Cotta replied clearly.

Before Marsha could speak, move, or think, Cotta's hand snapped up from her belt, the blade of a dagger sliding straight under the man's chin, piercing his neck and burying itself inside his head.

The man's eyes widened; his mouth fell open. There wasn't a sudden spray of blood; he didn't shriek or cry out for help. The blood just gushed out from under his chin and poured down Cotta's arm like a bucket had tipped over them.

He collapsed at her feet. Alive to dead in less than a heartbeat, just inside the castle wall.

Forced to kneel across his body, Cotta had to yank the blade out of his face She rolled her wrists.

"Now I know why Travis used to spend so much time lecturing his men on cleaning up after themselves. This is going to stick in the scabbard."

Marsha put her hands to her mouth to stop herself shrieking as Cotta wiped the blade with her gloved fingers so it fitted into its sheath. She was splattered in the warm sticky blood.

Cotta absently wiped her hands on her thighs, and when she was done, she stood straight and turned to Marsha.

"Before you say anything… I'll admit," she offered, "this complicates matters."

Kris finished hitching the horse to the wagon while Travis rechecked the wheel spokes and A'rrick stood talking with Rolo.

"It's time," Kris said as he finished belting the breeching straps into the trace.

Rolo reached up and set the foot iron free, releasing the brake.

Kris took the reins in hand and started leading the horse, pulling the wagon along the paths to the gatehouse to pick up Marsha and Cotta.

"This feels too easy," A'rrick uttered.

"Look around, m'lord," Rolo said as he walked next to him.

A'rrick did just that, glancing around.

Carts rumbled around, some carrying barrels or sacks of things into the castle, some taking things away. Men and women wandered past, all busy with their tasks, assuming everyone else was doing the same thing.

"No one is looking at an old wagon being taken somewhere they don't really care about." Rolo patted him on the shoulder. "Trust me, we know how to not be seen."

"Is it a huge risk, leaving your post like this? For this?" he asked.

"We'll keep the crown safe," was all he said.

They crossed one courtyard, then another, all four men walking at the same pace as everyone else. Passing through a tall archway, they crossed another courtyard and the gatehouse was just ahead of them.

"See," Rolo sounded confident, "just a few minutes more and it's done," he said as he opened the cast-iron gate and walked them through the short narrow tunnel that led to the relative quiet of the isolated street outside… and saw Marsha and Cotta… and a dead body.

"Don't stop," Travis ordered them quietly, "keep walking, go straight past them. I'll deal with this."

Sticking to the path, they turned and walked past the two women. For a moment the wagon obscured the scene, but after it passed, there was only one woman standing near the body, apparently being questioned by one of the city guard.

Marsha was force marched ahead of Kris, who had snatched her as they walked past.

A'rrick faded away into the first side street he saw.

"I have something I have to do," he said without a word more of explanation, and then he was gone.

"Keep looking straight ahead, Majesty," Kris said respectfully to the old queen mother, softly whispering, "I'm sorry if I grabbed you too hard," as he held her arms and pushed her ahead.

"It's all right, lad," Marsha said sternly, her face forward, old legs moving as demanded, her arms clutching the leather satchel Cotta had shoved at her just as she'd been taken away.

"At the next junction, I'll put you in the wagon and we'll be on our way. Rolo will leave us at the gate and meet us up the road. We're picking the squire up four miles outside the city gates, dumping the wagon and picking up a cart for the rest of the journey. I'll stay with you, but Rolo has to be back by nightfall. We can't leave our duty for any longer than that."

"I understand." Marsha started to shake at the pace she was forced to keep.

"Only a few minutes more," Rolo promised, coming up to her side. "Do you have the letter?"

Marsha nodded.

"Orania is a long journey. You'll pick up supplies along the way, enough to last until the next resupply point. The squire has some of your belongings, so you'll be comfortable enough."

"His name is Denny," Marsha said, eyes forward.

"He's leaving that name here," Kris replied. Marsha gripped the satchel a little harder, ignoring the pain in her fingers as she gripped the hard sides of what she carried.

They came to the junction and stopped.

Without hesitation, Kris lifted Marsha into the wagon. Rolo untied the canopy from the back and, fixing the frame in place, quickly hooked the waterproof canvas over her to shield her as much as possible. He fussed for a moment more, tucking a thick woollen blanket around her shoulders and making a pillow appear out of nowhere for her to lean on.

Kris settled into the driver's seat and adjusted the reins to the length he wanted.

Rolo stepped back, his face impassive. His attention fell on the satchel.

He bowed deeply to Marsha.

"My father served the crown, it was all he ever did, as did my uncle and my grandfather, who I believe served you when you first took the throne."

"I remember your father, easier now he's gone than when he was in my service."

Rolo nodded, understanding

"We served the crown, never the head wearing the crown."

"I never asked for the crown back," Marsha insisted. "My head carries all the deeds of my life and all the memories that go with it. I had assumed I'd never have to bear the weight of it again when I passed it to my son."

"King Lenard was a good man. King Orren was too." He looked at Kris then back at Marsha. "Tell me, is this what you want? Do you want us to take you out of Barclan? Do you want to go, with the crown, to Orania and ask for refuge with Queen Bris?"

Marsha felt the iron crown hidden in the leather satchel, so easily discovered if anyone bothered to look. Whoever wears the crown, rules the kingdom, she thought to herself.

"The crown goes with me to Orania."

Rolo bowed and stepped away.

Cotta shouted at Travis, her fists pounding on his chest, making a commotion to draw attention to them both.

"What's going on here?" A city guard approached them.

Travis knew the man. On instinct, he drew back his hood and looked straight at the guard, but the man didn't seem to know him, and Travis remembered his face was now disguised.

"I found this woman covered in blood and this man on the floor," Travis explained as Cotta hid her face in her hands, sobbing loudly. "She said she was walking past, heard a scream, and he stumbled out the gateway tunnel and fell on her as some others ran off."

"Street robbery?" the guard asked, making a move towards the body.

"Not sure, sir," Travis said respectfully. "Looks like one of yours though."

The guard kneeled and looked at the man. He got to his feet.

"A new one," the city guard acknowledged without sounding at all sad. "This isn't a rough area, but it's deserted a lot of the time, makes it a good spot for a mugging."

"Can't say as I know much about that," Travis replied. "What should I do with her?" He pointed at Cotta, who was playing up and being hysterical.

"Did she have anything else to say about the people she saw?"

"Nothing." Travis awkwardly patted her on the back a few times. "It was over in a couple of seconds. She only saw them running away, didn't say she saw them do it."

The guard sighed.

"All right then." He reached over and shook Travis's hand. "Leave this to me. Would you see the woman gets home?"

"Will do, sir." Travis turned and led Cotta away.

They walked in silence except for the sniffs and sobs that followed them into the city centre.

Eventually, Travis's pace picked up and they stopped pretending.

"Take this…" Travis unhooked his longer cloak and put it around her shoulders. "That blood will draw questions we don't need right now."

"Do you think they made it?"

"No one has sounded the city-wide alarm, and we know Marsha is wanted, so I think unless we see every guard in the city rushing westwards, we can assume they got out."

"Well done." Cotta slipped her hand into Travis's as they strolled back through the busy city streets.

"For what?"

"For today."

"Tell me well done when the crown I just sent out the kingdom is back on the Queen's head and on the throne."

Cotta smiled.

"What?" Travis asked.

"You said Queen. You mean An'eris."

"I said Queen. I didn't say An'eris."

Cotta shrugged and looked at him sideways.

"She's the Queen."

"She's your friend," Travis challenged her.

"She's both."

Travis stopped abruptly; Cotta was forced to stop with him, the crowd moving and parting around them like a river moving around two boulders.

"She sentenced you to death," he reminded her. "How can you stand here and call her a Queen when you know she's under his control?"

Cotta stepped up to Travis and put a hand to the back of his neck, intimately drawing him closer, but it wasn't for a kiss or a lover's sweet words. She put her lips to his ear.

"She is not herself. If she was, she would be sweeping through the castle halls, the very embodiment of revenge for every man and woman that has been slaughtered within those walls while she's been under that monster's spell. It is up to us," she released him, "to free her so she can take that revenge."

"No, she isn't the type for revenge. But you are."

Cotta stepped away, just enough to give him the space to lift his head.

"Is that what you want me to give you?" Travis asked, like a knight waiting for his orders. "Is that what you want?"

"Yes," she decreed. "I want a plan that gets me in front of An'eris. I want her to know, when that spell is unwound from her mind, that I never left her. And I want her to see and know about all the dead that fell while she did nothing, so when I take my revenge she will understand my rage and not step in the way of my wrath."

"What else?" Travis asked, a goading edge to his words that spurred Cotta on.

"I want war. I want men behind me ready to draw blood. Any face we don't know is a face I want dead."

"What else?"

"I want to cleanse the castle. I want to purge Kraner."

"More?" he goaded her. "What else?"

"I want the world to see that my kingdom is built on vengeance, the violence of my retribution is swift and the crown does not bow to anyone."

"*Your* kingdom?" Travis whispered.

Cotta licked her lips. She sucked her bottom lip into her mouth, biting it slightly before smiling up at Travis.

"My mistake," she said. "Caught up in the moment."

"Is that right?"

"Will you do it?" Cotta held his gaze. "Will you give me what I want?"

"I will," he vowed.

She turned her back to him, her hand snaking back into his again, their fingers locking together.

"Come." She began walking, pulling him behind her. "We've much to do."

A'rrick barged through the door into Kirin's shop, ignoring the startled customers that weren't expecting a tall stranger to rush past them and head up the stairs.

A few passed glances between them, but nobody did anything more than shuffle and wait to be served.

He took the stairs as quickly as he dared and banged the door once to alert Brennan that someone was coming in. A'rrick dashed across the small space, reaching Brennan in a few strides, reaching down and hauling him upright.

"A'rrick?" Brennan said as he tried to shrink away from the frenetic energy of the man who was pushing him to sit up against a wall. "What are you doing?"

"An'eris," A'rrick snapped. "I sensed her a little while ago in the streets out in the city. Put your mind out there, into the city, and see if you can find her."

"You're not making sense." Brennan put his hands up as a shield, but it was too late.

"Do it," A'rrick shouted. Without warning, he grabbed Brennan by the head and plunged their minds together.

CHAPTER 24

The endless desert became less stone and sand and sky and more arid grassland as the days wore on, and the four travellers let themselves be led north by their horses. They kept a brisk pace, only stopping to demand water and to graze on the wildflowers, long grasses and small bristling bushes that grew more abundantly with each mile they covered. Their feed bags lasted as long as it took them to notice there was more soil beneath them than compacted sand, and they hadn't seen a hill or dune in more than a day.

The further north they rode, leaving the deep desert behind, the more the sky returned to all the natural shades of blue they would expect; there were fewer streaks of neon lightning during the day, and at night the billowing ribbons of colour that cascaded and flowed above them started to thin out and dissipate.

As the visual reminders of the wild ethereal magic of the desert receded, the very real enormity of the task before them appeared in the form of the Raska mountains growing larger and more formidable every day.

Soon the mountain range became the only thing on their horizon, and the ferocious sun quickly turned meek, cool and subservient to chill winds and long shadows. Bode thought about the last time he crossed the mountains, the people who had ridden at his side. He had to force his mind off those sombre thoughts, finding ways to keep his sadness under control. Bode had taken it on himself to maintain the horses in good health, the routine of caring for them giving him a sense of purpose. But it wasn't enough, and he struggled to keep his mind busy for all the hours they were in the saddle. He had tried fletching an arrow he'd fashioned from a twig but his fingers were too unsteady and he struggled to pinch and hold the feathers. After a few futile hours he dropped it on the ground and never once thought to try again.

An'uek was absorbed in conversation with Calem as she tried to understand what he wanted to learn from her, but she was attentive to Bode behind her and she sensed when his sombre mood started to turn melancholy. That evening, as they settled down to eat after preparing camp, she took her turn at making their evening meal and asked Bode to help her.

He set the irons over their small fire and set up the small pots and kettles while she prepared the foods and set them to cook. She watched his movements, his hands and fingers still sore, arms moving more at the shoulder than the elbow or wrist, and he was tapping and scratching at the bandages across his chest more than usual.

She settled next to him, stirring her own small pot with a wooden spoon while he sorted through the bowls.

"I thought that after we've eaten I'd help you take the wrappings off." Her free hand skimmed up his arm.

She waited.

He searched through the satchel, pulling small wooden cups out and setting them down with the bowls.

"I can do it myself," he replied, "but thank you."

Feeling a little sore at being rebuffed, An'uek nodded, forced a smile that looked thin and mean in the light thrown up from the orange flames.

She turned her attention back to her food, reaching down to take the pot and set it on the ground to cool.

"Is it ready?" Raef interrupted, Calem a step behind him.

"Smells good," Calem rasped, taking the steaming bowl Bode handed over to him.

"What have you two been talking about all day?" Raef turned to Calem, ignoring the way Bode and An'uek sat angled away from each other.

"Learning words," Calem replied around a mouthful of mutton.

"Sounds dull," Raef teased half-heartedly.

"What have you done all day?" Calem asked.

"Watched your skinny backside trying to stay in the saddle." Raef blew away the steam and tucked into his meal.

Bode smiled. "What words?" he said, joining in.

Calem looked over at An'uek, who nodded her approval.

"It's learning the right way to say the words, so they're a song." He stared at the fire as he talked, moving his spoon in the air as if conducting the flames. In response, a flame the size of his hand rose up from the fire and hung in the air in front of them.

It pulsed and folded into itself to form a flower.

"I can do this without any thought. I just will it into shape." Calem put his hand out and the flame flattened and moulded itself into a perfect replica of his hand. He opened his fingers and the hand of fire did the same. "But the longer I do this, the more the other power starts to bubble and build up inside me." He closed his fist, and the flame died away into nothing.

Calem turned to Bode, to Raef.

"The right words, said in the proper way, are a way to control the flame, so I can put a dam around it." He turned to An'uek, as if checking his own words. "I don't really understand it yet, but it's the first lesson." He raised a hand to the druid. Bode flinched and put his arm reflexively around An'uek.

Calem put his hand down.

"It's supposed to work that way." He took another mouthful of food, wiping his lips on his sleeve. "But I keep coughing and I don't know if my voice is too damaged to ever get it right." As if on cue, he started to wheeze and gasp.

Raef leaned over without thinking and rubbed his back to help him through the coughing fit. Calem quickly doubled over and Raef scooted behind him, putting an arm around his shoulders to keep him up.

"Maybe that's enough talking for today then," he gently chided.

An'uek watched the exchange, seeing how naturally Raef forgot his animosity for Calem.

She turned to Bode; he looked at her and raised an eyebrow, shrugging into his meal.

An'uek shuffled forward on her knees, took Calem's cup and filled it with the tea she had brewed in her own kettle.

"Drink this, it'll help with the cough."

He took it with thanks, making no move to drink the liquid.

"Do it," Bode ordered without looking up.

Calem, managing to look remarkably sullen at the command, obeyed.

Raef, forgetting to move away from him, watched him drink.

"Come on, fool," he ordered. "I've seen newborn babies take more off a flat tit than you just sipped. Drink the damn drink."

"I'll start to clear up." An'uek got to her feet and started collecting the things from their meal. Bode caught her intentions and followed her away from the fire and into the shadows, starting to pack the food away.

"I was worried I'd need to keep them separate for the rest of our journey together," An'uek said quietly.

"Raef keeps forgetting he wants to hate Calem, he wants to blame him for Mason."

"Raef doesn't have it in him to hate as much as he needs to if he wants to work at that blame all his life."

"He doesn't know that." Bode fumbled on the satchel buckle, his fingers struggling to grip the frame.

An'uek reached over and put her hand on his, helping his fingers. He paused but didn't pull away.

"Raef, for all the deeds he's done in his life, is a good man. He just doesn't have it in him to be anything else."

"I'll talk to him," Bode said softly, allowing An'uek to help his fingers with the clasp.

"No," An'uek pulled back when the satchel was buckled up, "let him talk to Calem. I think there's something only they can help each other with."

Bode lowered his hands and moved the satchel towards the bundle of belongings. As he did so, the edge of one of the bandages on his hands caught itself on the buckle, pulling the binding enough that it started to unravel and fall away from his hand.

Bode didn't move. An'uek, reacting without thinking, reached out and pulled the bandage free of the snag, and then she proceeded to gently rewrap his hand.

"Wait," he implored, his other hand reaching over and holding hers over his, trapping both their hands together.

"Bode," she turned to him, "please let me help you."

Raef and Calem sat with their backs to Bode and An'uek.

"Should we go to sleep, give them some privacy?" Calem rasped.

"I'm not tired, are you?" Raef asked.

"No." Calem shook his head.

"They've got privacy anyway." Raef picked up a twig and threw it into the fire. "Can you hear what they're talking about?"

"No," Calem repeated, then turned to Raef. "What do you think they're talking about?"

"You," Raef teased.

"Me?"

"For sure," he said, looking for more twigs. "That's what I'd be talking about if I was with them. I'd be working out how to get you to be a bit more helpful around here, maybe cook a meal or brush your own horse down. You're lazy, you know."

Calem smiled and handed a small bunch of twigs to Raef.

"I'll try to do more," he murmured.

"Just don't accidentally kill us." Raef threw the twigs into the fire, smirking at Calem.

"I'll do my best," he said, his voice a little wheezy. He fidgeted with the edge of the cup. "Can I ask you something?" He turned to Raef.

The thief shrugged in reply.

"What do you dream about?" Calem asked.

"I don't dream." Raef's response was instant, his voice hard.

"I do." Calem looked at the sky. "Can I tell you about them?"

Calem told Raef about his dreams. He told him he had seen the whole world throughout time, what it was and what he could do to it if he wanted. He described seeing mountains falling into the sea, the sea rolling back, and the sky turning grey and hard and crashing down on the land. He told him he saw copies of himself, each one screaming at the other in languages he didn't know.

He said he would wake up sometimes and couldn't remember when he was. Raef corrected him, to "who" he was, but Calem was sure it was "when". He told Raef that sometimes he'd dream he was walking into a sea that was recoiling before him, that as he walked he burned the water away and the land rose up behind him. Raef listened, scared.

He asked him if he dreamed about A'taz. Calem told him he wondered if A'taz dreamed about him. He told him that his memories of Isaac had faded, that he only dreamed his own dreams now, and the things he saw were all the worse because he knew they were coming from himself.

He told Raef how hard it was not to let himself go, to start laughing, or crying, and let the thing growing in him rip away from him and be free. When Raef asked why it hadn't killed them all already, how he was managing to contain it, Calem didn't know. He thought maybe it was waiting for something, but he didn't know what. Calem lapsed into silence, waiting for Raef to get up and walk away from him.

Instead, and to Calem's relief and joy, Raef scooted a little bit closer. The thief took a minute, then told him that he had lied, that he did have dreams. He told Calem he dreamed about a home, nothing fancy, just a table with a comfortable chair in front of a warm fire.

Calem turned the cup round in his hands, now charred black. The sound of the tea sloshing around the bottom filled the silence. He put it down and put his head in his hands for a while. Raef waited. When Calem eventually sat back up, Raef reached over to look in the cup Calem had set down earlier.

"You didn't finish it." He handed it back to the sorcerer. "I can sit here all night until you do."

"It's vile… and it's wet." Calem grimaced at the sight of the drink and then yawned.

"Shut up and drink your vile drink, you lazy fool."

True to his threat, Raef sat with Calem while the boy forced the tea down his throat. The liquid burned from his lips to his belly, but he had to admit that by the time he finished it the constant nagging itch in his throat was a little soothed, and so was he. After the last sip, Calem held the cup in front of Raef, turned it over, and smiled triumphantly as not a drop spilled out.

Raef, raising an eyebrow, mock sighed.

"Do you want applause as well?" He reached over, taking the cup.

Calem sighed, and stood up, yawning. He stretched his arms above his head, rolled his neck, and sat back down, settling himself in his cloak against the cool night. He looked past the fire and over to where Bode and An'uek sat outside its glow.

"What are they doing?" he asked quietly.

Raef twisted to look over his shoulder.

"Best leave them to it, whatever it is."

"They do that a lot, talking quietly off together. I wonder what they can't say in front of us?" The mirth from earlier disappeared as he stared at them.

Raef, looking at Bode and An'uek, and then to Calem, momentarily closed his eyes before responding.

"Calem," he said to the boy, "not everything is your fault. We have to accept that, and so do you."

Calem turned and looked at Raef, his eyes wide.

"Thanks."

"For what?"

"For using my name."

Raef was about to reply, when An'uek and Bode stepped back into the light, coming to sit across the fire from them.

An'uek wrapped herself tightly in her long shawl, obscuring herself almost completely from view. Bode sat away from her, his hands stuffed into his pockets.

"Is there any tea left?" he asked.

"I'll make a fresh pot." Raef grabbed his waterskin and refilled the small kettle before putting it on the fire and throwing some dried leaves into the empty cups.

"No more for me." Calem put his hand up.

"No more for you," Raef agreed.

From somewhere else, the quiet night was split with a howl of a desert wolf, and for a minute they weren't alone.

"Is that nearby or far away?" Calem asked nervously.

"Why, scared it'll carry you off in your sleep?" Raef joked.

"Be nice," An'uek chided.

"I'm always nice," Raef said, snickering.

"I'm always nice," Calem said, imitating Raef's voice.

"Are you mocking me, boy?" Raef said in mock surprise.

"Wouldn't dare." Calem held up his hands.

"That's right." Raef picked up a cup. "Mind yourself or I'll make you another cup of tea."

"All right, Raef," Calem said, backing down, "no need to be so mean."

Unexpectedly, Bode broke out in a loud laugh that filled the night, drowning out the baying of the desert wolves.

They sat around the fire, sipping tea, making light banter, keeping each other awake long after they would normally have cocooned into their blankets and gone to sleep on the hard ground. Well after midnight, as Calem finally stopped coughing and gave himself away with soft wheezes and quiet snoring, Raef got his blanket and draped it over him.

"I didn't know you cared," Bode teased him.

"I'm not exactly tucking him in," Raef replied.

The silence hung between them, easier than it had been in previous nights.

"What changed?" Bode asked.

Raef took his time replying.

"I don't know." He scratched in the ground with a twig. "I've been talking to Mason." Raef's voice grew softer. "Constantly, in my head. And at first I thought he was answering me and was demanding revenge. Blood is warm, you know, and I've been so cold since he died. I wanted to be warm again. I wanted it to be Calem's blood."

He swallowed hard, staring intently at the ground next to him, crossing his arms over his chest.

"Then, when I was talking to him, I started to hear him less and hear myself more. And I didn't like what I was hearing myself say. I've played many parts, whoever I needed to be. But I was never the killer. Mason never let me take that role."

Raef turned to An'uek.

"I kept hearing you as well, in my head. Promising me that you wouldn't let me become a killer. When I went to talk to Mason, I heard your words in his voice, telling me kinder things than I've said to myself in a long time."

"And then what?" Bode asked, reaching out and taking Raef's other hand, as, with his other, he reached for An'uek.

"I stopped looking for him in the dark... I stopped looking for him... to talk to him."

Raef looked over at Calem.

"I don't know how Mason did it." Raef let his gaze fall to what was left of the fire, glowing orange embers in a circle of ash. "All the lives he took, all the killing. It never bothered him. I even think maybe he liked it, or felt... I don't know. I tried, I wanted to be like that. I thought if I could be like him then I could keep him with me and this feeling of empty space inside me wouldn't be so cold."

"You can't be someone you aren't," Bode offered.

"I'm not a killer," Raef confessed. As he spoke, he sighed, his shoulders dropped, and his body seemed to deflate. "I never will be."

"You're the same person you were, and the same person you always will be." Bode's deep voice filled the space between them. He held An'uek's hand as tightly as he dared.

"The more I accept Mason's gone, the worse I think I should feel, but I don't. I'm alive, and it makes me so damn guilty, until I get distracted and forget to be sad and angry or upset and ashamed." He let go of Bode and An'uek. They sat, still hand in hand, giving Raef the space he needed to weep. He cried into the dark night, curling up on the ground in the glow of the dying fire, eventually falling asleep next to Calem.

Bode and An'uek sat together in the darkness, heavy thoughts in heavy minds, quietly keeping vigil over their friends. Bode felt her shuffle as she folded her long legs under herself; he wondered if she was still getting used to being so tall now, and the thought made him smile.

She sensed the change in him, subtle, but enough to galvanise her resolve.

She shuffled again, uncrossing her legs and then recrossing them, and then, clearly irritated, she turned to him, huffing.

"This is ridiculous," she stated. "Move your arm."

He did as she said, and she immediately settled into his side against his body, pulling his arm around her shoulders.

She rested her weary self against him, and he felt her need him. He felt her lean against him.

"This is better," she murmured, gazing nowhere. She yawned so wide a low rumble reverberated through her.

Bode saw the dark shadow around her eyes, the lines too. Her skin was dry, the lustre gone from her hair, and in the light of the stars that should have exacerbated her beauty and vitality, she looked old and tired. It scared him more than his trembling hands.

"Are you going to get some sleep?" he asked.

"Maybe." A lazy smile crossed her features.

"Will you try at least?"

She didn't say no.

For hours, they sat in comfortable silence. He dozed against her, both supporting each other. As the dawn started to colour the darkness, he roused himself. He felt an itch in his trembling hands. Aware she was awake, he lifted his hands, letting her move against him to take them in her own. Even in the dark he could see the stains and frayed edges of the bandages that felt too heavy. Far away, he heard the wolves howling, but their voices didn't fill him with dread or fear.

An'uek stayed at his side, leaning into him under his arm as she started to unwind the bandages around his hands. She worked slowly, gently, so softly he thought if he closed his eyes he wouldn't be able to say if she was still touching him.

He did close his eyes. He didn't want to see what was left when the last wrappings dropped into the dirt.

"Open your eyes," she said softly.

"No." He squeezed them tighter. "Do the rest."

An'uek moved away from Bode's side and settled on her knees in front of him. He felt her close, felt her hands on his arms. She pushed his travelling cloak back off his shoulders, undid the buttons at the neck of his tunic and untied the strings at the cuffs. Lifting the hem, she pulled it up off his body, putting it neatly to the side.

With a hand on him at all times, she stood up and moved to sit behind him.

As the sun rose, An'uek unwound all the bandages across his chest and down his stomach, and the wrappings covering his shoulders.

She turned away to give him some privacy but wouldn't leave his side.

Pale yellow light bathed his body as he opened his eyes and looked down.

She heard him gasp and groan.

His once broad chest, covered in thick dark hair, corded with muscle and marked by battles was burned smooth, was now covered in angry thick red scars that branched off each other like arcane lightning had burst across his body. They radiated out from the point over his heart, traversing below his naval and up and over his shoulders, down his arms and along to the tips of his trembling fingers.

She watched him looking at himself, his eyes wide, mouth open but silent. She put her hands in his, her hands trembling as much as his. Closing her hands over his, she put them over her heart.

"They're beautiful," she said.

CHAPTER 25

At noon on the seventh day, Bode called a halt to the small group, ambling ahead alone for another hundred yards. His piebald stallion came to a stop under Bode's silent command, waiting patiently as the big man stared at the Raska Pass in the very near distance.

Raef moved up beside him, a hand on his pommel, another holding his waterskin, his chestnut mount doing its own thing. Raef drank the waterskin dry, wiped his mouth on his sleeve, then handed it over to Bode, refilled.

Bode drained it and pointed at the pass.

"We shouldn't be here already."

"I feel like we've travelled weeks in days." Raef reached over and took his waterskin back.

"I think we have." Bode reached forward and patted his stallion's neck, easing his fingers into his mane, craning forward to scratch his ears.

The horse whinnied and gently tossed its head.

"I'll be glad to be through the pass and out of the desert." As he spoke, his stallion stomped its hooves and Raef's did the same. Raef leaned down and patted his horse's neck, mimicking Bode's movements earlier. "No offence," he said soothingly. "I love it really. I just prefer a bit less sand and a bit more Barclan."

The horse flared its nostrils and flicked its head enough for its mane to whip back at Raef, who let out a small laugh.

"Easy." He settled back. Both horses turned around and led the men back to their waiting companions.

Bode chuckled.

"I really don't know why we even bothered with the bit and reins." He put his hands through the leather leads, but his thoughts were on the mountain range that loomed so close. Within moments, they were all together.

"Do we make early camp or make a break for the pass before nightfall?" An'uek asked.

"If we decide to ride we stay in the saddle until we make it through, there's no stopping midway and making camp."

"Agreed," Raef interjected. "The mountains are so high, they're like a wall between the kingdoms. We're either on this side or that side."

"We've got about four hours of light left, is that enough?" she asked.

"On these horses, I think so," Bode guessed.

The others waited on his decision.

"We ride."

"All right," An'uek said, turning to get Calem's attention. "Let's all take a break, enough to stretch our legs and dress in everything we've got. It's going to get very cold very fast. Then we trust that we'll make it through by nightfall."

Raef unrolled the spare clothes packed into his saddlebag and pulled them on. Over his long-sleeved light weave corn-coloured tunic he buttoned up a leather vest the colour of tree bark and covered in small bumps.

"This is nice," he mused, running his fingers across his chest.

"They have enormous birds here," An'uek explained. "Almost impossible to catch. Valuable to Bastion and his people."

Raef pursed his lips and looked around at the others, also donning vests of the same material, all stained in different shades of brown.

"He's very generous," he said, as he pulled his cloak back over his shoulders, tying it in place. He turned to Calem, expecting to see the young man dressing, then he smiled to himself.

"You're not going to get cold, are you?"

Calem shook his head.

"Then why all the blankets every night?" Raef asked, curious.

"It's comfy," Calem wheezed, stamping his foot on the ground, making the horses turn their heads toward him. "The ground is hard."

Raef shook his head, his lips curled into a smile.

Leaving Calem, he turned to Bode to ask if he needed any help, but he stopped when he saw An'uek with him.

She had helped him out of his thin tunic, displaying his scarred body to the others.

Calem paused, his eyes mesmerised by the marked skin.

Bode felt his heart start to beat against his ribs, acutely aware of the stares of his companions, and Calem's eyes in particular.

"Hand me the thicker one would you," he asked An'uek, pointing at his bag.

She handed him a long thick tunic, waiting for him to indicate that she could help him. She eased it up his arms and over his head, tying it close at the neck and wrists, smoothing it down his chest. He didn't flinch. Without being asked, Raef dug into his friend's bag and pulled out a leather vest similar to his own but longer. He handed it over and turned his back, letting them finish with a soft leather jacket that fell around his legs.

"Gloves," An'uek said to all of them. "Frostbite, remember. When I say it's going to get cold, I mean it."

Raef moved over to An'uek, who was wrapping her long shawl around her middle, up her back to cover her head and then down to wrap around her neck once and fall behind her back. He clipped her cloak.

"A few days ago this reached your ankles, now it's barely below your knees."

"Hopefully my knees won't get cold," she said, trying to joke, but they were all starting to feel uneasy.

"Are you going to be warm enough?" he asked, nothing light-hearted in his tone.

"If not I'll ride nearer Calem."

"Good enough," Raef replied, holding the stirrup for her.

She looked at him, a single eyebrow raised.

"Habit," he said, shrugging, waiting as she let him help her up.

Bode and Calem took to the saddle, Raef the last to seat himself.

"All right…" Bode turned to face them all. "When we came through the pass on our way here it was an easier ride. Winter was only a day old and the shadows weren't so long or so dark. We're riding back into the Barclan winter. It's no man's friend. There'll be shadows that look like passageways between the rocks, and at this time of year the pass may as well be in a cave. The mountains are too high, and the sun is too low and weak. It will be dark." His horse stepped around, agitated or excited, he couldn't tell.

"Calem, I'll be at your side." Bode looked at him, raising a gloved finger. "Don't be afraid. Do not do anything stupid in there." He spoke slowly, stressing each word.

"I won't," he said, nodding too quickly.

"I mean it, boy," Bode said sternly. "You keep your fingers in your sleeves, and if I even think I can smell a bit of singed hair or suspect you're thinking of lighting something up, I'll knock you out."

"I won't," he repeated.

"Bode," An'uek moved round, "don't scare him."

"I'm not trying to scare anyone," he explained. "But it can take more than a day to get through the pass in much better conditions that we're going into, and we want to do it much more quickly." He patted the horses to emphasise his point. "I just want us all prepared. We're going into the pass, but we're not in charge of getting through it."

They reached the shadow of the mountains long before they reached the mountain pass. The sun was barely three fingers above the flat horizon behind them when they stopped at the very edge of the gap between the mountain walls. Bode took the lead, Calem a foot to the right and behind. An'uek, her white mare seemingly muted to grey, kept as close to Calem as she dared, already shivering and chilled to the bone. Raef held the rear position, the blade Bastion had bestowed on him sheathed on his belt, his hands gripping the reins as tightly as possible.

Raef surveyed the pass. Looking upwards, it was impossible to say how high the mountains were. They seemed to lean together, touching, turning the pass into the entrance to a tomb.

"Why is it so different to when we first came through? I barely remember coming through here the first time," he wondered aloud to himself. An'uek heard his words, turned, and reached out to him.

"It's the first and last boundary of the magic in the desert. It reflects what we feel. On our way here, we didn't know what we were getting into. Now we know."

Raef whistled and let out a breath.

"We're in trouble then."

An'uek smiled.

"I think that's why Bastion set us up as he did."

"And that makes you feel better?" Raef asked.

"No." She crossed her arms over herself as she shuddered. "But I trust him to give us what we need to get through this. We just have to stay in our saddles."

"Ready?" Bode turned to them all. Without waiting for their replies, he dropped his reins and waited for his stallion to move forward.

Raef's horse took up the pace and moved forward, walking him into the darkness, to be lost and swallowed by cold and shadow.

Within minutes, An'uek started to see the things they'd all feared they might encounter. The shadows contorted into shapes of men and beasts that kept pace with their horses. Ice-cold blasts seemed to come from nowhere, striking just her, leaving the others unaffected. The sound of the horses, steady and sure, echoed off the sheer stone walls looming over them, repeating again and again until it was a crescendo of warhorses charging down on them. She had to bite into her hand to stop from crying out. She tried to close her eyes, but it was no use, she found herself staring ahead. She thought she saw the passageway start to collapse and shrink, surely about to come crashing down on them. She put her hands up over her head, covered her eyes, a hot sweat breaking out over her skin under her layers of leather and wool. She fiddled with her shawl under her cape, trying to unwrap it, feeling as though it was tightening around her, squeezing and suffocating her. She could taste her fear, and she pulled her feet out of the stirrups, pulled her knees up into her chest on the saddle. After the fear overwhelmed her, all she had left was despair.

And still her mare kept a steady gait, moving forward unburdened by the fears of its rider, the horse ensuring the woman in the saddle didn't slip out and fall to the ground.

Raef watched An'uek ahead of him, his thoughts settling on her as a distraction to the hurricane winds that thrashed his cloak against his body, trying to push him out of his saddle, but didn't move a single long strand of his stallion's mane. The shrieking blasts of wind hit him in the face, forcing excessive air through his nose, into his mouth, filling his lungs until he thought his chest would burst open, too full to breathe out.

Putting his hands up to guard his face, he looked away, but the wind moved to pummel him whichever way he turned. He tried calling to An'uek, to get her attention for help, but the wind stole his voice before it left his lips. She sat in her saddle ahead of him, relaxed enough to curl up and let her mare lead her through.

Desperate, Raef put his heels to his stallion hoping to spur the beast on; instead, the creature kicked up from under him, jarring him in his saddle enough to dislodge him for a moment. As he thumped back into his seat, the impact forced the air from his lungs, as if he'd been hit in the chest. His head rolled on his shoulders for a second, his vision blurred and then cleared. The wind was gone. Now, nothing but a gentle breeze stirred a few dry leaves in the darkness as he rode through the pass on his stallion contentedly taking sure steady steps.

Bode, ahead of them all, kept his gaze straight ahead. His eyes acclimated to the coal-black shadows within minutes, trusting that his stallion could see for them both. The horse didn't take any faltering steps, the steady clopping of his hooves almost monotonous. Bode, at ease in the saddle for the first time in months, let his gaze wander.

The grey stone cliffs pressed over him, crags and cracks in the stone face, sometimes the stark white carcass of a long dead tree still wedged in the crevice where it had grown, flowered and withered away.

"Whole lifetimes are lived and then lost in this place," he said to himself.

Around him, the echoes came back to him, his voice, softer, deeper, warning him not to get lost in this place.

The echoes didn't scare him. This place didn't scare him.

Beside him, with his hands in his sleeves, back bowed forward and head down, Calem shivered.

"Bode," he called out. "It's very cold."

Bode turned just enough to look at Calem riding beside him. He frowned and moved in his saddle as he looked at the boy. The ever-present flicker of orange fire light that pervaded his body was barely luminous in the shadows. He craned his neck back to look at the others: An'uek sat huddled on her saddle, Raef behind her had his head down and was hunched forward too. They were shivering so hard he could hear their teeth chattering over the sound of the horses.

Bode looked around again at the sombre stone walls, the hard grey earth under their horses' hooves, dry leaves, dead bushes, and on his left, which he hadn't noticed, the skeletal remains of some long dead animal. No life, anywhere, except their own.

Bode leaned forward out of his saddle, his face close to his stallion's tall ears.

"I don't know if you're really magical," he said softly, "or if I'm an idiot talking to a horse, but if you can understand me, as I think you might, then I think we need to get a move on." He looked back at the three behind him, An'uek had drawn more into herself, holding her face in her hands; he could see she was squeezing at her temples. Calem, next to him, was moving his hands and his arms in his long sleeves and shifting nervously. "We need steady speed." He reached out and ran his hand along the smooth neck. "Can you do that for us?"

The horse whinnied and flicked its head once, twice. Even through the thick saddle Bode could feel the way the stallion's muscles started to bunch, as if energy was being primed. He didn't need to look to know the other horses would be doing the same. Puffs of steam blew from the stallion's flared nostrils and it mouthed at the bit, passing its head from side to side for a few moments.

Bode reached out and grabbed Calem's reins in one hand, digging his heels into the stallion's flanks to tell it to slow.

The horse obliged but Bode had the impression it wasn't happy with the small delay. He kept his heels in until An'uek's mare was almost on them, reaching back to take her reins in enough time to tug her to his left. Holding them both, he called behind him to Raef.

"We're getting out of here, we have to believe that." His deep voice filled the chasm like thunder.

Raef's head snapped up. He nodded once, wound the reins around his wrists and grasped them tightly.

Bode turned to look ahead, made sure Calem and An'uek were at his side.

"All right boy," he said to his stallion, whose ears pricked up at the sound of his voice. "Go!"

CHAPTER 26

Bode and Raef lay on the frozen ground in a heap, limbs entwined as if they'd collapsed off their horses and fallen together, while the softly falling snow was slowly hiding them from view. Calem was a foot away, face down in the short, dry frost-bitten grass, the same snowfall melting before it touched him, turning to drops of rain then to steam at first contact with his body.

The four horses pulled at the short grass, ignoring the flakes of snow sticking to their long thick eyelashes. They swished their tails and walked around investigating clumps of earth that smelled like moss and nibbled on the leaves of bushes that hadn't quite fallen prey to winter yet, tasting and smelling everything new around them. They didn't venture far, braying softly, respecting the quiet winter morning.

Calem woke up, roused from a deep slumber by a bitter smell and the nauseating sound of someone gagging.

He opened his eyes, pulled his knees under himself and rolled forward to sit up, balancing on spindly arms.

"An'uek," he wheezed, shuffling over to her on his knees. He dropped down beside her, reaching out to her, and stopping himself at the last moment. He pulled his arms back, made his hands into fists, pushing against the earth to sit himself up. The druidess was on her knees, hands flat on the dirty ground, puking black muck into a small snow drift. It splashed back against her and mixed with the snow melting into mud that quickly smeared all over her pristine clothes. Her hair fell out of the tight long braid, stuck to her sweating face, caught in her mouth and then dipped into the puddle of sick near her face.

Her skin had lost its colour, her amethyst eyes a pale grey, no hint of anything left inside her.

Calem moved closer again, instinctively reaching to pat her on the back when she turned and shot him a warning glance.

"Water," she rasped.

He jumped up and went over to her mare. The horse that a moment ago had been sniffing around an old rabbit's burrow now stood still and let him take her waterskin. He rushed back to her, pulling the stopper out and handing it over.

She grabbed it with both hands, but instead of taking a long drink, she tipped it up and let the water fall on her face.

The water almost froze as it poured out, and as it splashed down on her, she started to shiver.

"Let me hold it." He didn't wait for her reply; he reached over and snatched it. Immediately the water turned from cold to gloriously hot, steaming in the air as it poured over her face. She sat back on her knees, filthy and stinking, with eyes closed, graciously accepting his ironic gift to wash the muck off her face and hands. She closed her eyes and raised her face into the stream—it felt so good. She leaned forward, lowering her head and letting it pour over her neck and forward into her filthy hair.

The water poured, and poured, not finishing until she finally felt clean and had washed the bile from her mouth.

The ground around her was a wallow of mud, but she didn't care. She sat down on her backside in the sludge and started to knead the muscles of her neck.

"Thank you," she said, as Calem carefully tied her waterskin to her satchel and came back over to her. He didn't notice that, at his last touch, the waterskin didn't refill. As he walked away from her mare, the horse shook out its mane, jostling the saddlebags just enough that the waterskin slipped from its fastening and fell unnoticed to the ground, sinking instantly into the snow, gone.

"Are you better?" he asked her, as close as he dared.

"I am." She looked at him, her gaunt face and grey eyes tired and empty.

"How did we get out? I don't remember anything after Bode took my reins."

"I don't either." She shook her head vigorously. "I don't care though. We're through, and judging by the cold, we're in Barclan."

She felt an unfamiliar emotion wash through her, and it took her a moment to recognise it as relief.

"But I can't even see the mountains." Calem pointed past her, over her shoulder. "I can't see a road. There's nothing around us for miles. Where are we?"

The druidess looked around. She didn't recognise anything as a landmark, and it didn't bother her at all.

"We're somewhere," she answered. "Wake them up would you?" She gestured to Bode and Raef. "I'm too tired to stand right now."

Calem kicked Bode's foot until he sat up. Raef woke up as Bode did, both taking a moment to untangle from each other.

As they stood, they both shivered and pulled their cloaks tighter, and looked around, blowing into their hands to warm them up, stuffing them under their armpits.

Raef turned around, gazing at the nothing around them.

"Before you say anything," An'uek held up her hand. "We've no idea how we got here, where here is, or how long we've been here."

"That wasn't what I was going to say." He kept looking around. "I was going to say... we're home."

"Yes, you are." She reflected the glee on his face with her own.

"You look awful." Raef stepped over to her. "The worst I think I've ever seen you," he said, frowning.

"I need a bath," was all she would say, the smile not leaving her lips. "Let's get ourselves together before we freeze solid. Feed and water your horses then we have to go."

They all moved at her command.

Raef helped Calem fit the feed bag over his colt's muzzle before moving to his stallion.

"Hello boy," he crooned, stroking the horse's forehead. "Did you get us out? I bet you did, good boy." He kissed the stallion's muzzle, reaching down with the other hand to tickle the groove under his chin. He sorted out his feed bag, belted it on, and set to checking over his hooves and coat while his horse munched at his feed.

Bode did the same, then started digging through his own saddlebags for the sticks of dried meat he knew were stashed somewhere. He threw some over to Raef, who caught them with ease.

"That's the last of it," he said, grinding the tough meat between his back teeth. "And just as well, I'd do anything for an apple or anything that isn't a bit of dry root and whatever animal this used to be."

"I feel like a new man now we're through the pass, but not a new man hungry enough to eat this ever again." Raef pointed with his stick of hard, dried meat. "I'll be indebted to Bastion forever, but I need to eat something freshly killed or just fallen from a tree." He spat out the food and dropped what was left in the snow next to him. "I'm done with this."

"Me too." Bode spat his out. He took a deep breath, filled his lungs and stretched his arms. "It's freezing cold, I have no idea how we made it here, but we're home." Bode looked at the nowhere and was happy. Until he saw An'uek when his joy became tempered with worry.

"She's getting sick you know." He nodded over to An'uek, who was discreetly changing her stockings and trying to wipe the mud off herself.

Raef looked over at her.

"She'll be fine."

"Are you sure?"

"I'm sure," he replied. "We all will be."

As soon as the horses were ready, they were too. Bode helped Calem into his saddle before climbing into his own and bringing his horse to An'uek's side. Raef took his time.

"Mount up, Raef," An'uek chided. "The snow's really coming down."

"In a second," he replied, moving around to the horse's other side, hiding himself from view. A moment later there was the sound of splashing, and Raef sighing happily.

"Ready now." He stepped back round, doing up his belt and pulling his gloves back on. "Anybody have any idea where to go?"

"We're lost for the moment," An'uek replied, casting a purposefully withering look at the thief, who wouldn't stop smiling at her.

"You're lost?" he countered.

"I'm lost?" She frowned as she turned to Bode. "Am I the only one lost? Do you have a map?"

"Of southern Barclan." He sounded shocked. "I'm a career soldier in my own kingdom, and you're asking me if I have a map." He feigned shock, touching his hand to his heart.

Raef started tutting, exaggerating the shrug of his shoulders, and with wide eyes, he looked at Bode and shook his head.

Bode rolled his eyes at her, all the more absurd for the dramatic gesture as he sat on his horse being pelted with snowfall that stuck in his dishevelled hair.

"I'm insulted." He yanked his reins, turned his stallion, and looked up at the cloudy sky. "I'll have us in a tavern by nightfall, and tonight, no sleeping on the ground."

They lined up and followed his lead.

An'uek sat on her mare without a clue to the direction they were going. She watched Bode as he rode ahead, talking animatedly with Raef. The change in him was extraordinary. As her thoughts started to stray to their passage through the pass, Calem came up beside her coughing and wheezing.

"The air is much colder and wetter," she said.

"It's so much worse," he said as his breathing settled. "Do you know how long we'll be on the road?"

"No idea. I don't even think we're on a road, and if we are, I can't see it."

"Bode knows where he's going."

"So does Raef."

"What do we do then?" Calem asked, a gleam in his eyes.

She turned to him, pushing wet hair out of her eyes.

"I teach, you learn."

They rode for hours, content to let their horses follow the lead of the stallions ahead. An'uek struggled to teach Calem the basic lessons taught to druids to control their own innate gifts.

"The words are the spell, but it's the inflection, the tone, that binds the power and releases it in the way you want to."

"I understand," he replied, "I do, but I just can't say the words right."

"You need to practise."

"When I practise, and I say it wrong, it hurts inside me." He danced his fingers over his arms. "It burns under my skin."

"When you draw on your own flame," she asked, "make it do whatever you want, how do you do it?"

"I just think it." He grimaced, knowing it wasn't a good answer.

"Yes, but what's happening when you just think it?"

He went silent for a while, trying to find the right words to describe what he couldn't really explain even to himself.

"I think about how I'm feeling, and what I have to do, and just let the rest of my mind go blank. I let it take over. I just think about what needs to happen right at that moment."

An'uek listened, asked, and learned as he talked about all the times he had called on his fire. She asked him about the times he had used his power but held the flame at bay.

"Those times, I felt like I was looking at what I was doing. It was like a memory, not instinctive."

"Isaac," she mused.

"How did he learn?" Calem asked.

"With time," she replied, knowing it wasn't an answer.

Calem sighed and unconsciously ruffled the sleeves of his robe and mussed his hair, slipping the hood further down over his face.

"Don't do that," she said, reaching out to pull it back. "Don't hide away from us."

"We're going to be in Penrose, and then we're going to be in Kraner, and A'taz is there and possibly the end of the world. Maybe I should hide." He turned sad solemn eyes to her. "We're riding towards a fight only I can win, and I feel like I'm going to lose."

She reached out, tentatively, and put a gloved hand on his arm.

"We have time," she promised. "I need to teach you differently," she said, leaning back, her hands clenched into fists on the reins. As they rode forward through snowdrifts, on a road neither of them could see, An'uek started to whistle a tune.

"We'll start with something much simpler, the tune before the words. Can you learn the tune I'm humming?"

The simple tune stirred memories from deep in his mind that filled his vision. He looked down and saw his hands, but smaller, like a child, and he was playing with sticks. His memories intensified, and he remembered being that child, he remembered Brennan and a sister, a father, a mother, he remembered humming that tune, and then, only light.

"Calem?" An'uek asked, hoping to get his attention.

His head snapped round, his eyes focused and sharp.

"I know that tune," he said. "I know it well."

She frowned. A sense of unease settling in her mind.

"How can you know it?"

He looked away, over his shoulder, as if looking to the past.

"No more questions today," he replied, his voice clear and strong, unlike himself.

An'uek felt the rebuff; irked, but wary, she dropped her questions and left him to brood in his robes on his colt. An awkward silence settled between them so she kicked her heels to spur on her mare and moved forward to ride with Raef and Bode.

"How far now?" she asked.

"Another mile," Raef replied. We'll come to a main road, follow it north, and there'll be a small town we can tie up in."

"We've come out east of the roadway we were avoiding on the way down. We won't run into the towns we passed getting here, and there's no need to hide ourselves anymore."

They rode on, passing the time with idle chatter. The snowy fields they crossed didn't change enough to say they passed a landmark, but both Raef and Bode knew enough to know when they joined the road, and after barely any time at all, they passed a small group of wagons heading in the same direction.

"Hold up ahead," Raef called out as they were close enough to be heard. He clicked his tongue and his stallion trotted forward.

Bode slowed his horse, and the others slowed as well and gave Raef time to chat with the travellers ahead. After a few minutes, he came back.

"We're headed to Fallowreach," Raef announced.

"Already?" Bode was surprised. "I overshot it a bit. We're further north than I thought by about a day." He reached down to run his fingers through the course mane of his stallion.

"It's a fair-sized town," Raef continued, turning to An'uek. "It has enough taverns and lodging houses that we can expect to find some rooms."

"It'll also have a garrison," Bode said, sitting a little straighter in the saddle.

"Well let's see if there's anyone still there or if it's been emptied before we pick out a banner, shall we."

Bode turned to Raef, frowning.

"Ale first," the thief smiled, "you promised."

They reached what passed as the town boundary after nightfall. It was nothing more elaborate than the name painted onto the side of the first building they passed, a dilapidated old wooden structure collapsed on two of its sides but with just enough slats and joints remaining to keep it upright. It might have once been a barn, or a school hall, a tavern or a brothel. It didn't matter. They rode into the town, in the night, back into Barclan.

Ten minutes past the edge of the town, set back off the road, they spied light shining from a sturdy house that fronted a gated yard. The long shadow of a woman split the light, her voice clear in the dark cold night, calling them over.

Bode dismounted and went to talk. When he returned, his eyes were bright, his shoulders relaxed.

"Her name is Nesrin, this is her livery yard." He sounded relaxed. "We can stay here too."

As he spoke, a young man came over with four older children; they each took up a set of the reins, and once the riders were down, they gently led the desert horses out of the snow into the dry stables.

"They'll be taken care of," Bode said as he handed over his saddlebags. He waited until the others were ready.

"Bode…" An'uek moved over to him, pressing her hand to his forearm to move him back to where they could talk privately. "Can we trust her?"

"We have no reason not to," he answered, his hands on his belt. "She runs this place as lodgings, rooms in one of the barns for men, in the house for women." He put his hands on her forearms, mimicking her actions. His hands easily circled the bony limbs; she was losing weight. "You need to rest," he stated. "We all do. We need proper food, a warm bed, and a bath. Sleep."

An'uek felt his gaze travel over her. He hadn't said anything to her earlier, but she knew he wasn't oblivious to the state she was in, even if she was pretending to be oblivious herself.

"It's my decision. We're staying here tonight at least," he said.

"And tomorrow?" she asked.

"Tomorrow… is the winter festival. We'll be staying tomorrow too or Raef will never forgive me."

She rolled her head on her shoulders, her jaw clenching.

"All right," she conceded. "Let's all go meet Nesrin. Who are we to you?"

"You're all my children." He threw a whimsical look at her.

An'uek glanced down at herself, and then across at his other two 'children'. She was as pale and gaunt as Calem; they could pass as twin ghosts. She called quietly to Raef, who came to stand between her and Calem; Raef, whose deeply tanned skin offset his rich dark brown hair and cinnamon eyes. An'uek raised her eyebrows at Bode, and looked pointedly at Calem and Raef.

"All your children," she said, grinning.

He smirked. "Different mothers."

An'uek sank into the hot water, holding her breath for as long as she could before forcing herself to come up for air. Tiny pink petals stuck to her face and in her hair, like little kisses from the flower heads that floated on the surface of the steaming bathwater. The lightly scented oils on the water coated her skin, and in the soft glow of the thick beeswax candles jammed onto the black wrought-iron candlestick holders in each corner of the room, An'uek almost looked alive.

Taking a deep breath, she sank under the water again, opening her eyes enough to see the shimmering surface dancing with shadows and orange light. Under the water, An'uek let herself feel as tired as she truly was, her limbs feeling thick and her eyes closing, the water comfortably heavy.

A moment of panic gripped her; suddenly afraid she wouldn't be strong enough to come back up, she jerked forward, breaking the surface of the water with a shout, sploshing water over the edge, spilling out across the slate floor.

She looked around, startled, and saw that the candles had all burned down and some had already gone out. She moved from reclining to sitting, an unexpected shiver, as the water, hot a moment ago, was almost cold against her skin.

An'uek scrambled over the side, her wet hands slipping on the wooden edges as she all but flung herself out and across the floor, grabbing for the thick robe she had been offered earlier.

Her wet feet left footprints as she scurried out the door and along the empty corridor to the room she had been given.

Without drying off, she dived onto the wooden-framed bed and rolled herself into the blankets.

Shivering, hiding from nothing in the bedroom, An'uek let the hours of night run into morning as she lay there, awake. Eventually, she started to notice sounds from outside the confining, comforting walls of her room, sounds she recognised. People with voices she didn't know were calling to each other from outside, the familiar knock and clank of doors opening, swinging back against latches, things being moved, or dropped, or dragged, normal sounds of people getting on with their day, talking, laughing, someone with a cough.

She moved under her blanket, her stiff limbs uncurling and stretching. Her back arched, she yawned and sat up.

Smells followed the sounds. Meat being fried in hot oil, fresh bread in an oven somewhere, all carried in on the pervading chilly air that defines a winter's morning.

An'uek let the blankets fall away from her shoulders, the cold air touching her skin, pebbling her flesh, reminding her that she'd neglected to tend her own fire and had watched as it burned out in the hearth through the hours she'd stared numbly at nothing.

Still stiff, she unwrapped from the bed; crossing her arms over herself, it was only a few quick steps to the chair where all her belongings had been laid out. Somehow in the night, or in the hours when she had lost herself to exhaustion staring at the dwindling fire, her clothes had been returned, freshly cleaned and folded neatly, waiting for her. Her dainty pale fingers, trembling from the cold, struggled to get a good grip on the woollen hose she pulled up her legs. She shrugged into the rest of her clothes, taking a moment to mentally thank Sona again, her last deliberate thoughts of the desert, the dangerous sun and hot winds already a faded memory as she pulled the grey shawl across her shoulders. Finally dressed, she took a minute to inspect the room. She hadn't noticed anything the night before, and now in the early morning she could see it all.

It was sparsely decorated, but it had everything a traveller might need. There was a single wooden cabinet in the room. On it was a small clay jug, a mug, and a bowl big enough to hold water to wash her face. There was also a single candle holder for anyone wanting to venture out after dark, a piece of mirror, only big enough for a small face, and a comb. On a shelf inside the cabinet was a discrete stack of thin clean linen strips for the needs of the female patrons in the guest house; An'uek smiled, something of the measure of the mistress of the house was spoken in that moment.

She closed the cabinet and noticed stacks of firewood in the corner of the room, and that was it. Everything she could need, barely anything at all.

An'uek moved back, sitting herself on the edge of the bed as she began to lace up her boots. She looked down at herself. As much of the mud had been cleaned away as possible, but on instruction to use only warm water, there was only so much even a diligent scrubbing brush could do on leather.

She reached for the comb, pulling the finely whittled wooden teeth through her long, knotted hair. It hurt to untangle the long strands but eventually her silvery blonde locks were neatly plaited and tucked away. She looked down when she was finished, mesmerised by the amount of hair pulled from her head entwined on the now ferocious teeth. For longer than she realised, she couldn't pull her gaze away, and she ran her thumb across the tips of the teeth, hearing a slight ping as her nail dragged over each tip. For some reason she couldn't fathom, she felt hot tears sting her eyes, watched them fall onto the comb wetting down her matted hair.

An'uek, still holding the offending comb, rested her head on her other hand and waited for the tears to stop. Eventually wiping her nose on the back of her hand, she put the comb down, pulled on her gloves, pulled her shawl over her head and forced herself to stand up and leave the four walls of the room that felt like the safest place she could ever remember.

Sighing, running her gloved hand across her head and down along the length of her braided hair, she opened the door and left to go find her men.

She walked quietly and slowly down a wide set of well-oiled dark wooden stairs that turned twice as they led her to the ground floor of the impressive house. She felt light-headed and thought perhaps she should go back to her room to the safety of her bed. She wasn't even sure if she wanted to eat, unable to work out if the sensation in her gut was pain or hunger. It felt more like pain. But the smell of fresh food all but dragged her into the big warm kitchen where she found Bode, Raef and Calem sitting at a huge oak dining table talking with their hostess and, she guessed from their easy manner with each other, the people who worked for her.

"Pass the cheese." Raef nudged Bode with an elbow, pointing at a plate too far away to stretch for. Bode handed it over, but not before taking a slab of the hard, dirty yellow stuff for himself and stuffing it into his mouth.

Calem spotted An'uek first, her lithe pale form resplendent in the bright morning light streaming through large clean windows, and she lingered shyly before rounding the corner to come into the room. The sorcerer, for once not obscured head to foot in clothes for hiding, patted his hand, motioning to the empty seat next to him. He had already finished a large plate of eggs and bread and was sitting back in a long-sleeved tunic and sleeveless vest, fidgeting with the lump of metal, which was almost always in his hands now.

"Morning." Bode smiled as she took her seat.

An'uek greeted everyone, thanking Nesrin, who handed her a glazed ceramic plate and mug, both white, decorated with finely painted green leaves that looped around the edges. She noticed her own wooden spoon had been laid out and she glanced at Bode, who for a second seemed to have seen too much of her. She pulled her shawl a little tighter around her shoulders, shuddering, cold despite the roaring fire warming the room.

Without much chatter, An'uek accepted a plate of fresh bread dripping in melting butter, a bowl of oats soaked in warm milk and some dried apple. She ate slowly, full after not much more than a few bites of the warm bread and a spoon of oats. Pushing her plates away, she heard a disapproving cough and looked up to see Bode staring; she knew why. She pulled the plates back.

Raef chatted with everyone, keenly aware of how quickly Bode fell away from the conversation when An'uek had joined them. He thought, as she sat down, that he imagined the sound of her bones rattling under her skin. There wasn't much left of her even hidden as she was under all the layers she wore.

"Put some honey on that," Raef muttered to her as she took another forced mouthful of bread.

"I'm fine," she said, thanking him, savouring the salty taste of the butter, but wishing she was already done. She asked for the honey and spread as much as she could across the slab of bread without it spilling over the sides. She sat and drank hot milk, her pale skin not taking on any colour in the warm kitchen, the grey of her shawl matching the grey of her eyes.

"Do you want something else?" Bode asked An'uek as she stirred her oats, his voice low, not meeting her gaze.

"No, this is plenty," she replied.

"Are you going to eat it then?" he said, staring at her.

Staring back, she put the wooden spoon to her lips, forcing the breakfast onto her tongue, swallowing it without tasting it. Her stomach ached.

"It's delicious," she said, forcing another spoonful in.

"Try the fruit." There was an edge of insistence to his words she didn't like, but she took a piece of apple and bit into it. The sharp tang of the cold stored fruit made her wince for a second.

He watched her as he chewed his own food: sausages, bread and eggs.

"There are raisins somewhere if you want, some nuts and berries?"

"No, this is enough." She took another bite of the apple, uncomfortable with how difficult it was to swallow the inoffensive morsel of food.

"Egg?"

"I don't like egg."

"Nesrin has beans somewhere if you want."

"Please stop," she said bitterly.

"Can you have some more of the bread?" He didn't stop.

"Would you like to chew it for me and swallow it too?" she said sharply.

"I will if it gets it into your belly." He took another bite of his eggs.

"I said I'm fine." An'uek stressed each word fiercely.

"I didn't ask if you were fine," Bode challenged her.

"I think I've had enough." She put her spoon down and sat back on the stool.

"You've not had even five mouthfuls of food."

"Leave it." An'uek moved as if to stand, but Bode called her name as if nailing her to her seat.

"An'uek, sit down. You're not leaving this table until you've eaten a meal." His words weren't loud, but they didn't need to be. He looked up, chewing.

An'uek glared at him, but she stayed sitting. He shrugged at her, refusing to acknowledge how angry he was making her.

"Did you at least sleep?" he asked.

"Did you?" she shot back.

"All right," Raef suddenly called out loudly, surprising everyone at the table. "I think we're all still tired from riding through the snowstorm yesterday, aren't we, dear sister."

Nesrin rose to her feet and started to clear away some of the plates, calling over for more drinks for her guests. When their mugs were full, she ushered her people away, leaving the four of them alone at the table. As she closed the door behind her, the façade of the four fell away.

"Well that wasn't obvious at all." Raef turned to glare at Bode and An'uek.

"What?" she asked, feigning ignorance.

"You two bicker like two people who hate each other so much you married to spite the other," Raef said, as he drained his drink, wiped his mouth on a bit of his sleeve, then got to his feet. "Father and daughter indeed, you're terrible actors, both of you." He reached over to Calem, hauling him to his feet by his shoulders.

"Come on, Calem, let's go and leave our sister and father to have an argument. When you're done," he turned to Bode, "come into town. I'm taking the boy here and going to look for something to steal, some honest drinking before noon, and someone who hasn't seen my dice game. There's going to be music and dancing at the festival and I'm going to be there. I'll be drunk later, so fix yourselves then come and get him."

He turned and dramatically stalked out the kitchen, all but dragging Calem along while the boy wailed that he didn't even have his boots on yet.

Bode and An'uek found themselves alone in the kitchen. He sat back, holding his mug of warm milk spiced with cloves in trembling fingers. He looked relaxed as he held her gaze, occasionally moving to ease some of the discomfort from his very full belly.

She watched him shift in his seat, raised his hand to cover his mouth, trying to hide a belch, wiping imaginary crumbs from his beard. Her anger, so quick to rise at his insistence on her selfcare, dissipated as quickly, replaced with a prick of guilt.

She picked up her spoon, frowning to herself as she moved the congealed oats around in the bowl.

CHAPTER 27

True to his word, as soon as Raef and Calem had reached the town centre earlier that morning they had gone straight to a tavern. Raef sent Calem to a corner.

"Wait for me. Stay out of trouble," he said, his finger raised to emphasise his words.

"Yes, I know." Calem rolled his eyes and made a show of stuffing his hands into his pockets.

"Keep them there," Raef ordered, then turned and squeezed his way to the bar to get the barkeeper's attention. He ordered a drink, and as he did so, he relieved the stranger at his side of his coin purse. Both men waited for their drinks, Raef striking up a casual conversation.

The barkeeper brought over their drinks together.

As Raef opened the man's coin purse and started to sort out the payment, the other man patted his belt looking for his money. Realising he'd been pickpocketed, the man began yelling and swearing. He spun, about to dash around, when Raef tapped him on the arm. The man swivelled and looked at him.

"No sense making a scene. He won't be here," Raef said casually, pulling some coin from the purse in his hand. He tapped the man's hand, and when he opened it and looked down, Raef dropped his own coins into it. He then reached over and paid for both their drinks.

"Take that, and have a great day." Raef slapped the man's arm as he spluttered his thanks. He reached over, put the man's drink in his other hand, and clinked their tankards together. Both men took a long drink. "I hope you find the man that stole your money."

"Thanks, friend, and thanks for the drink. I owe you one later."

"I'll look for you later then." Raef smiled and walked casually over to Calem.

Calem stared at him, bemused.

"I'm not sure I'm the one who needs to be told not to start trouble," he said, but he was unable to keep the edge of admonition out of his voice; Raef knew he was impressed. He grinned and winked and took a long drink.

"Skill," Raef said by way of explanation, taking another long sip. "After all, you don't think I've ever bought my own drink, do you?"

The thief led the young man out of the tavern and into the chilly winter day. Crowds had started to gather, and a small group of musicians were tuning their instruments.

Raef breathed deeply and turned to Calem.

"How long do you think they'll argue for?"

"Who, Bode and An'uek? I don't know, the rest of their lives."

Raef snorted a laugh, looking at Calem with a grin. He was starting to think the boy might have a wicked sense of humour if he wasn't so strange and serious all the time.

"Well, however long it takes, we've got that long to wander around and enjoy ourselves."

"Is this the part where you get drunk and I end up on my own," Calem asked, suddenly solemn. Raef sighed, the humour gone so quickly he wondered if this was the same boy who a moment ago was making a joke about their friends. He wanted to reach round, to sling his arm across the boy's shoulder and buy him a drink, get him drunk, get him laughing, maybe get him a girl. Instead, he found a low wall and put his tankard of half-finished ale down. He wiped his hands on his thighs and made to walk away, leaving the mostly full drink on the wall.

"Come on," he said, gesturing to Calem, who followed a step behind. "Let's go take a look around and see what there is to take."

"You mean buy."

"Did I say buy?"

"You said take."

"I know what I said."

Calem chuckled, Raef's eager mischievousness was as infectious as the grin that warmed his eyes, and Calem had a feeling this town wasn't prepared for a man like Raef in high spirits. As much as he wanted to join in and relax, he knew he couldn't. He kept his hands in his pockets, trying to ignore the way his palms itched and an unwelcome sensation of familiarity kept washing over him. He caught himself looking around the town centre, as if he recognised it, as if he'd been here before at some time in his life. Or maybe another town, just like this one somewhere else.

He kept following Raef, listening to the chatter of the people they wandered past. The man at his side stopped every few feet to say something to strangers. He charmed the women, he befriended the men, and all the children ran away laughing at the funny man. His smile was open and carefree, and he laughed louder than Calem had ever heard before. He politely declined every offer for them to join someone's table for a drink or a meal, and if anyone had noticed when he fleeced their pockets, Calem guessed they'd have probably forgiven him and let him keep what he wanted. The handsome man with the dark brown eyes had a way of belonging in the crowd that left Calem mesmerised, and as more people crammed into the square, Raef moved smoothly among them all.

For Calem, it wasn't so easy. He was careful not to bump into anyone, keeping his curious orange eyes away from people's glances, trying to be as forgettable as such a striking-looking young man could be. But inevitably, as the square filled and there was less space to move, he struggled to keep out of people's way. It didn't take long for him to feel like there was no way to be safe. A man accidentally stepped on his boot; as Calem jerked backwards out of the way, a small gang of laughing children barrelled past him, causing him to almost lose his footing. Instinctively he flung out his arms to catch himself as he fell, grabbing a fence post with both hands. Immediately, the smell of smouldering wood caught his attention. Snapping his head up, he wrenched his hands away, but already there was charring where he'd held on for mere seconds. He reached into his pocket and closed a hand on the lump of metal, feeling it start to throb in his grip. He stared at his boots, quelling the panic that was threatening to rise.

"Raef, I need to sit down," he called out loudly, hoping he was close.

Raef reacted instantly, the façade of the world's friend dropping away as he stepped close to Calem's side; he saw a scared boy standing next to a fence post marked with burned handprints.

"I've got you." He stepped close and carefully put his hand on the boy's elbow. He nudged them through the crowd, towards the outskirts of the stalls to sit on the edge of the stone fountain, water frozen in its basin, barely gurgling spurts of water through the mouths of hand-carved stone fish. Ice clung to most of the spouts, hanging down like white spears. There was no threat of even a splash touching the boy, but still, Raef wished there was somewhere else to put him. Then again, he thought to himself, maybe this was a good place.

"Sit here, sit down." Raef pushed gently to direct Calem where to go. The boy's hands were still in his pockets and his balance was off.

"You got your lump?"

Calem nodded vigorously.

"Good, keep with it," Raef said as soothingly as he could. He noticed the ice around the fountain starting to melt, Calem's body heat radiating from him.

Raef wasn't sure what else to do.

Without warning, the band struck up their instruments and the nervous quiet of the two men was interrupted with the sound of a jaunty tune.

Calem flinched in surprise, and all the icicles on the fountain shattered and fell onto the melting ice water of the basin.

Raef reached over, putting his hands on the boy's shoulders.

"You're fine," he said, unsure if he was reassuring himself or Calem. The boy was so hot, and Raef, looking down at him, didn't need to be reminded of just who he was, or what he could do.

The sound of a bow being dragged over protesting strings filled the air like a scream of pain. People around them roared with laughter as the person responsible stopped and started to fiddle with the tuning pegs. He tried again, and again the screech was torment; Raef saw Calem pull his hands from his pockets and covered his ears, the lump of metal, glowing red hot, falling to the ground near his feet.

The water from the fountain started to steam as it heated up.

Raef pushed the lump with his booted toe, too scared to reach down and pick it up, feeling a sense of dread as his stomach twisted. Looking down at Calem, he watched as the boy's lips moved, and he heard him humming the tune An'eris had been teaching him for the past few days, the one he couldn't get right.

Raef saw, just for a second, a pulse of flame flicker over the exposed skin of Calem's hands over his ears as the whine of the music carried on.

A sense of danger overwhelmed Raef; beads of sweat ran down his spine.

"This was a bad idea," he said to himself.

He was about to tell Calem to get up, that they were leaving, when someone tapped him on the shoulder. He turned quickly and saw the face of the man from the tavern.

"Hello, friend," the man said kindly. "Is he all right?" he asked, gesturing to the boy.

"He's fine." Raef made up an excuse. "My little brother is still hungover from last night. That man torturing his fiddle is doing his head in."

Raef was irritated; he wanted the man gone. He had to deal with Calem, to get him away from the crowd, from people in flammable clothes, leaning on bales of hay decorated with ribbons, sitting on wooden benches, chatting under wooden awnings, walking around on the ground littered with straw, children running around with lanterns made from dry parchment and twigs.

Raef, for a moment, had a vision of everyone, everything, on fire, the inferno raging around the centre of the town, but instead of the makeshift stage for the musicians, there was an old tree.

As suddenly as it flickered into his mind, it was gone.

"Honestly we're fine." Raef took the man's hand and forced him to step back. "Thanks anyway." He turned his back and hoped the man took his intent.

Raef bent down, picked up the cooled rock and dropped it on Calem's lap. He grabbed one of his hands and forced it onto the metal. It took only a second and it was glowing red hot again, Calem's fingers gripping it tightly. Moments passed and Calem used his other hand to hold the lump with both, the metal emitting a very audible thrumming as it reverberated in his palms. Raef, having lived a lifetime of survival based on holding his nerve, stood with him, waiting patiently for him to get himself under control. After a little while, the lump settled, the noise faded away and Calem looked up.

He didn't say sorry with his words, and Raef didn't need to hear them to understand the look in his eyes.

He kneeled in front of Calem.

"Are we good?"

Calem looked down at his hands, at the lump of insignificant cold heavy metal.

"M-Maybe I'll sit for a bit longer?" Calem stuttered, his voice deeper, older than earlier. "To be sure."

"No problem." Raef nudged him with a knee and, when he shuffled over, sat down next to him, close enough to be close, but not to touch him.

Neither spoke for a while, until finally Raef shifted on his seat and got Calem's attention. He pointed, Calem following his gesture.

"Look who finally decided to turn up."

Bode and An'uek had lost each other for a few minutes on the walk along the wide well-worn path into the centre of the town. People jostled them for their slow pace, too slow it seemed for everyone rushing ahead. An'uek snatched at pieces of conversation as people streamed past. She felt like a slow old fish caught in the current of the faster, happier fish, all swimming upstream together, because that's what they'd always done.

Their momentum carried her forwards when her legs wanted to stop and carry her back to the solitude of her small bedroom. People wanted to get to their favourite taverns, the best stalls, the comfortable benches, to eat delicious treats, drink their favourite warm spiced wines or cold ale, to spend the day with friends singing and dancing around bonfires late into the night. Their eager footsteps had trampled the snow-covered paths to mud, but everywhere else was a foot deep in fresh snowfall, as if the crowds were walking to a promise of happiness borne on the dream of perfect white clouds. As the delight of the crowds around her increased, An'uek felt her own emotions starting to lift; it was impossible to scowl at the face of laughing children running past, bumping into her legs, bouncing along with red cheeks, hand-knitted scarves loose around their necks, most already missing their winter hats or gloves or both. She forced her way to the edge of the crowd, which seemed more tolerant of her slower pace, and started searching for Bode. Never hard to spot, usually the head above most of the crowd, she moved like a stone in the current, against the crowd, finally reaching him with a slight gasp. She reached out, her hand slotting into his, and felt him tighten his grip before he turned to see her.

"I don't think we'll be the first ones there," she quipped.

"I only hope there's somewhere to sit when we get where we're all going."

As they walked with quick steps, the path took them into the town, and the sounds of music reached them above the banter of the jovial crowd. Looking up, as if searching for the music overhead, An'uek saw bright red and green triangles of bunting strung across the wide road from building to building. Balconies were decorated with thick ribbons hanging down shimmering in the slight breeze and most of the doors had beautiful wreaths wound through with deep red flowers nailed to the frames.

The smells captivated them next: roasting meats, the ever-present waft of fresh loaves and buns from the bakery, spices, herbs and the rich scent of pipe smoke as they passed groups of men leaning on whatever they could find, sharing a bag of dried leaves, clay mugs of ale and stories about the battles on the borders of the kingdom.

An'uek noticed Bode start to slow as they passed a particularly loud group swapping rumours of the King's demise. She yanked his hand, hard, and got his attention. Looking across at him, she shook her head.

"We're already strangers here, we don't need to be inquisitive strangers. People remember that."

He nodded and felt her tug him away, back into the shoal of people.

She felt a sense of relief at how easily he had relented, and she let herself smile, unconsciously squeezing his hand tighter in her own.

"Over there," she said loudly, pulling him over towards a stall that caught her eye.

When they stopped, he looked across at her, surprise clear on his face.

"Really?"

"Go on." She leaned towards him and nudged him with her shoulder. "We've got to join in, haven't we?"

He smirked at her excuse, dug in the pocket of his trousers and fished out a few small coins. Handing over a piece of copper, he took a small wooden dart offered by a young girl working on the stall and took aim at the board hanging on a crossbar ten feet away.

His aim was wildly off centre, but nonetheless, An'uek cheered when the dart bit into the board, and the young girl handed over a small prize for his efforts.

"For me?" An'uek feigned surprise, taking the small garland of lavender as her bounty. She put it to her nose, inhaled deeply, the sweet subtle perfume of the flowers reminding her of joy. Bode took a small piece of string from the girl and tied the garland to An'uek's shawl so it hung down over her shoulder.

"Matches your eyes." He offered her his hand, pleased when she smiled, and laced their fingers together.

His spirits lifted and then they walked around together in companionable silence.

Calem and Raef watched for a while as Bode and An'uek walked around the stalls. Their big friend had changed. His unkept hair had been trimmed close on the sides and neatly cut on top, taking the hair out of his eyes. His beard was trimmed close to his skin, covering the scars they thought he probably wanted to hide. He wore a thick long-sleeved black tunic under a grey vest, black leather trousers tucked into his boots, and a thick grey cloak buttoned almost to his neck.

An'uek, wrapped in her own white leathers and grey wool, leaned on his arm, laughing at something he said. Bode carried a bag of something, and they watched as he reached into the bag and pulled out a small handful of whatever it was and popped them into his mouth as he carried on with his story.

"Didn't expect that," Calem said, the sight of the two of them making him forget his own predicament.

"He looks older," Raef replied, staring. "He had a bit of grey before, but when did he get so much grey."

"When did the grey start to turn white?"

"She looks happy."

"He looks happy."

"Is she wearing a bit of twig?"

"It's a garland you fool," Raef chastised him.

"She's laughing?" Calem asked.

"I've not heard her laugh like that… ever, I think." Raef sounded stunned.

"I don't think she laughs like that except when she's with him."

"She frowns a lot when she's with him too."

The two men turned to each other, and a pressure valve released somewhere between them and they both sagged and suddenly felt tired.

Bode spotted Calem and Raef and headed towards them at a slow pace, tugging An'uek to follow.

"That's not a good sign." Bode finished the roasted nuts and threw the bag away, licking the sugary residue from his fingers.

"What? The two of them grinning like fools… or the blackened stone fountain behind Calem without any water in it?"

"Calem's clothes." Bode's voice hardened, and he stuffed his hands into the deep pockets of his cloak, his shoulders stiffening.

An'uek looked over and saw what Bode had seen.

"They look scorched." She quickened her pace a step before Bode picked up speed.

The two of them reached Raef and Calem, who was still leaning against the stone edge of the fountain, Calem's eyes downcast, Raef's smile as warm and convivial as it had been all afternoon.

"Glad you made it into town." Raef took Bode's offered hand, leaning over to kiss An'uek's porcelain cheek, which was tinged pink in the cold winter air.

"What happened?" she demanded.

"It's all right," Raef replied, "I dealt with it."

"You... dealt with it?" An'uek echoed his words. "What does that mean?"

"Means we're all alive." Raef reached over and pushed the two of them a step away. "And I'm taking Calem back to the lodgings."

"I can go on my own." Calem stepped in, standing straight, his head up, looking at them all with a confidence he usually didn't have.

Bode squinted at him for a moment, as if expecting to see another visage shift across his face, forgetting that the older mind was mingled more seamlessly with his own.

"I'll go," Raef said kindly.

"The festival has hardly begun," Calem argued. "You've not even found someone's wife to charm yet."

Raef smiled at Calem and laughed to himself.

"You're a fool," he muttered at Calem, but turned to Bode. He handed over several coin purses. "Here, go win her something decent, or at least buy her something decent. Good fathers spoil their daughters at festivals," he said to his big friend.

An'uek looked down at her simple lavender garland and fingered the woody stem.

"I like this," she said, chortling.

"Only because it's what you've got." He leaned over and kissed her cheek again. "Be warned, the music is terrible, and there might be some shouting later when people realise they've been robbed."

Without another word Raef reached out, pulled Calem forward with his hand on his elbow, and the two set off, heading away to the edge of the square, heading away from the laughing, the food and drink, the music and dancing, and everyone looking forward to a wonderful night.

Bode and An'uek were left alone, staring at the blackened stone of the fountain. The druidess reached down and put her gloved fingertips on the fountain edge.

"Still warm," she murmured.

"Best not to do that." Bode reached over and took her hand away, wiping the black soot marks from her fingers. "Don't want people to notice anything."

They stood in silence, both thinking. An'uek turned to Bode first.

"It wasn't long ago that I had to make him swear an oath on his life that he wouldn't try to murder the boy."

"Calem's changing. They've both are."

An'uek rubbed the back of her neck, suddenly tight with tension.

"Is that a good thing?"

"I don't know. I could ask you the same thing."

They both looked around, the festival colours seeming a little less bright, the chattering a little too loud, the crowds a little too close.

A cold breeze blew through the town, blew past them, the smell of burned stone so strange, so strong and sharp it assailed them for a moment.

"Come on," he said, turning, offering An'uek his arm.

"If we hurry, we can catch up with them. They're only a few minutes ahead."

Raef and An'uek sat together on a small bench covered in cushions near a large stone hearth that held a blazing fire, roaring flames, burning on nothing. Calem lay on the flagstone floor in front of the hearth, his head resting on his bent arm, staring at the fire. The bright orange flames changed shape as his mind wandered: flying birds, racing horses, faces in the flames they didn't recognise. An'uek got up from her seat of deep cushions; she went to the log store in the corner and brought over two stout blocks of dry hardwood. As she walked back, one slipped from her hand, the rough bark grazing her palm. She swore under her breath, bending forward and putting the wood into the flames. She got some more logs and stacked them so they at least looked like they were the cause of the fire. She brushed off her hands and stepped back, reclining onto the bench and moving the big cushions around to give herself a bit of comfort. She was staring at her palms, scowling. Raef draped a thick blanket around her shoulders and scooted closer to her. Wordlessly, he took her palms in his and saw the little splinters of wood sticking in her skin.

"Hang on," he said quietly and rose to go into the kitchen. A minute later he came back, a thin silver needle between his fingers. "I noticed a sewing basket in there earlier," he explained, settling in close to her to start digging out the painful slivers of wood.

"You'll be okay with this?" he asked, eyeing the needle.

"I've had splinters before."

She hissed once, looking at Calem but not moving her hand away.

There was a loud cracking sound; one of the logs had caught in the flames and was starting to burn.

"At least if Nesrin comes in there's a normal fire," Raef muttered, concentrating on not sticking the needle in too deep.

"I think Bode's still talking to her." An'uek grimaced as the needle slipped under a nasty bit of splinter, lifting some of it before it broke in half under her skin.

"Is the needle all right?" Raef asked, suddenly panicking as he realised he was pushing metal into the druid's body.

"It's fine. It's poisonous to us as children," she explained calmly, soothing his worries with her mind. "I can stand a bit of silver and whatever that's mixed with."

"If Bode sees this he'll go crazy," Raef said wide-eyed.

"It's fine." An'uek took the needle from him and put it against her cheek. As she lifted it off it left a thin red mark that faded in a second. She handed it back and let her head drop.

"Honestly," she said, "it stings but it's not too bad."

Raef nodded and went back to the splinters, as careful and gentle as he could be.

An'uek turned her head and stared at the snow falling against the small windowpane, the flurries building up quickly on the windowsill, a snow curtain building up to keep them from the outside world.

"What do you think they're talking about?" Raef asked.

"I have no idea," she scoffed, looking at the direction of the faint voices. "Maybe working on an explanation for why Calem needs to sleep on a stone floor tonight instead of the barn?"

"He slept fine last night, didn't char the bed or the blankets. Nothing for her to suspect anything at all."

"You checked on him?"

"We took turns."

An'uek smiled, wincing as Raef got the end of the splinter and dragged it almost out.

"Hang on," he murmured, then put her palm to his mouth. She wasn't expecting to feel the nip of his teeth or hard sucking on her flesh, and as quickly as he did it, he let her go, the tiny tip of the splinter on the tip of his tongue. He wiped it off against his hand, leaning forward for her to see.

"Got it," he muttered, pleased with himself.

"That hurt," she chided.

"But it's out." He shrugged, reaching for her palm and setting to work on the other slivers.

She turned again, staring at nothing, her focus on trying to hear what Bode and Nesrin were saying in the other room.

Raef focused on her palm, and he was aware of An'uek trying too hard to make it seem she was relaxed. The sound of Bode's deep voice laughing carried in past the closed door, and he noticed An'uek shift in her seat.

He smiled to himself.

The sounds of snoring crept up from the floor.

"I guess he's asleep then." An'uek nudged Raef with her foot and looked down at Calem. "For someone so dangerous he sleeps a lot."

"Sleeps better than any of us, that's for sure," he replied, nodding.

"Bode told me a story about when he used to visit Calem as a boy. He has an older brother, Bode's best friend."

"Brennan," An'uek interrupted.

"That's the name, yes." He bit into her palm and sucked out another splinter, spitting it out into the flames nearby. "He said Calem used to sleep on the floor with his dogs when he was a boy."

"Maybe this place feels like home to him."

"Might be why he managed to get himself under control in the town."

"That could have been a lot worse." An'uek winced, but she held her hand still as the needle drew a spot of blood.

"You don't need to remind me," Raef said, lowering his voice. "He's a lot more stable these last few days. Much less of the flicking between the old man and the boy."

"I thought about that," An'uek replied.

"You think it's from the stuff you're teaching him?"

"I've got no idea," she replied, turning to catch his glance. "I honestly couldn't tell you if I'm teaching him anything at all, or if it'll make the slightest bit of difference."

"But he is different," Raef insisted.

"How?" An'uek asked, curious to hear what the thief had noticed.

"He's terrified of his own power for a start." Raef stopped digging with the needle for a minute. "That makes me feel a little bit better."

"He's killed people with it. If that didn't terrify him…" She didn't finish her words.

Raef focused on the splinters.

"He's easier to be around I guess." Raef's voice was quiet.

"I think so too," An'uek agreed. "The less his mind jumps around, the easier it is to feel like we're getting to know him."

"Yes," Raef said, nodding.

"That's what makes him more dangerous now, more even than he was yesterday. The second we start to like him, start to think he's more, or less, than what he is, then we've lost."

Raef sighed; he stopped and looked at her.

"How can we forget how terrible he is, when we have you to remind us?"

She pulled her hand away slowly, looking down at the few remaining splinters in her palm. Opening her hand as wide as she could, palm up, she crossed over it with her other hand and the splinters disintegrated under her skin.

Raef, a flicker of annoyance across his face, sighed and sat back, stabbing the needle into the thick leather of his belt pushing it through the other side.

They didn't speak, they both just stared at the boy sleeping on the floor in front of the warm fire.

Bode and Nesrin talked into the night, longer than they needed to, about things that didn't matter to either of them, both finding they didn't want to say goodnight. But eventually they did, and Bode came into the small sitting room, took a spare blanket off the back of the bench and laid it out across Calem, the only one asleep, still on the floor.

"Do you think he'll want a pillow?" Bode asked playfully, but he paused, as without warning An'uek uncurled her bent legs from her seat on the bench and left the room.
Bode turned to look at Raef, his hands up.

"What was that?"

"Who knows with her these days," Raef spat back, getting himself up, taking a small cushion off the bench and kneeling to place it under Calem's head. The boy rolled over in his sleep.

Bode crossed his arms over his chest, stroking the underside of his chin with trembling fingers. He rubbed his eyes with the back of his hand and then, as if making a decision, settled into a faded armchair near the fire.

"You can go to sleep," Raef said as he settled down, leaning against the wall near the hearth. "I'm not tired. I'll watch him first."

"Not in the mood," Bode replied, turning his head to the doorway that Raef knew would lead to Nesrin's room.

He raised an eyebrow.

"Did she offer?"

"She made me think if I asked she wouldn't say no," he replied with a smirk.

"So?"

Bode held up his trembling hands.

"So?" Raef repeated, but he was asking a different question.

Bode unlaced his boots and pulled them off, put his feet towards the fire, and yawned.

"Things never quite go our way, do they?" he said wistfully, watching the dancing flames.

"You and An'uek seemed to have made peace after this morning though," Raef replied. "Although I don't think she liked you spending all evening talking to the lovely lady of the house."

"Is that why she stormed out?" Bode laughed ruefully at himself. "She was easier before."

"She's a lot more like us these days, a lot less like she was."

"That's our fault," Bode replied.

"You always do that," Raef said, exasperated.

"What?"

"Make excuses for her, for whatever she says or does." He raised his voice. "I heard her laughing today, and my first thought was, happiness doesn't belong in her anymore. She isn't kind to you. She isn't good for any of us. She's hard now. You can see it in her face, in her eyes."

"She's kind to me," Bode disagreed.

"Only when she remembers."

"Do you think I care about kindness anymore," he asked sceptically. "This thing we have to do, it doesn't need kindness… or goodness." He leaned forward, elbows on his knees. "It needs steel."

Raef stared at Calem.

"Ask me a month ago, I'd have agreed with you." His voice was solemn. "But now I'm starting to think we might have this wrong. And you're wrong." He looked at Bode. "You do care, it just makes you sad."

"We're leaving for Penrose tomorrow," Bode announced, ending the conversation.

CHAPTER 28

Cotta took a long drag on the smoke and handed it back to Travis.

"I'll never get the taste for sour old dry leaves," she said as she exhaled perfect rings of dirty smoke into the cold winter day.

"Really?" Travis pulled the smoke deep into his lungs. "Is that why you've nearly smoked my whole pouch?"

"It's nerves," she countered.

Travis nodded as he exhaled, dropping the stub underfoot.

"I remember your nerves," he said, taking his flask off his belt and offering it to her. "They tend to cost me money."

Cotta took a long deep pull, enjoying the burn of the brandy down her throat. Travis followed her, and between them they emptied the flask.

"I can't believe you agreed to this." Travis turned to face her, his thumbs hitched onto his belt, his head leaning against the cold stone wall where they'd been loitering for over an hour.

"I didn't have a choice, did I," she replied. "Brennan gets an idea in his head and it runs away with him. I can't tell him what to do, he's been talking about this for days."

"You know that's not true," Travis challenged her. "A'rrick's taking Brennan to the castle to find An'eris, and he's only gone because you didn't tell him not to."

Cotta looked everywhere except at Travis for as long as it took him to roll his last smoke, find someone to get a light, and hand it to her. He settled back to wait in silence at her side.

A'rrick and Brennan shuffled their way through the crowds celebrating the start of the winter festival. They stopped at every stall selling anything hot, Brennan cramming food into his mouth as often as he took a breath.

"Try not to choke to death before we get to the castle gates," A'rrick half joked.

"Hungry," was all Brennan could say around mouthfuls of meat and bread.

"At least chew," A'rrick suggested.

Brennan threw him an irritated glance, took another bite, and kept walking through the busy streets in the late afternoon.

"Remind me where?" Brennan asked as he chewed.

A'rrick turned a corner and started leading him towards the section of the city where he had started to sense An'eris earlier that week and been looking for her every day since. Brennan moved sluggishly, his body full of pain, but the surge of energy from all the food was fuelling his ability to put the pain out of his mind. As he walked, his limp subsided, each step a little surer, and he raised his head.

A'rrick noticed the physical change; looking at Brennan at his side with his other sense, he was amazed and troubled by what he saw. Brennan's aura was gone, now, a subtleness of something else that put him in mind of Cotta. He wondered how deeply the two were linked; could he be drawing his strength from her?

His thoughts were interrupted by a deliberate mental shove. Blinking, he looked over at Brennan, who was glaring at him.

"Stay out," he warned, an unspoken threat at the end of his words. A'rrick felt a sensation move over his skin, as if something was being dragged down his body.

"Sorry," A'rrick mumbled. "Bad habit."

"I know about those," Brennan replied, breaking the tension, rubbing his opaque eyes with the back of his greasy hands.

Changing the subject, A'rrick tapped his arm.

"Still hungry?"

"Why, what can you see?"

"Small cart, selling skewers of something."

"Get two of whatever's on the plate," Brennan said as he shuffled from the street to find some wall to take his weight.

As he waited for A'rrick to return with the food, Brennan kept his head down, down enough for a little girl wandering past to be able to look up straight into his face.

"What's wrong with your eyes?" Brennan heard a small voice that was too close. Putting one hand on the wall behind him, he lowered himself down to where he thought the girl might be standing.

"I got some lye on my face, it's burned my eyes," he said gently.

"Is that why they're full of muck?"

"Yes," he answered, making sure the little girl was forgetting him as she spoke to him.

"Will you go blind?" she asked.

"A bit but not too much." He smiled. "No, it's already better than it was a few days ago."

"Can you see my flower?" she asked, holding up a red winter rose, the petals almost as big as her hand.

"I can see it's very beautiful," he said kindly.

"My pa bought it for me." The little girl twirled it in her fingers.

"Maybe I should buy one?" Brennan asked.

"Do you have a daughter?"

"No, but I have a woman I love, and her favourite colour is—"

"Red, like my flower."

"Yes," Brennan nodded, "it's red."

"I think she'd like that." The little girl smiled, then turned around, forgot about Brennan, and walked back to her family who were being served salted hog crackling across the street.

"Who was that?" A'rrick asked, grabbing Brennan's hand and putting food into his palm.

"Little girl asking about the hunchback with the bleeding eyes."

"So stand up properly, I know you can. And they're not bleeding anymore," A'rrick reminded him.

"Well aren't I lucky," Brennan said as he started to eat, the grease from the fat running down his chin.

"You can see, can't you?" A'rrick retorted.

"Everything is still blurry, mostly shapes, no colour."

"A few days ago you were blind and dead. Stop being so ungrateful, eat whatever that is, then let's get going."

Travis and Cotta found enough space to squeeze onto the end of a seat at a table outside a busy tavern in the main market square. A barmaid brought over mugs of hot spiced wine and a plate heaped with chunks of hard bread and a bowl of thick gravy. Travis handed over coins and then enough to keep the wine from running out.

Cotta picked up her mug.

"I am so glad this isn't tea." She took a tentative sip, flinching as the hot liquid burned her tongue. Travis snickered at her impatience, watching as she brought it to her lips, blowing the steam away hoping to cool it quicker. He grabbed for the bread. They sat in silence, eating, drinking, listening to everyone talking around them.

The chatter was mostly idle gossip, drunken banter, and men and women placing bets on the outcomes of the traditional winter festival tournaments being run over the next few days.

Cotta could see the way the chatter caught Travis's attention.

"Want to place a few wagers?" she asked.

"Never say no to a bet," he replied quickly. "What do you fancy some silver on?"

They talked between themselves just loud enough to catch on with the people around them and were quickly drawn into the conversation around the table. Soon they were sharing fake names, false lives as man and wife, and encouraging some idle rumours.

It didn't take long before Cotta was able to subtly start asking questions.

"Have any of you taken up with that new morality then?"

"Not me," a middle-aged woman replied. "I'm not for prayer, but a lot of people I know have thought about it. It wasn't that long ago that we were starving to death. Makes you question who will look after your soul when you're in the ground."

"I reckon we've got the Gods for that," Travis said, mopping up the last of the gravy and waving to catch the barmaid's attention for more.

"True," a small bald man agreed, as he stuffed a pipe and lit it off the small oil lantern on the table. "But it doesn't hurt to offer up a bit of song to someone the Gods have blessed, in case your skin isn't as clean as you'd like when you go into the dirt and someone needs to argue for your place."

"Maybe some truth in that," Travis said thoughtfully.

Too thoughtfully for Cotta's liking; she knew the look on his face, could practically read the words he was thinking through his eyes.

"Don't you worry about your sins," she said to him. "I'll wash those clean off when the time comes."

He leaned forward and brought her knuckles to his lips.

"You say the sweetest things when picturing my death."

Their new friends roared with laughter and called for more drinks.

"What news of the castle then, is the Queen still in mourning?"

"I heard she is," someone replied, "but she's still going to come to the square later to light the bonfire. Apparently one of the council was going to light it but she's insisting."

"What?" Cotta shrieked, surprising the others.

"Tradition," someone replied, "been done since the first stone was laid in the city."

"That's right," the first woman replied. "Can't say as I would want to be her right now. Castle and coin and jewels aside, I'd want to mourn my man but I respect her. She's not from here, not one of us, but she's keeping our ways and our traditions."

Everyone started nodding.

"She's going to be a good Queen," the woman said.

"She is a good Queen," Cotta said to herself.

Travis watched as the slightly drunk Cotta stood; he knew it was time to go.

She didn't hear the excuses he made, but she smiled and shook hands and kissed cheeks and promised to find everyone later and let Travis lead her away, his arm around her waist, keeping her close to his side.

"We need to find A'rrick and Brennan. They're going to the castle but she won't be there."

"I'll find a way," Travis promised, leading her to a lantern column in the street for her to lean against.

"I want to see her," Cotta said, gripping his hands in hers.

"All right," he replied without hesitation. "I'll see what I can do."

"Hurry," she said, her voice taking on the edge of command as the alcohol in her veins disappeared with the surge of adrenaline she felt flood her body. "I want to see her, and if Troy is with her, or A'taz, I want them to see me."

As he walked away, with no idea of how he would accomplish anything she had just asked of him, he wondered if this was how he would die. Not from the addictive poisons he willingly took every day, not from drink or whatever he could find to smoke in his pipe. No, he thought to himself, he would go into the ground because he couldn't say no to her.

An'eris watched a maid brush through her long brown hair. She counted the strokes, losing track after she reached fifty as quick nimble fingers pulled her hair from her face and started to braid it into intricate patterns that resembled vines, accentuated by thin black ribbons wound through the knots.

They helped her dress in a full-length black gown cinched tightly above her growing belly. The maid was careful to smooth the gown down around the bump, tying a thick black satin sash around her waist, trailing it up over one shoulder, tucking it in at the back. The long sleeves flowed down over her hands, the edges of the tapered cuffs getting lost in the folds of thick warm fabric. A heavy velvet cloak was set on her shoulders, tied across her neck, while the hood, lined with bone to keep it stiff, sat over her head, keeping her features in shadow.

In the mirror she saw her face: no flowers in her hair, no laughter in her eyes, no smile on her face. And in her mind, there was the benevolent stare of Troy under his Ravi skin-mask, waiting outside her door, his words violating her mind, keeping her still, quiet, obedient.

"I'm almost finished, Majesty," the maid said, curtseying. "Only the boots."

An'eris stood and waited for the maid to help her into her boots, lacing them up to the knee. As she finished, the maid stepped away, bowed and left the room.

"Leave through the parlour door," An'eris ordered.

The maid did as she was told without question.

And so it was that An'eris, dressed for a funeral procession but preparing to ride out into the winter festival and open the celebrations, found herself alone for the first time since the madness in the throne room.

The words in her mind hadn't ceased. They tormented her and overruled her actions and her voice, but they didn't control what she saw. She turned to look at herself in the tall mirror. I look like I'm going to my own funeral, she thought to herself, except for the evidence of the life growing inside her. She put her hands on her belly, felt a timid flutter under her hands. She stroked her thumb over the folds of her dress that felt like a shield of smooth grief.

"I'm trying," she whispered to no one. As if her words were an instruction, she heard a polite knock on the door but knew it for what it was. Without waiting to be called to enter, Troy stepped through the door.

"You shouldn't barge into a woman's dressing room," An'eris said, as she felt the effects of Troy's spell, augmented by A'taz, force her lips into a smile.

"You don't tell me what to do, Majesty," Troy reminded the Queen. "Where is your maid?"

"Wherever maids go when not in service," she hissed back.

He tugged her forward to the door, then let her go. Turning, the monster that wore Ravi's kind gentle face carefully smoothed her dress out and pushed a few strands of hair back into place. He checked that the stiff hood of her cloak rested comfortably on her shoulders and, taking her hands in his own, tenderly pulled the black silk gloves over her long fingers, the bones like twigs under her pale skin. He started to squeeze, a rush of excitement rising in his blood as he thought about how easy it would be to break all the bones in her body, one by one. He released her, trailing the tips of his fingers across her hands.

"I'll be at your side the whole time." His accented words sounded so kind as he pulled the glove off one of her hands. He lifted it to his face and sniffed along her fingers, his soft wet tongue darting between his lips to lick at the tips.

She shuddered, desperate to look away as he tasted her skin.

If she closed her eyes, she knew she would believe it was really Ravi and she wouldn't feel so scared and furious, so alone and helpless.

She kept her eyes open and turned her head, the simple movement taking all her willpower and strength.

"Let's get this over with," she said, trying to force as much steel into her words as she could, but even to herself, she knew she sounded weak.

Regarding her, hating her even more than he thought possible for her refusal to submit to his will, Troy forced more of his power into the spell that bound her. He watched as she physically recoiled for a second as his magic rammed into her; when she next raised her head, it was in supplication.

But it didn't please him, it only made him angrier. Anyone else would have broken within days, yet somehow she continued to defy him, to defy his master.

"Come, my Queen," he said, gently pulling the glove onto her hand again. "Let's go meet your entourage and head into the city. I'll sit with you and hold your hand, and whisper in your ear, reminding you that your beloved is dead. Your castle and your kingdom belong to us now. No one is coming to help you, and when you have your baby I'll make sure she's handed over to me before you even get to hold her. When my master is done with you I'll drag you away and put another brat in your belly and keep you as my sow. Some things are just fate."

A'rrick and Brennan reached the bottom of the street that would lead them up the hill to the castle gates.

"Ready?" A'rrick asked.

Brennan was about to reply but his words were cut off by a trumpet blast. The sound ripped across the city, announcing the opening of the gates.

From their spot at the bottom of the hill, A'rrick and Brennan turned to watch the ornate heavy black iron gates being pushed open by six men in polished steel armour. A procession of city guards on horseback rode out ahead of a large open-topped carriage, and therein sat An'eris, and on one side of her sat Ravi, wearing the mark of the House Master in her service. On the other side was A'taz.

Brennan felt A'rrick's intentions and reached out to throw himself around him before he could take off at a run up the hill.

"Wait… don't!" Brennan held him tight, weighing him down.

"Get off." A'rrick pushed at Brennan, trying to untangle his arms from his waist.

"Not now, not yet," Brennan said, knowing his words were useless. "Wait," he said into A'rrick's mind, stopping the man's body with the force of his command.

A'rrick turned panicked furious eyes on Brennan.

"I can get to her!"

"If you do, he'll kill her," he said quietly, his words a vow.

"I can reach her."

"So can I." Brennan released A'rrick from his vice-like grip. "Find out where she's heading, take me there."

"What are you going to do?"

"I don't know… something."

At the sounds of the trumpets blaring from the castle walls people started to move towards the bonfire set up in the middle of the square. It wouldn't take long for the Queen's procession to make its way there and everyone wanted a good spot to see her, to hear what she had to say and to watch as the bonfire was lit. The sight of the flames licking up the sides, igniting as the sun settled on the city, was something everyone loved to watch.

Cotta and Travis pushed their way to the very front of the crowd that had gathered around the bonfire to wait.

It was understated, Cotta thought to herself, looking around at what Travis had done. Every few feet stood a man she recognised, known from the days when Travis was just a guard in one of the city patrols.

"How many did you manage to find?"

"Between Kirin's efforts and my own, maybe seventy in the city we can rely on. About twenty-five of them are here in case things don't go your way."

Cotta smiled.

"I just want to see her. I want them to see me. They need to know I'm here. She needs to see me here, standing in front of her."

"And if they do see you, and come towards you?"

"I don't think they'll make a scene in in the square… too many people."

"I think that's exactly why they will, too many people, you can do a lot of damage if you have a riot as an excuse."

"Is that what you would do?"

He thought for a while.

"Yes," he replied. "It's a risk we shouldn't be taking. Most of the city guards are A'taz's men. If they decide to come for you, a crowd won't stop them, and my handful of men will be almost halved before we've even tried to run. They'll be slaughtered to give you a chance to get away." He held her gaze. "Is that acceptable to you?"

"The fightback starts here, it starts now." She turned to him. "I can sound my own trumpet of war without a drop of blood falling in the street."

"See that you do then," he replied, unusually bold. "Just because this is the right place for a fight, doesn't mean we want a fight."

"We'll only fight if we have to," she promised.

Annoyed at the flippant attitude to the danger she was creating, he turned to her.

"You talk of fighting. Have you even got a weapon on you?"

"My weapon is coming." Cotta searched the crowd for Brennan. "I don't see him yet," she admitted, still looking.

"They'll have heard the trumpets, they'll know she's heading here."

"Brennan won't know where to go."

"A'rrick will, you need to wait."

She turned to yell at him but caught sight of the face she most wanted to see; all the rising heat at the talk of fighting and warfare drained from her blood, replaced with a different heat.

A'rrick and Brennan materialised out of the crowd beside them; Cotta flung herself at Brennan and his arms closed around her, pulling her close; her own arms winding round his neck, she pushed her face into his chest. She wasn't prepared for the overwhelming sensation of relief.

"I've got you."

She clung to him for a moment more before turning her face up to his.

"Kiss me," she whispered.

Hidden in the crowd of strangers, the lovers kissed desperately. Brennan crushed her body against his as she dug her fingers into his neck. And then it was over, and they pulled apart, gasping for breath, mouths still touching, the feel of their lips ghosting over each other sending a surge of energy between them. Brennan kissed her again, but with less urgency, and felt her warmth absorbed into his cold body, their intimacy marred by a much closer trumpet call marking the entry of the Queen's carriage into the square.

Cotta wrenched herself from his embrace, one hand holding his shoulder, the other reaching instinctively for Travis. A'rrick pushed toward the lovers, forcing himself between Cotta and Brennan.

"Are you ready?" he demanded.

Brennan nodded. He reached for Cotta's hand, opening her palm and kissing it. He closed her hand and pushed her to Travis, standing at her side.

"Don't let me fall," Brennan said to A'rrick, then he turned to face the Queen, Troy and A'taz, and threw his mind against them all.

The bonfire in the middle of the square was built up from old pallets, wagon wheels and broken furniture that couldn't be repaired by lathe or hammer and nails. Bales of straw were placed at intervals, bunches of sticks and logs jammed into spaces between spindles, floorboards, bags of sawdust and mounds of woodchips. As high as five tall men, it would be set alight at sundown and mark the start of the winter festival celebrations in the city and all the other towns and villages across the kingdom.

Before she could set the spark, An'eris had to speak to the gathered crowd. Visibly shaking with grief, words she hadn't planned started to play out in her mind, and she felt a brush against her consciousness, one that was familiar and kind, like a twinge behind her eyes.

"Don't fight me," it whispered to her... just to her. An'eris felt a flutter from her unborn child, a joyous movement, and gave up space in herself for Brennan.

His words started to come from her lips, and the crowd fell silent.

"People of Kraner, I'm standing here before you all, again, to tell you that your King is dead. He was killed in a battle. He died protecting a border town from invaders. He died because he put his body between an innocent and a sword. He died because he was a man who fought for his kingdom himself, never asking more of his men than he was willing to give himself. Our child will never know her father," she put her hands on her belly, "but she will be his legacy. I promise you all, in her father's name, I will bring peace to Kraner. We've all been through too much in the last year. We need steady times, we need things to return to normal as they were before the famine, before Orren left. We need Kraner to be Kraner again."

Brennan, his control over An'eris welcome, firm and holding, eased his consciousness out and over the crowd. He could feel the minds, curious, open to the words he put into her mouth. They just needed a little nudge to be a little more enthusiastic to what she was going to say.

"I've been in the castle, but I've not been locked away."

A'taz jerked his head up at her unexpected words. He dived into her mind to search for her intent but came up against a barrier.

"I've heard the worries from you... too many strangers, too much change, too much uncertainty in the city. You are fed, your bellies are full, but you don't feel content."

Brennan pushed on, and the crowd, as one, realised the Queen was speaking truth. They were happy, but there were a lot of unfamiliar faces these days, there was a lot of change happening around them, and it had been making them uneasy. They all knew, at that moment, that the Queen was right.

"There will be no more demolition. The clerics in the city will be asked to cease their prayers that you tell me are to a God that is not your God, that keeps you awake and makes you fear for your souls."

Brennan nudged the crowd; every man, woman and child felt relief at the Queen's words, as if she had promised to save their souls herself.

The crowd cheered, and A'taz got to his feet behind An'eris, Troy standing beside him.

An'eris turned to Troy, to Ravi, and Brennan stared at him from behind her smile.

"Lord Ravi has been of great assistance to me for many months but he has asked that he be relieved of emissary duties to return to his own kingdom. I have granted his request, allowing him to leave tomorrow. He will be replaced by a member of the serving council, ensuring continuity for you, the people of the city."

There was a cheer and clapping from the crowd.

"The stonemason, who has also been of service to me, has also asked to leave the city, and he will be leaving, tomorrow—our arrangements with Aquam have changed."

A'taz, overcome by surprise, began an incantation but found he couldn't throw his will over the crowd, over An'eris. Whatever was moving in her had touched enough of the crowd and pulled them into a single mind enraptured by her words. It was a single, enormous mind, too big for A'taz to pierce and grasp.

"People of Kraner," An'eris raised her hands, "tomorrow, when their entourages ride out of the castle to leave our city, I beg you to line the streets and watch them leave, remembering all they've done here, seeing them out beyond the castle gates."

The crowd erupted in cheers and surged forward towards her.

She turned to A'taz, speaking only to him and Troy. "I told you, you should have killed me."

A'taz heard An'eris, Troy heard Brennan.

As Brennan kept his hold on the people, he prodded An'eris, giving her the urge to look into the crowd at the faces staring back at her.

He was in her mind when her eyes fell on Cotta. The surge of relief and joy he felt in her almost threw him out of her mind. As he struggled to hold his place in the flood of emotions that rushed through the Queen, he tethered her own self-control to those feelings.

"Think of Cotta." He put the words into her mind. "Remember her faith in you. Use her strength. She has enough for us all, for everyone. Remember your friend."

An'eris closed her eyes for a moment, getting a grip on herself that she had been denied for so long. She couldn't shake off A'taz's control, knowing that as soon as Brennan slipped from her, she would be back where she was, but she knew events were now in motion and his hand was forced. Once out of the castle, his control would weaken until she could break free.

"I'll put things right," An'eris said, herself, to the cheering crowd, but her words were for Cotta.

"And now," she called out to the crowd, "for the fire."

Cotta stepped forward as the crowd surged, until the only thing separating her from An'eris was the body of men who, loyal to Travis, had gravitated towards her and become a living wall between her and the Queen, who had stepped out of her carriage to light the bonfire and was mingling with the crowd.

Travis, his hand not leaving his sword, had to decide to put himself between Cotta and the Queen or help Brennan. He stepped away from Cotta and went to help A'rrick take the meagre weight of the man who held the mind of everyone in his grasp.

Troy sat on the edge of the seat in the carriage, utterly confused. He couldn't make sense of what had happened, or how it had happened. The scent of the mind working against him was familiar, but it had grown in power and was now something entirely different to the simple mind reader he had taken Brennan to be. Sitting alone in a sea of people all cheering and clapping for the Queen, who was still susceptible to his control, Troy felt lost. He didn't know what to do. The happiness of the crowd was overwhelming, and as the joyous emotions hit him like a physical onslaught, he felt himself weaken. From nowhere, memories of his youth jumped out from the places where he had banished them. Troy, in his madness, remembered what it felt like to be lonely. It angered him, and he fell back on familiar rage and anger to rebuild the barriers around his mind. Regaining his self-control, He stepped down from the carriage, and as Ravi, he wandered into the crowd. He found his way to the Queen's side, but instead of grabbing her and pulling her away, giving in to the urge to stab a blade into her throat, his hands were caught by strangers who wanted to thank him for all his help and wish him well on his journey.

As he accepted their gratitude and thanks, he had no choice but to endure the smirk on An'eris's face. He was so busy keeping up the fakery of Ravi that he lost his words when a pair of hands gripped his and he looked up into Cotta's eyes. She held him and leaned forward.

"I'm coming for you," she promised.

Snatching his hands away, he turned to find his master. Stepping back up into the carriage, Troy sat down next to A'taz. The two men, holding their false smiles and waving at the crowd, looked out at the Queen surrounded by hordes of people, protecting her with their goodwill, a wall of armour. They watched her melt into the crowd, watched her find her way to Cotta, and watched as the two women reached out to each other. For a moment their hands briefly touched, before the waves of people moved them past each other.

Troy turned to A'taz.

"What must I do, Master?"

"Gather my things," A'taz replied calmly. "We leave tomorrow."

"We're leaving the castle?"

"We're leaving the city," he corrected him.

"We can't let her win surely?"

"We can't move against her like this. Look around, the minds of the people have shifted. There are members of the council in the crowds. This is a royal decree. If we move now, the streets will be full of the dead by tomorrow, and who will sustain my power then? No, she hasn't won, we just need to relocate, reposition."

"But why, you didn't find what you're looking for?"

"And I won't as long as An'eris and those people are alive." He turned to stare at Troy, the implications in his words clear.

"Get our men out of the city, have them come in groups. I'll pick a place."

"And then what?"

"Have them prepare for war."

"Master?"

"If I can't find what I want using gentle measures…" He smiled to himself. "I was going to let them live… most of them anyway. But now, they'll be mine, and I'll take their lives, all of them, all at once. I'll gorge myself and I'll get what I want."

Brennan gasped in A'rrick's arms, coming back to himself, out of breath and desperately thirsty. Licking his dry lips with a parched tongue, Brennan clawed at Travis, who had turned and taken the first cup of anything out of the closest person's hand.

He drank it down in one go, dropping the empty mug, leaning into A'rrick.

As Travis and A'rrick held him up, they walked him through the crowd and headed for Kirin's shop.

"I don't know how you did that, or how much of that you did." Travis sounded angry. "But well done, you've just handed Cotta her war."

Brennan smiled, thinking of Cotta and An'eris, of the joy he felt as the two of them had seen each other.

"My pleasure," he slurred, then passed out.

The sounds of laughter, music, cheering and dogs barking in the street below carried into the small room on the soft breezes of the winter night.

Brennan sat near the small brazier eating fried fish and bowls of thick crab soup, plate, after bowl, after plate, his appetite insatiable. He decided keeping his mouth full of food was the best way to keep from answering any of the questions Travis kept throwing at him.

A'rrick, wrapped in his long dark cloak, was keeping to himself across the room.

Travis paced the floor, occasionally rubbing his hands over his mouth as if trying to scratch his gums. His steps were light, his pace quick; he was talking softly to himself as his mind raced through options, searching for a thread from which to stitch a plan.

Cotta watched him, looking profoundly sad, something clenched so tightly in her fist her knuckles looked like dice under her skin.

He kept pacing, clicking his fingers, shrugging his shoulders, cracking his neck, muttering to himself.

"For pity sake," Cotta snapped, "sit down, you're driving me crazy."

Travis stopped, turned on his heel, and sat on the closest stool, a foot immediately starting to tap the floor.

Everyone was silent, wrapped in their thoughts. It was only the absence of chewing and slurping that made them realise Brennan had stopped moving; he was as still as the dead. Cotta moved cautiously from her seat, kneeling, crossing the floor towards him slowly.

"Bren?" she called out softly.

"Is he there?" Travis asked, breathless.

They all yelped when, without warning, Brennan twitched as if asleep, and a second later, he shouted out in surprise as he suddenly jerked upright.

The plates and bowls clattered around him as he scrambled to his feet. He rushed to Cotta, pulling her up, grabbing for Travis and dragging him over, doing the same to A'rrick.

"You have to go to Penrose. Leave now, tonight," he shouted.

"What, Bren, what are you talking about?" Cotta asked, surprised.

"Go, go now." Brennan hurried them out of the room. "Go to Penrose. Calem will be there, go get him."

CHAPTER 29

Cotta ran her fingertips across Brennan's lips as she stood on her toes to place light kisses over his eyes.

"Please be safe," she begged.

"I will," he promised. Pulling her closer against him, he turned her hands palm upwards and kissed the wounds on the pale skin of her exposed wrists. She pulled them from his grasp.

"I promise when we're done we'll leave this place, we'll forget all of this." She kissed his cold lips lightly.

"Falconfall," he said, breathless. "When we're done, we'll go there?"

"Yes." She kissed him again. "We'll go home."

When they finally broke apart, Cotta stepped away first and moved to stand between Travis and A'rrick. If there had been a hint of sadness, of fear or grief as she kissed him goodbye, it was gone by the time she turned around.

"We leave on the midnight tide. We'll be at sea for four days, maybe more if the weather turns bad. As soon as we have him we'll turn around and come right back."

"I don't think I'll be here when you get back, but you'll know where to find me. Calem will find me." Brennan gestured towards the tall druid, who looked at him sadly.

"Keep my daughter safe?" A'rrick asked. "This idea you got in your head while inside hers, it's up to you to play it out now."

Cotta, hearing A'rrick's words, was reminded of the Tradefair, and the last time Brennan had run away with an idea.

"He'll figure it out," Cotta said, looking at Brennan. "You do what you need to do, so when we return, we end this."

She reached down and picked up a small hessian satchel. Slinging it over her shoulders and tying it across her waist, she moved to the door.

"Come on," she called to Travis and A'rrick, "we'll barely be on the back of the tide, the captain won't wait for us."

She didn't spare him a lingering glance, but as she moved past him, her fingers brushed his one last time.

Kirin locked the door after the three of them had left and hurried up the stairs. Alone for the first time with the strange man who came to her shop more as a corpse than warm body, she felt the weight of her task before her and wondered how she had ended up in such bizarre company.

Reading her mind, Brennan thought for a moment of what to say.

"Kirin," he said softly, calling her by name. "I don't need you to do anything for me. My task now is…" he looked for the right words "…my task is laid out. You only need to do what Travis has commanded."

"I can do that," she said, wondering what he saw with those bulging white eyes that wept blood.

"Do you think there will be enough men?"

"No," she stated, not hiding the anger in her words.

"There's no way of defending Kraner now anyway," Brennan muttered.

"That's your fault, isn't it?" she demanded.

He thought about her question.

"Yes," he said clearly. "And no. A'taz, he would have waited An'eris out, maybe for a day, a year, or a hundred years. This thing that he wants, that he's hunting for, he can't find it without her, and she could live for hundreds more years. And so could he… by taking lives. Kraner, everyone in the city, was doomed the moment he entered the gates."

"I don't know about doom, and taking lives, but I'll do as Master Travis asked and get our men armed and have them start keeping guard near the gates."

"Thank you," Brennan said.

"When can we expect an attack?"

"I don't know, but soon. He won't wait for a reason." Even to his own ears, it was a terrible answer.

"Why don't we clear the city? Surely it has to be better than leaving everyone oblivious. We may as well be leaving them to die."

"I can't order everyone to leave the city; where would they go? Do they leave now, tomorrow, next spring? I don't know what the next play from A'taz will be. I can only do what I need to do right now to save the Queen."

"There are children in the city," she said, heat in her words.

"There are children everywhere. I can't think of the children in Kraner. I have to think of the children in Barclan."

"How noble of you," she sneered.

"I'm trying to save a kingdom," he said slowly, patiently.

"Lofty words from someone who used our Queen to challenge a monster to a game of cards."

"Is that what you think I did?"

"Yes," she said, and she shrugged. "But what do I know, I just sell fish."

She slammed the door behind her, leaving Brennan alone in the room. He looked around, everything was a grey shape or a black shadow. He couldn't remember the last time he had been alone. It didn't bother him, not at all. Taking a minute to fumble his cloak around his shoulders and find some boots to slip over his feet, he let himself out and headed north into the city, heading for the castle.

"See that?" Travis pointed at a thick line of rope threaded through the ship's railing that the deckhands were grabbing. "Get on the rope, and when the captain calls, pull on it with everything you've got."

A'rrick looked at Travis, clearly confused.

"You've never sailed before, have you?"

A'rrick, about to answer, was cut off by Cotta coming up behind them.

"Just do as you're told until we're at sea," she told him, as she took up her own position, unwinding the line off the deck cleat, holding it tight to herself, ready to release the sail as soon as they were away from the dock.

The captain of the sloop called orders from the bow; the crew reacted and the small sailing ship sprang from the dock on the heaving tide. Cotta released the line and the mizzen sail caught the wind. She quickly wrapped the trailing rope around a cleat and hauled back. The sail helped turn the ship as the captain steered the craft out the harbour clear into the open sea under heavy grey storm clouds in a moonless night.

By the time the lanterns of Kraner harbour had blinked out and the lighthouse at the end of the pier was invisible, the storm had broken above them. Travis and Cotta did their best to work with the deckhands, ignoring the lashing rain and freezing winds heeling the ship into the wind while the captain rolled the wheel and moved the tiller, steering them through the squalls. As the storm grew fiercer, their own sailing skills proved deficient and they were soon a hindrance, not a help.

"You should get below deck," the captain called to them from his place at the helm.

Taking it for the order that it was, and drenched through to the skin, they both headed below to find a place to wait out the storm. A'rrick was already at the stern, banished below as soon as they'd cleared into open water and he wasn't needed. The small oil lanterns fixed to the wooden beams by chains swung wildly as the ship rolled, moving the shadows left and right, up and down. Everything not secured in nets bolted to the sides were strapped down with thick cords of leather sewn into harnesses that tied all manner of everything together. A'rrick had found a space between barrels of preserves and bales of wool, wrapped himself in his cloak, and focused on warming himself inside the bottom of the freezing cold vessel.

"What type of ship is this? Who are we sailing with?" He had to shout to be heard above the waves pounding the hull and the wind screaming as it tried to tip them over.

"The type of captain that doesn't ask questions and is always ready to leave for enough coin," Travis yelled back, peeling his saturated clothes off his shivering body as Cotta pulled their satchels free of a net and rummaged inside to find dry clothes for the two of them.

"Do I want to know?"

"Do you need to know?" Travis grinned, taking the clothes Cotta tossed him and pulling them on as quickly as he could. Pushing his feet back into wet boots, he grabbed a net with one hand to steady himself, offering Cotta his other hand for balance as she began stripping off. Travis looked away rather than see her exposed skin still covered in bruising that was slowly fading to mottled greens and jaundiced yellow. The scabs had pulled away, with her wet clothes breaking the skin again. The bruises would fade, but there would always be scars.

A'rrick, remembering an image of Cotta as she had stumbled to them only a few days ago, muttered a short incantation, and shadows jumped to cover her for long enough to offer modesty in the cramped space. As she rubbed her arms to get some warmth back into tired muscles and weary bones, she thanked him.

"What do we do now?" A'rrick asked.

"We wait," Cotta replied, nudging him with her foot. Taking the hint, he scooted over as much as he could to make space for her. She sat down and huddled up. A'rrick could feel her shuddering at his side, the cold radiating from her skin. He opened his arms, turning around in the small space, manoeuvring her until his legs were either side of her, and ignoring her protests he pulled her against his own warm body, wrapped his arms around her and locked her in his embrace.

"Stop squirming," he murmured, as she shifted and tried to pull away.

"I don't need you to hold me like an infant."

"You're shivering like one." He ignored her words, holding her tightly.

It only took a moment for her to give up and relent; as soon as she did, lethargy overcame her. She felt too heavy to move and surrendered herself to lying on A'rrick's broad chest, his calming steady heartbeat a soothing rhythm that helped her forget the groans of the great oak boards riveted together, all that kept them safe and dry from the fury of the sea barely a foot away.

As he felt her relax he dared to raise a hand and stroke her head, humming gently to himself, the tune reverberating into her body.

"Are you trying to put me to sleep," she asked softly.

"I don't think I need to," he said, soothingly. "I think we're all tired."

He felt her nod.

"I am tired, but I've never been able to sleep through a storm."

"Are you afraid of thunder then, my girl?" he asked.

"No, I'm afraid of badly built ships that fall apart in rough seas drowning all the rats in the hold."

"We're not rats." He patted her shoulders. "And I don't need you scaring me on my first time aboard a ship."

"Sorry," she whispered, grinning. "It was only a joke."

"You and An'eris always shared a terribly dark sense of humour." He sighed. "Do you think Brennan can help her?" A'rrick asked, a father scared for the life of his child.

Cotta, eyes closed, yawned and pressed her face into his chest, the gentle touch of his hand running across her head more potent than any spell.

"I think she can help herself," Cotta assured him. "Brennan is going to break her out of that prison they put her in, and then… well, we'll see what happens next."

"I came to Kraner to help her, to save her, and I've not been able to do anything beyond stand in a crowd and watch her give a speech," he confessed to the top of her head. "I'm her father; I should have done more."

Hearing his words, the heavy weight of failure in his tone, she shifted to gaze up at him.

"A'rrick," she said, getting his melancholy attention. "Let me tell you this." She sat up, held his face, made him see her. "You are a good father, and An'eris is strong because you taught her well. She isn't sitting waiting to be saved. She's fought for herself and for everyone else every minute since they imprisoned her."

"How do you know?" A'rrick asked.

"I know because she never gave him what he wanted. I know because we're all still alive." She pulled his head down to kiss his forehead.

A'rrick stroked her hair, lost in his thoughts for a while, mulling her words. She dozed on his chest, not quite slipping into a deeper sleep, not quite able to get past the dreams that made her flinch and twitch in his arms. After a particularly bad dream that made her hit out as she jerked away, clenching her jaw and holding her head, she lay back down against him, exhausted.

"Please," she asked him quietly. "Can you put me to sleep for a little while? I don't want to dream."

He kissed her head and sang to her, only stopping long after her breathing had evened out and deepened and her fists had finally uncurled.

As the ship violently tipped and rocked through the night, battered by the heavy winter storm, he held her tighter, grateful for the words that eased the burden of his guilt and lifted his spirits.

From close by, shrouded in shadow, Travis had watched and listened to their quiet conversation, and he waited until he was sure she would sleep through what was left of the night.

"She's quite something," A'rrick said, turning to Travis.

"You don't have to remind me," he agreed, but there was a tone in his words that made A'rrick frown.

"What is it?" the druid lord asked.

Travis looked down at his hands, picking at the shredded tips of his bitten nails.

"Cotta, she's a force," he said to himself more than A'rrick. "People meet her and they either fall in love with her or hate her for fear of her. Her will is indomitable, and people, they want to do what she tells them to do, they want to please her, they believe in her, and she always wins. She's so rational but speaks with such passion she's mesmerising. And she doesn't fail—even when she loses, somehow, she wins. She plays people better than anyone else ever will. She's even bent Brennan to her will."

"She didn't make him fall in love with her," A'rrick countered.

"But he did, and as much as she didn't knowingly do it, she uses that love to control him."

"Why would you say that?" A'rrick held her protectively, defending her but not disagreeing with Travis.

"Because she's been doing it to me since the day we met," he said, smiling.

"You're in love with her?"

"No, but I do love her. She was my first love and she'll always be that to me."

"I didn't take you for a lover of women." A'rrick sounded surprised.

"I'm not. It's just who she is. She does it because she's terrified of losing control, because she wants to save everyone." Travis swallowed, fidgeting with something in his pocket. "Because she's afraid of the pain of losing. She wants me to build her an army because she can command men. She can turn her mind to military strategy, and if we were going to war with Reve, or Vaden, I'd defer to her and follow her into battle knowing we'd win. But this…" He gestured with one hand to the dark interior of the ship. "We're sailing across the most dangerous sea crossing on our world, in winter during a storm, to pick up a sorcerer and bring him back to Kraner to wage war using spells, fire and magic from the Gods."

"She can't control what's coming towards her."

"No." Travis watched her sleep. "She'll try to though. She'll throw herself in the path of lightning if she thinks she can redirect it."

"So what do we do then?" he asked.

"We do as she says." Travis shrugged. "With Cotta, there's no other way."

"So that's your plan, your grand idea. Build an army, line up behind her, and when she calls for the charge, raise a banner in her name and aim at the nearest enemy?"

"That's how men fight," Travis said clearly. "We follow our general towards our enemy with our swords out. A'taz will have an army between us and himself. That's where Cotta will place herself, right at the front, and so we must fall in behind her. I think Brennan sent us, sent her, to get his brother so she can work out how to use all of us to win this war once and for all."

"What a terrible thing to say about someone you love."

"It's not so terrible," Travis replied, "when you think of what's at stake. And I think she'd agree with me."

"I think your mind is seeing fantasies because of all the poison you put into your body every day."

"That poison gives me a clarity that lets me see where events will lead. It lets me see the inevitable conclusion once I untangle the threads and can see the path."

"I think you're mad."

"I might be." Travis pulled a little vial of jebam oil from his pocket, looked down at it impassively. "I think I'm right though."

"And when everyone is dead because swords can't fight magic, and the only ones left standing hold the power of the Gods and can raise the dead with spells?"

"Then Cotta will be the first of the dead to rise, and I'll rise right behind her and point my dead man's sword and go where she tells me. And I'll keep rising, and all the men behind her will keep rising, until the day is won and we never have to fear things that men can't control ever again."

In his arms, lying comfortably against his chest, Cotta rolled over in A'rrick's embrace. Instinctively, he loosened his grip until she settled then held her again, smoothing his own cloak over her, keeping her warm and safe, soothing her with gentle caresses of his hands, making sure she stayed asleep, resting in dreamless slumber.

Travis smiled at the irony of A'rrick's innate reaction to Cotta. After a minute, A'rrick looked up and met his gaze, an unspoken acceptance and admission on his features.

"On the battlefield, where will you stand?" Travis asked him.

A'rrick kissed the top of her head; he didn't need to answer. Instead, he curled his hand into a fist, muttered a chant under his breath and threw it across the small space at Travis. The simple spell hit him like a gust of wind and Travis toppled over, asleep before his head hit the deck.

A'rrick resumed stroking Cotta's head, content to stay awake through the night, watching over them both, keeping them warm and dry, giving them rest; as if that was enough to save them from what he thought might be the end of the world.

CHAPTER 30

Raef rummaged through the storage chest in the entrance hall of the lodging house. Finding a heavy woollen jacket he threw it behind him, grinning at the sound of it hitting Calem.

"I don't need all this." Calem threw it back at Raef.

Grabbing it in mid-air, expecting it, Raef threw it back without looking over his shoulder.

Calem, exasperated, threw it back again.

"Are we playing a game now," the sorcerer asked, stepping out of the way to let it land on the floor when Raef threw it a third and fourth time.

Equally exasperated, Raef got to his feet, walked over and picked it up.

"Stop arguing with everything I say and put this on," he ordered.

"I don't need it," Calem said softly. "I don't get cold. Every inch of snow in Barclan could fall on me, I wouldn't even feel it."

"It's not for you, it's for the sake of appearances." Raef pushed the jacket at Calem's chest. "If we ride through a town in the middle of the blizzard, all dying from the cold but there you are, in a vest and trousers rolled up to the knee, sweating like a hog on a feast day, someone might think that's a bit odd, and maybe that someone will be a spy for A'taz, and a mile up the road we all get arrows in our backs and then we're all dead." Raef jabbed Calem in the chest. "Put it on."

Begrudgingly, he held it up and looked at it. He put his face to it, sniffing suspiciously.

"It stinks."

"It's been in a trunk for years with all the other forgotten things, of course it stinks."

Raef turned and delved back into the horde of old things. The heavy sound of heeled boots arrived moments before Bode stepped into the hall.

"Are you ready?"

"We need a bit more time," Raef said. "Nothing here is to Calem's exacting standards."

"Hurry up," Bode said, gruffly. "An'uek is already in the stables."

Raef turned to Calem, holding a short coat triumphantly in a hand.

"This might be for a short woman or tall child," he said, walking over and manhandling it over the sullen sorcerer. "Obviously, it's perfect for you."

"I'll finish him," Bode interrupted Raef. "You go get yourself ready, we need to leave. The day looks clear but I want to get up the road to Eldermire before nightfall. It's too cold to set camp now."

"We have a problem," An'uek shouted from the hallway as she stormed towards them. "Our horses are gone. By now they're probably halfway back to the desert."

It took Bode less than an hour to work out a price with Nesrin for four horses and a wagon from her yard. They didn't have time to find another seller and couldn't explain their haste, so had to take her price. But it was Raef who handed over the silver coins, counting slowly, deliberately, to fifty. Taking the payment, she called to her steward with instructions.

"It'll be another hour at least before we can leave," Bode said, clearly annoyed, pulling his gloves off and stuffing them into a pocket. "And how did you end up with so much silver?" He turned on Raef.

"Are you seriously asking me that question?" Raef put his hands up, looking around the room.

"We've been here a day, did you rob the whole town?"

"I wasn't keeping score." He stood in front of Bode, closer than he needed to be.

"You always keep score." Bode's voice dropped.

"I'm sure there were people I missed," he mocked.

"Well aren't they lucky."

"I think we're the lucky ones," Raef said, seething. "The fool creates fire not coin, and if I hadn't had a few handy pouches of silver, we'd be in trouble now, wouldn't we."

"I'm not a fool," Calem muttered from the corner of the room. "We have the coin Bastion gave us."

"Enough to pay Nesrin for the clothes we've taken from the piles of things people have left behind, nothing else."

"One or two, Raef, that I could understand, but all that silver?"

"One or two or twenty, who cares?"

"We don't need to draw attention to ourselves, you know that." Bode sounded disappointed. "Do you think people aren't going to wake up with empty purses, talk to each other and remember the happy stranger they all bumped into yesterday. What if we have someone from the town patrol knocking on the door before we're on the road?"

"Then I'll tell them I was also robbed." Raef lifted an empty coin purse, turning it inside out to emphasise his point. "I'll tell them a thief stole all my coin and then ran away with two horses and a small wagon."

"Stop it," Calem said, pushing to stand between them. They both stepped away from him, the heat from his body slamming into them as much as shoving them apart.

"It's all right." Raef put his hands up, talking to Calem.

"Everything's fine." Bode mimicked Raef's gestures.

At that moment, An'uek walked back in and saw the two men with their hands up and a third standing between them, orange eyes glowing, fingers tipped with flames.

"Calem…" An'uek stepped slowly, inching towards him, her voice calm, "what's wrong?"

"Nothing, they were just arguing." He didn't sound that upset.

"Then why…" An'uek kept creeping closer, pointing at his hands.

He looked down, and his mouth opened in surprise and he shook his hands, flicking the flames away.

"Sorry!" He looked ashamed, confused.

"It's all right," Raef repeated, glancing between Calem and An'uek. Without thinking, he put his arm around Calem's shoulders and started walking him out the room.

As he passed Bode and An'uek, Raef smirked at the druidess.

"Let's go find something to eat. You can put your hands on the iron stove if they itch."

"That's happened twice in two days now." Bode didn't need to elaborate.

"We need to get on the road." Her voice, always so calm, quivered just enough for Bode to see how shaken she was by Calem's slip.

"Can you think of a reason for it?" he asked.

"Not one I want to share right now."

"I don't like that answer." He reached for her hands. "Calem is not a subject for secrets."

"I need you to give me time to think it through," she prompted. "Can you do that?"

"Of course." He dipped his head. "But you will tell me, won't you?"

She held his hands, studying his face, working through something else in her mind.

"An'uek?" he asked, waiting for her reply.

"I'm going outside to try and contact the others," she said, sidestepping his question. "Do you want to come?"

Nodding, he followed her out into the bitterly cold clear morning. The moment she stepped outside she started to shiver. Bode shrugged out of his coat, laying it over her shoulders.

"Are you ever going to warm up?" he asked. Just then, from the nearby kitchen window, the silence was split with the sound of Calem shrieking at something Raef must have done.

He couldn't help but grin, feeling warmed himself when she mirrored his reaction.

"Come on," she said, reaching out to pull him along, "let's go see what news there is from the borders."

Calem stood, fascinated, in front of the large map that covered most of the wall in the kitchen. With a pointed finger, almost but not quite touching, he traced the lines marking rivers, streams, mountains, valleys and roads. There were smudges the size of a thumb to mark them as town and villages, with the names scrawled around them. Around the edges of the land, someone had scrubbed in some light blue paint and drawn small boats clustered around the smudges.

"Kraner," Calem said to Raef, pointing at the map. Raef stood up and came to stand beside him.

"It looks like it's been drawn by someone who doesn't know much about map-making," he said, lightly touching the wall.

"It's been drawn by many people," Nesrin explained from her seat at the table. "I can't remember who started it exactly; it was when my mother was alive and ran this place."

"A lodger?"

"A lodger," she replied, nodding, stacking plates. "A man was finishing up, paying his coin but he didn't have enough. He promised to come back, but my mother was no fool."

"Promises are empty payments."

"She told him he could do a day's work to pay off his charge." She carried the dishes to a table at the back. Wiping her hands on her apron, she came back over to them, staring at the map on the wall. "He did some repairs, it was enough, so mother bade him leave, asking where he was heading. It was a town she didn't know. He tried to explain, but she didn't travel much and couldn't think of the place, but I think she just enjoyed listening to him talk about his travels. She kept asking more about where he'd been, so he drew his wanderings on the wall, promising to wipe it off. In the end, he stayed for a few more months, the wall never got wiped clean, and now most people who stay, if their place isn't on the map, they add to it."

Raef regarded the map with newfound wonder.

"That's a wonderful story," he said.

"Is your hometown on here?" she asked.

He looked across the map, tapping his mouth with a finger. He recognised hundreds of places he had been, but none that were his home.

"I don't have a hometown," he mused.

"Everyone comes from somewhere."

"No," he replied, "not everyone."

She let it go, turning to Calem.

"And you?" she said, catching his attention. "Where are you from?"

"Penrose," he answered, "but I'm going to Kraner." Forgetting himself, he put his finger on the spot marked on the map. Raef reached out, smacking his hand away. Too late. The mark on the map was instantly blackened, the city mark and name burned away.

Stepping closer, Nesrin tutted.

"Looks like you wiped it out." She touched the spot, surprised to feel it was warm. "Never mind." She wiped her hands again. "Someone will come and put it back on one day. My people are bringing your horses round from the yard now, we need to get you set and on your way."

The wagon was hitched to the horses' harnesses, and in just over an hour they loaded themselves up, said goodbye to their hostess and were heading north to Penrose. Bode and Calem sat in the back of the wagon under the bonnet talking quietly. Raef sat up front with An'uek, barely needing to tug the reins to control the obedient horses.

"I think I preferred my stallion," he lamented.

"They weren't ours to keep," she conceded. "But I miss my mare."

He looked across at her, trying to find a softness in her features. She was as white as the snow clouds that were slowly building and, he thought, as cold.

For hours they sat in silence, content to stare at the road ahead, watching as mile after mile fell behind them. They ate a cold lunch in their seats of bread, cheese and dried fruit. An'uek picked at her meal wrapped in clean muslin, offering what she didn't eat to Raef, who took it, thanking her, wasting no time in demolishing everything she'd left.

"How did you do it?" she asked, the randomness of her question surprising him.

"What?"

"In the square at the festival. Calem. How did you do it?"

"I didn't do anything," he exclaimed. "Calem, whatever it was, he did it himself. He calmed himself down, maybe with that tune he was humming. I don't know."

"A tune?"

Raef replied by trying to hum the melody as much as he could remember. After humming a few bars, An'uek put her hand on his wrist.

"That's enough, thank you." He could feel her hand shaking.

Her tone irked him. There was fear in her voice; she was keeping secrets. Flicking the reins in his hands, he dislodged her touch. She looked away as he did it.

"Is it progress?" he asked her, no warmth in his voice. "Is he learning what you're trying to teach him?"

"I'm not sure," she said thoughtfully. "But I think I'm beginning to understand just how broken he was, how many pieces he had inside him that didn't go together. He has the power, he has the knowledge, he had the lives, the experience. But they didn't fit. And then the desert happened, and it's like he's had the space to file the edges down and smooth out the cracks and make it all fit together. He's grounding himself and gaining control. But I don't think it's the words or the songs of spellcasting that's doing it. Before, he was confused, scared, never in his mind long enough to know who he was or what was right or wrong. He was doing what he was told to do, what he was told was right." She finally looked over and met his eyes, and for once, she didn't hide. He could see how drained she was, fading, withering away.

"Now?"

"Now I think he's realising he can do anything he wants to." Her voice changed and she was quiet again. "I think he controlled himself because he didn't want to hurt you. Because he knew if it got free of him, you'd be the first to die."

"Somewhere between wanting to kill him and wanting to buy him his first mug of ale, I've ended up liking the fool."

"I'm glad," she confessed.

"Will you still teach him?"

An'uek, instead of answering in her emotionless clipped tone, surprised him by turning away and putting her head in her hands.

"No," she replied. "There's no time anymore. I told him once, his power is something I can't fathom, something I can't affect. Maybe the lesson wasn't in how to control the power. Maybe it was getting him here safely with both of you."

"When I was learning to steal, I didn't learn to lift purses, I learned people."

She laughed at his analogy.

"Yes," she nodded, "teaching him is just like that."

He flicked the reins, not needing to.

"I think now he has the ability to remember, when the time comes, that there are reasons not to let it overwhelm him."

"How did you do that?" Raef asked.

"I'm not the one who's done it. It was always there. He just needed to find an anchor to stop himself going over the edge."

"And you think he has that now? That anchor?"

She reached out again to take his hand.

"I do."

Raef let her hand rest in his, the meaning of her words warming him despite the cold wind.

"I'm glad," he said.

"So am I. That's something I could never give him, even if I wanted to."

"I didn't think I could ever do anything but hate him."

Sighing, giving in to an urge she hadn't had in a long while, An'uek wrapped her arms around Raef's waist and rested her head on his shoulder, letting her mind touch the edges of his, seeking that intimate bond she had with him, like she had with Bode, that was as devastating to her as it was nourishing for them.

"You're not capable of hate. It's not in you. Haven't I told you that already?"

Sitting still, letting her take whatever comfort she needed from him, wanted from him, Raef smiled as his spirits lifted and he felt energised at her honesty.

She sat holding him, the gentle sway of the wagon and the burden of obligation momentarily lifted from her heart.

The wagon rolled on into the late afternoon and evening. By the time they reached Eldermire, the town gates were closed and they had no choice but to hand over more coin than they wanted to get them opened. There was also nowhere to rent a room for the night. Eldermire was barely a town, but more than a village off the main route north, and everyone who had a spare room had filled it with someone. Their stomachs empty, they found somewhere to buy a warm meal then Raef resumed the search for somewhere to sleep. After a while he stopped bothering and came back with the news that they'd have to pull up somewhere out of the way and sleep in the wagon.

"Did you at least find a stable for the horses?" Calem asked.

"I did," Raef replied, nodding, "but it's late, and no one is going to come out in the cold to take care of them for us, but I have someone who'll tend them if I take them there."

"That means?"

"That means it's expensive and we've run out of coin," he said as he started to change. "But I'll see to that."

"Not the whole town, please?" Bode threw a comment over his shoulder.

"Just what we need, I promise."

And with that he was gone with the horses.

An'uek shared a glance with Calem as she climbed into the back of the wagon.

"So, we're all sleeping here tonight then?" he asked.

"We've not got a choice," she replied. "You've slept just fine every other night. I'm sure it'll be safe."

"Still..." he ran his fingers through his white hair, "probably best if I wrap up under the wagon or something." He looked at the cloth bonnet, the wooden wheels, the wooden... everything. "Or maybe on the ground a few feet away."

"I'm sure it'll be fine," An'uek repeated.

"I'm not." Bode took some blankets from under the seat in the wagon and unrolled them in the back. "Find somewhere close by out of the wind. Raef and I will take turns staying with you when he gets back."

"No," An'uek snapped, then said more gently, "no. You and Raef sleep, I'll stay with Calem."

There was no changing her mind. By the time Raef returned, Bode was dozing in the back of the wagon and An'uek was sitting beside Calem, the two of them seated opposite each other around the small stack of kindling Bode has set for them earlier.

An'uek set herself to make a pot of tea.

"Before you ask, I don't want any," Calem joked.

"Before you ask, I can start the fire myself," An'uek retorted.

"I wasn't going to offer."

"Neither was I." She chuckled, setting the sticks she'd gathered over some bigger pieces of wood she'd found strewn around the ground.

"If it's damp, it won't light," he pointed out. "Wood taken from snowdrifts is like that."

An'uek dropped the wood.

"I forgot," she mumbled, annoyed he was right.

She sat down in front of the small unlit campfire.

"Do you think you can…?" she asked, pointing at the sodden logs, "without it becoming more?"

"I do," he said, settling next to her.

Sitting close, but not touching, Calem reached out to a log. A flame sprang from his fingertip, lengthening and snaking towards the stack.

"It's really quite beautiful," An'uek commented, her gaze drawn to the soft orange glow of the unnatural flame.

"It feels amazing inside me, like it's alive, but even more so when I let it out." Calem breathed the words like a prayer.

Fixated, An'uek felt herself drawn towards the flame.

"Careful…" Calem's voice deepened as he warned her. "Not too close, Druid."

She had to force herself to stop leaning forward, all at once afraid of how her body and her mind had reacted to the barest display of his power.

She tried to look away but couldn't.

"It's hot?" she asked, her own body perpetually numb.

"It's burning," he answered, "but it's the best feeling there is."

Calem added his mind to his power and the lazy ribbon of winding flame from his fingertip thickened and fattened, leaping to the other fingers until five ribbons of light oozed from him, coalescing into a single thick chord of fire emanating from his fist. His face changed; the soft ever-present orange glow of flame from his eyes pulsated and became more luminous, his expression going from one of pleasure to one of encouragement, as if he was coaxing a shy creature to come out of hiding. His flame responded, stretching out further to touch the logs and wind through the spaces where they lay piled on each other, like a snake coiling through tree roots. The damp wood hissed and steamed as it dried at the touch of the flame. And then, without warning, one of the logs ignited, the sap inside it exploding with a deafening pop.

An'uek shrieked, the sound surprising Calem, who, without thinking, turned to her and reached out to grab her with his burning hand.

She kicked at his hand with her boot and threw herself down on the ground to get away from him. The fire roared, encasing him in flames. As quickly as they sprang from him, they died away, absorbed back into his body. Calem sat staring at her, nothing in his eyes but shame and sadness.

"I'm s-sorry," he stuttered, the fire instantly dying away, leaving only the burning logs. He reached out to help her up, looked down at his hand, and annoyed at having done it again, he swore to himself, stuffed his hands in his pockets and backed away. As he passed the pile of logs, they all ignited into a cheery fire. He sat down opposite her, finding his lump of rock in his satchel, and began passing it between his hands.

Out of breath from fright, it took An'uek a moment to compose herself. After a while the cold winter night forced her to move closer to the fire for warmth. She put her hands towards the fire, the irony of her actions prompting a scornful smirk.

"Don't be sorry, Calem," she said, surprising him. "I shouldn't have done that. I should know by now, you forget sometimes. I shouldn't have let my guard down around you."

He was quiet for a long time, long enough that An'uek watched the logs burn away to nothing but ash, but still the fire kept burning, keeping her as warm as her body allowed. Calem's eyes were fixed on the flames but his mind was on An'uek. A part of him, once older and detached but now sewn into his self, thought deeply about her. He forced memories to return, of druids, of their lives, of their deaths. Knowledge came to his mind of druids and mankind, who looked so similar but were so vastly different. He imagined a painting of a butterfly, swirling patterns of purple and amethyst on silver wings. Around the butterfly, pencil sketches of three stone ravens, black beaks, black eyes, black wings, angry. He imagined the small butterfly lift off the parchment and start to fly around the ravens, specks of coloured dust from its wings falling on the birds, slowly coating them in the colours of its body. After a while, the butterfly started to struggle to stay airborne, it dipped and looped, faltering and crashing into the birds, clumps of its colour splatting the dark feathers, turning them from menacing to beautiful soft-feathered songbirds. As the last of the colour fell from the butterfly's wings, it crashed down back onto the page, nothing more than an outline of something, nothing more than a scribble.

He couldn't get the image out of his mind. He could feel the parchment as if he had drawn the tiny creature and the ravenous birds. He imagined touching the parchment, seeing the edges scorch and start to curl, the smallest lick of flame waiting to consume everything. As he let the image play through, he watched as the three birds unfurled their wings and lifted themselves off the parchment to fly away, leaving just the empty husk of the butterfly in the path of the flames. Impassive, Calem waited as the fire licked over the outline of the delicate creature. But to his surprise, instead of consuming it, the fire found a little break in the sketch and crept into the butterfly, filling it with colour.

Sitting across from him, An'uek watched beguiled as Calem absentmindedly conjured visions in the flames of a little butterfly and three large birds made from his own flame. An'uek was defenceless when, without warning, Calem raised his glowing orange eyes to hers and released the butterfly from his control. It flew up high over the campfire, seemingly dancing over it, before looping, swooping, and then falling straight into her body.

She felt the flames penetrate her skin, felt the ache and the burn as it burst inside her chest, filling her being. Too much... the pain and the heat was too much. Before she had time to scream for help, even to turn her eyes, An'uek fell unconscious next to the fire, and Calem, confident and sure of what he had done, shuffled over as close as he dared to watch her, satisfied.

She woke up to the sensation of someone shaking her gently. Opening her eyes, she felt groggy and sat up slowly.

"What?" she asked, disorientated.

"You've been asleep, actually sleeping." Bode sounded happy. "We're ready to go though, you need to get up."

All through the morning, Bode and Raef watched as An'uek changed. As each hour passed, she looked better than the last. At first it was subtle; she climbed into the wagon with a little more energy than she had before. She was more talkative. Then they noticed the physical changes. Her skin looked smoother, plumper. Her faded bone-white hair regained its silver lustre; it looked thicker as it settled and curled around her shoulders and down her back under her shawl. Her grey lacklustre eyes had reverted to the captivating deep amethyst and her blue lips were now as pink as the flush on her cheeks. She didn't look like the weight of her body was too much to bear.

They didn't ask, she didn't say, and as they rode through the day into the night, no one thought to ask Calem why he looked so happy with himself.

On the third day An'uek spent the daylight hours in the driving seat with Raef, her face impassive as her mind travelled the length of the kingdom while she sought out the minds of the other far-criers. There were only two left she could find, still serving with the armies in the north; those with the troops interspersed along the western border were gone.

"Bode," she gasped his name, "the attacks in the north are slowing."

"Did you find out why?"

"The weather, in part," she explained. "The roads are becoming impassable. Heavy snowdrifts mean they can't cut through. Some of the rivers are flooding, and troops from Vaden are starting to patrol around some of the routes in and out of the kingdom."

"It's taken them a long time to decide to act. There's no way they didn't see the attacks on our border, it's their border too." Bode slammed his fist on his leg. "Bastards, I bet they've been waiting to see if the threat to us is a threat to them before doing anything."

"Whatever they've decided, they've cut down some of the mercenaries attacking the towns."

"That might raise a new problem for us," Bode remarked, still angry.

"A problem for spring if we're lucky."

"And if we're not?"

"We can't do anything about Vaden right now."

"We'll have to if they've been watching and have worked out what we have. The kingdom is as weak as it's ever going to be."

"They won't invade in winter, will they?"

"I don't know. If it was me I'd wait through winter and let it play out, but Vaden, they're brutal, they like war. They aren't predictable."

"Well, they aren't our problem right now."

"What else?" he asked. "What about the other squads along the west and to the south."

"I couldn't find them."

He raised his head at her words, reading the look in her eyes.

"Are you sure?"

"There's no question," she said, fidgeting with the laces of her gloves, tied as tightly as possible at her wrists. Bode could see she was composing herself, swallowing sobs. "I don't know how they died, but I know they're dead." Her hands were shaking but her voice was even.

"If they are, then the armies with them probably are too?" Bode asked.

"I think so," she replied. "If his men are going to pour into the kingdom from anywhere now, it'll be the west."

"Orania and Aquam border us on the west, but the border is mountains and valleys, not many people live there. An army could pull itself together and there wouldn't be many eyes in those remote places."

Bode conjured a map of the kingdom in his mind.

"We don't know though, do we?"

"No." An'uek shivered. "I can't tell you anything more. Only that winter is on our side in the north, but we're blind in the west."

"Vaden in the north, or Aquam and Orania in the west," he mused.

"Bode, what are you thinking," she asked, worried by the look in his eye.

He tapped his chest, sorting through the options and consequences of the strategies that might be playing out.

"North or west," he muttered. "West, I think. Orania."

"Bode?"

He didn't reply. He was away travelling through Barclan on the map he summoned in his mind. He saw it as a battlefield, all the lines of rivers, forests, great plains and valleys as familiar to him as his own face. He pictured troops crossing open ground, digging under attack, places for cavalry and infantry and which roads would take them where. He thought about numbers, of men who might still be alive and able to regroup, of weapons, machines of war, of all the logistics and support that would be needed if he had to defend the kingdom in the north or rout a full-scale incursion in the west.

An'uek wished his thinking wasn't so clear to her. She sat quietly as he strategised, the flashing of his thoughts occasionally touching hers, felt his spirits lifting as he imagined organising and leading the troops. It occurred to her that as they had travelled, she had forgotten who he was, who he had been before they had come together. Sitting in the wagon in silence, the man next to her was mapping out the kingdom's defences in his mind. She smiled a rueful smile. He didn't need a sword in his hand when he could see every sword in the kingdom.

The third day passed into the fourth. It took three days to cross the Irondale lowlands, a monotonous expanse without a hill or a tree to break the horizon. The land was as barren as it was flat, not good for farming, grazing, not good for anything. There were only two small villages that existed purely to supply travellers on the road with somewhere to sleep, somewhere to eat and somewhere to keep their horses. In both places they found rooms, the payment down to Raef, who would empty his coin purse every night but have it refilled by each new morning. They passed the time idly talking about nothing, no one acknowledging the growing feeling of dread as they came within a day of Penrose, which mean Kraner. And so, as the last empty mile became a slow drive on a road filled with other travellers on horses, carts, wagons and foot, their false cheer gave way to silence. Except for Calem, who was always humming his tunes or singing the songs An'uek had taught him.

CHAPTER 31

Brennan left the shop on the docks and headed towards the castle. Hunched over in a cloak with his head down, no one spared him a glance as he shuffled past. With his eyes now open he saw only murky grey images that confused his senses and made him uneasy. After tripping over cobblestones and his own feet, he stepped off the street to lean against a dry wall. He reached up to rub his stinging eyes and his fingertips came away wet and smelled sweet. He'd rubbed them raw.

"What have I done," he thought aloud. No one answered him, only the sounds of a busy city full of people living oblivious lives.

"This won't work," he muttered, the urge to scratch his eyes a distraction. He felt the sensation of something wet trickling down his checks and knew his eyes were oozing.

"Are you all right?" The voice of a little girl broke his self-reflection.

"I'm all right," he replied, putting a hand up over his face as if shielding his eyes from the sun.

"Ma…" He heard the girl calling to someone. "This man looks sick."

He heard the sounds of someone rushing over to him.

"Come away, Cilla…" A women's worried voice, then the sounds of small feet being rapidly pulled away.

"I hope you get better soon," the little voice called out.

Brennan raised a hand, calling softly, "Thank you." He wished he would get better soon, the sight of the little girl with new leather boots dyed green and polished made him ache.

Green boots.

Brennan turned his head and looked again. Sure enough, he could see the little girl, her boots, and as she walked out of sight, he saw other people, and the edges of the cobblestones under their feet, and the buttons on their coats and the lines of weathervanes high up on rooftops far away, and all through closed eyes.

Brennan gasped and looked down at his hands, seeing them as clearly as if his eyes were open and healed. But no, he tentatively touched the bloody mess on his face. This was something else. He gave himself a few more minutes of looking, seeing with his new sight until he was sure it wasn't a trick of his imagination. The longer he looked in this new way the stronger he felt; it was the same wave of energy that he had experienced in the square during the festival. Seizing it, he stepped back into the road, and still with rounded shoulders and his hood over his face hiding his dribbling eyes, he continued towards the castle, forgetting that he didn't know what to do once he got there.

His vision never wavered or flickered; as he walked, he felt it come more under his control. By the time he reached the city square he had started to experiment with his new ability and was directing his sight towards the people he passed. He could see through his closed eyes; he could see men and women; if he chose to, if he wanted to, he could brush past their thoughts and see through their eyes for just a second.

The sensation of that second was captivating and he felt a rush of excitement flood his body; he wanted to do it again. So he did. For a mile and a half, he dipped in and out of the minds that passed him by, never lingering for long, just a scant taste of their thoughts, desires, fears or ambitions. He was giddy with it, not careful, and so when he skimmed the thoughts of a man sitting in a doorway contemplating the man he had murdered for revenge only minutes before, he wasn't prepared for the onslaught of the man's shock. It crashed into him and he fell forward in the street; unable to bring his own mental defences up in time, Brennan was pulled into the man's guilt.

He was drowning in it, regret, remorse and the burning acid of shame that was coming from the murderer. He saw flashes of an argument between two men over a gambling debt, images of a fight, a knife, and rage.

In the street, on his knees, Brennan covered his head. He didn't want to see it, and he felt from the man in the doorway that he didn't want to be seen. He wanted to hide away, and Brennan in that instant also wanted to hide. All the fear he had ever felt in his life was focused on that moment, and he wished he was invisible, that no one would ever see him, ever catch him.

No one stopped to see if the man lying in the road was all right. No one noticed him.

The man in the doorway recovered before Brennan did; he got himself together, got to his feet and ran away.

Brennan, feeling the break in the connection like a twig snapping in his mind, sprang back up, gasping and wheezing. Still, no one noticed, they just walked past.

Confused, instinctively reaching out with his sight, he floated around their minds, dipping in to see through their eyes, to make sense of what had happened.

It took a while for him to realise that he couldn't see himself through their eyes, while at the same time, he still felt the desire to hide as strongly as the need to breathe within himself.

His confusion quickly gave way to understanding.

"They don't see me," he said. A grim smile broke out across his face as he once again set off for the castle.

No one saw the hunchback on the streets of the city as he headed for the castle.

As Brennan walked straight up to the eastern gates, he threw the hood back from his cloak and looked at the face of every man and woman he passed as he headed into the grounds and then into the castle itself. He was there when A'taz and Ravi rode out on horseback, a trail of men behind them. The sheer number of mercenaries following them out stunned Brennan; they truly had amassed an army of killers inside the city. A cold dread filled him as the men filed past, and he wondered where would they go. He put the thought out of his mind. He knew there was no way A'taz and Troy were leaving, they were merely going somewhere else. An'eris, even if her own mind was saved, was no match for them and their power. Brennan just hoped there was a mind left in his friend to save.

He shuffled through familiar hallways and corridors hunting for An'eris. He guessed she would be in her rooms and headed straight for her private chambers. The people he passed never knew he was there, but he waited until he was sure the hallway was empty before opening the door and slipping into her room.

Her despair pulled him like a tide. He found her huddled in the corner of her bedroom, shaking, sweating, her arms locked around her knees crying like a madwoman in desperate need of a drink or a smoke of a pipe.

Kneeling in front of her, it took him a moment to understand what was happening to her body and mind.

As gently as he could he pulled her into his arms to cradle her.

He held her through the worst of her tremors, nothing more than a hallucination to her as her body and soul suffered the sudden withdrawal of the spells cast into her mind for so long. Her thoughts hurt, it stung just to be aware, to be conscious of the wretched emptiness where once they had held her so completely.

He sat with her through the night, soothing the edges of her need, diffusing her desire to retreat to the deceptive simplicity of their domination of her words and actions. Eventually he was able to lull her into a fitful sleep, the final vestiges of their heinous authority only slipping away when Brennan made space in her mind for the soothing sound of her baby's heartbeat. He gently lifted her into her bed, pulled the blankets over her shuddering body, smoothing them around her quaking limbs. Climbing into the bed himself, settling next to her with his hand on her head, he kept her asleep until the morning, when it was time to wake up and rise as the Queen.

He was there when she opened her eyes, there to wipe the frantic tears as he soothed her distress, promising her again and again that A'taz was gone, Troy was gone, that he was real, he was there, and no, he would never leave her side even if she couldn't see him. Her servants couldn't understand why she sobbed as they dressed her, trying to sooth and comfort her but failing to do more than pass her small squares of cloth to dab her eyes and blow her nose. Brennan gave them ideas that it was just a phase; everyone knows pregnant women sometimes cry for no reason. They started to cluck around her, and she had no choice but to let them. As her tears finally dried away and she sat staring at her reflection in the mirror, she saw the mirage behind her. Brennan reminded her he was there, the man she knew. He showed her how he remembered himself, with his dirty blonde hair, neatly trimmed beard, green eyes and mischievous smirk.

At midday he was in the great hall standing behind the throne, behind An'eris in full view of everyone, visible to no one.

She was exhausted, barely able to hold her head up, so he did it for her. He helped her find words to speak to the assembled council, guilds' leaders, merchants and eminent city men and women. She ordered all places of worship closed; she didn't know it but there would be no places left for the clerics of A'taz who fed him night and day, draining life from the city as they chanted his name.

An'eris began to tell them a true story, spoken in Brennan's words. It was about attacks on the kingdom, sabotage, and murder. How Orren had gone to try and find out who was behind it all, how it had cost him his life. Brennan spoke through An'eris, telling them that they had thought the treachery in the castle had been discovered, but those small plots had been set as bait, just enough to keep them from seeing the wider ruse, putting all the pieces together.

She explained that Mistress Cotta had in fact been cruelly and unjustly accused of crimes against the crown, and that all the evidence against them had been fabricated.

As he spoke through her about Cotta, Brennan decided his own fate.

With sad eyes, An'eris announced that the body of Master Brennan had been found in a mass grave, along with dozens of men and women from the castle.

He switched the narrative. An'eris talked about Master Travis, who had, under her direction, been working in secret to investigate and understand the disappearance of so many men in the patrols, now understood to have been murdered. If he was ever found, if the investigations ever came to an end, An'eris announced, the kingdom would honour Travis, would honour all three, for their love and dedication to the crown.

The same councillors who had been the first to call for Cotta's execution refused to believe her. They made accusations themselves and the men and women on the floor fell to arguing between themselves.

Brennan, as if blowing hair from his eyes, reached out and changed the minds of anyone who didn't believe. He let them argue, letting their change of heart take just the right amount of time. Then, convinced of the legitimacy of the Queen's words, the councillors called for the reinstatement of Cotta if she was ever found alive.

"It's taken the lives of King Orren, hundreds of our soldiers, good people loyal to the crown, our own House Master. In truth, all we know is that we are under attack, but we can't say for certain by whom. Vaden, Reve, we can't assume it's our old enemies. We don't know. We aren't safe from the threat yet, we must be vigilant. There is still fighting on our borders and we must never stop working to uncover what poison festered in the kingdom, for how long, and from where it came. We have been complacent. It mustn't happen again."

The day dragged on, and An'eris, who would have collapsed if not for the man behind her, brought the matters of the kingdom back under her control.

As the evening meal was laid out for the councillors who would be sitting through the night, the full extent of the disarray was revealed. Over plates of meat, pies, vegetables in gravy and loaves of bread, orders were drafted to recruit soldiers, guards and healers. After enough wine and ale, there was the matter of how to deal with all the bodies in the pits that had been discovered outside the city limits.

An'eris presided over it all, never wavering in her words, her strong clear voice never once faltering as she set out commands and made decisions.

It was after midnight, when the work was finally done for the day, that someone called out a question from the back.

"All those disappeared, all those dead," she asked, "why didn't anyone say anything?"

No one had an answer.

From behind her, Brennan pushed them to be more honest.

"I noticed people disappearing," someone replied, "but I thought they were leaving for the war effort on the borders."

"A lot of people go home to their families for the winter festival," someone else said. "I noticed but didn't think much of it. I just thought someone else would do something if there was a problem."

Homen, Brennan thought to himself. These people were complacent because men like Homen and women like Cotta lived to serve the court and the kingdom. They could enjoy fine food, endless drink, prestige, and luxury, occasionally putting their seal where it was needed because everything was taken care of by someone else. It made Brennan angry.

Everyone had a reason for not looking too closely at what was going on around them. As he listened, Brennan realised just how easy it had been for A'taz to come in and take over. Looking around the men and women who supposedly played a hand in running the kingdom, it occurred to Brennan that all he had to do was change a few of their minds, and if he wanted it, the kingdom would be his. But the night was long, and even he was tired.

An'eris found her way to her bedchambers assisted by servants who hovered around her. No one saw Brennan, the puppeteer who got her back to her bed, releasing her as soon as her head nestled into the feather pillow and a maid pulled her boots off her feet.

"Majesty?" the maid called out nervously.

There was no reply. The girl didn't know what to do. Could she leave her Queen fully dressed in bed? Brennan created a quick image for the girl, and off she went, content that she had helped Her Majesty out of her elegant green gown, unwound her hair from the circlet that kept it in place, and helped her slip her sleeping shirt over her head before tucking her into bed.

Brennan pulled a small chair over from the corner of the room and put it beside her bed, ensuring he didn't wake her. He settled, leaning backwards over the edge of the backrest, hearing the gratifying click of the bones down his spine as they settled into place. He relaxed into the seat, not hungry, not thirsty, not tired nor awake. He sat content to watch An'eris sleep, her guard against monsters in the night who would sneak in and rob her of her rest.

The next day was more of the same, but instead of holding court An'eris spent the morning with castle stewards and officials. The scale of the murders and disappearances was becoming clear, and it left her numb.

She could pretend to be shocked, but every name on a growing list of the missing was a soul on her back. The worst ones were the names without faces, people she realised she hadn't even known, who might have served her, walked past her in the halls, maybe bowed or curtseyed as she passed, and she couldn't even remember if they had black hair or brown eyes.

Eventually her feet led her to the empty healer's halls. What should have been a space for bones to knit, wounds to scar and heal and minds to rest as the broken healed was nothing more than draughty cold rooms. An'eris sent out a decree to six of the biggest towns in the kingdom that at least three of their most skilled healers were to come to Kraner without delay. She didn't care who they were, she just needed them back in the halls; she knew, soon, there would be wounded.

If she refused to walk the passages that led past Cotta's offices, no one thought it deliberate, but she could only avoid it for so long. Refusing to stop for a meal at midday, An'eris sent her attendants away as the bell tolled. As their footsteps faded behind her and she was momentarily alone in the hallway, she called softly to Brennan. He let himself be seen, materialising in front of her as if stepping out of a haze of smoke.

"Will you come with me?" she asked.

"Of course." He took her arm, knowing exactly where she didn't want to go.

They walked to a wide stone staircase, and he led her up, keeping her steps firm. Men and women passed her as they made their way by on their duties, seeing the Queen walking alone. In the sombre mood of the castle they didn't question it.

She stood outside the door to the rooms Cotta had worked in for nearly half her life.

"If I open the door, she won't be there, will she?"

"No," Brennan said gently.

"But you're here? Why can't she be here?" She almost sobbed, her guilt an acid taste in her mouth.

"She's not here." Brennan took her hand, eased the door open and led the Queen into the study.

An'eris's hand flew to her mouth to stop herself from crying out as she stepped across the threshold, seeing everything exactly as it was the last time they had been there together. The embroidered red cushions were still stacked against the arms of the heavy dark-wooden double-seated chaise where they had shared their last cup of hot tea. There were parchments scattered everywhere, on the floor around her desk, stuffed between the seat of her favourite reading chair, her inkwell and quill where she had left them the last time she had put her name to anything. The room still smelled of Cotta, a unique perfume made just for her from the flowers that grew on the hills around her family home.

"We might have joined our staff and our offices in the new rooms across the castle," Brennan choose his words carefully, "but when she wasn't there, working with me, she was here. She loved this place. These walls are crammed with the books she's written on the laws that all the kingdoms adhere to, her treaties, her accords, charters and pacts." He stepped further in, admiring the books that lined the shelves from floor to ceiling. "She did all this."

"Tell me how she is?" An'eris asked.

"You saw her in the square," Brennan reminded her.

"Please," An'eris begged. "All I can see are the chains around her wrists rubbing her skin away. Toxic metal cutting into her flesh."

"She'll learn to ignore the scars."

"I called her a traitor."

"She knew they weren't your words."

"I slapped her."

"She didn't feel it."

"She said she'd never lied to me." An'eris was crying. "She loved me."

"She still does."

"I ordered her death."

"She escaped."

"I sent her to that place. The things they did to her are my fault."

Brennan, the memories of men brutally violating her coming into startling clarity, couldn't reply. Instead, taking a minute to steady himself, he waited until he was sure he could hold his words, then he stepped over to her.

"They didn't break her. Not because they didn't try, because they couldn't." He reached up and wiped her tears. "Enough," he said gently. "Stop crying. There's no one left who wants you to cry for them."

"What then?" she asked him, looking for his guidance. "I've brought this kingdom to its knees. All the dead are mine. If not sorrow and guilt, what should I feel, what should I do, what should I look for? Revenge?"

"No." He shook his head as he looked around the room one last time. "No, leave revenge to Cotta." He turned to her. "Take me to what A'taz was looking for."

The makeshift camp settled ten miles outside the city. There were no silk pavilions or proper tents, just hundreds of squares of cloth stretched over ropes hammered into the frozen ground. The fighters didn't have cots to keep them off the ground as they slept in pairs under the canvas, but they had hot food, drink and evidence of so much gold coin coming their way that they were prepared to stay in service to A'taz. Gold was gold after all.

Only A'taz and Troy had somewhere warm and dry to sit. In the centre of the encampment Troy had erected a small waterproof awning that he had managed to snatch just as he was leaving the city. It kept a patch of dirt relatively dry, a fact of which A'taz was not aware.

The sorcerer sat on the ground, legs crossed. His eyes stared at nothing, his slack mouth hanging open, a slow constant intonation barely audible. In front of him on the ground was a small box, the lid open, and inside were three small stones. A'taz's hands were raised, palm down, hovering just above the stone. He had begun the chant at daybreak on the second day, and since that moment Troy had paced back and forth, never stopping, never taking his eyes off his master.

He wanted to drop to his knees and put his ear to his master's mouth, to hear the spell, to learn the spell, but it would be death. He could see his master, could hear something coming from his lips, but he could no more grasp it, understand it, than a deaf man can appreciate music. He had no idea what his master was doing or how long it would take; all he could do was do as he was told and wait.

Troy didn't notice when some of the men didn't wake up on the third day. There were so many of them that a few dozen not opening their eyes, lingering in sleep, wasn't cause for alarm. A perpetual mist had risen from the ground at some point in the night; he had noticed it but didn't care. All he cared about was doing as he was told, if his master suddenly snapped back, he would be ready to serve. By the fourth day, Troy knew something was wrong. The mist was unnatural. What it was he couldn't say, but it was thick enough that he could feel it against his legs every time he took a step. He would occasionally glance around the camp, some of the canvas tents lost to the mist as if it had swallowed them up along with the men inside, the men who wouldn't wake up.

On the fifth day no one woke up, and A'taz, with every inhalation, took the mist into his being. Troy paced, the mist swirling around him, pushing against him like a strong tide. He had stopped worrying for his master and now was walking back and forth, afraid to stop in case the mist swallowed him too.

On the sixth day A'taz got to his feet, no longer a man. The creature that he was reached out and touched Troy, penetrated his body, and gave him new words to say.

Tethered to the creature of mist A'taz had become, Troy walked through the black night across hills and along the road, a thin ribbon of mist tracing each of his steps, winding back, connecting him to his master's hand. He walked until he came to a hill; standing at its crest, he looked over the city spread out in front of him.

With a new voice, Troy incanted the spell of new words, the mist curling, swirling, slowly unfolding from him, flowing down the hill inexorably toward Kraner.

An'eris led Brennan through the castle. He wasn't sure where they were going. She turned left into corridors he was sure were in the wrong place, and when they started to find staircases where there had never been a staircase, he began to understand why A'taz had never found the place himself. The stairs looked old, worn down from thousands of feet over hundreds of years; white granite became older grey stone, then ancient rickety wood.

"Have we left the castle? Are we still in Kraner?" he asked.

"Yes... and no," she replied, hurrying forward in the dark. "We've left the now, we're in long ago."

He followed her downwards, niggles of fear and doubt slowing his steps.

"You want to know what will happen when we get there?" she asked, seeming to sense his unease in the slowing of his footsteps.

"I need to know what A'taz was looking for," Brennan explained. "I need to understand it, so when he attacks, I know what to do."

"And you think you will know what to do?" An'eris slowed her pace and Brennan caught up with her.

"No," he replied. "But Calem will."

She stopped.

"Brennan," she turned to him. "We're here."

He looked around, oblivious to the darkness, seeing regardless of the lack of light. He heard water lapping at a shore and realised he was at the edge of a lake. Kneeling, he reached his hand out.

"Careful!" She grabbed his wrist.

"What happens if I touch it?"

"You'll wake the Gods."

Brennan looked at himself in the reflection of the lake. He saw himself, the man, then the reflection shimmered, and he saw himself... a hunchback without eyes.

An'eris watched him lean over and look down at its mirror-like surface. She saw his face, the one she knew, the man who had freed her from A'taz and had been with her since she wakened from his control. She knew him, Brennan, her friend.

And then the image changed and she saw another face.

CHAPTER 32

Before the road became a highway running into Penrose, they found a merchant who was willing to buy the horses and wagon. It wasn't a good price.

"I've been robbed twice because of you," he accused Bode, pocketing the meagre bronze coins as he walked back to the group huddled out of the way.

"Think of it as the turning of the wheel," Bode threw back at him as he hoisted his gear on his back and buttoned up his coat.

"Coin and philosophy are poor bedfellows," Raef mumbled.

"Are we ready, gentlemen?" An'uek rebuked them, the stern words softened by a smile. "We need to buy passage on a boat across the sea today. Raef, have you got enough coin, the price will be high this time of year?"

Raef, dropped his gear on the ground, put his hands on his hips and pouted.

"Are you joking?" he whined.

"No need for a boat." A familiar voice intruded on their huddle. "Your places are booked and paid for, we leave in one hour. Calem, your brother sent us to fetch you home."

Cotta stepped towards them, raised her hands and drew back her hood as Travis stepped forward and did the same. Bode felt relief at seeing their familiar faces as visceral as a mouthful of brandy.

"Lady Cotta," he rejoiced.

Raef lunged for Cotta, capturing her in his arms, hefting her up and swinging her around. She laughed and clung to his neck, kissing his cheeks and calling him filthy names.

"Well, I take it you know each other," Bode quipped, introducing himself to A'rrick. The two men shook hands before Bode turned and ushered An'uek forward.

"And of course, you know An'uek, although perhaps not so well now," he said as she stepped forward. Surprising everyone, A'rrick pulled An'uek into a strong embrace after staring at her in shock for what felt like the longest time.

"You've grown," he said. "How?"

"On the ship, Lord A'rrick," she replied. "Plenty of time to talk on the ship."

"Yes," Cotta agreed, still caught in Raef's arms. "If you all don't mind, I'd like to take this reunion off the road." She turned to Calem. "Can you make the voyage?"

"I can." His voice was sure.

"Good." She manhandled Raef into letting her go. "Come on, we have just enough time to get to the dock."

Bode and Travis slipped into step with each other. As quietly as they could, they both rushed through what they knew, their talk quickly falling to fighting.

Raef insisted on holding Cotta's hand. Even when she tried to shake him loose, he just hung on tighter, his long slender fingers knotted with hers.

Cotta couldn't stop herself smiling at the rogue; the fact Mason wasn't with him and he hadn't mentioned his brother chilled her heart. She let him keep hold of her hand, pretending to try and untangle his fingers, gauging something in how he clung to her. She wondered if he knew about Homen. She would bet money that he didn't, and that if the constant babble coming from him was any indication, he had equally horrible news for her.

Calem was the last to step onto the ship. With each foot up the gangplank he remembered a sea voyage with Brennan and another with Orren. As he jumped over the final step, landing with an ominous thud on the deck, he felt something kindle, a longing that surprised him. He turned immediately and went to the stern of the ship, found somewhere to sit and put himself out the way, just as he had done on that first voyage with Brennan. As the ship cast off and men walked past him, around him, avoiding him, he thought of his brother. The longing, he realised, was love. He missed him. Calem looked down at his hands, saw the glimmer that shimmered across his skin, felt the itch and sizzle inside his body. Brennan, he thought to himself, get back to Brennan. He found the lump of metal in his pocket, took it out and held it against his chest, squeezing it with both his hands.

Cotta watched the young man scurry out the way and hide himself as best he could. Unlike on the outward journey, they didn't need to help, the tide took them right out of port and into the open sea.

"Will he come below deck do you think?" she asked Raef.

"No," he replied, "best to leave him. I'll check on him every few hours, make sure he doesn't burn the ship."

Cotta stared at him, her expression unreadable.

"I'm joking," Raef replied, grinning.

"I hate your jokes," she stated.

"Impossible," he said, and kissed her cheek.

Cotta sighed, knowing there was no way of escaping what was coming. She took his hand.

"Come on," she led him toward the steps that led below, "we need to talk."

Raef sat with his back to the bulkhead, Cotta opposite him, her back against a barrel. They passed a flagon of cheap strong wine between them. If anyone thought they shouldn't be drinking so much, no one said it, and when they opened another, everyone turned away.

When Raef passed out, An'uek snuck over and made sure he was on his side, covering him with her shawl.

Cotta regarded the young druid woman.

"You're very kind to him," she commented, her words slurred but her eyes steady.

"I'm not really," An'uek replied, taking a seat on the floor beside the woman with black hair and faded bruises that almost, but not quite, disappeared in the dim lighting below deck.

"He told me what you did for him, for all of them," Cotta said.

"And A'rrick has told me what you intend to do when we get to Kraner."

"There's a man who needs to die." She took another pull on the flagon, knowing better than to offer it to An'uek, and not wanting to share.

"And that will bring peace?" An'uek asked.

"It doesn't need to," Cotta replied, "it just needs to even the deck."

"War isn't a game of cards."

"No, it's a game of chance." She took another drink, looking at Raef. "That's what he said to me once, many years ago. We argued for days about it, Mason too of course. Matters of state, the rules of kingdoms, right and wrong. He wasn't interested but he always had something to say. He would do anything Homen asked of him, but when it came to taking anything seriously, not a chance. Everything was a game."

An'uek glanced over at him, tucking her shawl in tighter around his shoulders.

Cotta raised her flagon.

"All this talk of war…" She took a drink. "Do you know how much blood I've seen in the last few weeks?"

"Are you ready to see a lot more?" An'uek challenged her.

"I am." Cotta put the flagon down and rubbed her wrists. "I keep thinking how much I want the fight, but now it's near, I think what I really want is peace."

"A'taz doesn't want peace." An'uek shook her head.

"I know. That's why it has to be war. You want him dead as much as we do." Cotta gazed at An'uek.

"I do," she agreed. "I'm going to stand with you on the battlefield. I need to know it's done."

Travis and Bode waited until Cotta passed out next to Raef and An'uek had settled with A'rrick, the druids talking without speaking.

"That's very unsettling," Travis muttered.

"You get used to it," Bode said, smirking.

"I don't think I want to get used to that." Travis was drumming his fingers on his knees.

"So tell me," Bode put the full weight of his attention on the man fidgeting at his side. "Why is one of the most powerful people in Barclan hiding fading bruises and disguised as a commoner?"

Bode didn't utter a word as Travis narrated events in the city. They both fell silent, minds working to the same goal. It was Bode who broke the contemplative quiet.

"I had planned to leave the city and head west as soon as we docked and Calem was delivered up."

"We've heard the same reports as you have, and it would seem like a good idea. War begets war, and we both know we'd invade if we had our sights on another kingdom in the same state as we find ourselves."

"Borders aren't a fat man's belly. They don't grow over time, they're taken."

"No," Travis agreed, "and I'd rather we didn't shrink our borders at the cost of saving our skins."

"But?"

"But," Travis was still tapping his fingers. "I need you at the back of the battlefield. I need you coordinating whatever effort we can gather."

"Isn't that your role?"

"It might have been a while ago," Travis said ruefully. "But not now. I'm the man pointing the sword. I need you to be the man behind all the pointed swords."

Bode frowned and Travis read his silence.

"It's not what you want to hear, is it?"

"No," he replied honestly, then raised his hands so Travis could see the way his fingers trembled. "It's why I wanted to head west, to be useful in some small way."

"You have no idea how much I need you on the battlefield." Travis let his voice dip.

"Do we have men? Horses? Weapons?"

"I have someone in Kraner pulling that together, I'm hoping when we get back she's worked some magic and put more boots in our ranks."

"How many?"

"Maybe if we're lucky we'll have a hundred."

"A hundred what? Infantry? Cavalry? Heavy horse?"

"People, Bode. If we're lucky, we'll have a hundred people."

"Oh," Bode said, shocked.

Travis put up a hand.

"We can talk more, maybe tomorrow." He got to his feet, and bending low, he went over to Cotta. He nudged her awake, hands constantly moving at his sides. Bode didn't hear what he said to her, but he was surprised when instead of berating him for waking her up from her drunken slumber she got straight to her feet, put her arm around his shoulders and walked with him to find a private space behind some barrels. Turning away from something that was none of his business, Bode crossed his ankles and began to think about what he could do with a hundred men, besides order them to dig their own graves.

The druids talked for hours in silence. An'uek bore the full weight of A'rrick's grief, his guilt and his fear for what was coming. The words he used to describe himself were as sharp and cut as deep as any blade: feeble, useless, unnecessary. She didn't offer platitudes or ill-placed compliments in an effort to ward away his turmoil, but she demanded he consider the sanity of his self-inflicted enmity.

"Tell me your thoughts," she commanded, "and I will tell you truthfully if they are justified."

"I could have done more to help my child break free from under the monster's hand."

"False," she replied without emotion. "Your power has limits. A power greater than yours held sway over her mind, you couldn't have helped her."

A'rrick looked at An'uek, seeing a stranger, but was compelled by the stranger to continue.

"I gave up too easily. I couldn't get to her, and I gave up without trying again."

"Again, false. You found the people who helped her. You did help her in that way. You are still helping her in that way."

He sat back, his tense shoulders starting to drop.

"I'm a bad father."

"Not true, you're here. If you were a bad father you wouldn't be feeling how you feel right now."

A'rrick started to feel some of the heaviness lessen. At last he said the words that he had refused to say even to himself.

"I wish An'eris had never left our lands, never come to Barclan, never met Cotta or that prince."

"That is a shameful wish. It's wrong to wish away love."

A'rrick felt the sting of her words. There was only one more confession he had left, the heaviest of them all.

"An'eris might die."

"An'eris will die," An'uek said as she soothed the druid lord's feeling without him even realising it. "One day. We all will. That is a fear you must bear regardless of the day or night."

He looked away.

"When did you become so cruel. And so wise?"

"When you sent me to these men, and I loved them, and I changed for them." She reached up, cupping his cheek with her hand. "I can't tell you what you want to hear," she admitted. "You can't sneak in and steal An'eris away and turn your back and pretend you aren't as caught up in this as we all are now."

"These people that we're surrounded by that you suggest we stand beside on a battlefield that isn't of our making are flawed and broken. They're erratic, volatile and lead with their emotions."

"Yes," An'uek said, nodded and smiling. "But they're a part of the world, and whether we like it or not, we have to help them, if for no other reason than a selfish one."

"If they lose, our kind are next."

Nodding, An'uek broke contact with the druid lord.

"There is no choice, is there?" he mused, calm.

"There is always a choice," she acknowledged. "But some choices are wrong. Make the right choice."

On the third day Raef stopped drinking with Cotta. He made his way up on deck to the fresh cold sea air, the spray from the waves as sobering as he hoped they would be. He picked a spot out the way, unlaced his trousers and relieved himself over the side.

"I thought you'd have checked on me before now," Calem called to him, his voice carrying over the heavy crash of the waves and the boom and snap of the sails catching the wind.

"Can you wait until I've at least tucked myself back in before you bother me," Raef croaked. "I can't see straight, and I'd like to avoid pissing on my boots."

"Too late for that," Calem scoffed.

"Don't stare, it's rude," Raef mocked, doing his trousers up. Holding the railing, he timed his steps to the pitch and roll of the ship and came to sit beside Calem in the only dry spot on the deck. He looked at his wet boots.

"That's from the spray," he drawled.

"Sure," Calem agreed too readily.

Raef put his head back, closed his eyes and groaned.

"What did you drink?" Calem asked.

"Everything."

"You and Bode?"

"Me and Cotta."

"Is she in the same shape as you?"

"Not a chance," he griped. "Damn woman could drink ten men under the table if she wanted... and wake up perfectly fine the next day."

"You look terrible."

Raef cut him a hateful glance, then chuckled.

"I bet I do. I'm sorry I didn't check on you."

They lapsed into silence.

"Do you think we'll be there soon?" Calem asked. Raef heard something else behind his words.

"What is it?" he asked, his hangover receding by the second.

"I'm not sure really." Calem creased his brow, looking down.

Raef waited, anxiety chasing away the last of his haze as Calem raised his hand.

"I thought it best to sit here, out of the way, you know. I kept it in my hand, but after a while it got so heavy, and hot, even for me it felt hot."

"Calem?" Raef implored, apprehensive and clear-headed, "what's happened?"

"I kept ignoring how hot it was, ignoring it when it got soft, just kept holding it, squeezing it."

"Calem, where is the lump of rock that Bastion gave you?"

Calem opened his hand. Resting on his palm was a small round stone.

"Will you take me to my brother?" Calem asked in a quiet voice. "He'll know what to do with me, with this."

Raef, eyes bloodshot, mouth as dry as a cupboard of spilled flour, barely able to stand on his own two feet, slowly closed Calem's fist around the little stone in his hand.

"I'll get you to him," he promised.

Raef stayed with Calem for the rest of the journey, as close as he could get without burning himself. An'uek brought them food and water, a blanket in the night that neither of them needed. Raef fell asleep, woke up, shifted on his backside and rolled his ankles when he lost the feeling in his feet. He taught Calem foul words in all the languages he knew. He showed him sleight of hand tricks with coins, the irony of parlour tricks entertaining the sorcerer not lost on either of them. He ignored the way Calem fidgeted with the stone in his hand until it got too much for him and he made him stuff his hand inside his sleeve.

On the last day, with the promise of Kraner starting to grow on the horizon and the voice from the crow's nest calling out, Raef saw nothing but fear in the young man.

"Do you know something?" Calem said quietly to Raef as everyone sprang to action preparing for their entry into the harbour.

"What?"

"I've never been to a party." He sounded far away. "I've never danced, or got drunk, been robbed," he smiled at Raef, "or woken up next to someone and had my heart broken when they regretted the night before." Calem set his gaze on the rapidly approaching vision of Kraner, the castle on the hill already visible, a grey stain on the winter sky. "But I have to go kill someone today."

Raef sighed.

"Calem, that might be the saddest and truest thing I've ever heard."

"It'll be sadder if I fail."

"Don't fail then," was all Raef could say.

Calem turned to him.

"Have you ever set out to kill someone and done it?"

"No," Raef shook his head. "I never had to."

"It should be a horrible feeling." Calem got to his feet and went to stand at the railing. "But it isn't. It was, but it's not now."

Raef stepped up beside him.

"I'm glad," he stated. "Everything is at stake. We made a mistake at Ipcriss. We can't make a mistake again."

"I can't," Calem corrected him. "You can. When we get to port, you can turn around and I'll walk up to the castle myself, find Brennan, and he and I will get this done."

"But I won't do that." Raef bumped Calem with his elbow. "Only a fool would think I'd abandon him now."

"And you're no fool," a deep voice interrupted them.

Raef and Calem turned to see that Bode and An'uek had come up behind them. Towards the bow, Travis waited with Cotta and A'rrick.

"Time to go," Cotta called to them.

"We're ready," Raef called back.

The ship slid into port. Thick coils of rope were unwound and tossed to waiting hands on the quay, and the thundering clatter of the anchor as it was released and slid out of its bracket caused everyone to flinch and jump. Sails were pulled in, orders shouted and answered, the gangplank locked in place.

Without delay, they walked off the ship and were in Kraner.

CHAPTER 33

A'taz focused on the gems, channelling the life of the men around him through their crystal facets, magnifying the energy; he fed day after day, and through every night. When there was nothing left in the men who had withered away to dry husks of skin and brittle bones locked in a misty white tomb, he redirected his search for life and strength through Troy into Kraner. For four nights his loyal servant stood looking down on the city, home to tens of thousands of oblivious, ripe, rich souls.

It was a feast, just for his master. The mist crept through the gates into the north-west sections of the city, slipping under closed doors, through the cracks in windows, rising through the seams of floorboards and reaching up from under beds to coil around a foot not tucked under a blanket, snaking and covering bodies, to be breathed in, but never breathed out.

A'taz gorged on men, women, children, babies, day by day, drawing closer to the castle, covering more of the city. As he grew stronger, he could see the ribbons of power that Brennan had laid around the people that had undermined his control so effectively. Part of him could admire the simplicity of Brennan's riposte, acknowledge even that the man had some power, some skill. But that was as much as A'taz would grant. He watched those streams of power, mesmerised by their trail, following it back to the castle, back into the halls that he felt were his. He followed Brennan's footsteps as if he was a few minutes behind him, seeing the echo of where he had just been. A'taz moved, downwards, into the foundations of the castle, into the depths of Kraner.

At a juncture in the journey, the trail he was following split, and he could sense two distinct lives travelling together: Brennan and An'eris.

A'taz, at the realisation of where they were going, where he was going, was so overcome with excitement that he nearly missed the moment when he felt An'eris's living being move past him, retreat from this ancient place. He waited, hidden and away from Brennan, who passed a moment later, then he turned to walk down the path they had left for him.

A'taz had the scent. He followed the trail at his leisure, taking all the time he needed to follow Brennan's footsteps until he came, at least, to the lake.

A'taz stopped at the edge, dwelled there for an age outside of time as he began his preparations to step into the water.

Brennan felt him, somewhere, somehow; he passed A'taz as he walked back into the castle. He wondered why he wasn't scared, why he wasn't overcome with fear and dread. And then he knew.

Brennan felt him the moment he stepped off the ship and his feet hit dry land.

"Calem is here," he said as he followed An'eris through the castle.

She turned, falling into step beside him.

"Are you sure?"

"There's no doubt."

She nodded.

"What?" he asked, aware there was something he was missing.

"How long were we gone for?" she asked.

"What do you mean?"

"Look around." She gestured to the empty halls echoing with their solitary footsteps. "Where is everyone?"

Calem stood on the docks.

"I need to hurry." There was a measure of confidence in his voice none of them had heard before.

"This is where we part then," An'uek replied. "I feel like I should hug you goodbye."

"Probably not a good idea though," he suggested.

"Probably not." She looked away. "I don't know what to say."

"Then let me say it… thank you." He touched his hand to his forehead and bowed to her.

An'uek stepped away as Calem turned to Bode.

"Stay safe," he said to the big man.

"You too, Calem."

Raef, waiting quietly at Calem's side.

"This is the wrong place for sad goodbyes." He tugged Calem's sleeve, making the young man turn around. "It'll take an hour to get to the castle, are you ready?"

"Are you?" Calem countered.

"Time to go." Raef roused his bravado and leaned in to kiss An'uek before turning to shake Bode's hand.

"This has been the worst job I've ever done." He tried to grin, but his lips quivered. "And it looks like now I won't even get paid."

"You saying my company wasn't payment enough?"

Raef opened his mouth to speak but was silent. He tried again, but the jokes died on his lips.

"Let's have a drink," he said, "after this is done."

"I'd like that." Bode held out his hand. "You're paying."

Raef couldn't help the chuckle that spilled out.

He turned to An'uek.

"I remember my vow," he said softly to her as she reached up and took his head in her hands, bringing her lips to kiss away some of his anguish.

"I do too," she replied, sighing, "and I release you from your vow, because the man you are now doesn't need to be bound to anyone to do the right thing."

Raef took her hands from around his face, brought them to his lips and kissed her.

"Go now." She pushed him away, pushed him towards Calem, then said to them both, "Hurry, your brother is waiting."

Bode reached for An'uek's hand, lacing their fingers together as they watched Raef and Calem walk away.

"All roads lead to Kraner."

"That they do," Cotta said, stepping over to the two of them. "And now we have to go."

"Go where?"

"Travis left Kirin with orders to assemble the fighters near the south gates."

"Horses? Weapons?"

"If she's done her job, they'll be waiting for us."

"And then?"

"We mount up and ride out. We know A'taz and Troy won't be far away. They left by the western gate. They'll most likely be camped somewhere nearby."

"We can't just ride to battle. We need to come up with a strategy."

"Isn't that what you were doing on the boat?"

Cotta started walking, assuming the others would follow her. As she did so, she turned to Bode.

"Well, Knight. What's the plan?"

As they walked, A'rrick and An'uek were the first to notice the increasing panic in the streets.

"What's going on?" Bode asked.

An'uek concentrated for a few minutes, her hearing cutting the background noise away. "People are talking about a sleeping sickness that's in the north of the city. There's a fog." She looked perplexed. "Something like a fog that's in the streets and around the houses." She concentrated again, listening. "It's thick though, like sponge, and the people in the houses are missing... they're gone or... somehow locked inside the fog."

"A'taz," A'rrick announced. "Who else could it be?"

"It's spreading," An'uek continued. "It's rolling through the city. It sounds like it's at the castle, almost all around it, and it's heading south."

An'uek stopped walking, a hand to her head, her eyes squeezed shut as she concentrated.

"People are missing. And everyone else is scared."

She opened her eyes and turned to Bode.

"Panic," she said. "They're on the verge. One more thing and it'll spark a riot."

Calem and Raef walked quickly through the streets.

"Something's wrong," Raef said as they pushed passed groups of worried men and women.

"We can't stop," Calem said, starting to wheeze. Raef looked over at him. He wasn't sure if it was a trick of the insipid light filtering through gloomy winter skies, but he thought Calem looked... bright.

They carried on, with all the focus on keeping to the main roads and avoiding any delays. Raef kept looking at Calem.

"You all right?" he asked, his voice unnaturally high.

"Yes, why?"

"You look strange."

"What does strange look like?" Calem asked, his eyes forward.

"Like there's fire at the end of your fingers."

Calem, still walking, looked down at himself.

"How far are we away from the castle?"

"Ten minutes."

"Then maybe you'd better leave me here?" Calem said, still looking at his body, which was starting to change.

"I said I'd get you to your brother."

"I know the way from here."

"I don't doubt that," Raef said, still walking.

"I might kill you." Calem kept pace with Raef.

"You might," he agreed, grinning. "But then, considering the life I've lived, if nothing's got me yet, what chance do you have?"

Calem looked over at Raef.

"Promise me you'll leave me once we get to Brennan," he stated.

Raef understood what Calem was asking but refused to let this be their goodbye; instead, he increased their pace.

"I will," he replied. "I'll wait for you, I'll come get you when it's done."

They broke into a run up the last section of streets that led to the open gates of the castle wall. No one was on duty; the whole place was deserted. The only thing living was a thin veil of mist covering the ground. It hissed and recoiled as if in pain as Calem strode through it to the enormous oak doors of the castle main. The mist seemed to lunge for Raef but was kept away by the distinct flames that now covered Calem's body, his fists incandescent.

"Can you open the doors for me?" he asked. "Brennan is somewhere inside, and so is A'taz."

Raef stopped, his hand on one of the doors.

"I open this door, you step through, there's no turning back?"

"No, you open that door, we trust that fate has something in store for us, all of us."

"What if fate will have us dead?"

"Then you'd have died in the desert." Calem said. "I am surer of that than I am of anything. You'll live."

Raef opened the door and stepped aside for Calem.

Brennan forced An'eris up the stairs, physically moving her ahead of him.

"I can't get you out like I planned, something's changed."

"Let me make a run for it." She clung to the railing trying to anchor herself against him as he pushed her ever upwards.

"There's no way out of the castle. A'taz has created something... it's alive, some sort of poison. It's breached the castle and it's coming in. I don't know what else to do but put you in the highest place and hope it can't climb."

She pushed against him.

"Let me try save myself," she half sobbed. "Let me do something."

"Please," Brennan shouted to snap her out of her despair. "Please," he said, more softly a second time, "just find a place, find somewhere to hide, do what you need to do to save yourself and the baby. There's no more time, An'eris, please."

Brennan pushed her up the final steps, opened the door and forced her into the dusty remains of Homen's study.

She stepped inside, turned and reached for him.

"I'm scared I'll never see you again." She reached out and touched his face. "Before it's too late, I'm sorry... for everything."

"You never did any of this," he said, gesturing widely.

"But I never stopped them either."

"You did, or A'taz would have found what he was looking for before help arrived and we'd all be too dead to be saying goodbye."

"So this is goodbye?" She let the tears fall.

He didn't say no.

Brennan walked away, the sound of the door closing behind him booming loud enough to shake the foundations of the castle, to shake the bones in his body.

He headed back the way he had come... was it an hour ago, a day, a week, or a hundred years. He couldn't remember, but he knew where he was going. As he set off, lost in his own thoughts without any idea of what to do, he heard a familiar voice calling his name.

He turned and ran, following the voice calling for him, turning left and right, up and down hallways that led to the entrance hall. He saw a man he didn't know, tall, slender, with dark hair, standing in the doorway, daylight streaming in beside him, and for a second he was confused. It lasted until his sight recognised that the glowing radiance next to him wasn't daylight at all.

He rushed down the stairs to the pillar of light.

"Hello, brother," Brennan said, his voice breaking, tears of blood streaming from his mangled eyes.

"Hello, Brennan," Calem replied raising his hand to brush away his brother's tears. At his touch, Brennan's body absorbed some of his brother's light. As if drawn in on a deep breath, Brennan took in as much power as he wanted and was changed.

Raef, unable to look away, watched as the disfigured hunched man re-formed. He stood straight, his face healing itself, his eyes open, sparkling and luminous.

"Thank you," he said, and he grinned.

"I'm sorry I couldn't come sooner."

"Now is soon enough."

"I hope so."

"A'taz is here. He's found the lake."

Calem turned to Raef.

"Time to go."

He nodded,

"I'll wait outside."

"You can't, the mist..."

"Then I'll find somewhere," Raef assured him, gesturing with his hands as if to push the radiant man away. "I'll find somewhere safe."

"Homen's tower, do you know it?" Brennan asked.

"I do."

"Then head for the tower."

Calem nodded and turned to Brennan, who reached for Raef.

"Go," he said kindly. "Your job is done."

Raef shook his hand, then turned and ran.

Cotta mounted her horse, gripping the reins tightly.

"Kirin, how many?"

"Barely a hundred, hardly any with more than a year of service on their boots. Less than twenty have ever seen battle."

"It'll have to do," Bode said, clicking his teeth and pulling on his reins to get his horse moving.

It took them almost an hour to reach the south gate. The streets were packed with people and it was slow going regardless of the imposing horses.

As they left the city behind them, A'rrick pulled in close to Bode.

"I can see the fighters. Do we make camp?"

"No." Bode shifted in his saddle. "From what Kirin's reported, this mist seems to be coming from A'taz. It's killing people, suffocating them in the city. We have no time, we have to attack straight away."

"We have no idea what we're riding into."

"We know we're outnumbered by probably fifty to one." Bode turned to the druid lord. "Do you believe in fate?" he asked.

His question surprised A'rrick.

"I do," he replied. "I've communed with the Gods. I know they see us, they have a hand in our lives."

"Then can you believe you have a purpose, that you are here to help us?"

"I can."

"Good." Bode looked relieved. "Then tell me, Lord A'rrick, I know what An'uek can do for us, what can you do?"

Travis rode beside Cotta, his armour and weapons in place, holding loosely onto the pommel of his saddle.

"Seeing you in your armour, it makes me nervous." She kept her eyes ahead.

"For someone riding into their first battle, you should be a lot more nervous than you seem."

He looked at her, waiting.

"I'm terrified," she admitted. She wore no armour; there was nothing to fit her. Her sword was too heavy, and the scabbard on her belt pulled at her waist like heavy hands.

Travis coughed to keep her attention when he saw her mind start to drift to fearful places.

"Stay with me," he said, winking at her.

Neither spoke as they continued up the short road that would take them to the lowlands west of the city. Armour or not, there was no weapon she could wield that would make a difference now.

As the miles started to fall away, An'uek rode up beside Cotta.

"You remind me of my friend," Cotta said, to steady her own nerves.

"An'eris?" An'uek asked. "I met her, but I was younger, different then."

"She's in the castle," Cotta said, a darkness edging her words.

"We need our minds to be here," An'uek said, drawing her attention. "If you are thinking of your friend in the castle, a sword will be in your belly before you get off your horse."

"Have you been in many fights?" Cotta asked, painfully aware that the woman beside her exuded more confidence and battle readiness than she could even hope to fake.

"More since knowing your people than most druids have known in their whole lives."

"Is it terrible?" she asked, feeling compelled to voice her fear.

"It's..." An'uek searched for the right word. "It's an end," was all she could say.

Cotta mused on her words.

"Why are you here? I know what you said, but why here, at the front, with me and Travis? Why aren't you at the back with Bode? I thought he was going to die when you refused to stay beside him."

An'uek actually laughed.

"I can help you here," she explained.

Cotta, on hearing such simple words spoken from someone she knew to be powerful, felt a surge of comfort. It renewed her confidence and she felt stronger, eager, the rising energy a wave she was happy to let overwhelm her.

They reached the crest of a low hill, and it took no time at all for the small band of fighters to rein in and stop. Below, stretched out like an inland sea, a thick mist, like paste, covered what they could just make out as makeshift tents set up around a scrawny awning. There, under the awning, was a familiar face.

From half a mile away, Troy turned and magnified his vision. He sought out Cotta's face, turning to look at her, licking his lips with his forked tongue.

CHAPTER 34

A'rrick got off his horse and walked the short distance to place himself in front of their small army.

He sat down on the frozen ground, put his hands on his knees, and began a slow chant. At first it was nothing more than a murmur, a sound no louder than a cat purring at the bottom of a bed. The fighters around him felt the hairs on their arms stand, a tingle run across their skin, and they all took a step away. It didn't take long for the chanting to grow louder; the utterances start to change as the spell was crafted.

A'rrick pushed and pulled at the forces he could draw from nature until he had a pulse of energy he could put into his spell. Without a loud cry or grand gesture, he changed the pitch of his voice, and the sound of his song carried across to the ground blanketed in A'taz and Troy's creation.

"What is he doing?" Cotta whispered to An'uek.

"The mist is a twisted druid spell," An'uek hissed.

She heard Cotta take a sharp inhalation, guessing she had been witness to other spells, and remembering what she knew of what happened to Brennan, she understood the nervous gestures of the woman beside her. To alleviate some of her fear, she offered what explanation she could.

"A'taz draws life from others. That's what the spell is doing. Something this powerful, over so much distance, so much life, must be augmented by the gems."

"Can he break the spell?"

"No, he isn't strong enough, not when the gems are involved."

"What then?"

"He's making a path," An'uek said, getting down from her horse.

Cotta frowned.

"A path for what?"

"For me."

Cotta watched as An'uek walked to A'rrick, towards the sea of mist, towards the army camp, towards Troy.

She had to wait, and watch; when An'uek was less than a hundred yards from the edge of the camp, in a clear voice that filled the air, the druidess shouted for Troy.

Getting his attention, An'uek took off her gloves and raised her hands above her head, palms towards the sky. Above her, the grey winter clouds started to swirl, and a moment later a maelstrom appeared above her, angry and heavy, seeming to pull the sky down towards her commanding hands.

"What are you doing, little druidess," Troy taunted, stepping towards her.

"I'm raising an army," she announced.

The clouds pulsed at her words, the grey transforming into hues of deep magenta and violet, reflecting off her silver hair and alabaster skin. Troy stood dumbfounded as, behind her, shimmering into existence, hundreds of soldiers appeared. In his shock, his mind went blank for a moment and he lost the threads of the spell he had been casting. Unbound, it snapped away from him, unleashed, rapidly unravelling, the power of the gems that held it in place withering and taking the mist with it.

Bode saw the mist start to dissipate as An'uek created the illusion of thousands of men called at her command. It was what they had been hoping for, a distraction so stunning it broke Troy's single-minded focus on maintaining A'taz's spell, shattering the magic cast all around them.

"Now!" Bode shouted, and his army advanced.

The men swarmed down the hill towards the tents. It wasn't until they were almost upon them that the first of A'taz's men stumbled to their feet. Disorientated, emaciated, skin on bone, it took hardly any time at all for Bode's men to begin the slaughter.

But as weak as they were, there were more than hundreds of them, there was over a thousand, and soon the frenzy of battle spurred them on, and weak arms lifted swords with a lifetime of experience, and the man-shaped husks started to fight back.

In the castle, Brennan led Calem down to the lake. With each step they could feel the earth beneath them start to shake.

The steps took them back in time.

When they finally reached the cavern, the utter darkness was banished by Calem's presence.

They stopped, the brothers, and saw A'taz at the edge of the lake. He was on his knees, scooping up water with his hands.

Time slowed. Calem saw him raise his hand to his lips, drops of water slipping between his cupped fingers, each drop that fell setting off a rumbling in the foundations of the castle, of the very kingdom. The chamber shook, threatening to collapse as great cracks appeared in the cavern walls and above their heads.

"Don't, you can't contain it, it'll destroy the world," Calem pleaded. "You're not a God."

"I think I will be though," A'taz said, smirking.

"Please don't."

A'taz smiled and drank the tears shed by the Goddess Evram. He took them in one gulp, the water dribbling down his chin.

Brennan watched impassively as A'taz stepped toward Calem, then stopped and began to transform.

A'taz's body grew larger as the cavern shrunk in size, the booming becoming a rolling thunder, the heartbeat of the earth itself rebounding around the echo chamber, drawn into A'taz as he gathered the vestiges of the very echo An'dorna had used to shape the earth.

All around him the walls shimmered, cracks flashed then disappeared, mirages of mountains rising from the sea played out across the floors, on the walls, images of mountains erupting, lands cracking and falling into the sea again and again. The hard rock became course stone, then sand mixed with water, a brown earth that slowly turned green as time changed all things and the images showed the creation of life on their world, all played out in the shadow A'taz cast around him.

"See where it started," he called into the cavern. "See where I can go back to, what I can do."

His shadow reached back, pushing mountains down, under the sea, banishing the land.

A'taz felt the water in his veins mingle with his blood, and the essence of all the lives ever lived coursed through his body. He felt the beating echo of creation in his chest. It pulsed within him, merging with his being, coming under his control.

He turned to Calem.

Calem waited. There was nothing he could do. He couldn't touch the water. He couldn't harness the echo. A'taz stood before him, flush with the power of the two Gods who had formed the very world itself.

Calem felt a pull towards A'taz, as if he was drawing Calem's own power out from under his skin. He pictured his body rending apart, A'taz sucking the flames out of his veins. He imagined the loss of the heat, a life without the itching effervescence inside himself that he loved so much.

Calem let himself be pulled forward, his feet stepping towards A'taz. He went down on his knees in front of him, his head back, exposing his neck.

A'taz knew absolute power. Invincibility.

He reached out, his long fingers wrapping around Calem's glowing throat, squeezing with all his might, calling the boy's power out, demanding it for himself.

This was what he had waited for. The heat, the spark, to have it, to take it back in time, to keep it for himself.

As the pain of A'taz's grip overwhelmed him, all he wanted was to hide, but there was nowhere left to go. Calem cast his mind back to his journey across the lake with Isaac. He searched his memory for what Isaac had said to him, recalled his voice in the chamber.

It wasn't enough. A'taz could still find him. He had to go further, to the darkest place he had ever been, where there was only himself.

"Burn." The word echoed in the cavern, a voice from the past; Calem heard it, and then, from a time forgotten, "Find the light."

Calem inhaled all the air in the chamber, drawing it into his lungs, into his body, the very air of life the fuel for his flame, ignited in the darkness.

Brennan stumbled back, his hands over his face, trying not to see as Calem surrendered to A'taz, his submission unleashing world-breaking devastation.

Travis fought alongside men; some fell, some got back up, most didn't. His armour was dented inwards until it was so bent it cut into his side and he had to take if off or choose to stop breathing. Behind him he could hear Bode calling out orders; Travis obeyed blindly. He ran left when he was told, he pulled back, he regrouped with everyone around him, he went forward when they attacked. The dry husks of men kept coming. He didn't know how many he had cut down.

Cotta had stayed with Travis as he wanted, but in the chaos of the melee they'd quickly got separated. She'd only swung her sword once, the momentum of it almost taking her off her feet. Instantly she'd dropped it and grabbed for the daggers on her belt. About to launch at the nearest enemy, she heard Travis shouting behind her.

"Hang back, kills only."

She understood. She kept herself away from the main attack, kept to the edge. Every time one of her fighters dropped an enemy she would rush in, stab her daggers into their throat and then retreat. Bode, seeing what she was doing, called out a change of tactic, and the men surrounded her, their death dealer. Now focused on just bringing the enemy down for her to finish them, the army moved with ruthless efficiency, buoyed by the constant confusion caused by An'uek's illusory fighters.

Cotta killed every single man she could reach. As the fighting moved and they edged ever closer to the centre of the camp, she drifted further and further from Travis.

As she stabbed a man in the throat, leaning on his chest to steady herself as she stood, she turned and saw Travis fighting.

She saw him swing and miss.

She saw the other blade strike true in Travis just as he twisted and brought his own sword down again.

She saw them both fall.

Leaving her blades in a mercenary's throat, she ran to Travis, screaming his name in terror.

The enemy, mortally wounded, took Travis down under his own body weight, and by luck, landed on top. Travis, under the man husk, scrabbled to change his grip, to get enough leverage to stab the thing somewhere, anywhere, to end it. He could feel it rolling over on him, its knees jerking upwards and connecting with his ribs. He felt them break, felt a harsh pain in his chest. He shouted out, tried to take another breath to heave the body off his chest, but couldn't quite fill his lungs. He tried to breathe again, feeling something gush up his throat, filling his mouth with something hot that tasted like blood.

He kept trying to breathe, losing his grip on the body on top of his, losing the strength in his hands as the sounds around him started to fade away.

The last thing he heard was Cotta's voice, a scream of rage and sadness he'd never imagined she could conjure. He heard her screaming a name, he thought it might be his, but he couldn't quite remember.

He felt a weight dragged off his chest, hoped he would at last catch his breath, but there was just no air left in the world.

He saw her, her beautiful face, no bruises, her dark hair, those green eyes he had been lost in all his life, so vibrant, seductive, loving.

He could feel something splash on his face. He knew she was crying; he felt her thumbs wiping her tears over his cheeks like she was cleaning him, and he knew.

He heard her call his name one last time; she was telling him to do something. His vision faded away, but in his last moments he heard her clearly.

"Go to Falconfall, Travis, go home. Wait for me there. I'll see you one day soon, I promise."

"Yes, my lady," he said with his last breath.

Cotta rested her head on his chest, knowing it would never rise again.

She got to her feet, tears flowing freely, cleaning her blood-covered face. She spun around, taking stock. It was too hard to count, too many men, maybe hers, maybe Troy's.

Troy.

She looked for him in the crowd.

An'uek, calling illusions out of the sky, watched Travis die, and watched as Cotta stood up from his body.

She had never seen an expression of such hatred on a living face.

An'uek knew what she wanted.

Casting her mind around, she found Troy.

She called for Cotta, getting her attention. When she looked over, An'uek raised her arm and pointed.

Cotta, seeing her prey, walked towards him. As she passed the druidess, An'uek stopped her and handed her a dagger: a white pommel and grey blade, like smoke trapped in a mirror.

Cotta gripped it in one hand and continued.

Troy saw her coming towards him, a puny single blade in her hand.

Confident, full of swagger, he turned to face her, incanting a spell that would slow her down enough to give him all the time he wanted to rip her to pieces with his fingernails.

She stalked towards him, covered in the blood of hundreds of men, but now only seeing one she wanted to kill.

He felt small, momentarily nervous. Turning around, he looked for an escape.

It was all she needed. In the moment it took him to turn, she crossed the last fifteen yards and pounced on him.

He felt himself knocked to the ground, her weight on his. Still smiling, he started his spell, but the words didn't sound right; his split tongue and torn mouth couldn't form the words and the magic wouldn't come under his control.

Looking up at her, his smile faded.

She waited, made sure he knew who she was, made sure he had enough time to remember everything he had done to her, done to An'eris.

"Remember me," she put her lips to his ear, "and know this. I will forget you and everything you've done. You are, no one."

Then she took the grey blade and pressed it against his lips.

He clamped his jaw shut, but it made no difference. With all her weight behind the blade, it shattered his teeth as it slid into his mouth. He felt the tip bite the back of his throat, pierce the skin, his blood gushing, sliding down his throat into his lungs, bubbling up as he breathed it in, breathed it out.

With both hands on the hilt, she put her weight on it, then twisted. The blade plunged through him, splitting his head in half.

She tried to yank the blade from his body, but it was so heavy she could barely lift it.

Cotta fell off him soaked in his blood.

A cold calm crept over her as she lay next to his corpse. She turned her head, and across the ground she could see Travis.

Lying between them, she thought she might take a minute to rest. She was so tired, and the blade was so heavy.

But no, she could hear An'uek shouting, yelling at her to do something.

Dragging herself to sit up, she focused on the druidess.

She nodded once, then hauled herself to her feet, barely able to stand with the weight of the blade in her hand. She stumbled towards the awning where Troy had been hiding, dropping to her knees when she reached it.

She found a little wooden box with three jewels inside, vibrating, knocking against each other.

In the cavern, A'taz stood engulfed in Calem's flame, immune to the heat of the inferno, protected by the equalising measure of Evram's water, the power resonating inside him, controlled by his mastery of the gems in his possession.

Calem could sense the water in A'taz, could feel it drawing his flame out, but still he burned. The sizzle in his skin changed for a moment, and Calem remembered the tea he had drunk with Raef. He remembered the water he had sipped. He remembered what happened in Ipcriss, when Orren did what he did.

Calem abandoned any sense of control of his flame; he let it free. It sprung from him, a living thing, surrounding A'taz, piercing him, flowing into him.

And still he absorbed it, still he took everything Calem had.

Calem, letting it loose from his body, was able to turn to Brennan.

"I need your help, brother."

"How, what can I do?"

"The gems," Calem said, stepping forward, stepping into A'taz, melting their bodies together. "Cotta, it has to be her. You have to take us all to her and bring her here to us. Put us altogether, here at the end of the world and there at the last battle."

Brennan looked behind him, as if the fighting was at his back. He sent his sight out and found his lover crying over Travis's dead body.

Brennan reached for An'uek and put the thought in her mind. He reached for Cotta, paused her pain for just long enough to do as An'uek commanded. In his eye, Brennan put them all together.

He watched her get to her feet, kill Troy, and then turn to the gems.

He wove his vision, everywhere, and gave them each their purpose.

He told her what to do.

As she brought the hilt of the dagger down on the first gem, he sighed to hush the crowd of killers around her, reminding her of her vision.

Miles away, Cotta felt a gentle sigh brush the hair away from her face, heard Brennan telling her to be calm, to strike true.

Cotta looked at the blade in her gloved hand. So much blood. She put it down and serenely pulled off the gloves, revealing the clean skin of her hands. She picked up the blade, wiping it on her leg as much as she could, surprised at how easily the blood came off. She dragged the grey blade across her palm, sharpening the edge with her blood, then raised it above her head and brought it down with all the force of her vengeance.

She smashed the first gem.

In the cavern, their bodies entwined in flames, A'taz screamed as a quake ripped through the cavern.

He convulsed in pain, ripping his body away from Calem, who fell out of him, falling between him and the lake.

Cotta raised the blade and took aim at the second gem. Brennan breathed strength into her arm as she smashed it to pieces.

A'taz, his mouth as wide as a barrel, drew all the air in the cavern into his lungs, taking it all until there was nothing left, choking screams turning to gasps.

Cotta grabbed the blade in both hands, barely able to lift it, the weight pulling her to her knees. She managed to hold it barely an inch over the last gem, and with the weight of every life on her back, she slammed the hilt down, and it shattered on contact, destroying the third gem.

In the cavern, lying on the floor, Calem felt a heaviness smash into his chest. He imagined it shattering every bone in his body, the shards piercing his flesh. Beside him, the incandescent flames A'taz had consumed spluttered out for a moment, replaced instantly by angry red fire.

Calem, unable to move, to make a noise, know of anything beyond pain, thought he could hear the world ending... or perhaps starting. Instead of shadows, the cavern was filled with the mythical creatures of the deep desert that he had consumed, brought back to life, created from his fire. One after another they erupted from his body, took flight, and turned on A'taz. Calem turned his head, eyes wide in surprise, and with something like joy, turned to face A'taz.

"Burn," Calem said in the darkness, to himself, to the creatures coming to life from his body on the cavern floor.

A'taz, howling in rage and agony, was alive until the very moment his blackened flesh dropped away from his charred bones, the echoes of his screams alive for as long as Calem chose to keep the fires burning.

Across from the city, Cotta collapsed on the ground next to the empty wooden box. The ground was littered with crystal shards, dull, ordinary. The mist was burning away in the daylight. She heard a sound, a piercing shriek, and turned to look over her shoulder at the city. From above the castle she thought for a fleeting instant she could see the outlines of golden creatures taking flight, spiralling upwards on great wings, disappearing into nothingness.

Brennan watched as Calem, and Cotta, killed A'taz.

When the monster was nothing but dust, he waited for Calem to destroy even that. He might have sat for years waiting for the flames to flicker out. He thought, perhaps, it had been a thousand years before Calem, lying prone on the floor, weakly called him over.

"I'm here," he said, shuffling over, trying to gather him in his arms. His fires, gone.

"Don't," Calem yelped. "It hurts, please don't." He started to cry, tears slipping down his cheeks.

"I've never seen your eyes like this, little brother." Brennan smiled down at him.

"I'm so cold," Calem said, sobbing. "Is it done?"

"It is." Brennan leaned down, careful not to hurt him, using the barest of touches to push his hair out of his cobalt blue eyes. "You did a good thing."

Brennan could feel the cold seeping from his trembling body.

"In my hand," Calem said, starting to gasp.

Brennan gently opened his clenched fist and found a tiny stone.

"It's the last one," he sobbed. "You know what you need to do."

"No." Brennan shook his head. "No, he's gone. We don't have to."

"Please," Calem whimpered. "It hurts. I don't want it anymore."

"Please no," Brennan begged. "We've only just found each other."

"Please," he asked again.

Nodding, Brennan leaned down and kissed his brother on the forehead.

Brennan closed Calem's hand around the stone, squeezing it tight. He leaned over him and picked him up.

Calem cried out in pain.

"Just a few steps," Brennan said soothingly. "Hold on for a second, then it won't hurt anymore."

He felt Calem turn his face into his chest, felt him sobbing in his arms.

"I love you," he whispered.

"I always loved you," Calem replied. "Even when I didn't know anything, I know I always loved you."

Brennan walked into the lake, carrying Calem in his arms. He waded out as far as he could go, far enough to lean down and let the water lap at Calem. By the time the water splashed at his hands, he wasn't crying anymore. The pain had gone. Calem's hand fell open, and the water swirled around the stone that dissolved at its touch. Brennan took one more step, let the water cover Calem's body, then let him go under the surface of the lake.

He made his way back to the shore, sobbing into the dark cave. With each step he took away from the lake, it progressively dried up until there was nothing left.

The sound of his cries filled the chamber, his own grief returning. His sobs grew louder, his cries becoming wails, then howls. As he walked away, he felt a tremor in the ground beneath his feet.

He turned, in the dark, in the emptiness, and felt a stirring of something warm across his cheek, like a sweet caress.

"Calem?" he cried into the dark. But there was no small voice calling back to him. Just a rumble that grew louder.

Brennan turned and ran.

The ground under him shook as if to break apart. He made it to the castle, seeing cracks appearing in the walls and floors, windows shattering and ceilings starting to fall.

He heard someone calling his name; Raef ran into him, An'eris a step behind, knocking them off their feet. The thief jumped up, pulling him up as they ran.

"Calem," he screamed, "where is he?"

Brennan could only shake his head.

Raef squeezed his eyes shut.

They stood in the hall as the ground quaked and the castle shook apart around them.

"We have to go," Raef shouted, gripped by memories of falling stone and brains smashed out on the floor. "Come on." He grabbed Brennan and ran, pulling him along behind him.

Raef saw a way out and put everything into his efforts, helping An'eris, and reaching the exit, they just made it through as the great wooden beams fell from the ceiling, crashing down behind them.

They all ran and didn't look back as the ground heaved and tore itself apart under their feet. The city fell in on itself, buildings falling, roads collapsing, lifting, dropping, the land reforming itself. The chaos spread from the castle down into the city, unrelenting. The crowds were running everywhere and anywhere. Lost children cried for their mothers; fathers screamed for their children. Brennan saw it all around, the chaos as the city fell.

He stopped running.

Raef skidded just ahead then turned and raced back, grabbing him, trying to pull him forward. But Brennan pulled his hand back and shook his head.

Raef felt the touch; it skimmed his thoughts and he had the urge to run; he knew where to go, how to escape.

He saw the same look settle on the faces of everyone around him.

He closed his eyes, his feet already moving.

He looked back over his shoulder just long enough to see Brennan standing calmly in the crowd, a smile on his face, the same smile on the faces of everyone around him as they all rushed to safety, families reunited, running away to safety as the ground tore apart.

And so Raef ran with An'eris, racing with the swarms of people fleeing the city in orderly panic.

Raef and An'eris reached the western gates and burst onto the lowlands beyond the city walls as Kraner fell to ruins behind them, burying its sleeping dead in the rubble.

Brennan watched them go. He watched everyone go from where he stood, not in the middle of a collapsing city, but from the top of a grassy hill covered in tall red flowers. The air was heavy with a sweet scent that he could taste on the back of his mouth. He felt the warm sun on his face and sat down on a white shawl laid out on the grass to wait.

Raef knew the inevitable had happened when the passive looks on everyone's faces changed to fear and the people started to scream and run. But by then they were out, they were safe.

It reached the harbour, the waves smashing into the docks again and again, getting higher and higher until they breached the walls and started to surge into the city. But by then the land had changed. Rising up, the seabed was forced upwards until the sea itself started to fall away, further and further back as the new land rose up as Kraner fell.

Cotta couldn't move. It wasn't until An'uek rushed over to her, A'rrick at her side, both picking her up between them, that she was able to put her feet on the ground and stand.

"Help me with her," An'uek muttered. "Then go, go find An'eris, take her home. Find whoever is left and see them safe, see they find somewhere else to go."

She sounded different.

Cotta looked at An'uek, grabbed her face in her hands, pulling her head close to her eyes.

She moved her head from side to side, searching her face.

An'uek saw herself reflected in Cotta's eyes. She touched her face, felt the wrinkles, touched her hair; it came away in her fingers: grey, brittle, old. She looked down at her hands and saw them as shrivelled, covered in spots she only saw on the longest-lived druids, whose bodies were weary of life.

She lifted Cotta over to A'rrick, who held her upright, looking at her.

"What had this cost you?" Cotta asked, unable to believe what she was seeing.

"The cost was mine to bear. So be it," An'uek said.

There were no more sounds of battle behind them. There were no more enemies to fight, only bodies of the dead, and a scant few of the living. They heard the sound of heavy boots charging across the battlefield, announcing Bode, who barrelled into them.

"There's an earthquake," he blurted out, "in the city." He was breathing hard. He looked at the three of them, registering shock, but they didn't hear what he had said. He reached for An'uek, for her hands.

He stepped round to see her, to see that she was all right.

For a moment he simply stared before raising his head and looking out at the field where they had won an impossible war because of her illusions. He raised trembling hands to his head, covering his eyes for a moment before she reached up and took his hands.

"Bode..." Her voice, still so soft, called his name.

He looked at her, his face in her hands.

"Bode," she said again. "I've not got much time left. Maybe a season, maybe a year, but no more than that. I'd like to spend it with you."

He pressed her hands to his lips, nodding, unable to speak.

"I'll find us a home," he promised. "No more camping on the ground, no more root stew. No more cold blankets. You'll have warm fires and easy nights."

"I'd like that." She stroked her thumb over the scars on his cheeks. "As long as we're together, wherever we go, for however much time we have left."

He put his arm around her shoulders, letting her lean on him. "Come on." He reached round and found Cotta's hand with his own. "Time to go."

EPILOGUE

Late into spring at the turn of summer, with the horrors of winter finally receding, Cotta stood in Penrose, her back to the small crowd that had silently gathered around her. She gazed at the horizon, at a point across the new land, where she knew Kraner lay in ruins.

She sensed the pressure of the crowd behind her, waiting for her to say something, to do something. They were happy, smiling, excited at the promise of the future.

All she wanted to do was rest.

The weight of everything that had been done and everything still to do was almost enough to make her turn and walk away.

Almost, but not quite.

"It's time, my lady," she heard Denny say, his voice deeper than she remembered.

He stood at attention beside her, flanked by Kris and Rolo, who held a satchel between them. Rolo leaned towards her.

"Are you ready?" he asked, tapping the satchel. "This means you won."

"It means I lost."

Cotta put her hand on Denny's arm and let him turn her to face the crowd.

She looked at the people. So many she didn't know, but they knew her. That ever-present weight of expectation made her heart hurt; she had to force herself to take slow steady breaths.

Her eyes roamed the small crowd looking for faces she so desperately wanted to see, but they weren't there, not even a ghost.

She felt a stab of sorrow and loss and the unmistakable sensation of the threat of tears. Blinking twice and taking deep breaths, she tore her thoughts away from them and looked at the crowd again.

Men and women looked back at her, waiting.

"Ready," she whispered to Denny as she stepped forward. Denny stepped forward at her side, and then took another step, turning to stand before her. Rolo reached into the satchel and handed Denny a crown to set on her head.

Cotta bent low, then let him raise her up, Queen of Barclan.

The End

Printed in Great Britain
by Amazon